D-Day
In The
Capital

D-Day
In The
Capital

Rob Shumaker

For Earl W. Black and Harold E. Shumaker

Army Veterans

United States of America

— .... .— —. —.— / —.—— ——— ..—

Phantom: (a) something (as a specter) apparent to sense but with no substantial existence;
(b) something elusive or visionary.

– *Merriam-Webster's Collegiate Dictionary* 868 (10th ed. 2000).

CHAPTER 1

Milan, Italy

"As soon as her bra comes off, we're going in."

There was a noticeable silence before the walkie-talkie crackled to life, like the recipient of the message was running through the mountain of possibilities that might change the plan. The man worried he might set off his sometimes surly boss, but the question had to be asked.

"What if she keeps her bra on?"

There was no delay in answering back. "It'll come off," the man in the van grunted. He had been in the business long enough to know the bra always came off in a situation like this. And when it did come off, it was sure to keep the male viewer occupied – like the frisky kitten who can't stop playing with the bouncing ball of yarn. "The bra coming off is the signal. She'll do it."

"Roger that."

Stan Evans had been with the Central Intelligence Agency for 25 years, spending much of the last decade leading his team of special operations officers across the globe in the clandestine services. If Evans had a valid passport, it would show stops in Afghanistan, Iraq, Yemen, Somalia, and an assortment of other worldwide hellholes where he gathered intelligence, subverted local terrorist regimes, and otherwise caused serious mischief in service to his country. He spent the last three years immersing himself in the tribal areas of Pakistan – making contacts, killing enemies. The intelligence he learned led him to his current position in the bustling metropolis of Milan, Italy.

The CIA had been watching the man entering the Royal Suite of the Four Seasons for over a year now. Late forties with a nicely trimmed beard, Assad Khan would fit in on any Ivy League campus. Given the tone of his skin and jet-black hair, he would most likely be found in the faculty lounge of the political science department – perhaps the Middle Eastern studies wing. He himself was educated – an economics graduate of Pakistan's Punjab University. Following his graduation, he traveled across

Europe in search of himself before settling in the outskirts of Paris amongst the non-native Muslim population – a bubbling cauldron of anger and discontent that was beginning to frighten neighboring Parisians. Unfortunately, like so many others, Khan fell under the spell of a radical Islamic cleric whose bombastic rants had caught the attention of multiple law-enforcement agencies around the world. It was then that Khan's life took an ugly turn. He learned to hate the West, and he especially loathed the United States with its ever-expanding influence in every corner of the globe. He wanted the Great Satan out of Iraq, Afghanistan, and, above all, his homeland of Pakistan. After months of indoctrination in the hatred of America, he now had a new calling in life. He decided to use his education to help finance the resurgence of the Taliban in the country of his birth and take it to the enemy once and for all.

His father, Wallid Khan, was the Interior Minister of Pakistan, and his son used the family connections to develop his financial acumen. Fraud, bribes, and kickbacks swelled his bank account. Assad Khan slowly worked his way up the government's ladder. Lately, his side job had been keeping him busy.

Quietly, but on behalf of the Government of Pakistan, Khan had worked his financial magic across multiple continents, traveling to faraway places to implore Muslim leaders to support the fight against the infidel Americans. He received most of his donations from Saudi Arabia and its oil-rich royal family, who secretly despised Americans but outwardly loved taking their money. Side deals with Iran and Russia brought in huge caches of weapons to fight U.S. forces in the mountains of Pakistan and Afghanistan. Khan-supported madrasses began springing up all over Pakistan – the religious schools teaching the next generation of jihadists on the finer points of global terrorism. Mosques sent out their new wave of angry recruits to further the cause. Militant groups prepared for another holy war. Much to his delight, Khan's heavily funded Army of Jihad would soon find its name on the U.S. State Department's list of foreign terrorist organizations.

Within the last two months, Assad Khan and Pakistan military leaders were starting to see the fruits of their labor – real results indicating they had made substantial progress in their war against America. Ten U.S. soldiers were led to their death by a Pakistani undercover operative acting as a local guide. It was the second time U.S. forces had been ambushed after relying on a so-called Pakistan friendly.

Another red flag was raised when an American defense contractor was abducted in Pakistan following a U.S. missile strike on a suspected Taliban hideout. The American was well-known in Islamabad and believed to be friendly with Pakistani leaders. But the abduction and subsequent beheading of the man appeared to be an inside job – payback for the U.S. bombing on Pakistan soil. Although it could not be confirmed, it was believed Assad Khan personally decapitated the American with his own sword.

Naturally, U.S. officials were growing disillusioned with the Pakistan Government, some in the State Department openly wondering which side of the war on terror Pakistan was really on. Diplomatic relations were becoming increasingly frosty. U.S. military transports had to be rerouted after the Pakistanis closed the Khyber Pass to Afghanistan. The relationship between the two countries was going downhill fast.

When the CIA discovered Khan was the Taliban's new moneyman, Evans and his operatives on the ground wanted to have a few words with him and learn who was really calling the shots in the Pakistan Government. Maybe the U.S. could find out whether Pakistan was really an ally or an enemy. After a full briefing, the President gave the go-ahead.

Evans had drawn up the plan of a "snatch-and-grab" over six months ago. It would be a simple operation, so said the CIA Director after being briefed by Evans. Hell, his team of ex-special forces soldiers could do it on the streets of Karachi in broad daylight without any problems. No one would even know the CIA was on the ground.

But the operation came to a screeching halt when Khan's brother, Pervez Khan, became Pakistan's intelligence chief. This new wrinkle had intelligence officials in Washington rightly worried. The Pakistan Taliban's financier now had an intimate relationship with the head of Pakistan's ISI. Everyone from the President on down knew this couldn't be good news. If the United States was going to continue having a base of operations north of the Arabian Sea, the military needed to know who it could trust. Something needed to be done. Grabbing Khan off the streets of Pakistan might lead to another war that no one in Washington wanted. When the CIA assured the President they could do the job quickly and quietly outside of the borders of Pakistan, the President signed off on "Operation Roundup."

As the second largest city in Italy, Milan sits closer to the border of Switzerland than the Italian capital of Rome. In the Lombardy region of northern Italy, Milan is home to a million-plus inhabitants, and the streets swell with buyers and aspiring models every February and March for the annual parade of high-end merchandise from Milan's very own Valentino, Gucci, Versace, and Prada during fashion week. In the summer, tourists from around the world make the trip through the Swiss Alps to visit the Santa Maria delle Grazie monastery and admire Leonardo da Vinci's *The Last Supper*.

Assad Khan had traveled to Milan on five other occasions, all under the watchful eye of the CIA. Notwithstanding his terrorist leanings, Khan was very good at keeping his nose clean, saying all the right things in public and doing his dirty work when no one was looking. Some day, he knew his violent cause would require him to give up his globe-trotting ways and hole up in Pakistan for good. But he wasn't there yet. He was still known to fly to Geneva, Switzerland, several times a year to check on his family's secret bank accounts. There, he would make deposits and get a little spending cash to do as he pleased. From Geneva, he would cross the Italian border and head straight for Milan.

The trips to Milan, however, were not to raise money for the cause or to round up militant recruits. No, Khan traveled to Milan "because that's where the beautiful women are." Under orders from his brother, the playboy Khan was to promise great riches to the bevy of aspiring models in exchange for trips to Pakistan to satisfy the upper echelon of the regime. Khan's brother apparently thought good government included using the people's money to satisfy his and others' sexual urges. There was no shortage of beautiful women in Milan – leggy blondes, tall brunettes, waifs of every color and nationality. And in his mind, Khan's brother thought even the model castoffs were better looking than what they had back home. And he wanted nothing but the best for him and his men. He would become Pakistan's Sultan of Brunei and with that moniker Pervez Khan would enjoy an endless parade of beautiful women strutting down his own runway. He left it to Assad to do the shopping. While he was at it, his brother told Khan to get a little for himself on the side, maybe sample the local fare before he brought it back to Pakistan for the others to enjoy. Never one to disappoint his brother, Assad Khan traveled to Milan as often as possible.

"The door is closed."

Milan, however, was not the ideal destination for Agent Evans. The one-way streets of Milan are incredibly narrow, barely enough for a car and a half. And the tightly packed buildings make getting your bearings difficult. It was like trying to work in a land of miniature. The place was ideal for mopeds, bicycles, and foot traffic, but hauling a body through the streets on a bike or over one's shoulder was out of the question. Moreover, Milan's police were constantly on the prowl, always looking to stick their noses into anything that might look suspicious. It wouldn't be long before a blue *polizia* car would make a stop so officers could check out Agent Evans' "dry-cleaning" van or tell the driver to move along.

Evans hated working in places like these – civilized societies with laws and courts and security cameras. He would much rather work in the lawless streets of the Third World where acts of retribution and swift justice were commonplace. It was a much easier environment to do business in, at least in his mind – the shadows providing the necessary cover for his covert activities. In areas of Afghanistan or Iraq, a dead body along side of the road was not out of the ordinary and wouldn't draw the satellite trucks and cable-news hounds raising holy hell and snooping for clues.

The cultured streets of Milan, however, made Evans nervous. The 50-year-old veteran of numerous secret wars wiped the sweat beginning to collect in the upper reaches of his dyed mustache. He needed his plan to work flawlessly.

Four CIA operatives sat in the fourth floor Executive Suite at the Four Seasons. The hotel was a converted convent that dated back to the 15th century and, needless to say, the vow of poverty the former occupants might have taken did not carry over to present times. Located in Milan's ritzy Quadrilatero della Moda, the posh hotel was steps away from seemingly endless high-end fashion boutiques. Given its prime location, rooms didn't come cheap. Assad Khan's Royal Suite, all 3,000 square feet of it, occupied the entire fifth floor and cost well over 2,000 euros per night. The suite had its own terrace and private garden as well as a view of the Duomo. It was Milan opulence at its finest.

One floor below, the Executive Suite housing the team of CIA agents was a third of the size, but still pricey. The beds were made and the bags were packed. The black and white pictures from the hidden camera were playing out on the agents' TV like some in-room pay-per-view movie.

The woman with Khan was Asian with long dark hair and even longer legs. Her $2,000 Valentino bow dress was way too short on the bottom and a size too small on the top. It looked like it might pop at any second.

The $720 Prada patent leather pointed toe platform pumps made her five-eleven, an inch taller than Khan, and he loved looking over every inch of her body. The two had met three times before in the Royal Suite and Khan made sure to ask the escort service to make her available on every visit. Against his brother's wishes, he had stopped trolling the fashion houses for women desperate for modeling contracts and the bright lights of Paris and New York – Karachi or Islamabad having little appeal to them even with the promise of big money. Instead, Khan headed straight for the high-end bordellos and brothels where he knew services would be made available for the right price. Negotiation was much quicker that way. Although it went without saying that the anti-American backers who ponied up big bucks would no doubt be dismayed to discover their donations marked for jihad often went to pay for $1,000-a-night whores.

The CIA had also put its own moves on the woman now on Khan's arm. She had dreamed of becoming a model since her early teens – the clothes, the runways, the magazine covers. It all excited her. She craved the click of the camera, the bright lights of the flash, and the eyes of everyone on her. She left Hong Kong when she was twenty and spent five years begging for modeling jobs in Milan with only modest amounts of success. When the younger models arrived on the scene and started landing all the top contracts, she knew her time on the catwalk had passed her by. An older model, who was in her early 30s, convinced her she could start a new career – one that would earn her as much as she wanted. With the hopes of filling her closets with the best fashions Milan had to offer, she joined one of the top-flight escort services in the city.

Codenamed the "Dragonfly," she initially balked at the idea of working to satisfy the needs of the Agency. Sex with strange men was one thing – prostitution simply being a way to make a living. Moreover, the associated occupational hazards could be lessened with certain precautions. But sex with men who were under surveillance by U.S. intelligence agents made her think twice about her occupation – getting caught in the crossfire a more immediate risk than an STD. When CIA agents promised her more money than she could make in half a year, she decided to cast her concerns aside. Once she signed up, she was told to lure the man into the room, lock the door, and do what came natural. The CIA reassured her that agents would be nearby, and as soon as the bra came off, they'd be inside.

"Subject is getting a drink from the bar."

Three CIA agents sat in a van down the street from the Four Seasons listening, waiting for Alpha Team to tell them the deed had been done and the package was ready for transport. The CIA had considered grabbing Khan on the Via Gesu as he walked to the hotel, but the thought of him on his back and in the buff proved to be a better plan – one likely to draw less attention from the locals and tourists and to catch Khan with his pants down.

"Dragonfly is in the bed."

The four agents sitting one floor below kept one eye on the TV and the other on their weapons – a silenced pistol, two tasers, and a black bag full of syringes with enough chemicals to sedate a charging rhino. The weapons were chosen for stealth – the quieter the better lest any nosy hotel neighbors or maids become suspicious. Although they knew Khan was always armed, they were confident they could get inside before he reached for the revolver in his suit coat. The door connecting the Executive Suite to the private staircase leading upstairs was silently unlocked and opened.

"We might have a problem here."

Every agent froze in place and put a finger to his earpiece. Those in the Executive Suite looked at the TV again. The foreplay hadn't even started yet. And Khan wasn't known for needing a Viagra. But there was a problem outside on the sidewalk running parallel with the Via della Spiga on the north side of the Four Seasons. The statement of concern came from Agent Evans in the van. He had noticed the three men from a half a block away making their way toward the hotel.

"What's up?" asked Agent Thomas, whispering into his microphone and maneuvering the curtains for a quick peek outside. He needed to know whether the show was still on.

"Dragonfly might be having some company."

Agent Evans grabbed the binoculars and zeroed in on the three men. The men had stopped outside of the Cinzia Rocca boutique so they could ogle the mannequins wearing the latest and sexiest lingerie. "Son of a . ."

"Who is it?" Agent Adams wondered.

"The Pakistani ambassador to Italy," Evans whispered. He started shaking his head in disgust. The CIA had a thick dossier on the man and at least a third of the file dealt with his proclivity for prostitutes. He had to use his diplomatic immunity on a number of occasions when he refused to pay his escorts for a night in the sack. Evans couldn't stand the scumbag. "Fuckin' horny bastard."

"Shit!" Adams exclaimed, his mind putting the pieces together. "They're probably going to meet with Khan."

Agent Thomas stepped into the bathroom and put his hand over his walkie-talkie. "Are we calling it off?" he whispered. "Are we off?"

Evans made the call, and the urgency in his voice indicated things could get ugly real quick. His perfect plan was in jeopardy.

"Stick with the plan," he said. "Stewart and Bronson, get the elevator to the top floor and keep it there as long as you can." The last thing Evans wanted was for his team to struggle with Khan or, heaven forbid, allow him to escape the hotel room. If the Ambassador's bodyguards made it upstairs before the agents apprehended Khan, Evans, the CIA, and the United States Government would have a whole lot of explaining to do.

"Alpha Team, be ready. We might be going early."

One agent opened the door to the Executive Suite and quickly stuck his head out. With no one in sight, he hauled ass down to the end of the hall. Seeing a housekeeping cart outside the last suite on the floor, his check of the room revealed the maid preoccupied in the bathroom. He grabbed the cart and rolled it to the elevator. When the doors opened, he pushed the cart in between the doors and hurried back to the suite. He grabbed the maid's vacuum on the way back.

The agent monitoring the video feed gave his next play-by-play. "Subject has disrobed. Suit coat is on the floor next to the bed."

"Come on, you pervert," Evans said, peering into the tiny surveillance monitor in the van. "Hurry up and get in bed."

The CIA agents tiptoed up the staircase and unlocked the door to the Royal Suite. One floor below, an agent plugged in the vacuum, turned it on, and left it running in the hall. Then the agents waited for the order.

The Dragonfly motioned for Khan to come closer and then positioned herself for the taking. Khan got on top, as the Dragonfly said he would. But it wouldn't be long, she said, before she'd take over and put on a show just like he wanted. Khan was a creature of habit. Like clockwork, the Dragonfly grabbed him in a deep kiss and rolled him over. She then straddled him at his waist.

"Standby for entry."

She told him to just let go and let her have her way with him. He did not protest. She held down his arms and dove in for another kiss on his lips. Her long dark hair fell over her bare shoulders. Her tongue tickled his earlobe. This was why he kept coming back to Milan, he thought to himself. She then pushed back and slowly ran her long fingers down his bare chest. She gave him that familiar sultry look from her deep dark eyes, her smile indicating pleasure was forthcoming. She knew what was next. Khan thought he knew what was next. She grabbed the rear clasp of her Dolce & Gabbana leopard-print bra and then let it all hang out. With visions of sugar plums now dancing in his head, he closed his eyes to let his mind savor the moment. Ah, the wonders and beauty of Milan.

"Alpha team, go now!"

Boom!

The door to the suite burst open and the only thing bigger than the Dragonfly's breasts were the eyes of Khan as he watched four armed men lunging toward him. They said nothing. The only noise heard was the faint sound of the vacuum cleaner below.

"What the . . . ?"

He managed to scramble to one knee on the bed and lunged for his suit coat and the gun, but the dart from the taser struck him in the chest in midflight. With two muffled screams as his muscles suddenly locked up, his stunned naked body landed with a thud against the wall. One agent grabbed the Dragonfly off the bed and another stuffed a rag in Khan's mouth. The agents grabbed him by the arms and legs and hauled his mostly limp body back onto the bed. Zip ties cuffed his ankles and his wrists. A black hood covered his head.

"Package is secure."

When the maid had finished scrubbing the toilet, she retreated to the hall only to find her cart and her vacuum were missing. She found the former at the elevator, which was buzzing in anger at not being able to close its doors.

"Damn kids," she muttered under her breath. She freed the cart from the clutches of the elevator and the lights above the door slowly counted down to the lobby level.

"The ambassador is getting on the elevator," Agent Stewart announced, having run down from the fourth floor. He had caught the elevator again at two and lit up every number on the board again to slow the trip up.

"Guys, we need to get the package out of there!" Evans announced, the intensity in his voice rising. "Get him out. Now!"

The agents grabbed Khan's clothes, one remade the bed as best he could, and one hulk hoisted the now-drugged Khan over his shoulder.

They scrambled down the private staircase, back into the Executive Suite, and closed the door behind them.

Agent Stewart was downstairs in the lobby watching the numbers of the elevator display creep upward. "Elevator has stopped on two."

"They're gonna start asking questions if he's not there," Agent Evans said out loud to himself.

Evans didn't like the way things were shaping up. With yet another wrinkle, he needed to think fast. "Michaels," he said into his microphone. "Put the Dragonfly back into Khan's suite. Have her tell them Khan found another girl, but he thought the Ambassador would like some alone time with the Dragonfly."

"Roger that."

"Elevator has stopped on three."

As two agents stuffed the slumbering Khan into a body bag and loaded him and other assorted luggage onto a baggage cart, Agent Michaels informed the Dragonfly of the plan and promised her she would be royally compensated if she played the part and kept her mouth shut. She agreed, but she wanted double the money.

"Done," he said after running her back up the staircase. He then pushed her inside. "Get in there."

"Elevator has stopped on four."

Agent Michaels locked the door to his side of the suite and told his men to get ready. He radioed the others. "We're gonna take the garbage out in three minutes."

"Elevator has stopped on five."

Via the hidden camera, the agents heard the Ambassador's knock on the door and saw the Dragonfly throw on the rest of her clothes. Forgetting to put on her bra, she lifted up the mattress and hid it underneath. She adjusted the dress one last time and stopped just short of the door to catch her breath. She opened the door after the second round of knocking. She brushed back her long hair, creating quite the profile against the door. The agents peered into the TV and saw the Ambassador with his two bodyguards standing behind him. They could not hear what the Dragonfly was saying but it was enticing enough that the Ambassador smiled broadly and followed her inside. The bodyguards came in as well to check out the place – the bathroom, the closets, underneath the bed.

All clear.

When the agents heard the door shut in the suite above, one pulled the surveillance cable out of the TV and they were on their way.

"We're moving," Agent Thomas whispered into his microphone.

The four agents, two carts with plastic-wrapped "dry cleaning," and the baggage cart carrying Khan made it down the hall, maneuvering around the housekeeping cart, the maid now vacuuming up a storm. Then it was around the corner to the elevator. The agents took the elevator down to the second floor where they exited and walked quickly to the service elevator that would take them to ground level and the side door exiting out onto the Via Monte Napoleone.

Two agents in a dry-cleaning van moved quickly down the narrow street and pulled to a stop at the side entrance.

"In position," the driver said. He then made a sweep of the area. "All clear."

The side door to the Four Seasons opened and two agents pushed out the dry-cleaning carts onto the sidewalk. The cart carrying Khan was then rolled out in between them. At the rear of the van, the agents dragged Khan off the cart and loaded him into the back. The dry cleaning was thrown on top of him. The carts were returned to the hotel and left unattended. All four agents then got on board.

"All in," the driver announced into his microphone. "To the airport."

"Roger that," Agent Evans said in the van out front. "Get him in the air." Evans breathed a sigh of relief. All had gone well. And all had been quiet. He checked the scene. Nothing but people going about their business on the streets of Milan. The van carrying Khan drove by on its way to the airport without a second look. "Stewart and Bronson, you may stand down."

As Agents Evans and Adams prepared to close down the operation and meet the rest of the team at the rendezvous point, Evans noticed movement on the surveillance monitor. He decided to give it one last look before he switched it off. He caught the image of the Pakistani Ambassador smacking the Dragonfly across the cheek and throwing her on the bed. Apparently the Ambassador liked to play rough.

"Aw, hell," Evans said. His bosses might have told him that it wasn't his concern. Sometimes bad things happen to confidential informants. It was the nature of the business with the CIA. The operation was a success and that's all that mattered. But watching that horny Ambassador throwing off his clothes, Evans couldn't stomach the thought of what was about to happen.

"Agent Stewart, are you still on site?" Evans whispered into mike.

Stewart pulled the microphone in his collar closer to his mouth. "I'm about to exit the side door."

With the Ambassador now on the bed and ready to pounce on his prey, Evans gave the final order of Operation Roundup. "Pull the fire alarm."

With the alarm blaring and the emergency lights flashing, Evans saw the Ambassador's bodyguards rushing in to pull their boss from the bed and get him dressed before the fire department showed up to search the rooms and ask questions. They scurried out of the suite and left the Dragonfly on the bed.

Evans saw her sit up and straighten her clothes. He was satisfied enough that he could sleep soundly tonight.

"All right, let's go have a talk with Mr. Khan."

CHAPTER 2

The White House – Washington, D.C.

"In God We Trust," William E. Cogdon said in deep contemplation, as if a matter that had slipped his mind for some time now needed his full attention.

It was a Friday afternoon, and Cogdon and his boss, the President of the United States, were seated in the Oval Office tying up loose ends before they, along with the First Lady, took off for a weekend of relaxation at Camp David. Cogdon, however, was bored. As President Anthony Schumacher's chief of staff, he craved the nonstop action of the Oval Office and all the attention that went along with it. He was always on the move, always making some important decision or plotting ways to make his boss look good. He felt like he should be doing something – skewering some lib Democrat for his or her opposition to the President, twisting the arms of recalcitrant northeastern Republicans on an upcoming vote, or peppering the media with his insightful and brilliant commentary.

Called Wiley by the President and his friends, Cogdon's Secret Service codename was "Coyote," which was befitting his image of the beloved cartoon character and the foibles that were discovered over the years as he sought to catch his desired prize of the moment. He had failed mightily on occasion (mainly with women and the bottle), but he was never deterred. He would simply get up, dust himself off, and march on. His bullheaded determination finally paid off when he orchestrated President Schumacher's landslide victory in last year's election. Now he believed he was on top for good. Conservative admirers from across the country flooded his mailbox with plush Wile E. Coyote stuffed animals, and they now lined shelves and cluttered the desk in his West Wing office as some sort of shrine to his brilliance. Liberal detractors would send him pictures of an anvil crashing down on his head or a box of ACME dynamite blowing up in his face. Wiley reveled in the love he received from like-minded Republicans, but he cherished getting under the skin of Democrats even more.

With his reading done for the afternoon, Cogdon had looked in his wallet, pulled out a dollar bill, and turned it over.

"In God We Trust," he said again.

"Our national motto," President Schumacher said, not even looking up at Cogdon. The President was signing a stack of letters, a nice easy chore for a Friday afternoon. "What about it?"

"It's on the back of this dollar bill."

"It's on the back of *all* U.S. coins and currency," the President reminded him. He still hadn't looked up.

The phrase "In God We Trust" first appeared on U.S. coinage in 1864 and paper currency in 1957. In this day and age, the motto finds a prominent display near Washington's ONE, Jefferson's Declaration, Lincoln's Memorial, Hamilton's Treasury, Jackson's White House, Grant's U.S. Capitol, and Franklin's Independence Hall.

"You're probably going to tell me it has origins in the Bible."

The President hesitated. He was usually pretty good at reciting chapter and verse of well-known biblical passages but this one had him stumped at the moment. "I'm pretty sure it does. Let me think about that one for awhile."

"I'm sure that has been a subject of litigation over the years," Cogdon said. He thought of how it must gall those angry atheists.

"Of course."

Cogdon turned his eyes to left of the dollar bill. "What's this '*annuit coeptis*' phrase above the all-seeing eye and the pyramid?" He had either never thought about it before or just plain forgot about it.

"It's Latin," the President said. "It means 'he has approved our undertakings.'"

"He who?"

"God."

"Oh boy," Cogdon said in mock despair. "More litigation. Separation of church and state they'll yell."

The President nodded his head and began shuffling through a stack of papers on the desk. He had something to show Cogdon. "Let me find that proclamation I just signed," he said. "Here it is. My 'National Day of Prayer Proclamation. Now, therefore, I, Anthony J. Schumacher, President of the United States of America, by virtue of the authority invested in me by the Constitution and laws of the United States, do hereby proclaim the first Thursday in May as a National Day of Prayer.' Then I ask Americans to pray for God's protection and his continued blessings."

Cogdon's left hand slapped his forehead in feigned shock. "You are going to get sued."

The President nodded. "I do every year." He then smiled. "And they'll probably come after me again when I issue another proclamation this November."

"Thanksgiving?"

"Yep," the President said, he had now moved on to a stack of photos that needed to be autographed for recent visitors who were lucky enough to get a "grip and grin" in the Oval Office. He then offered a big smile. "Of course, maybe they'll take it easy on me since I have so much to be thankful for."

He did indeed. He had a loving wife, three healthy and productive children, and a grandson who liked to romp around the White House when he visited. Oh, and one other thing that he could be grateful for.

He had lived to see another day.

President Schumacher had much to thank the Lord for considering what he had been through over the last eight months. On Election Day of last year, the President and the First Lady survived an assassination attempt by Islamic terrorists at the First Family's home in Silver Creek, Indiana. The heinous plot with VX nerve agent was thwarted by the great work of the United States Secret Service and the Federal Bureau of Investigation. Other than the six dead terrorists, the only casualty was ol' Wiley Cogdon himself, who was slightly exposed to the VX. The fifty-state landslide, however, quickly cured him of any lasting ill effects.

In a nod to the media calling President Reagan the "Teflon President," Schumacher had become known as the "Kevlar President." The last six months had been peaceful, however, and the President's relentless assault in the war on terror had resulted in numerous high-value targets being captured or killed. Still, many Americans wondered when the next attack would occur.

The President stood six-two and still had the athletic build that made him a special agent with the FBI back in his younger days. But the signs of presidential aging were starting to appear. The gray hair was becoming noticeable, the temples having already given way. Political commentators had even mentioned the crow's-feet around the eyes when he smiled. Cogdon did his best to reduce the President's stress by scheduling high-profile events before eight o'clock at night. Otherwise, the heavy eyelids would appear with the President's loss of focus soon to follow. Cogdon offered the President his Red Bull, but the President dutifully stuck by his morning Diet Coke. With a little caffeine and the fresh air of spring, President Schumacher was ready to kick it into high gear.

Just a month earlier, the President had unveiled his "All-American Energy Plan." He put an end to the remaining drilling moratorium off the U.S. coasts and opened the Arctic National Wildlife Refuge and other federal lands to U.S. oil coffers. Oil companies that had once been rebuffed with endless amounts of paperwork were unleashed to commence drilling. Like runners at a starting line, they sprinted toward the finishing tape with renewed optimism in an American energy revival. The regulatory process for clean coal, natural gas, and nuclear power plants was also streamlined. Tax breaks sought to encourage wind, solar, and biomass power. Every available energy source America had to offer was put on the table.

But some people weren't happy.

The Democrats had held their tongues long enough. The President had enormous approval ratings since surviving the terrorist attack. Since the inauguration in January, he had worked to focus the country's energies on American energy. The cost of a barrel of oil had been cut in half. Americans were no longer cursing their every stop at the local gas station. The economy was humming right along.

And the Democrats couldn't take it much longer. They despised Schumacher. He was becoming the most hated Republican President of all time – the smile, the pretty wife, the favorable poll numbers. Sure, the Republican Lincoln took his lumps – cartoon caricatures of him as an ape or in love with black women, but the printed word only went so far. Reagan took his darts on the nightly news – purportedly stealing beans from the homeless in Lafayette Park and threatening World War III by walking away from the Soviets at Reykjavik. But, even then, viewers would move on from Uncle Walter to the Cosbys or J.R. and the Ewing clan at Southfork. President Schumacher, on the other hand, had to endure twenty-four hours of nonstop vitriol led by the left-wing nuts at MSNBC, the bloggers on the Internet, and those manning the war room at the Democratic National Committee.

The Democrats now had to start plotting for the midterm elections. So liberal antagonists started dipping their toes in the water to see if attacks on President Schumacher would stick or backfire in their faces. Articles began surfacing on the web and in print railing against the energy bogeyman. The readers were told that the evil Big Oil companies sought only to enrich themselves at the expense of the American people, coal producers were said to have raped the earth and scarred the lungs of American children, and, last but not least, the nuclear energy sector – which the lib environmentalists said was only one meltdown away from bringing Armageddon to the world.

But it wasn't just average, everyday liberals looking to tear down President Schumacher. The real enemies were those with serious financial skin in the game. Middle Eastern oil kingdoms, communist despots, and the Russians were none too happy with the drop in oil revenue. To those countries, the most glorious sight in the world was American consumers at the gas pump paying a price per gallon that increased on a daily basis. For years, the foreign oil producers had manipulated the price of crude depending on how much they wanted in their bank accounts. Private jets and secluded island paradises don't come cheap, and once one becomes accustomed to a lifestyle of largesse, he will take any and all measures to keep it.

The quiet stillness of the Oval Office was broken when the phone on the President's desk started ringing.

"Yes," he said.

"Mr. President," the President's secretary said. "Director Parker is here to see you."

Schumacher looked at his to-do list and then over at Cogdon. "Did we forget something on the schedule for this afternoon?"

Cogdon shook his head. "No, he's not on the schedule."

The President looked noticeably worried. Surprise visits from the CIA Director often brought bad news. The tension in the room went up a couple of notches. It was a calm Friday afternoon no more.

"Send him in."

The President walked out from behind his desk and started for the door. "Bill, I hope you're the bearer of good news," he said as he greeted the CIA Director with a handshake.

Director William Parker stuck out his hand and offered a smile. The fifty-five-year-old former intelligence analyst had worked hard to gain the President's trust and respect over the last year and a half. It was an uphill battle, however. The President's relationship with the CIA had been rocky to say the least.

When he was Vice President, Schumacher uncovered a plot between President Ronald Fisher and CIA Director Jillian Franklin to assassinate Schumacher, blame it on the terrorists, and give Fisher the opportunity to appoint Franklin, who just happened to be his lover, to the vice presidency. The plot unraveled, and both Fisher and Franklin took their own lives rather than face a life sentence in prison. Needless to say, President Schumacher proceeded cautiously in his dealings with those at Langley. But considering Parker came highly recommended by FBI Director Tyrone Stubblefield and Joint Chiefs Chairman Hugh Cummins, the relationship was off to a good start.

Director Parker knew his visit would be a surprise and one that might raise alarm bells with the President. But today was not that kind of day. "Sir, I do indeed have good news. We have captured Assad Khan."

The President let out a sigh of relief. "That is good news." He then motioned Director Parker and Cogdon to have a seat on the couches near the fireplace.

"We picked him up in Milan, Italy," the Director said, opening a file marked "Highly Classified."

"Milan?"

"Yes, it's one of his favorite haunts."

"Was it clean and quiet?"

Parker knew this was important to the President. "Yes, sir," he said. "We caught him with a prostitute while his pants were down. We put him on a plane and we have him at a black site in the Seychelles."

"Have we learned anything yet?"

Parker shook his head. "Not yet. We have everyone we need on-site so I imagine it will only be a matter of time before we start getting some information from him."

"Good."

Cogdon stirred in his seat. Now refreshed from the jolt of good news, he started thinking all things politics. If the secret nature of Khan's capture became known, his boss could have a mess on his hands. The Democrats would have a field day upon hearing the news. They would love nothing more than to gin up concern over President Schumacher's way of doing business in the war on terror.

"Won't somebody wonder where Khan is if they don't hear from him?"

Director Parker did not seem concerned with the question. "Khan was well known for dropping off the radar for weeks on end. He traveled alone and kept his communications to a minimum. When you're dealing with thugs and terrorists all over the world, you don't advertise your itinerary or call home to mom and dad very often. We've already hacked into his e-mail accounts and phones so we'll know if anyone becomes suspicious."

"I'm sure it would be quite the topic of conversation at the G8 meeting next week in London if it leaked out," Cogdon said.

The President nodded. "I'm sure the Italians wouldn't be too happy to find out the CIA was snatching people from hotel rooms in their beloved Milan."

"Nobody is going to find out, Mr. President," Parker said confidently. "If somebody gets suspicious we can always put him back where we found him." He then chose his next words carefully. "And this time the hooker might have other things on her mind than just a romp in the sack."

CHAPTER 3

Founders Park – Alexandria, Virginia

"Mommy, look!" the child yelled, tugging at her mother's hand. She was all of three years old and enjoying the walk in the park with her mother on a warm spring day. "Mommy, look! A balloon!"

The child's free hand was pointing excitedly to the tree to her right. It was a matter of great importance.

Her mother took notice. "Oh yeah, I see it. Somebody's balloon got stuck in the tree."

The child, proud of her discovery, agreed. "Yeah, it got stuck in the tree," she said. Her mood then grew somber, the sadness evident on her face. She imagined what it would be like if that was her balloon. "Poor little balloon."

The balloon was red, and given the amount of helium still left inside, it had probably floated to its current resting place amongst the forest of green leaves within the last couple of hours. But it didn't wrangle its way off the wrist of a young child. And it hadn't found its current resting place after some celebratory send-off.

It was right where it was supposed to be.

The man running along the path saw the little girl point to the tree from a hundred yards away. He was in the first mile of his usual Tuesday run, the sweat just starting to trickle down the side of his scarred cheek. After parking his car, he had gone north to Oronco Bay Park, making his way parallel to the Potomac, then turned around and jogged back. The dark Oakleys shielded his eyes from the sun and gave him the chance to scan his surroundings without anyone noticing. The man passed by the woman and the child and gave a friendly nod. Had they been paying more attention, they would have taken notice of the man's slight limp, which caused him to rock to the left with every other step. He gave one last glance at the red balloon and picked up the pace. His increased heart rate began to feel good and the wheels in his mind were spinning at a good clip.

It was time to go to work.

The man was Russian. He went by the name of Vladimir Patrenko, and he slipped into and out of the United States with multiple diplomatic credentials. He went virtually unnoticed in the U.S. nowadays – American law enforcement too busy looking for bearded Middle Easterners carrying bombs in their turbans or their underwear. Since the Cold War was over, white Russians didn't raise as many red flags as they used to.

The Russian Embassy vouched for Patrenko as a simple courier, but his secret employment history showed he was much more than just a messenger carrying notes back and forth between Moscow and Washington, D.C. His father worked for the KGB in Stalingrad from 1960 through the end of the Cold War. Hoping to follow in his father's footsteps, Patrenko joined the *Sluzhba Vneshney Razvedki Rossi*, otherwise known as the SVR, Russia's Foreign Intelligence Service and the successor to the KGB, in hopes of resurrecting the Soviet bear to its former superpower status.

Known as Vlad the Impaler, he preferred gutting his enemies to shooting them, and the Russian Federation never seemed to run out of enemies for Vlad to slice, dice, and ultimately silence. If he accompanied a comrade to Siberia or just some quiet place outside Moscow, it meant there would be one empty seat on the ride back.

Patrenko limped to a stop at the trunk of the Russian Embassy's leased Mercedes. He had run two miles, and that was the norm unless he thought he was being followed. He had once gone eight, but that was only until he realized those in the park were training for a half-marathon. On this spring day, however, the park was nearly empty. The tourists taking the water taxi down the Potomac to visit Old Town Alexandria had yet to arrive. Perhaps they were still in D.C. looking at the cherry blossoms or the monuments to great Americans. Or maybe those in their cars were still stuck in morning traffic on the Capital Beltway.

Patrenko toweled the sweat off his bald head. He was a muscular five-eleven and his weight fluctuated between one-eighty and two-hundred pounds. Of course, sometimes he gained weight on purpose, just another way to conceal his identity when need be. He threw the towel in the trunk and put on a pair of black athletic pants over his shorts. A black athletic jacket completed the ensemble. He zipped it up and got in the car.

The red balloon signaled he was to head to the Berrett Branch Library at Queen Street and North Washington in Alexandria. Sometimes the balloon was green and then it was off to a park in Arlington. A blue balloon meant he would head to the parking lot of the Wal-Mart in Chevy Chase, Maryland. It would normally be a five-minute drive from the park to the library, even less if he caught the lights just right. But Patrenko never took the direct route. He was never in a hurry. He would drive endless loops around his destination, sometimes stopping for gas or lunch but always on the lookout and always watching his mirrors and studying the endless stream of cars and faces he encountered. He once drove down to Mount Vernon and took the tour of Washington's home on the Potomac thinking he was being followed by U.S. agents.

Patrenko didn't particularly like the library drop site, but it was quiet, dry, and offered ample places to store hollowed out books that would not get a second glance. He always went to the library during the busiest hours, thinking the librarians would be less likely to notice him snooping around the stacks. He entered the sliding doors of the main entrance and checked his surroundings – the multi-purpose room on his left, the restrooms on his right. The black athletic suit was still on but he topped it off with a brand new Redskins cap covering his bald dome. His chin was perpetually down and he used his cell phone to conceal one side of his head. The security cameras were never able to capture a full view of his face.

He walked beyond the main desk where the librarians were busy showing the old folks how to work the Kindles and iPads. No one even noticed him. He took the stairs to the second floor and then walked to the far corner of the building. He didn't need to look for Dewey's decimals or subject signs to find out where he was going. It was the sports section – full of biographies on the athletic greats of years gone by – the Galloping Ghost, the Big O, the Golden Bear, the Mick. That corner was never busy, no kids scampering about the dusty shelves or regular patrons frequenting those parts.

As he was walking, Patrenko saw two old-timers talking at a table near the elevator – a safe distance away. Other than that, he had the whole second floor to himself. The smell of aging books filtered through the air. There was little noise, save for the air conditioning system humming right along at seventy-two degrees. He walked to the second to last row and then to the second-to-last shelf near the wall. Five rows from the bottom, he pulled back the last two books – out-of-date tomes lauding the exploits of the famed Secretariat. By the looks of the covers, the books might have been sitting on the shelf since Secretariat's Derby win in '73. Patrenko noticed the dust on the shelves. Most of the books hadn't been moved in ages. With the plastic dust jackets, he practically had to pry the books apart from their neighbor. It was a good spot.

After a check of the second floor through the gaps in the stacks, Patrenko reached his hand in and grasped the Mentos gum container wedged between the backs of the two shelves. No faux book this time, just a place where nobody would go looking. He took the container out and shook it twice. It was clear the rattling wasn't coming from any pieces of fresh mint gum. He opened the lid, turned the container upside down, and out fell a SanDisk Cruzer eight-gigabyte flash drive. He dropped the flash drive back inside and snapped on the lid.

Mission accomplished.

He turned to replace Secretariat on the shelf. It was then he saw a pair of eyes staring back at him.

"Geez!" he blurted out in a whisper, the Mentos container falling to the carpeted floor.

"It's me!" the man across the shelf whispered back. His eyes were wide with fear. "It's just me."

Restraining himself from punching the man through the stacks, Patrenko let fly a string of Russian profanities.

"Shhhh! Not so loud!"

Patrenko picked up the container off the floor. His eyes again met the man on the other side. He jerked his thumb over toward the far wall. "Get over here!" he grumbled under his breath.

The two met against the wall and no one spoke until both of them looked in every direction. Patrenko didn't think they had been heard. He looked through the shelves and over the tops of the books. There was no movement on the floor.

"You know I don't like meeting like this," he grunted.

The man on the receiving end nodded his head in agreement. He knew he wasn't supposed to meet with Russian spies. That was the point of signal areas and drop sites. The man should have known better.

That was the first thing they teach you at the CIA.

Roland Barton had worked for the CIA for close to thirty years. His career was unremarkable – a few commendations here and there but he had been passed over for promotions multiple times over the last decade. He hated those working above him and treated those below him with utter disdain. His wife left him years ago, and she took the house, the kids, and got the hell out of his sad pathetic life. With the little money he had left over after rent and alimony, he took to smoking two packs a day and found solace in the bottle, spending most of his time at the corner bar scarring his lungs and drowning his liver. There, he also discovered his love of gambling – first the bar's video poker machine, then the casinos, then Internet gambling sites when he was too lazy to leave the apartment. Pretty soon, he had lost everything. Now, heavily in debt, he took out numerous loans that he couldn't pay back. With no hope, he considered suicide. He tried but failed in that endeavor as well. Now he was desperate. He had to do something to save himself. He decided his only hope was to sell out his country.

And the Russians had lots of cash to wet his whistle.

"You are such a fool!" Patrenko whispered again in disgust. The glare in his eyes told of his exasperation. Barton had no hat on, no glasses, not even a fake mustache or beard, nothing that would conceal his identity from anyone passing him by on the street or cameras peering down on him from above. Perhaps he should have spent time in the section of the library dealing with Spycraft 101.

"I'm sorry," Barton said, putting his hand on Patrenko's shoulder to calm him down. He then looked around and tried to sound confident. "Relax. Nobody is around. I come in here all the time. I consider it part of my cover."

"Kinda like that hole-in-the-wall where you get drunk every night?" Patrenko snapped. Vlad the Impaler suddenly had a desire to bring out his knife but he restrained himself. "What the hell are you doing here?"

"I needed to talk to you."

Patrenko cursed under his breath. He wondered if Barton was too much of a risk, maybe he might out the both of them before all was said and done. "We have plans to contact each other. No face-to-face meetings. Remember?"

"I know, I know."

Patrenko relented for the time being. He glanced down at the Mentos container. "Did you bring what you promised?"

"Yes," Barton said. "There are names of covert operatives in Afghanistan and Iraq. There are also copies of American plans to undermine the Iranian regime. The U.S. wants to cut off Iranian oil exports unless Iran ends their nuclear weapons program. I'm sure your comrades in Moscow will be very interested considering the billions of dollars Russia makes with Iran every year."

Patrenko nodded. Barton had been providing names of covert operatives and secret plans for over eight months. The Russian SVR had already killed three U.S. operatives who were set to unmask Russia's unsavory deals with America's enemies – Iran, North Korea, and Venezuela. U.S. officials also believed Russia was providing aid and support to various terrorist organizations throughout the world. Without its superpower status, Russia felt impotent in the world community. And now with President Schumacher promising to get out of the energy import business and rely on North American oil, natural gas, coal, and nuclear power, the higher-ups in Moscow decided it was time to wake the old Soviet bear from hibernation, time for old man Gorbachev's policies of *glasnost* and *perestroika* to be put on the back burner. The SVR would travel the world befriending every unsavory person or group with a bone to pick with the United States and entice them with large stacks of whatever currency the traitor, mole, or sell-out wanted.

In the United States, Roland Barton was their guy.

Patrenko met him late one evening at Barton's favorite watering hole. Barton had let it slip on one too many occasions that he worked at the CIA. While his inflated ego wasn't so large as to tell any tall tales that he was an actual spy infiltrating foreign governments and saving the world, he did like to boast that he was in the upper echelon of the Agency.

Russian surveillance agents had been tailing him for several months and discovered Barton went to the bar every night at nine o'clock. Sometimes he would stumble out to his car and then weave his way back to his dump of a bachelor pad. Other times, the bartender would throw him in the back of a cab and give the driver five dollars to drive him home and keep his loud mouth out of the bar.

Patrenko initially told Barton that he was in the Russian oil and gas business and was looking to find someone in American Government who could help facilitate exploration deals. With dollar signs in his eyes, Barton seemed intrigued. Thinking himself the most brilliant person America had to offer the world, he thought he knew everything about every subject known to man.

Patrenko could tell he was reeling in Barton ever so slowly. By striking up a conversation and then a friendship with Barton, he lent him a sympathetic ear so Barton could lash out at his "stupid" superiors, the "incompetent" underlings at the Agency, and even his "slut" of an ex-wife. Patrenko fed Barton's deep-rooted ego and, before anyone knew it, they were talking serious money.

Patrenko and Barton started setting up meetings outside of the bar, usually in a different place depending on the month. Patrenko moved forward slowly, asking Barton for menial U.S. secrets that were one step away from being declassified anyway. Patrenko could have found those secrets in the garbage that an analyst put out by the curb. He went slowly just to make sure he had definitively hooked Barton for good.

Barton found the security at Langley left more to be desired. When the now-deceased Director Franklin was at the helm, national security secrets found their way to the outside world on a regular basis. Whatever then President Fisher's henchmen needed to cover their asses when things went wrong were promptly delivered to the news media so they could be leaked and written about in the next day's news. While Director Parker was trying to change the culture at Langley, it was slow going. And the changes were being made from the bottom up. The old dogs at the top were resistant to learning any new tricks. The revamping of the Agency would be a long and arduous process, but it was one that Parker was determined to make.

Barton, a few rungs below the top but still well above the wet-behind-the-ears rookies, saw this as his best time to get out. And make some money while he was doing it. Now all he had to do was give the Russians what they wanted without him getting caught. Then he could vanish to some tropical getaway and never have to worry about his crappy job, his exorbitant alimony, or his meddling creditors. He would tell the world to go to hell and laugh all the way to the bank.

Barton made sure never to take out a laptop or a briefcase full of folders stamped with "For Eyes Only." Instead, he faithfully carried his Mentos into work every day. When he went through the metal detectors, he'd throw his keys, his loose change, and the gum container into the tray. Once through, he put everything back in his pocket and went on his way. He'd then download what he needed onto the flash drive. He covered his tracks as best he could. It helped that the Russians were seeking information on matters Barton was privy to on a daily basis. Internal inspectors who might be watching wouldn't see any red flags by Barton searching certain records or looking in recent files.

On the way out at the end of the day, Barton would repeat the routine at the metal detectors. Sometimes, he'd even open the container and plop in a fresh mint with green tea extract piece and chew to his heart's content. The guards at the employee entrance paid little attention to him or his belongings. They couldn't stand him any more than the colleagues that worked side-by-side with him day after day. They simply wanted the blowhard to get the hell out of the building and leave them alone.

"My people are very happy with your work," Patrenko said to him. He could see Barton swell with pride. He knew the man was getting his satisfaction by sticking it to the Agency that had wrongfully held him down for so long. He should have been deputy director by now. At least that's what Barton had been telling himself for the last several years.

"There's something else," Barton said.

"What?"

Barton looked to his right and then bent down slightly to look through the gaps in the shelves. He turned back to Patrenko and whispered, "Something big has gone down."

"What do you mean?"

"It's really big. I can't give you all the details just yet but it involves the Pakistani intelligence service. I've given you a little taste on the flash drive. That's why I took the chance to meet with you," Barton said. His ego told him he was now running the show. "The stuff I've been giving you in the past is routine Agency information. You could get it off the Internet in a Google search. But something has happened. The higher-ups at Langley have been very tight-lipped lately. The Schumacher Administration is doing some very questionable stuff."

Patrenko was intrigued but he didn't show it. He wanted to get the hell out of the library. He kept looking over his shoulder. "Well, hurry up and tell me what it is."

Barton shook his head with great pleasure. He had them now. "You think I'm going to fork over all the information for nothing, Patrenko. You know me better than that."

Patrenko had no patience for being jerked around. "Listen, Roland," he grunted. "If you have information you want to give us, then follow the proper procedure. I'm sure my people will be happy to make a deal."

Barton knew it was time to drop the hammer with his demands. "Like I said, I've given you a little taste, something to chew on. But the other information I have is worth more than double what your 'people' are currently paying. Your bosses are a bunch of cheapskates. Tell them I have information that could put a serious roadblock in the path of President

Schumacher and his administration. It could put an end to the All-American Energy Plan as we know it."

Patrenko nodded his head. He turned to leave but added one last directive to make sure there were no more surprises. "Follow the procedure," he whispered. He stopped short of calling Barton an idiot. But he wasn't afraid to issue one last threat. "Or there will be consequences." He then fired off an imaginary bullet from his finger.

Barton, now totally full of himself, pretended to catch it with his left hand. "Have a nice day," he said with a smirk. He could see the palm trees and sandy beaches in his mind. Just a few more days at Langley to get the goods and clean out his desk and he'd be set to lounge around in paradise.

CHAPTER 4

Quantico, Virginia

The explosion rocked the building, the ground shaking underneath the shockwave of the blast. Glass flew everywhere. Those close enough to the building could hear yelling inside – gunshots ringing out, more explosions echoing throughout the surrounding streets. The five masked men who had entered were now on their way out, having not found what they were looking for. Armed with the best weapons money could buy, they were now walking in the direction of one man.

And he just happened to be the President of the United States.

Smoke still wafted through the air, a siren blared in the background, and nobody felt the need to surround the President or get him the hell out of there. There should have been an army of agents springing into action to save the most powerful man in the world. But none of the men with dark glasses and earpieces moved a single step. Some just watched. Of course, the President was on friendly territory so the Secret Service felt they could stand down for the time being. Or at least stay at a reasonable distance.

FBI Director Tyrone Stubblefield approached from behind. He was smiling from ear to ear. The men dressed in black battle dress uniforms with full body armor and carrying their Heckler & Koch MP-7s were his boys. He could not be prouder of them.

"They look good," the President said to him.

"They should," Stubblefield boasted. "They're the best we've got."

Despite the President's security resting in the hands of the Secret Service, Director Stubblefield took it upon himself to make sure all the bases were being covered. It was something he had been doing for over thirty years.

Anthony Schumacher was a fresh-faced lawyer from Indiana when he entered the FBI Academy and was assigned to partner with ex-football star Tyrone Stubblefield. After graduating from Quantico, they became partners at the FBI's San Diego field office. During their time together, they busted drug-trafficking rings, gun-running operations, and human-smuggling plots. The two spent much of their free time together – running, carpooling. Stubblefield and his wife Tina even welcomed the then bachelor Schumacher into their home. Both men envisioned a long career in the FBI.

That all changed one day during a botched bank robbery. Special Agent Schumacher had entered the bank to withdraw some money on a lazy Friday afternoon after work. While he was waiting in line, shots rang out and two heavily armed men in full body armor shot up the place and demanded the bank's cash. Special Agent Schumacher returned fire and killed one of the gunmen. The second masked man managed to fire off one round that struck Schumacher in the chest. The only thing that kept the gunman from finishing him off was Special Agent Stubblefield's deadly aim once he ran into the bank after the shots rang out. Schumacher nearly died, and he considered Stubblefield his guardian angel ever since.

After the shooting, Schumacher left the FBI and entered politics – first as a member of Congress, then Vice President, and finally President of the United States. At the same time, Stubblefield was working his way up the FBI ladder – breaking down racial barriers with every step. The two never lost touch with each other. And Stubblefield never stopped looking after the President. When then FBI Director J.D. Bolton was killed in the helicopter crash that injured Vice President Schumacher, Stubblefield headed the investigation. When President Fisher committed suicide, President Schumacher nominated Stubblefield to head the FBI. And the guardian angel didn't take a break. Stubblefield saved the President's life when then Justice Ali Hussein tried to detonate a suicide vest on the floor of the House of Representatives during the President's speech to Congress. When terrorists attacked the President's compound in Silver Creek, Indiana, Director Stubblefield was on the phone with his agents to help thwart the attack. He seemed to have the magic touch when it came to protecting the President.

Stubblefield was a proactive man. He wasn't one to sit behind his desk on the seventh floor of the Hoover FBI Building and shuffle papers from one box to another. He wanted to be on the offensive, not just react to matters after they happened. Given their history, their friendship, and the importance of the President's security in the world, Stubblefield devised Operation Phantom, a plan to shadow the President wherever he went.

And if need be, a plan to rescue the President in case of an emergency

– one where something has gone horribly wrong.

"Have you run this by Director Defoe and Agent Craig?" the President asked, thinking the Secret Service might like to know what Director Stubblefield and the FBI had in mind.

Stubblefield expected the question. Both men had deep respect and admiration for the United States Secret Service. Special Agent Michael Craig, the head of the presidential protective detail, was first with Schumacher when he was Vice President and had put his life on the line on several occasions to protect him. The President had the utmost confidence in him and his team of agents.

"Mr. President," Stubblefield said, a slight grin forming in the corners of his mouth. "I think you can understand that I believe it would be best to keep the operation quiet for the time being."

The President nodded. "I figured as much."

"Mr. President, I would like to introduce you to the team members of Operation Phantom."

"Nice job, guys," President Schumacher said, greeting the men. "It looked good. Sounded good too."

"As I told you, the Phantom team is led by Special Agent Schiffer."

President Schumacher reached out a hand to the masked man in front of the team. Although they had never met, President Schumacher was well aware of Agent D.A. "Duke" Schiffer and his heroic exploits on behalf of the United States of America. Schiffer was six-two and tightly packed with closely cropped hair and dark steely eyes. One of the FBI's most decorated marksmen, he had more commendations and service medals than any other active agent. A member of the Tactical Helicopter Unit and the Hostage Rescue Team, Schiffer was on duty, at Director Stubblefield's request, when the attack on the President's compound took place. Schiffer fired the shot that ended the terrorist plot. Now as team leader, his job was to train the men for any high-risk tactical operation they might encounter.

"What we have here is a quick strike team, Mr. President," Stubblefield said. "These five are the best the FBI has to offer. Snipers, counterassault, SWAT, HRT, they can do it all. Each agent has been cross-trained by the CIA for covert operations in foreign lands – allowing them to fully immerse themselves in the culture and customs of any country they enter. They can eat, drink, and dress like any local citizen would. If you make a stop in Moscow, they'll be wearing *ushanka* fur hats and eating *borscht*. On the Arab peninsula, they'll blend in with *keffiyeh* headdresses, *thawb* robes, and maybe even a *hookah* pipe if the situation calls for it."

The President nodded appreciatively as he began to understand the effort Stubblefield put into the Phantom team operation.

"Also, the team has been fully trained in survival, evasion, resistance, and escape. We've designed plans for each major city in Europe, the Middle East, and Asia. The men have scouted routes from the *Autobahn* to the *Champs-Elysees*. They have trained tirelessly, and they'll be quiet as mice."

"Well-armed mice," the President said, smiling.

"Yes, sir," Stubblefield responded.

He then introduced the rest of the men to the President. He pointed first to the massive six-foot-six figure at the end of the line. "This is Agent Olivera – our tool man, breacher, and driver. He is in charge of dispatching any obstacles that might come our way. He is also a master locksmith. He can pick any lock from here to Kathmandu."

Stubblefield continued on down the line.

"Agent Jenkins is our tech man – surveillance equipment, cameras, and bugs. Alvarez is our licensed pilot – everything from jet fighters to Piper Cubs and Little Bird helicopters. We call Agent Guerrero here 'the Detonator.' I think the nickname speaks for itself."

The biceps of two of the men were inked with, among other things, the trident of Poseidon, the Greek god of the sea. Both were on loan from the Naval Special Warfare Development Group. Stubblefield knew it could never hurt to have a couple of SEALs on his team.

Once the meet-and-greet was over, the President and Stubblefield discussed the FBI Director's plans.

"Mr. President, we'll take everything we need. Sniper rifles, MP-7s, flash-bangs, smoke grenades – all military grade and FBI approved. With night vision and thermal-imaging capabilities, we'll be able to act under the cover of darkness. We'll have anything we need to react quickly in an emergency. And we'll move it around to the FBI legat offices in each country's embassy and store it there. No one will see us and no one will hear us."

President Schumacher took it all in. He was always impressed when FBI firepower was being discussed but he felt the need to state the obvious. "You know, the Secret Service has a few good men and women at their disposal as well."

"I know, sir. I know. This is simply an extra layer of protection. If a terrorist would happen to infiltrate the inner perimeter, the Phantom team members will be able to coordinate with the Secret Service and respond in a matter of minutes. We're just going to be in the shadows. No one will know we're even there."

"Won't even know you're there, huh?"

"Yes, sir."

"Did my wife have anything to do with this grand plan you've cooked up?"

Stubblefield laughed. "Well, sir, she has mentioned your security to me on several occasions. And, of course, the First Lady and Tina talk on a regular basis. I promised the First Lady that I'd be with you every step of the way."

"Well, I guess it's better than her contacting the astrologers."

Stubblefield nodded and added, "We're a little bit more reliable too."

"You're not going to be on site with the team, are you?" The President's tone indicated his thoughts on the matter. He too was looking after his friend's well-being. When Democratic vice-presidential candidate T.D. Graham got himself kidnapped by Mexican drug cartels prior to last year's election, Stubblefield led a team of FBI agents down to Mexico to rescue him. Stubblefield was shot during the operation. Thereafter, President Schumacher ordered him to be more careful and let the younger FBI agents be the heroes. A hands-on Director, Stubblefield said he would consider the demand.

"Sir, I'll be in the shadows just like the rest of them."

"I don't think you're capable of blending into the shadows."

"I'll just quietly be in the background," he promised.

"You know the last time you were on site you got shot."

Stubblefield waved off the reminder. "That was a fluke deal, Mr. President."

"You're too famous to be in the background anyway," the President said. "Mr. *Time* Magazine cover man."

Director Stubblefield had indeed been on the latest cover of *Time* Magazine, his large hands on his hips, his suit coat opened revealing his massive chest. You could almost see a big red "S" on the front. A closer look at the right edge of the photo showed the Director's shoulder holster, no doubt carrying his own brand of justice in case America needed him to save the day yet again. The story inside was a wonderful biography of

America's top man at the FBI.

"I'm going on your Europe trip to talk security with my foreign counterparts."

"Just tagging along, huh?"

Stubblefield nodded his head and smiled broadly. "Yes, sir, just tagging along. Maybe check out the tourist hot spots."

CHAPTER 5

Eagle Station – Republic of Seychelles

"Wake up!" Stan Evans yelled, his right hand slapping Assad Khan across the face.

Khan's heavy eyelids had closed for the third time in the last sixty seconds and Evans was determined to make sure it didn't happen again. It was a hot and humid eighty-five degrees outside, but Evans and Khan were seated in a mobile industrial refrigerator that kept the place at an uncomfortable thirty degrees. The constantly churning generator vibrated the fillings in their teeth.

Evans' beard and mustache were gone, and his once full head of dark hair was cut short. He changed his appearance whenever he entered a new country. And the sweltering heat outside was good reason for a shave and a trim.

"I said wake up!"

Roughly a thousand miles east of Africa, the archipelago making up the Republic of Seychelles had seen a growing number of Americans invading its shores within the last several years. The remote outpost had seen a parade of U.S. Government Gulfstream C-20s and C-37s, Cessna UC-35s, and an occasional C-130 Hercules occupying the airspace. The American military had laid the runway within the last two years along with others in Djibouti and Ethiopia. From there, MQ-9 Reaper drones could patrol the Horn of Africa searching for al-Qaeda terrorists training to kill Americans and the Indian Ocean for pirates trying to capture American container ships for ransom. It was also the site of the CIA's East African site for operational interrogation.

"This is the last time I'm going to ask you, you schmuck," Evans promised with a hand slap to the cold metal table on which Khan was trying to rest his head.

Khan was handcuffed to the table, each wrist secured on the opposite end. His ankles were similarly shackled to the floor. He couldn't move, couldn't bring his arms together to warm himself. The only thing he could do was shiver uncontrollably.

He had been kept awake for thirty hours and he was beginning to succumb to the interrogation techniques of the CIA. Every terrorist thought he could endure the CIA's tactics. They bragged about it to others, always promising they would hold out and never give in to the evil Americans. Khalid Sheikh Mohammed was allegedly waterboarded 183 times before breaking, and every terrorist thug since then had promised to set a new record for interrogation obstinance. But no matter how much one crowed to his cohorts, the relentless CIA always got its way.

Evans, of course, knew this, as did his fellow operatives. Those joining him in the Seychelles even had a pool – fifty bucks to enter with the pot going to the closest one to predict the breaking point. The newer operatives always went high, putting too much stock in the jihadist psyche. They were all in double digits as to Khan's expected resilience. Evans, however, the wise veteran learned in the art of interrogation and coercion, quickly sized up Khan and went low. He'd break after six rounds of the waterboard, he proclaimed. Khan's playboy and pampered lifestyle would be no match for the water. Evans could already count the money.

Khan's boxers, the only clothes he had left on him were soaked, partly with ice water that had been thrown on him for the past two hours and partly with his own urine. His skin felt like it was being pricked with a thousand needles. And every hit from Evans made his skin crack. He was tired, hungry, and cold.

"Who in your government tipped off al-Qaeda that led to the killing of the ten U.S. soldiers?"

For a few minutes, the only sound heard was the humming freezer. Khan looked at Evans. "Fuck you Americans," he mumbled through chattering teeth. He didn't even know he said it. It just came out like a reflex.

In his parka and stocking cap, Evans wasn't going to put up with it much longer. He would just as soon end the interrogation and dump Khan into the Indian Ocean for the sharks to take care of. "You want the waterboard again?" Evans asked.

He didn't expect an affirmative response but he asked again.

"Huh, you want the waterboard?" He started unlocking the handcuffs shackling Khan to the table. Evans kind of liked the idea and was glad he could make it happen. "We can do the waterboard again if you want."

Khan could not control his shivering. His head was pounding. His entire body ached. The sixth round of waterboarding almost broke him. The water kept getting colder each time, the drowning sensation that much quicker. Despite his tough talk to his friends, he finally told himself that it was enough. If they threatened him with it again, he would just relent. They would break him sooner or later. He knew they always did. No sense prolonging the inevitable.

Evans turned to the table behind him. He grabbed a gallon jug of ice water and began pouring it slowly over Khan's head just to remind him what was next once they strapped him to the board. Khan recoiled at the freezing chill. It felt like he had an IV of ice water pulsing through his veins. He shook his head side to side.

No more. He was ready to talk.

Evans put the jug on the floor and opened a heated cooler sitting in the corner. He grabbed a warm towel and threw it around Khan's bare back. It was the first sense of heat in over a day. Khan wanted more and knew what he had to do.

"Who in your government tipped off al-Qaeda and the Taliban?"

A moment of silence. Evans expected another American slur. He made sure Khan saw him reach for the water jug again.

"No," Khan whispered, letting it be known that his mind was just slow in getting the information out of his mouth. "Major Assafa."

"Major Assafa," Evans repeated to make sure he heard right. Khan nodded. "Of the Pakistan Army." Evans knew of a Major Assafa, but he wasn't in the army.

Khan shook his head no. "Air force," he said softly.

"Assafa of the Air Force?"

"Yes."

"How high up did it go?"

Khan stiffened slightly. He didn't want to say any more.

"Was the Interior Ministry involved?"

"No."

Evans didn't believe him. "Was your father involved?"

"No," Khan said, his voice the strongest it had been since he arrived.

"No one in the Interior Ministry at all?"

"No."

"Defense?"

"Yes."

"Who in Defense?"

Khan stopped to think. He was having trouble remembering names.

"Come on, Assad," Evans said, his fingers drumming on the cold table. "Who in defense knew about the attack?"

"The Defense Minister," Khan said.

"Minister Mularah knew about it?"

"Yes."

"Did he order it?"

Khan nodded his head, although he might have been drifting off to sleep.

"Why?"

When Khan's head tilted downward, Evans slammed a fist down on the table. Khan's neck snapped back and his eyes awoke yet again. "Why did he do it?"

"Bin Laden," Khan mumbled. "Because of the U.S. take down of bin Laden . . . the NATO airstrikes . . . and . . . President Schumacher's threatened sanctions against my country." He exhaled, his breath showing in the frosty air. His body looked deflated, as if he was ashamed he had given up the information.

Evans nodded his head and turned to the see-through mirror, slightly fogged because of the chill. Even though he couldn't see those on the other side, he rubbed his fingers together and smiled. He had done his job for his country and came out a little richer too. He then twirled his finger to signal the next round of questioning could begin. A new interrogator would get all the specific information Khan had to offer while rewarding him as they went. By the time it was over, Khan would be fully clothed and enjoy a nice hot meal.

Evans stepped out of the freezer and into the midday heat. He took off his parka and stocking cap and soaked up the sunshine. He walked over to his sedan and grabbed his secure satellite phone from the trunk. He punched in the numbers and then stared out across the vast expanse of the Indian Ocean.

"Director Parker, please. It's Evans."

Director Parker was on the line in less than ten seconds. He was eager to hear what Evans had to report.

"Director, the subject has confirmed what we expected."

"Pakistani involvement?"

"Yes, sir. At least as high up as the Defense Ministry. We are still extracting the details as we speak."

"I want a full report that I can brief the President on," Director Parker said.

"Yes, sir. I'll have it by tomorrow morning."

CHAPTER 6

Palazzo Chigi – Rome, Italy

"Don't you threaten me, you bastard! I am the Prime Minister of Italy!"

The profanities that followed were part Italian and part Sicilian slang – although the only ones who could understand the latter weren't talking. Giovanni Scarponi slammed down the phone, the veins in his neck pulsing with great intensity. He stared at the phone for a couple of seconds, silently cursing whoever was on the other end. His deflated body slumped into his chair and he tried to rein in his breathing – in deeply and then out with a couple good long exhales. He closed his eyes hoping it would calm his nerves.

His whole world was crashing down upon him.

Scarponi had been Prime Minister of Europe's fifth most populous country for eight years, having used the billions he made from his media empire to keep hold on his position through two different Italian Presidents. As head of the People's First political movement, he had ushered in a wave of social programs demanded by his supporters. After years of generous welfare handouts, free university education, reduced working hours, and a lifetime pension for all Italians starting at age fifty, the bills were accumulating with no end in sight. Like much of the socialist-leaning Europe, Italy was drowning under a mountain of debt, and responsible politicians were finally coming to the realization that the big-government nanny state could not go on forever. Bond rates were on the rise, the Italian national debt skyrocketing. Members of Parliament were growing antsy and were tired of being looked upon as the laughingstock of Europe. Some feared Italy was on the verge of collapse, and Scarponi had been taking heat from every member of the European Union.

Scarponi, who relished the power that came with the job, had to pivot and introduce reforms to save his country as well as his backside. Once the austerity measures were proposed, the gloves came off and the long knives came out. Opponents smelled blood in the water, and even his friends started to cash in their chips.

Once intimidated Italian media outlets let loose with stories of Scarponi's womanizing with females from both ends of the spectrum – prostitutes, beauty queens, politicians, and even some who were barely old enough to consent to any of the Prime Minister's amorous advances. A notorious ladies' man, whose six-foot frame and dashing good looks made him a natural in front of a camera and a catch in the eyes of women across Italy, his exploits filled the pages of sleazy European tabloids for years on end. He had mistresses from Calabria in the south to Verona in the north. Along the way, he had a list of beauties from Naples to Bologna that he called upon whenever he was in town. If things got out of hand – a rough night in the sack or an unforeseen pregnancy, Scarponi's billion-dollar fortune came in handy. And he had made many a woman a rich one over the years.

The citizenry had been known to overlook Scarponi's sexual dalliances as long as their free handouts kept coming. But revelations had leaked out that Scarponi had been violent to his wife and booted her out of their Palazzo Chigi bedroom with such a lack of grace that even Scarponi's defenders could only shake their heads at his callousness. When pictures surfaced on the Internet of teenage hotties being escorted into the Prime Minister's residence, his hotel suite, and onto his yacht, Italians wondered whether Scarponi was really looking out for their best interests.

The door to Scarponi's office opened without a knock, and his chief of staff cautiously stepped toward his desk.

"Mr. Prime Minister, I have made the call for the cabinet to meet later on this evening," Luciano Rossi said quietly.

Scarponi did not respond. He was still slumped in his chair with his aching head buried in his right hand.

"Mr. Prime Minister?"

Scarponi nodded to Rossi, at least showing he was still alive after another brutal round of beatings in the press and still more violence in the streets of Rome. He could not get away from the madness. A glance out the window revealed clouds of smoke – some of it tear gas, but most from the piles of burning garbage that striking sanitation workers had not picked up in over a week. The stench of human waste hovered over the Prime Minister's residence and Italy's Parliament like a toxic cloud. The nightly news on Sky Italia showed masked anarchists and torched cars. Instead of tourists lining up to spend their money, signs on doors told them to go elsewhere because the museums and theaters were closed for business. Chants and whistles filled the air on a nonstop basis. The flag-waving rallies seemed to never end. Just outside in the Piazza Colonna, the protesters' incessant pounding of drums made Scarponi's headache that much worse.

"I brought you some aspirin and water, sir," Rossi said, approaching the man who still had not looked up at him.

Scarponi grabbed the bottle and shook out two aspirin. Thinking better of it, he poured out two more. With the way things were going, he thought about taking the whole bottle and ending it all. He washed the four pills down with the water and leaned back in his chair. He licked his parched lips and tried to blink the tired from his aching bloodshot eyes. He closed them, hoping the pills would have an immediate effect.

Rossi, his mouth also dry as cotton at the moment, made mention of the next item on the agenda. It would not be pleasant. "Sir, we have Mr. Zhukov from the Russian Federation here to see you."

Scarponi cursed under his breath. Riotous crowds and jilted lovers were problems he thought he could handle. He had done it before. His massive ego got him the job and it would work its magic to help him survive in office. But those damned Russians were a completely different story.

"Do you want me to send him away?" Rossi whispered. "I can tell him you have an emergency conference call with the EU." After a further thought, he added. "Or maybe that you are ill."

Scarponi liked the idea. He had no desire to talk with the Russians today. Plus, Zhukov was a notorious ball-buster – always threatening dire consequences if Mother Russia's demands were not met. Trade deals with Zhukov were never pleasant affairs. He had become known in certain circles as "the Mad Russian," and it was not a term of endearment. When Scarponi stood to scurry out the back, the door to the office burst open.

"Mr. Prime Minister, so good to see you," Viktor Zhukov bellowed loudly, barging in unannounced and uninvited. The Prime Minister's diminutive secretary made a worthless effort to try and stop the two-hundred-eighty pound Zhukov. With a full head of steam, the five-nine Russian shot straight toward the wide-eyed Scarponi like a cannonball.

Before Scarponi could take another step, Zhukov had already accosted him and there was no escape. "Mr. Zhukov," he said. "Hello again."

"I hope I'm not interrupting something important," Zhukov said, gripping Scarponi's hand with such force that he didn't dare pull away and excuse himself until a later date. Zhukov had huge calloused hands, strengthened by years of toiling in the Russian potato fields and rail yards as a youth and hoisting vodka by the pint as an adult. The hands led to a massive set of forearms that furiously pumped a handshake with great force. The intimidation factor was felt by even those who weren't on the receiving end of Zhukov's vice-like grip. "I've been looking forward to seeing you."

"I am glad you are here," Scarponi said without an ounce of sincerity. Zhukov was the last guy he wanted to see in his office.

"Now is a good time to talk," Zhukov said. It was not a question.

Scarponi eyed the man still crunching his hand. "Wouldn't you find it more productive to talk to the Interior Minister?"

"No, I wouldn't," Zhukov said slowly. He then leaned forward to make sure Scarponi felt the full force of his next statement. "It is *you* that I must deal with."

Scarponi's hand must have gone limp because Zhukov let go and motioned the Prime Minister over to the couch. Scarponi relented to the demand for a meeting, but the wheels were already turning on how to save himself from a prolonged chat. "Yes, I have a few extra minutes to talk."

As Rossi made himself scarce, the two men sat on the couch away from the windows. Without the rays of sunshine hitting them, the coolness of the shadows gave a slight chill in the air. Scarponi loosened his necktie, the tension squeezing his already tight throat.

"What can I do for you today?"

"My people in Moscow have discovered some interesting information about our Black Sea oil pipeline."

"Are you sure you don't want me to get the Interior Minister?"

Zhukov smiled and shook his head. "That's not necessary. Only you have the information I need."

Scarponi gulped. He didn't like the sound of Zhukov's tone.

Zhukov was the head of Russia's Ministry of Gas Industry, and he had personally inked a deal with the state-owned energy companies of Russia and Italy. The multi-billion-dollar deal promised to bring oil and natural gas from Western Siberia underneath the Black Sea to Bulgaria and then further west until it reached the Adriatic before ending at the southern boot heel of Italy. It was a massive political and financial undertaking, and one so big that corruption and graft would undoubtedly become a primary player. On the Italian end, the company set for the biggest payout was headed by Scarponi's brother – a sweetheart deal that would fill the family bank accounts in cash and gold. Unfortunately, Scarponi, his brother, and their agents decided to take a little more off the top than what the Russians had offered.

And now Zhukov was coming to collect.

The abrasive Zhukov decided diplomatic tact was not on the agenda. Phone calls and angry letters had made little headway. It was time to get tough.

"You have stolen from Mother Russia, you thief."

The charmer Scarponi feigned shock at the accusation. "I have done no such thing! You have a lot of nerve coming in here and calling me a crook!"

When the famed Scarponi finger wag made an appearance, the seated Zhukov lunged at Scarponi, grabbed him by the wrist, and twisted his arm behind his back. Scarponi howled in pain but only until Zhukov lodged one of his massive forearms in Scarponi's Adam's apple. Scarponi, zapped of any strength and giving up at least a hundred pounds to the raging bull Zhukov, who now had one knee perilously close to Scarponi's groin, could do little more than gasp for breath.

"The Russian people do not like it when people steal from us," Zhukov growled. Magnified by Zhukov's thick glasses, Scarponi could practically see the hammer and sickle in the madman's bulging eyes. "We warned you not to screw with us."

Scarponi, remembering he was the Prime Minister, managed to shove the barrel-chested Zhukov off of him. "Don't you threaten me, you prick," Scarponi said, massaging his neck and moving a safe distance away. He looked at the closed door to his office and wondered if he should hit the panic button for his security guards. "I've been threatened enough today and I'm not going to take any more of it from the likes of you."

Zhukov adjusted his glasses and stared straight at Scarponi. He reached into his suit coat and pulled out a folded group of papers. He threw them onto the Prime Minister's lap. "Ten-point-three billion dollars," he said, letting the figure sink in.

Scarponi looked over the list. "This is meaningless. It proves nothing," he said. He didn't mention that the number was actually lower than he thought.

"Ten-point-three billion dollars," Zhukov said again, just for the benefit of Scarponi's spinning mind.

"You have got to be kidding. That's just a rounding error to you Russians."

While that might have been true, given the state-owned energy company had $130 billion in revenue last year, the Russians did not take kindly to people stealing any amount of their money.

"We have phone conversations of you and your brother. We have banking records. Both prove that you have been shaving thirty percent off the top."

Scarponi stood and started the finger wag again. "You are just upset that the world oil market has tanked, my friend. Just because your energy coffers have dwindled does not prove that I am to blame. If you want to place blame on someone, maybe you should be looking at the United States and President Schumacher." The wag became more pointed. "He is the reason you are losing billions!" Scarponi yelled. The argument that Russia was a victim at the hands of the Americans made him feel good so he included his country as well. "He's the reason we're all losing billions!"

Zhukov stood, a coffee table the only thing between him and Scarponi. "Ten-point-three billion dollars," he repeated. When he reached into his suit coat again, Scarponi took one step closer to the panic button on his desk. He was about to make a lunge for it when Zhukov brought out a mini-cassette recorder.

"I have here a conversation between you and your brother and the deal you have cooked up to steal billions from the Russian Federation."

Scarponi said nothing. He just stared at the recorder. He remembered the conversations with his brother and the deal that had been struck, the offshore accounts that had been set up, the plans that were made for their life of luxury. But he was dubious as to whether the Russians could have eavesdropped on their calls. It was possible, he thought to himself.

"You have no such thing," he said. "You are lying."

At least one of them was.

Zhukov's thumb depressed the play button and the voices of Giovanni and Alberto Scarponi filled the air in the Prime Minister's palatial office. It was all there, the whole scheme laid out in grand digital fashion.

"You're a piece of shit," Scarponi hissed.

Zhukov knew he had him. He figured now all he had to do was issue his demands. "We expect you will make full repayment by the end of the month."

"Screw you! What the hell do you think you can do to me? I am the Prime Minister of Italy!" He had hoped that the title would carry some weight with someone on that trying day. So far, not so much.

Zhukov replaced the recorder back into his jacket pocket. "Mr. Prime Minister," he said with sarcastic deference. "As you know, we have people who are experts in matters of collections."

Scarponi readily understood the threat, but he wasn't one to shrink at the first sight of intimidation. "And may I remind you that my people do not like being threatened and will respond accordingly."

The "people" both were referring to were the Russian and Italian Mafia, both of whom could make Mexican drug cartels look like the Little Sisters of the Poor. When diplomats and ambassadors couldn't get the job done, the mob was oftentimes called in to break some legs and bust some kneecaps for the good of the country.

"By the end of the month," Zhukov said again.

"Get out of here!" Scarponi snapped. "Get out!"

Zhukov did an about-face and excused himself.

Scarponi's head was pounding again. When the door to his office closed, he picked up a glass paperweight on the desk and hurled it against the wall. Everything seemed to be closing in on him. His country was failing, his personal life was in shambles, and now some very threatening people were determined to force him to do things he didn't want to do.

He had to do something. He had to come up with a plan. Survival was now his number one goal.

CHAPTER 7

CIA Headquarters – Langley, Virginia

Seated at the conference table on the third floor, Director Parker had the look of a man who had the weight of the world on his shoulders. His tie was loose, and the top button of his white dress shirt was undone. His sleeves were rolled up, and his pale white arms indicated he had not been enjoying the spring sunshine during his off days. Of course, he hadn't had an off day since he started, and the bags under his eyes indicated he needed one badly.

Parker oversaw the Agency's operations in every nook and cranny throughout the world. He was a micromanager, some thought too much so, but he was determined to regain the trust of the President of the United States and that of the American people. The Khan capture was big, although no one in the outside world knew about it. The CIA couldn't really send out press releases tooting its own horn when matters of national security and international espionage are at stake.

While the successes made it worthwhile to get out of bed in the morning, the setbacks caused his hair to turn gray at an alarming clip. The weight gain was noticeable to him as well as his wife and his secretary. If he didn't take better care of himself pretty soon, everyone in the Agency would notice his growing girth.

Seated next to him, the head of the Agency's National Clandestine Service was ominously tapping his fingers on the table. Hank Fengler was in charge of the collection of human-source intelligence around the world, and, unfortunately, his trusted sources had been dropping like flies. Something was wrong and it was making his job very difficult.

Besides Director Parker and Fengler, four members of the CIA's internal affairs unit sat around the table. None of them looked like they were having any fun themselves. The faces were long, and the eyes intense. Everyone knew the CIA had a mole in its midst, and it was about time to force the traitor out of his hole.

Agent Tony McCoy grabbed the remote control, dimmed the lights, and then pressed the "Play" button. "Director, we believe this is our man."

The picture on the screen showed the official CIA employee photo of Roland Barton. The poor comb over made it look like he had a really bad toupee. A look of smugness was permanently etched on his face, like he thought he was the finest employee ever to have walked the grounds at the Central Intelligence Agency.

"Roland Barton," McCoy continued, "has been with the Agency for almost thirty years. With TOP-SECRET security clearance, he has worked as an analyst in the Office of Russian and European Analysis for the past fifteen years. He knows all the players in Iraq, Iran, Russia, Afghanistan. Over the years, he's written some good stuff for the CIA World Intelligence Review, provided plenty of good analyses on issues ranging from Russian arms deals, drug trafficking in Afghanistan, and Iranian nuclear technology. Over the past year or two, however, his attitude toward the job has deteriorated. Around the office, he's known as a control freak and a smart ass. Three complaints have been filed this past year concerning his behavior toward several of the secretaries. He was reprimanded once and ordered to undergo sensitivity training, which he successfully completed. He is recently divorced, and apparently he did not do well in the dissolution proceedings. He is also the father of two grown sons."

The six men seated around the table looked at the picture, peering into Barton's eyes to see if they could uncover what was going on. Some of them knew him, and none of those men liked him.

"Why do we think Barton's the mole?" Director Parker asked.

"There have been four analysts working on the Afghanistan and Pakistan operations in the last six months. They all have access to the same classified intelligence. We believe some of the information has been divulged to a Russian spy here in the United States."

"What type of information are we talking about?"

"We're talking highly classified material – NOFORN and WNINTEL both," McCoy said ominously.

The acronyms made Director Parker squirm in his seat. NOFORN stood for Not Releaseable to Foreign Nationals; WNINTEL for Warning Notice: Intelligence Sources and Methods Involved.

McCoy continued with the bad news. "Names of covert operatives, meeting sites, friendlies in Afghanistan, Pakistan, and Iraq. Three of the operatives have been killed in the last two weeks."

With a forlorn look on his face, Fengler nodded his head, indicating the information was accurate. Parker was not surprised with the news. With the loss of three operatives, he knew something wasn't adding up. "How was it divulged?"

"We believe the intelligence was downloaded on one particular work station on the second floor and saved to multiple flash drives."

"I thought we implemented a rule that says you can't take flash drives out of the building," Parker said.

"We did," McCoy said. "But we believe Barton smuggled his own flash drives inside and downloaded the materials."

"More than one?"

"Yes, a different one each time. And we have codes in all of the Agency's flash drives that indicate the material was not saved to them. It had to go to an unapproved one."

"Shouldn't it be impossible to download material on an unapproved drive?"

"The IT guys are working on it."

Parker didn't like it that the CIA seemed to always be one step behind. "So you think he brought in multiple flash drives and made it past the metal detectors?"

"Yes."

"On the way in and out?"

"Yes," McCoy said.

"And that didn't cause any red flags to go up? Any warning bells to sound?"

"Barton had TOP-SECRET security clearance, and he wasn't downloading the information on off days or at 3 a.m. on Christmas Eve. All of it took place within his regular office hours and involved material he was privy to."

"So he just walked out the front door?"

"It appears so. We're in the process of reviewing the security camera footage for the past two months."

Parker felt the need for an antacid. Something felt like it was eating away at his gut. He had been warned on entering the job about the lax security during the previous administration. It was just one more thing he'd have to fix. "Go on."

"We checked stores in the area that sell flash drives – Best Buy, Wal-Mart, Target. It was a shot in the dark given that flash drives are becoming so prevalent in today's world. But it didn't take long before we found something interesting at the Walgreens on Sycamore Street. When questioned about flash-drive sales, the store manager said they only sold one or two per week. But recently the manager recognized a man purchasing a flash drive on consecutive days and that same man had made similar purchases in the past few weeks. They were eight-gigabyte drives, and, as an anti-theft measure, they each had to be unlocked from their display by a store employee. The manager did so on two occasions and said the guy reeked of cigarette smoke. Given the amount of data storage available, the manager thought the guy must be downloading lots of porn. He remembered the man came in two days before we showed up. We asked to see the surveillance video and the manager readily agreed."

"Does Barton smoke?" Parker asked.

Two of the men nodded their heads. "Like a chimney," one said. "And it is obvious when you're around him," he added, shaking his head in disgust as he remembered the filthy stench emanating from Barton's clothes.

McCoy grabbed the remote again, pushed a couple of buttons, and up popped a black and white surveillance video showing the Walgreens checkout counter. McCoy turned up the volume and let those around the table have a listen to the transaction between the twenty-something checkout girl and a man wearing a Washington Nationals baseball cap.

"Did you find everything okay?" The big block letters on the name tag indicated her name was "Cassie." She was very polite. She had been trained well.

"Yes." The man said little. He also had been trained well.

"I like these flash drives," Cassie said, scanning the bar code twice until she heard the ubiquitous beep. She was very talkative and let everyone within earshot know what was on her mind. "I use them for all my classes. They are so much easier to use than compact disks."

"Yes."

"And you can put so much more information on them."

"Yes."

"It would take me forever to fill one of these up."

"Uh huh."

The chatty Cassie dropped the flash drive in the plastic bag and stood poised to total up the charges. "Is there anything else that you need?" She was very helpful.

The man looked behind the counter and pointed with the index finger of his right hand. "Give me a carton of Marlboro Gold," he said clearly.

The men seated at the conference table, trained at looking for identifying clues, saw no ring, no watch, no tattoos. It looked like the man had all five fingers on his right hand.

The young woman turned around, opened the cabinet, and grabbed a box. She then scanned the bar code, but the sound of the double beep kept her from reflexively putting the box in the plastic bag.

The man slowly glanced to his right, his left, and then back over his right shoulder. He made sure to keep his head down and only move his eyes so the camera wouldn't pick up his facial features. His worried mind told him the transaction was taking too long. He was ready to leave. An elderly woman with a head of white hair was pushing her cart toward the checkout. Out of the corner of his eye, the man saw her approaching and turned slightly to keep his back to her.

"I'm sorry, sir," Cassie said sincerely. "I'm supposed to ask for your date of birth." The man obviously looked old enough to buy a pack of smokes. She felt silly asking, almost embarrassed for having to do so. "But my manager will read me the riot act if I don't."

The man glanced to the left as the sliding door opened and in walked a customer. A ring of perspiration began to form under his ball cap. The old bag next in line scooted closer and started putting her containers of Metamucil on the counter. She then slapped a dollar-off coupon on the top of each one. The man was being boxed in.

"March 24, 1956," he said without a thought.

Cassie punched in the month, the day, and the year, and the computer responded with another beep that indicated the man could lawfully purchase cigarettes in the Commonwealth of Virginia. He paid with two fifty dollar bills – the cigarettes costing almost twice as much as the flash drive. Cassie took out her marker and gave a quick swipe of President Grant. Satisfied the security line indicated the man with the hat wasn't trying to pass a fake bill, she gave him his change and his receipt. He grabbed it with his left hand.

No ring, no watch, no tattoos, and no missing fingers.

"Thank you for shopping at Walgreens."

The man nodded but said nothing. Then he was out the door. The surveillance camera never got a good look at his face. The camera covering the parking lot showed the man walk to the corner of the store and then disappear into the concrete jungle of modern suburbia.

McCoy pressed pause. Those seated around the table said nothing, all of them waiting for Director Parker to chime in with his questions.

"We didn't get a clear view of his face," he said. How was he supposed to confirm the identity of the mole if they didn't have something more concrete to go on? There were probably a million people out there that buy flash drives and Marlboros.

McCoy was ready for the query. "Sir, we don't need a picture of his face. Roland Barton was born on March 24, 1956."

Parker leaned forward and rested his chin in the palm of his left hand. The chances of it being just a coincidence were slim to none. He wanted more concrete evidence, but he wasn't going to sweep what they had under the rug. Many an intelligence chief had been thrown under the bus for not recognizing the obvious clues and putting the pieces of the puzzle together. Parker was determined to stay on top of things.

"Let's put Barton under twenty-four hour surveillance. I want to know his every movement. I want to know who he is meeting with, who he's sleeping with, everything." Parker then made a motion with his hand. "Put up his last performance review."

McCoy grabbed the remote and scrolled down the computer screen until Barton's last annual review popped up on the wall. "He's due for his yearly polygraph next Thursday morning at 10 a.m."

CHAPTER 8

The National Mall – Washington, D.C.

"Hey hey, ho ho, that dirty Schu has got to go!"

So went the chant from the protesters as they paraded up and down the sidewalks lining Constitution Avenue and the National Mall. The new-age hippies were out in full force, signs decrying the Schumacher Administration and corporate America and claiming the Republicans and big business wanted to rape the earth of its natural resources and enslave the citizenry in menial minimum-wage jobs. Drums and bongos filled the air with dull monotonous tones. A few flags fluttered in the wind, but most of them were of the hammer and sickle variety. The protesters used the Stars and Stripes as floor mats and made sure to desecrate Old Glory in front of every TV camera they could find.

"Down with Schumacher!"

Grunge was the apparel of the day – communist green the favored color of the troubled masses. The anti-capitalist peaceniks contradicted themselves with Che T-shirts that were mass-marketed across the world. The protesters' shunning of most things capitalist apparently went so far as to include soap and deodorant. The place was beginning to smell like urine. Trash was piling up. Rats infested the place at night and feasted on discarded food. A bacterial meningitis scare brought out a haz-mat crew from the CDC. The ragtag gang had been there for three days, some sleeping on the bus, others with the homeless in D.C. They spent their nights singing songs and trolling the Anacostia area looking for weed, their stash apparently having been consumed in a short period of time. Most of them were high by midmorning.

"Down with the U.S.A.!"

Their numbers had swelled to four hundred, although the liberal media claimed the number was in the tens of thousands. The commentators called it "a movement," and some even likened the group's plight to those brave Chinese demonstrators in Tiananmen Square – the only exceptions being the absence of rumbling tanks and summary executions by a communist government. Most of the reinforcements had been bussed in from all over – union members from Baltimore with nothing better to do, anarchists from New York looking to smash some bank windows and overthrow the government, and environmentalists from Boston hoping to end drilling for oil and setting America on the course for "wind-only energy," although not in their backyard like the Cape, of course. One young chap lamenting America's oil addiction doused himself with the contents of a quart of Pennzoil every hour on the hour, although some of the tourists making their way to see the sites couldn't help but smell chocolate syrup in the air. Probably Hershey's. Maybe Nestle's. No doubt bought from those evil smiley-faced capitalists at Wal-Mart.

"Impeach Schumacher!"

The self-described progressives, the "Liberal" moniker having become a four-letter word in this day and age, were well-schooled in civil disobedience. The Democratic Party had succeeded in brainwashing them at an early age, which wasn't difficult given that most of their parents had once lived in the hippie communes in California and protested across the fruited plain every chance they could get.

They marched, they chanted, and then marched some more. They wanted health care, welfare, a college education, and a nice retirement. And they wanted it all paid for by their fellow American citizens. It was all-out class warfare. Although the liberals had taken a beating at the polls since President Schumacher came into office, they all thought the time was now for a return to the glory days of yesteryear. This was what all of America wanted they told themselves. And they were determined to let everyone know they were the future.

"It's a beautiful sight, isn't it?"

Arthur J. Brennan put down the binoculars. He could not stop smiling. With his trademark cigar in his mouth, he looked like a proud new father gazing admiringly through the glass in the maternity ward. He loved all his little children – little dirty rug rats that they were. The pugnacious head of the ultra-liberal Civil Liberties Alliance was looking south out the window of his Pennsylvania Avenue office. Even without the aid of the binoculars, he could see the miscreants and malcontents on the National Mall – all of them raising the hell that he was paying for. It was like Christmas morning to him.

Art Brennan had been a notorious thorn in President Schumacher's side ever since he took office. As head of the CLA, he took on every liberal cause he could and blamed all of the world's ills on the Schumacher Administration, the Republican Party, and the United States of America. If Muslims attending a Catholic school didn't like the atmosphere that "they were forced to endure," he'd sue to take down the crucifixes and statues of the Virgin Mary. If the terrorist detainees wanted legal help to get out of the detention camp at Guantanamo Bay, Brennan was by their side with an army of lawyers. If anarchists needed representation after being charged with destruction of property, Brennan swooped in with a helping hand. If protesters needed funding for transportation, Brennan made it happen. He was a man of action in Democratic Party circles.

He spent his time shuttling back and forth between New York and Washington, D.C. – wherever the fight was taking place, wherever the TV cameras were on so he could lambast the American way of life. He believed America needed to be taken down a peg, its superpower status an affront to the rest of the civilized world. Who was America to impose its brand of justice on others in every corner of the globe?

When not fighting for the liberal cause in the courts or on the streets, Brennan spent the remainder of his time gathering donations for the Alliance. Hollywood leftists and San Francisco liberals took up most of the donor lists. But lately Brennan had stepped outside the usual liberal haunts for his cash. He had started looking overseas in places where socialism was still hanging on by a thread. His friends in Italy, Greece, and Spain were always good for cash in hopes that a less powerful America would help their cause at home.

"I thought the demonstration would be bigger."

The man standing next to Brennan sounded disappointed. He was not impressed. He had been promised the protest would rival any the National Mall had ever seen. Brennan had even gone so far as to say Washington, D.C. would be shut down, the U.S. capital grinding to a dramatic halt. "It looks like a Sunday afternoon picnic."

Brennan's cigar tilted downward and his jaw clenched. He could feel his heart rate increasing. Brennan didn't take criticism very well. Now offended, he tried to save face. "No, there are more of them out there," he protested. He then pointed across the way. "You just can't see them because they're obscured by those buildings."

The man next to him grunted. It was obvious he didn't believe Brennan. His limousine had driven by the Mall just an hour earlier and he was not impressed by the size of the crowd then.

"I got more coming from the slums of D.C. in less than an hour." Brennan smiled again. "Just in time for the evening news."

Maxwell Warner turned away from the window and headed straight for Brennan's liquor cabinet. The silver-haired Warner, known as Max the Ax, was dressed in his finest Armani suit. The billionaire financier had made his way to Washington at the request of Brennan, who was hoping for a big fat check to fill the CLA's coffers. It was Brennan's job to feed Warner's ego, promote the CLA's agenda, and then pry the money from his clenched fists.

"Art," Warner said, licking his lips after a nip of scotch. "Have you ever worried about getting into bed with the wrong person?"

Brennan was twice divorced. He hadn't been in bed with a woman in years. The only thing he took to bed was an underlying hostility to all things Republican. His dreams centered on defeating conservatives, bringing down the United States, and replacing it with the social utopia found only in the minds of big-government central planners. Those were his loves, and he never cheated on them.

"No, I can't say that I have."

Warner stared straight at Brennan. "Well, that's what I'm worried about right now." He took another swig. "Why should I support the CLA when this is all I'm going to get for my investment?" He then pointed out the window. "My household staff could make more noise than those bums out there."

Max Warner was all about the money. He made billions of dollars in the green energy movement. His outfit was the first to photograph the lonely polar bears floating "helplessly" on the supposed last iceberg left on the planet. The pictures were then sent to grade schools across the country so little Johnny and little Jane would run home to mommy and daddy and tell them the world was going to end if they didn't vote for the Democratic Party. Donations poured in. Handwritten letters, some even penned in crayon, begged politicians to save "the" polar bear. It was a brilliant campaign – a tug-at-your-heartstrings tearjerker that conveniently paid little attention to the truth.

Warner then spent his money propping up climate scientists who shared his view of man-made global warming. Seeing the gullibility of the American liberal, he started the first business devoted to selling green energy credits. For a large amount of greenbacks, buyers could assuage their guilty conscience knowing that Warner and his company would promise to plant a tree or a bush or turn off a light and claim carbon dioxide levels were drastically being reduced across the globe. Warner laughed all the way to the bank.

Until President Schumacher showed up.

The Schumacher Administration rolled back job-killing EPA regulations put forth by prior presidents. "World renowned" global-warming alarmists were outed as frauds – only sounding the warning bells in hopes of continuing to receive their big-government grants and advance their liberal agenda. With the President's All-American Energy plan focused largely on oil exploration and domestic drilling, Warner's business of green energy offsets took a massive nosedive. The public-relations hit caused his other businesses to tank. He lost a hundred million dollars in the last six months. And the future wasn't looking any better. He needed help to stem the tide.

Things had gotten so bad he was willing to slip under the covers with the smarmy Brennan. As liberal as Warner was, he didn't like Brennan's brand of gutter politics. And he didn't like getting in bed with a snake. He'd rather just buy off politicians with fistfuls of campaign cash like he had done in the past. But the current political climate made bribery a waste of money.

"Max," Brennan said. "I need you. And you need me." Brennan had done his homework. He knew Warner had billions in the bank but was losing a good deal of his portfolio every month. Warner would be desperate for a change in policy and, more importantly, a change in administration.

"I need you like I need an STD," Warner hissed.

Brennan bristled at the condescension. He had made his mark in the world, and Democratic pols sought him out at every election. He wasn't some stooge, he thought. The backroom brawler took the cigar out of his mouth and pointed it at Warner. "Max, I think you know I have been having some troubles lately. I know you have been going through a rough patch as well."

Warner nodded.

"And I think we can both agree that the cause of our problems is that bastard down there at 1600 Pennsylvania Avenue!" The octave in his voice rose, and the blood was flowing generously to his round face.

Warner nodded again.

"If we can join forces, we can cause him so much trouble that the Republicans won't even want him running for reelection."

"That's almost four years away," Warner reminded him. He didn't want to wait that long. His bank account might not make it to the next election cycle.

"I know, I know," Brennan said. "That's why I have a plan. We need to hit President Schumacher hard on oil drilling and his energy plan. With your expertise on the global warming hoax . . ."

"It's not a hoax, Art," Warner protested slightly but not very convincingly. He wasn't ready to give up on his one-time moneymaker just yet. He was hoping the green energy indulgences would make a comeback.

Brennan, however, couldn't care less. "Whatever," he said. "Just like you did with those polar bears, we'll do with oil. We'll show sandy beaches full of oil . . . and . . . and birds!" he exclaimed. "We'll throw some oil on some birds and we'll show the pictures to school children and they'll send letters to the White House demanding the President stop polluting the world. We'll saturate the airwaves with commercials warning of the destruction of Mother Earth."

Warner tried not to roll his eyes at the small-minded man. "I don't know if that'll work any longer, Art." Warner turned toward the window and stared at the Capitol dome to his left. "The right wingers are on to us. The polar bear myth lasted, but only until people learned the truth that it was just one bear taking a respite on a floating piece of ice. There are more polar bears prowling the world than there ever have been. And the only animals in any danger are the baby seals that the polar bears are feasting on."

"I think it would work," Art said. He just knew he was right.

Warner, on the other hand, thought differently. Brennan knew the street, but Warner knew the market. "Art, you need to start dreaming big. You're never going to make anything of yourself unless you think out of the box."

"Screw you," Brennan huffed.

"I'm serious, Art. Your answer to most everything is a lawsuit or a protest. You want a couple of commercials showing oil-soaked ducks?" He didn't hide his utter lack of support for the idea. "What we need is President Schumacher out of the White House."

"No shit," Brennan snapped. Tell me something I don't already know,

Brennan thought. "If it was only that easy."

Now it was Warner's time to pump up the other man's ego. "With the people you associate with, you could make it happen."

Brennan stopped and looked at the floor. The people he associated with, he thought. He took a breath to watch what he was about to say. He was smart enough not to mention the "A" word. He was a deeply suspicious man, and he didn't put it past Warner to be wearing a wire. For all Brennan knew, President Schumacher's FBI might be listening in on the conversation as they spoke. He thought he had better protect himself.

"We can't take him out, Max," he said, lecturing him like a Boy Scout telling his cohorts that stealing candy from the corner store was wrong. For the benefit of anyone else who might be listening, he self-righteously added. "That's wrong."

"I'm not talking about that, Art." Warner wasn't stupid enough to say it either.

"Well, what's the plan?" Art wondered. "Impeachment? How do you plan on getting the Republican majority in the House of Representatives to bring charges of impeachment against a Republican President with eighty-percent approval ratings?"

Warner smiled again as he looked out the window. "Again, Art. You're thinking way too small. Impeachment is a nonstarter. It would never happen. Not with this Congress."

"Well?"

Warner turned to Brennan. "Do you have a copy of today's *Post*?"

"Sure." Brennan walked over to his desk and rummaged through a mound of paper. He pulled out his copy. "Here it is."

Warner grabbed the paper, walked over to the couch, and laid it out on the coffee table. He flipped through the pages and stopped on page four. There, under the Foreign News banner, were the goings-on from around the world. He motioned Brennan over.

The story above the fold showed a masked man in a cloud of tear gas throwing a Molotov cocktail at riot police in the chaotic streets of Rome. The protesters were fuming at the Italian Government's austerity measures. Unlike the mostly serene nature of those on the National Mall, the rioters in Rome were mad as hell that their political leaders were attempting to cut back on their free handouts. That Italy was broke was not their concern. They had been promised an easy life and were willing to get violent to protect their entitlements.

"See here, that's how it's done," Warner said, mocking Brennan's coddled, new-age hippies with their iPods, cell phones, and bottled water. But that was not what he was looking for. His finger worked his way down the page and found it below the fold.

"President Schumacher to meet Pope on foreign trip," read the headline.

Brennan looked it over. The President's first foreign trip would take him to France, England, and Italy in conjunction with the upcoming D-Day anniversary and the G-8 Summit. After skimming the story, he turned his eyes back to Warner.

"And?"

"This is our best shot," Warner said, pointing at the story. "We have to get him on foreign soil."

Brennan's back stiffened slightly. He wasn't sure what Warner meant by "get him."

"I know you have friends all over this world, Art. Friends in low places, friends in dark corners of the globe who only come out when it is in their best interest to strike. For goodness sakes, your last client was a 9/11 conspirator. Your legal bills were paid by the Saudi royal family."

Brennan interjected, "Muqtada Abdulla was entitled to a defense against the aggression of the American legal system!"

Warner threw up his right hand to stop him. "I know that, Art. But you cannot deny that there are rich people in this world who would like to support your cause."

"So what do you want?"

Warner pointed again at the picture of the rioters in Italy. "Maybe you should start out with this." He intentionally used the word "you" and not "we."

"You want me to take some of my protesters across the pond?"

Warner started shaking his head in disgust. "*Your protesters* are worthless. Look at these people," he said, pointing at the picture. "Molotov cocktails, rocks, and that's just what they can get their hands on. They torch cars, burn down buildings."

"What do you want out of my people?"

"Chaos," Warner said ominously. It was so simple, he seemed to say. "You start in France. You create chaos and let the world community know the problems President Schumacher is going to bring during his administration. Then you go to England and the chaos grows – massive protests that fill the streets of London and shut down the city. President Schumacher is a danger to the world, the template will go. Then it's on to Italy. By that time, some of your *more well-off friends* might be able to exact a 'regime change' for the benefit of us all."

Brennan pushed his stocky frame off the couch and walked over again toward the window. He didn't know what to make of the plan. He was looking at the protesters on the Mall when something farther south near the Potomac caught his eye. He thought he saw something ominously red and there was a bunch of horses crowded around. Thinking the riot police and their horseback posse were readying to shut down his march on Washington, he hurriedly picked up his binoculars and peered through the lenses. Then his jaw dropped. He could barely believe what he saw.

Brennan adjusted the lenses again just to make sure. He saw television crews, cameramen, handlers, gawkers of every stripe. On the far south side of the Mall under a stand of cherry trees stood one of the most treasured symbols of corporate America – the Budweiser Clydesdales. The dignified and stately beasts of the field with their reddish-brown coat and white stocking feet, along with their familiar red wagon fully stocked with Bud, two drivers, and the dalmatian, were on site for a TV commercial and calendar shoot with the nation's capital as their backdrop. They had an appointment at the White House later that day. With the eight-horse hitch preparing for a day in the spring sunshine, passing government workers marveled at their beauty, tourists flocked to their side, and young children with big smiles posed for pictures to send to grandma and grandpa at Christmas.

Americana at its finest.

On the north side, which might as well have been the other side of the world, Brennan turned his binoculars to his dirty, unkempt hooligans – the beasts of the human race, the great unwashed, what Lazarus must have meant by "the wretched refuse from your teeming shores," railing against corporate greed, President Schumacher, and American exceptionalism. He zeroed in on two scruffy looking members of his mob who were currently engaging in fisticuffs. Apparently, they had come to blows after one had stolen the other man's weed.

The difference in the two scenes was striking. The regal horses had more class and self-control than Brennan's rent-a-mob. He couldn't help but sigh. Feeling half-defeated, he turned back to Warner.

"Maybe you're right, Max. Maybe I need to start thinking bigger, maybe take the protests to the next level. I'll start working on my contacts overseas to see if we can make something happen." He then snapped out of his funk. "It'll take money though. And a lot of it."

Warner stood and offered a hand to Brennan. It was what he wanted to hear. "The check will be in the mail tomorrow."

CHAPTER 9

Camp David

The conference table inside Laurel Lodge was full, not a seat to be had. It was not out of the ordinary that all of the seats would be taken on the weekend before a foreign trip by President Schumacher. The logistics had been worked out, and now all the participants wanted to make sure they were on the same page.

"After the D-Day ceremonies in Normandy, we're heading straight for London," Wiley Cogdon said as he read the trip's itinerary.

As the President followed along on his copy, so did FBI Director Tyrone Stubblefield, Chairman of the Joint Chiefs of Staff Hugh Cummins, Defense Secretary Russell Javits, Secretary of State Mike Arnold, Secret Service Director Allen Defoe, and Special Agent Michael Craig, the President's lead security man. The latter six men had only one thing on their mind – the safety and security of the President of the United States.

It was a monumental undertaking, and the bulk of the work landed on the shoulders of the Secret Service and the military. Armored limousines and helicopters had to be flown over in advance of Air Force One's arrival. Agents from multiple Secret Service field offices across the nation had to be pressed into action overseas to protect against any eventuality. Advance agents had to go over proposed routes, cooperate with local authorities, and double check every potential threat over and over again. A nervous Director Defoe wished the President would just stay at home in the White House bunker.

"London looks clear," Director Defoe said. England was rarely a problem given the bond between the U.K. and the U.S. "Scotland Yard and MI-5 have reported no credible threats."

"And I'm sure Buckingham Palace has a pretty good security system in place," the President said.

Wiley then returned to his list. "And then we're off for just a day in Rome. First, a meeting with the Pope at the Vatican and then an early evening get-together with Prime Minister Scarponi at the official residence."

Defoe had no problems with Vatican City other than getting in and out. Rome on the other hand was a bit of a concern. "Mr. President, I'm sure you've seen the news that Rome is burning."

The President nodded. "First Greece, now Rome. They are having some fine demonstrations over there."

The Secretary of State nodded in agreement. "Some are peaceful, others require the riot police. It could get ugly."

Director Defoe had that worried look on his face. "It wouldn't bother me a bit if you decided to visit Rome some other time. Maybe like in your retirement years."

The President grinned. "That could be awhile."

Defoe nodded. "Yes, but I do have some concerns."

The President made an executive decision. "Well, we'll keep it on the schedule for now, have everyone in place as planned. If we change our minds, then we'll just skip it and tell Prime Minister Scarponi I need to get back to the United States."

"Yes, sir."

The trip planning was nearly complete when the President's personal secretary knocked on the door. "Mr. President, Director Parker is here to see you."

"Oh no, the CIA," the President lamented in jest. He was only half-kidding. Director Parker had taken to personally briefing the President on nearly everything that was going on at Langley. Day and night. Sometimes it would be two or three times a day. The President knew Parker was just trying to rebuild the trust with the CIA but for goodness sakes put it in a memo or something.

"Bill, come on in and have a seat," the President said, waving him into the conference room. "Something must be up if you're going to come all the way up here."

Director Parker nodded hellos to those seated around the table and took a chair a military aide just brought in and squeezed between Directors Stubblefield and Defoe. The others at the table stared at the new guy in their midst. He was the outsider, the one who had yet to fit into the club.

Parker cleared his throat. "Mr. President, I have good news and bad news to report to you today."

The President grumbled under his breath. "You always seem to carry some bad news with you, Bill. What is it this time?"

Parker opened up his file but the President stopped him before he could open his mouth. "Tell me the good news first this time."

"Mr. President, we have been getting quality intelligence from the capture of Assad Khan."

"That is good news," the President said. The rest of the group nodded their approval. The President placed his elbows on the armrests of his chair and folded his hands in front of him. "At the black site in the Seychelles?"

"Yes, sir," Director Parker said, turning over a page in his file. "We can confirm that Pakistani defense officials were involved in the deaths of our ten soldiers just a couple of months ago."

The President nodded, his clenched jaw noticeable to all in the room. "Are we already on to the bad news?"

"No, I'm sorry, sir. Confirmation of the plot by Pakistani insiders is the good news. Although I'm sure it is not much of a surprise to those of you here."

They all nodded.

"Pakistan has been on shaky ground with us for some time as far as I am concerned," General Cummins said. He was already thinking of an attack plan.

"As I remember Pakistan wasn't too happy with us after the SEAL raid that got bin Laden?"

Cummins nodded in agreement.

So did Secretary Arnold. "They were livid," he said. "If they had the ability to retaliate against us I think they would have. They have never forgiven us, and with our flourishing relationship with India, the grudge keeps getting stronger."

"It doesn't help that Pakistan's leaders keep getting more radical in their ideology," the President said. "What else?"

"Mr. President, we still believe we can get some more useful information from Khan and we will continue to use every lawful avenue to extract it from him."

The President gave one quick nod. Nothing else needed to be said.

Director Parker took a deep breath and squirmed in his seat. He could feel the eyes of everyone at the table looking at him. He still felt he needed to earn the trust of his colleagues, all of whom were slowly allowing the CIA back into their good graces.

"As for the bad news," he said, turning to the next page. "We have lost another operative."

"Another one?" the President asked. "Where?"

"Afghanistan."

"What do you mean by 'lost?'" the President asked. "Do you mean he's gone offline or AWOL?"

"No sir, we know where he is. He's dead."

"Murdered?"

"It appears so, sir. A gunshot wound to the head at close range – execution style."

Wiley felt the need to ask his own question. "Could it just be that your operative was hanging out with the wrong crowd?"

"It's possible, but losing three operatives in two weeks concerns me greatly." The CIA took great care in protecting their assets on the ground, and given the amount of time and money expended on them, losing one was always a matter of grave concern.

"You think the bad guys are getting tipped off?" the President asked.

Director Parker let out a defeated breath. He looked down at his notes. "Mr. President, I know I told you I had good news and bad news. But I'm afraid that I have some disturbing news that you and everyone else at this table are not going to like to hear."

The President gritted his teeth. The problems at the CIA had caused him sleepless nights. Sometimes he wondered what the hell was going on over at Langley. He leaned forward. "How bad is it?"

"Mr. President," Parker said, steadying himself like a good soldier and preparing for the bullets that would soon fly his way. "We have a mole in the CIA."

The President slammed his closed fist on the table, rattling the glasses of water that had been put out but not touched. "Damn it, Bill." The pulsing veins in the President's neck were not a good sign. The others at the table sat forward in their seats, almost begging the President to say the word and they would pounce on the new guy. Director Stubblefield glared at the man next to him and jotted a note down on his legal pad.

"Am I going to have to clean everybody out over there and start from scratch?" the President asked.

Parker, prepared to take his lumps, nodded in deference and held out both of his palms. He wanted to give the President the facts as he knew them and what was being done. "Sir, I have been worried about a mole for approximately two weeks, since we started losing operatives. I put internal affairs on it. We believe we have the mole identified. We have him on round-the-clock surveillance. If the man is in fact a mole, we will get him."

"Do I need to put Ty and the FBI on this?"

Stubblefield crossed off the note he had made and then turned his head toward Parker. The CIA Director could almost feel the massive Stubblefield getting ready to snap him in two.

"Mr. President, I don't think we're there yet. I have my best and most trusted people on it. And, as I said, we have the man under surveillance."

Stubblefield shook the room with his deep voice. "When are you going to take him down?"

Parker glanced slightly at Stubblefield and then the President. "I'll think we'll do it in a matter of days. We're still analyzing data and putting the pieces of the puzzle together. Obviously, we want to make sure we have the right guy." He then made eye contact with Stubblefield again. "Within a matter of days."

The President sat back in his black leather executive chair, the one with the presidential seal in the headrest. Contrary to the CIA Director, the President did not like to micromanage things. He tried to put the best people in the job and then let them do their thing. And he would have to do so now.

"Okay, keep on it, Bill. We need your operatives alive so let's make sure we get this guy. If you need help from the FBI, let Ty know."

"Yes, sir."

"Let's call it a day then," the President announced. "I need to start worrying about our so-called friends in Pakistan. Thank you, gentlemen, I'll see you all back in Washington before I leave for Europe."

Those around the table rose and excused themselves except for Director Stubblefield.

Once the door to the conference room had closed, the President looked over at his long-time friend and former partner at the FBI. He shook his head like he couldn't believe what was happening. "Tell me again why I took this job."

Stubblefield couldn't help but smile. "I told you not to." He then started counting on his fingers. "I warned you about it. My wife warned you about it. The First Lady warned you about it."

"All right, all right." The President didn't need any "I told you so's" today. He raised his arms above his head and gave them a good stretch.

"You want me to keep an eye on what's going on over at Langley?" Stubblefield asked.

The President didn't want any unnecessary squabbles between the FBI and CIA. He was willing to let Parker do what he said he was going to do. "We'll all keep an eye on him," the President said, hoping things were on the upswing over at the CIA. "You said you wanted to go over some things after everyone left."

"Yes, sir," Stubblefield said, opening his own folder. "I want to let you know where we are on Operation Phantom."

"Are all of your guys ready to go?"

"Yes, sir. The training is complete and they'll be on the ground when you get there."

"But you're coming with me, aren't you?"

"Yes, and I have some meetings set up with my counterparts following the welcoming ceremonies."

"Sounds good."

Stubblefield shifted in his seat. "I do have one other thing for you," he said, reaching into his pocket. He pulled out a container of ChapStick.

"Ty, I have plenty of ChapStick," the President said, reaching into his own pocket and pulling out his container. He never left home without it. If it would be appropriate for the President of the United States to hawk products on television, ChapStick would have a devoted pitchman.

Ty smiled. "I know, but this is the new super-secret ChapStick."

He scooted closer to the President and pulled off the white cap. Although he had several different varieties to choose from – cherry, strawberry, botanical berry, green tea mint, not to mention a medicated version for irritated lips and Ultra 30 for beach goers, Stubblefield went conservative and chose Classic Original. No reason to draw any unnecessary attention with strange or exotic flavors of lip balm. The tube looked like every other black and white tube of ChapStick the President had always used – a little padimate, white petrolatum, and carnauba wax among the regular ingredients.

"Mr. President, the guys in the FBI's gadget department have been working on a communication device that would be available to you in an emergency – in case a terrorist is able to grab you and take you hostage."

The President frowned and shook his head. "I can't imagine a terrorist getting close enough to take me hostage. We'd probably all be dead before that happened."

Stubblefield, however, lost sleep at night at the thought of a presidential kidnapping. A terrorist organization holding the President of the United States would create a crisis the world has never seen. Markets would crash, foreign governments might look to cash in on the confusion, dictators might try to expand their murderous reach. Chaos would be the order of the day. Stubblefield took it upon himself to never let it happen.

"Besides, the Secret Service already makes me carry around this panic button," the President said, reaching into his other pocket and fishing out his oversized Lincoln penny that, when the clasp was pressed, sent a signal to the Secret Service that the President was in an emergency situation.

Stubblefield nodded, indicated he readily understood. "But I wanted something a little more sophisticated than a panic button. All that does is tell someone you're in trouble. The Watergate burglars hid microphones in ChapStick containers, but that wouldn't do us any good in a hostage situation. I wanted something that would enable you to hear us and then communicate back. I know you have a locator device in your shoes, your belt, and the pen in your suit coat, but there's always a chance that a terrorist will make you discard everything on your person. I thought about your watch but they might make you hand it over as well. At any rate, even if you have a locator device on you, knowing where you are doesn't help that much as to what is going on around you."

"Yeah."

Stubblefield then looked directly into the President's eyes and held up the ChapStick. "Do not give this up," he ordered. "If they make you change clothes, hold it in your hand until you can store it somewhere."

Stubblefield then turned the dial at the end of the ChapStick container until the waxy end popped out. A wide-eyed President oohed and ahhed over the inner workings of the canister – an antenna acting as the shaft and an earpiece encased underneath the balm.

"If something happens, you'll need to get to a safe place," Ty said, as he carefully took out the earpiece that was slightly larger than a pencil eraser. It would be virtually unnoticeable once inside the ear canal. "Maybe get to a bathroom stall or a closet. Once the earpiece is removed from its housing, it'll send us a signal that it's operational. Put the earpiece in and you should be able to hear us."

"Okay, so I'll be able to hear you. Then what?"

Stubblefield then demonstrated the next step. "Replace the waxy part back into the container and put the cap back on. Once you screw in the other end far enough, you'll hear it click and know it is where it needs to be. Someone on our end will then be able to ask you questions, 'Are you okay?' or 'Is your security detail nearby?' or 'Are there more than ten terrorists in the room?'"

The President nodded.

"Then it's one click for yes. Two clicks for no. The good thing about this is you can click it in your pocket even with a terrorist or kidnapper in the room with you." Stubblefield then demonstrated for the President.

"I guess it'll be easier than learning Morse code."

"Yeah, but just click your answer and then wait for the next question."

The President nodded again, but he had a concern. "What if in the excitement of the moment I get the clicks wrong and you think I'm injured?"

The FBI had already thought of that. "Let me see your container. See where it says 'Net Wt 0.15 oz.' We've changed it to 'Yes W/ 1 cl.' Clear enough?"

"Yes."

"If the terrorist would happen to want to take a look at it, he's probably not going to read the ingredients and directions on the side."

"I hope not."

"Plus, we can always ask if your one click meant yes or no so we know we're all on the same page." Stubblefield held the ChapStick in front of his face. "With this, we'll be able to gain intel on how many terrorists there are and let you know that we're coming. Maybe tell you to hit the ground right before we barge in."

The President nodded as he grabbed the container. He pulled off the cap and applied the balm to his lips. He approved. "It's good."

"Just treat it like you do the normal one. If you run out, all we have to do is put in a replacement cup."

The President nodded his head and put the new ChapStick in his pocket. "Let's just hope I never have to use it."

CHAPTER 10

Oriole Park at Camden Yards – Baltimore, Maryland

Roland Barton's appointment with the CIA polygraph examiner came and went without Barton showing up. He had called in sick the previous two days. The flu was his excuse, and his hacking smoker's cough helped sell the lie over the phone. CIA agents had tracked Barton for the last week, shadowing his every move. On Tuesday, they saw him go to Founders Park in Alexandria, walk around for a half hour, and float a red balloon into the trees. They then watched as he walked into the library, where he spent ten minutes inside returning two books and perusing the stacks before leaving in his rusted white Taurus. Agents reviewed the surveillance video and were able to find the hiding spot in the sports section. There they found a Mentos container with a USB flash drive inside, the same brand sold at Walgreens. There was also a ticket to Thursday's Baltimore Orioles game with a note that read "10 grand cash, two envelopes. Then I'm done." The agents made a copy of the ticket, the contents of the flash drive, and put them both back on the shelf. Director Parker called Director Stubblefield at the FBI, told him what the Agency knew, and both recommended that Barton be taken into custody. Parker contacted the Attorney General, and the warrants were drawn up and signed off on by a federal magistrate.

After a weeklong investigation, the FBI, in conjunction with a team of CIA agents, made preparations for the arrest of Roland Barton.

In downtown Baltimore in the early part of June, the sun was shining, the sky was blue, the grass was green, and the Orioles were already eight games out in the American League East. In the city of the Bambino's birth, the first-place Yankees were in town threatening to sweep the three-game series and further bury the Orioles in the division basement.

Barton arrived an hour before the start of the game while the Yankees were taking batting practice. Since the Bronx Bombers were in town, he knew there would be a decent crowd even for a Thursday afternoon business persons' special. Enough of a crowd that he could blend in with the fans and still meet with his Russian contact. He walked along the field-box level, milling about the season ticket holders and beer vendors. His Orioles cap covered his head and his black windbreaker concealed his train ticket to New York tonight and the plane ticket to Sao Paolo tomorrow morning.

Barton had already shifted thousands of dollars forked over by the Russians to various offshore accounts throughout the world in numerous banks located in Switzerland, the Grand Caymans, and his future home in Brazil. He also had five thousand dollars tied to his right ankle and another five grand tucked behind a false wall in the suitcase in the trunk of his car. Never feeling like he had enough money stashed away, he left the ticket and demand for cash for Vlad the Impaler, which would give him another ten thousand to see and feel without the worry of his bank account being frozen by U.S. authorities once they inevitably found out about him and the selling out of his country. Of course, only after he had fled the United States and faded into oblivion.

Barton walked behind the visitors' dugout, soaking in the atmosphere of America's pastime for the final time. He would most likely never go to another baseball game again. Not in the United States at least. He wondered if they had baseball in Brazil. No Brazilian ballplayers came to mind. He thought he would probably have to learn to love soccer, which he couldn't imagine doing. He had skipped over the books about Pele in the library.

Barton started looking for Vlad, figuring the Russian would stick out like a sore thumb. He wanted to slowly make his way out of D.C. – first by car to Baltimore, then by train to New York. He thought meeting Vlad outside of the Washington area was the safest plan. He noticed a group of grade-school kids, no doubt on an end-of-the-year field trip, and their chaperones. The young boys were hurling insults at A-Rod, who was taking grounders at third base. He blew some bubbles but otherwise paid no attention. The girls, with their hot-pink posters and folded hands were begging Jeter to marry them, and the screams of glee when he waved to them as he trotted off the field indicated the outing had been worth it for the girls even before the first pitch had been thrown.

Two men next to the group of kids caught Barton's attention, snapping him out of his nostalgic trance. The men were dressed alike – khaki pants and black jerseys with "Ripken" and "8" on the backs. There were a thousand people wearing Ripken jerseys, even though the Hall-of-Famer hadn't put on the uniform in years. Barton thought sure they were eyeing him. Behind his dark sunglasses, he looked the men over from top to bottom out of the corner of his eye. When one of the men put his arm around his third-grade daughter, Barton moved on.

The FBI and CIA had purchased twenty tickets to the game, and a whole cast of federal agents were roaming about the ballpark. Several wore suits and ties – obviously businessmen playing hooky, maybe taking a "long lunch." The others blended in nicely – another Ripken jersey, a pinstriped T-shirt with Jeter's number two on the back. One CIA agent, a lifelong Orioles fan, brought his Jim Palmer jersey out of the closet. Another became a vendor for the day, hawking beer up and down the aisles like a seasoned veteran. The agents chatted on their phones, texted their positions, and downed a few hot dogs while they were on the job. It was a beautiful day for a ballgame.

Or the take down of an American traitor.

"Suspect has taken his seat."

The agents had all eyes on the seat that Barton had left for Vlad – Section 54, Row E, Seat 3 – not too far from the third-base coach's box. They were regularly $60 tickets, but since the Yankees were in town, the Orioles bumped up the price to $95. It was prime foul-ball territory with lots of good view of the action. Barton sat down in the second seat.

"Seat three is still empty." There was silence. "Seat one is taken. White male, gray hair, seventies."

The lead FBI agent in charge, Chris Bennett, radioed all units to keep an eye out for Barton's seat companion. He reminded them not to spook whoever was supposed to be sitting next to Barton, most likely his fellow conspirator. No one knew who they were looking for – male, female, young, or old. One agent sat three rows behind and used his iPhone for a ten-second scan of the field in front of him. And then, as any good Oriole fan would, he put down his phone and finished off a plate of Boog's barbecue to blend in. Another FBI agent knelt down in the camera well at the end of the first-base dugout. He pointed his long lens toward Barton's section across the field and got close-ups of everyone in the vicinity.

"Everyone in position?" Bennett radioed. All units checked in, but no one noticed anything suspicious. They all gave the unknown man in seat one a good long look.

The CIA and FBI had followed Barton to Founders Park, but nobody showed up to look at the balloon in the trees. No one showed up at the library to pick up the ticket or the flash drive either. It was possible the recipient would just buy a general admission ticket and then meet up with Barton during the game or even after.

"Ladies and Gentlemen, would you please rise and remove your caps as we join in the singing our national anthem."

The federal lawmen in the vicinity of Barton rose but kept a close eye on him behind their dark glasses. They all wondered what Barton was thinking. He held his Orioles cap over his heart and looked at the American flag fluttering in the breeze above the center-field scoreboard. Less than two miles away, the flag at Fort McHenry was flying high over Baltimore Harbor – just like Mary Pickersgill's 15-star version did on the morning of September 14, 1814, when Francis Scott Key penned what would become *The Star-Spangled Banner* after he witnessed the British bombardment of the fort from the Patapsco River. The "rockets' red glare" and the "bombs bursting in air" obviously had an impact on young Francis.

Apparently not so much on Barton – a sell-out and turncoat to his country.

After the anthem concluded, Barton took his seat and watched the Orioles take the field. He bought an $8 beer from one of the vendors making his way down the aisle. The guy in seat one next to Barton kept score, dutifully noting in the first square that Jeter led off the game with a sharp single to right. The third-grade girls in the upper reaches of the ballpark squealed with great joy at their boyfriend/future husband's triumph at the bat.

"All units report in," Bennett radioed. He was starting to get nervous. He began to wonder if he should reposition his men. They might be on the move shortly.

By the time the sixth inning rolled around, the Yankees were up by eight runs. Jeter was three-for-three and the girls in the upper deck were loving every bit of it. The Oriole Bird mascot was prancing up and down atop the home-team dugout trying to will some offense out of the lethargic O's. It wasn't working. The only birds taking flight in the ballpark were the boo-birds, the die-hards tired of the mounting early season losses.

The seat next to Barton's right was empty. It had been the whole game. Barton hadn't moved, not even to use his cell phone. The man to his left was still coloring in the diamonds on the Yankees' side of the scorecard. The only comment the man made to Barton was his desire that the Orioles fire the manager and replace him with Ripken – the last great hope for a return to the glory days of the famed Oriole Way. Barton gave a couple of nods in agreement but said nothing.

As the game wore on, the surveillance team began noticing Barton look around more frequently – his eyes glancing to his left and then his right, down the rows, and over his shoulder. Instead of watching the game, he was obviously searching for his guest and wondering where he was. Maybe the Feds were on to Vlad. If so, it wouldn't be long before they were on to him. The worry caused him to shift uncomfortably in his seat. His dry mouth could have used another beer. The five grand he had hidden on him felt like it was getting soaked with the sweat rolling down his leg. He had expected to meet Vlad, get his last envelopes full of cash, and then leave after five innings. He should have been at the Amtrak station by now.

It was getting late, the Orioles needed base runners, and Barton wanted to get the hell out of there.

Once the Yankees made the third out in the top of the seventh, Barton excused himself from the row while the crowd stood for the seventh-inning stretch. While the faithful broke into song, he hustled up the steps to the main aisle.

"Suspect is on the move," one agent announced into the microphone hidden in the collar of his jacket.

"All units look alive. Suspect is on the move and heading down the first base side of the seating area."

Jim Palmer, Cal Ripken, and Eddie Murray, or at least someone wearing their respective jerseys, started making their way in Barton's direction. The beer-man agent sold his last brew of the game.

Barton had gotten a bad feeling, the kind that told him he needed to get moving, to change plans and save himself from whatever might be around the corner. He felt it deep down in his gut, and his gut was telling him to run. Better safe than sorry, he told himself. He exited the stadium near the right-field section – the area teeming with Orioles fans wanting to leave early and beat the workday traffic jams. Barton looked right. He saw the grade-school girls lining up for the bus with their giveaway pennants and their cell phones full of Jeter pictures. Barton went left.

"Suspect is heading north on Eutaw Street."

The street ran parallel to the right-field fence and the B&O Warehouse, past Boog and his barbecue tent, and then exited behind the center-field scoreboard. He looked toward the west. He had parked his Taurus down near the Babe Ruth Museum. The agents following him noticed he took a good long look, like he was thinking about what he should do. His car still had his bags and ten grand stuffed inside. Something didn't feel right – Vlad was a no-show and Barton needed to get to New York. He could do without the cash, he told himself. He had plenty more hidden in his bank accounts. He pulled out his phone and stared at it. His mind told him not to make the call and let the Feds learn his position.

Time for Plan B.

"Suspect is now heading east toward the Inner Harbor."

A breathless Agent Bennett radioed from an unmarked car. He had four agents sitting on Barton's car, and now Barton was headed in the opposite direction. "Let's get some units down toward the waterfront. Right now! Call the Coast Guard and the Baltimore PD! He might be meeting someone on a boat. Let's move!"

Barton's steps quickened as he hustled down the sidewalk. His head never seemed to stop turning from side to side. As he walked, he checked the interior of every car, the eyes of every fan that had left the game. He looked in the rear windows of vans to check if anyone was following him. Storefronts gave him a chance to see if someone was closing in on him from the opposite sidewalk. He saw a man on a bench reading a paper, another man walking had a phone to his ear. They were all CIA, he thought. His heart rate spiked and the sweat was rolling down the side of his face.

"Suspect is nearing the USS Constellation."

Agent Bennett radioed the FBI field office in Baltimore and requested assistance. Bennett could not let him get away. A chopper was ordered and would be in the air above downtown Baltimore in five minutes.

"We need agents on foot and support vehicles," Bennett ordered. "Keep an eye out for Barton getting into a vehicle. Let's get some people down to the train station!"

Barton kept heading east, trying to figure out what to do. The Amtrak station was in the opposite direction and north several blocks. He could backtrack, he thought. But that would take time. He could take a cab, but if the CIA or FBI were on to him, he knew a train ride wouldn't do any good.

"Suspect is heading in the direction of the Hard Rock."

Bennett and his driver were three blocks behind Barton. From the front seat, he was trying to get a visual on Barton through his binoculars. "How many agents do we have nearby?"

Four agents were within two blocks of Barton and six others were stuck in traffic.

Barton turned around and looked back west. He heard nothing but the sounds of normal rush-hour traffic of Baltimore. Maybe he was being paranoid. Maybe it was nothing. It was then that he saw red and blue flashing lights of two unmarked vehicles stopped in a line of cars behind him. Four other men, who definitely weren't out for an afternoon jog, were running straight for him a block and a half away.

"Shit!"

Barton looked north but saw no way out – nothing but the concrete jungle that would eventually box him in. He thought about stealing a car but he knew that would end badly. He just needed to put some distance between him and the men coming to get him. Then he could contact Vlad and demand the Russians save his ass from American law enforcement or he'd out every last one of those SOBs.

Barton took off in a sprint for the Inner Harbor. The water was his only way out.

"He's running! He's running! He's heading for the waterfront!"

"All units, he spotted us! Take him down!" Bennett yelled before switching on the siren.

Barton was now in full sprint, the five grand taped to his ankle causing his right leg to lag slightly behind in his gait. The world was passing him by in blur. He scanned the scene in front of him. A large crowd was ahead – some coming from the game, others exiting the National Aquarium. He weaved in and out of school buses and charter coaches lining the street. The evening trolley tour had just started and he hopped on one side and leaped out the other side.

"He's on the trolley! Check the trolley!"

Two agents with their badges on full display brought the trolley to a screeching halt, the passengers jolted in their seats. They climbed on board the trolley and checked every seat, but they didn't find Barton.

"He's running along the busses toward the Harbor!"

Two others agents were closing in. The badges were visible and hanging from a chain around their necks. They had restrained themselves from unholstering their weapons. They hoped it didn't come to that.

"Barton! Stop! FBI!"

The whole scene played out like a movie. Everyone not involved in the chase stopped to watch what was going on. Some pointed. Others thought better of it and headed for cover.

"Don't move Barton!"

The fifty-six-year-old Barton was gasping for breath. His frantic eyes tried to ward off the blackout that was sure to follow from the lack of oxygen making it to his brain. He hadn't run this hard in years, and his tar-scarred lungs felt like they were going to explode. With every step he took on the pavement, his head pounded in agony and his heart struggled to keep the blood flowing.

He looked at the water and forced his aching legs to keep moving. The Big Red Boat was shoving off. His only hope now was the water taxi and it was starting to motor away from the dock. He could feel the agents closing in, the gut-wrenching feeling of the long arm of the law ready to grab him and not let go. He let out one last primal scream as he made it to the end of the dock and launched himself through the air. He landed with a thud against the side of the moving water taxi, his ribs taking the brunt of the collision.

"Aghhh!" he grunted in pain. His hands desperately tried to keep hold of the railing of the pontoon boat.

"Oh my God!" one of female passengers screamed. "Oh my God!"

The rest of the stunned passengers felt the boat rock slightly to the right whenever the breathless Barton tried to pull himself up out of the water. The rocking motion increased with every heave Barton made. When several large passengers from the left rushed over to the right side with its own fair share of obese patrons, the boat felt like it was going to tip over.

Then all hell broke loose.

One passenger acting as a Good Samaritan tried to bring Barton aboard and save him from the murky depths. Another man in a Yankees cap, apparently thinking Barton was a terrorist or just some cheap bastard who didn't want to pay for a ticket, tried to kick the interloper off the railing. The taxi captain stopped the boat as it rocked back and forth in the chaos. Purses flew through the air. Screams echoed off the water. One elderly lady passed out in the commotion and fell to the deck. Two passengers, not wanting to go down with the ship, jumped into the harbor and swam for shore.

A gasping Barton was still hanging on for dear life, although the kick to the head by the Yankees fan just about did him in. The money that was once strapped to his ankle started to surface on the water.

Agent Bennett, his team of FBI agents, and those from the CIA reached the harbor and found the Baltimore police department's marine unit fishing Barton out of the water. Once they hauled in their catch, they laid him on the deck of their police boat. Barton looked like he was dead. They brought him to shore and handed him over to the FBI.

Agent Bennett took the lead as one of his team members applied the handcuffs. A line of police officers and federal agents kept the crowd from getting too close. A drenched Barton said nothing. His breathing was labored. He coughed up what was left of the harbor water that he had swallowed. He had a welt above his left eye.

Bennett stepped forward. "Mr. Barton, you are under arrest for conspiracy to commit espionage and acting as an agent of a foreign government."

Bennett walked Barton over to an unmarked car and put him in the back seat.

It was all over.

Roland Barton would spend the night before his planned retirement in a six-by-ten jail cell.

Air Force One

The President had his feet up on the footstool in his office near the front of Air Force One. The reading material in his hands was his speech for the upcoming D-Day festivities. He had had a good week. First, it was a Memorial Day weekend at the Indianapolis Motor Speedway for his annual pilgrimage to see the "Greatest Spectacle in Racing." On Monday, he attended a wreath-laying ceremony at the Congressional Medal of Honor Memorial in downtown Indianapolis. After a much needed three-day vacation at his home in Silver Creek with the First Lady, their three children, and two grandchildren, one of whom was just a month old but already well spoiled, it was time to head overseas for his first official state visit as President of the United States.

The President and his entourage of fifty Secret Service agents were currently somewhere over the Atlantic – Air Force One at its cruising altitude of 40,000 feet and a speed of 600 miles per hour. A Boeing C-17 Globemaster had ferried the President's limousine, codenamed

"Stagecoach" and nicknamed "The Beast," as well as the rest of the presidential security caravan, which was already on the ground in western France. A second C-17 was currently flying at 35,000 feet with twenty pararescue jumpers ready to pull the President of the United States out of the Atlantic if necessary. Two fully armed F-15E Strike Eagle aircraft escorted Air Force One on the flight over. It was the safest the President would ever be save for the White House bunker. He was the most guarded man on the planet.

But he would soon be in hostile territory.

"You're probably going to get a lot of crap from the leaders of Spain, Italy . . . Russia," Cogdon said, going through his checklist.

"Don't I always?"

"Damn communists. The American economy is on the upsurge, but we have all these socialist countries that are mired in an economic slump that they can't seem to pull themselves out of."

"Well," the President said, smiling. He could tell Cogdon was getting hot under the collar. "Maybe they need to make some tough decisions on how to run their countries. I'll just talk tough to them and tell 'em to shape up."

Cogdon nodded. As the President's political guru, he was always concerned about public perception, how things would play out in the media. He didn't want the President to look weak, to let his foreign counterparts walk all over him and make him the laughingstock of world leaders. He went over his list of things every President should avoid doing while on a foreign trip.

"Make sure you don't bow down to them when you first meet. You don't want to look like Obama."

"Okay," the President said, dutifully noting the warning. He then stopped, trying to think of something to get Cogdon's blood pressure up. "What about the Pope? He's old, a bit feeble. What happens if he's sitting down when I'm introduced to him and I have to bend over?"

Cogdon tapped his pencil on his lips. His contemplative state indicating this was a matter of great importance. "Bend at the waist, not at the knees. No genuflecting."

"No genuflecting," the President repeated.

"Just a good firm handshake."

"Got it."

"And don't throw up on a foreign leader at dinner like the elder Bush did." Cogdon was crossing items off his list as he went.

"No bowing, genuflecting, or vomiting. Anything else?"

"Don't give in to their demands either," Cogdon ordered. "You're the President of the United States. It's okay to say no."

The President gave that smile that said he was thankful for the half-neurotic Cogdon's advice. "Don't forget I'm multilingual. I can say 'No' in eight different languages."

Wiley chuckled.

"No, *no, no, nej, nee, nein, non,* and *nyet.*" The President started counting on his fingers. "I think that's English, Spanish, Italian, Swedish, Dutch, German, French, and Russian."

Wiley started shaking his head. "I don't think you can count 'No' as three different languages."

The President shrugged. The conversation was interrupted by a ringing phone.

"Yes," the President said.

"It's Director Parker." The communications office on Air Force One was ready to patch the CIA Director through to the President.

"Okay, I'll take it. Bill, it's Anthony Schumacher, can you hear me?"

"I can hear you loud and clear, Mr. President."

"What's up?"

"Mr. President, I am proud to report that we have taken the suspected mole into custody."

"That's good news," the President said. He placed a hand over the phone and relayed the news to Wiley. He then returned to Director Parker. "What's the man's name?"

"His name is Roland Barton, a thirty-year veteran of the CIA. We believe he was involved in selling secrets to the Russians."

"Did we get anybody else?"

"Sir, I'm afraid to say Barton is the only one in custody at this point. We thought he was going to meet with his Russian conspirator, but he or she was a no-show."

Director Stubblefield walked into the office and the President motioned for him to take a seat. Stubblefield was preparing to break the news to the President but Parker beat him to it. He gave the President a thumbs-up.

"Do you think we can get any information out of this Barton guy?"

Parker paused slightly. "We'll try, but I wouldn't hold out much hope."

"Okay, good job, Bill. Hang on just a second."

The President put his hand over the receiver. "Should we let Bill take the lead on this?"

Stubblefield nodded. "Let him put a nice big red bow on it."

The President agreed. "Bill, why don't you get together with the Attorney General and the U.S. Attorney and make the announcement in D.C. We'll make a statement once we get situated on the ground in France."

"Yes, sir."

"Good work again, Bill. Keep on it."

"Thank you, sir. I will."

CHAPTER 11

Central Detention Facility – Washington, D.C.

A stiff and sore Roland Barton awoke at 6 a.m. with a massive headache. He had spent several hours in a Baltimore hospital being treated for various cuts, scrapes, and a few kicks to the head. Once discharged, he was transported under heavy guard to Washington and the Central Detention Facility. For the two hours he spent alone, he did not sleep well – the bed in jail not being the most comfortable place to lay one's aching head. But mostly his mind could not stop racing through the events of the previous day. He cursed Vlad Patrenko and the Russians. He told himself he should have never trusted them. He wondered if they had tipped off the American authorities.

He had been so close. Now he was looking at spending the rest of his life behind bars as a guest of the government for which he used to work.

The unlocking of his cell door roused him from his slumber. Two guards entered and ordered him to "cuff-up." It took a few seconds for him to move his stiff extremities, but he finally stood, cursing under his breath. The orange jumpsuit they gave him smelled like it hadn't been washed since the Nixon Administration. Once Barton was securely shackled, the guards brought his aching body down to an interview room.

Special Agent Chris Bennett walked in and placed his yellow legal pad and folder on the table. Barton's movements were slow, and he could do little more than scowl at the man.

"Can I get you a cup of coffee, Roland?"

Barton shook his head but only until the searing pain reared its ugly head inside his brain.

Bennett noticed. "Maybe a glass of water and some aspirin?" Thinking about Barton's daring escape attempt yesterday in Baltimore, Bennett could not suppress a grin as he looked at the disheveled man.

"Go screw yourself," Barton croaked, barely audible.

Bennett took a seat, flipped over the top page of his legal pad, and clicked his pen. He then took out a sheet of paper from his folder and laid it in front of Barton.

"Roland, I'm going to read you your *Miranda* rights first," Bennett said before rattling off the well-known rights – right to remain silent, anything he said could be used against him in court, right to an attorney, and right to a court-appointed attorney if he couldn't afford one. "Do you understand the rights I just read to you?"

Barton nodded slowly and just once. Bennett then placed a waiver-of-rights form in front of him. Without any further prompting, Barton reached out for Bennett's pen, made notations after each listed right, and then signed a name with great flourish at the end. He could feel the energy starting to return to his body. He then slid the paper back over.

Bennett looked at the form, saw that Barton had written "FU" after each right before signing it "Fuck You" in his own elaborate script at the end.

"I take it you don't want to make a statement or answer any questions."

Barton thought about spitting in Bennett's face, but his head hurt too much to rare back and let it fly.

"We'll take you down to the federal courthouse in about two hours, you'll have your initial appearance, and then we'll see what happens after that. They'll get you some breakfast here pretty quick."

Barton said nothing verbally, but the daggers he was throwing would be understood in any language.

Bennett picked up his materials, put his pen in his jacket pocket, and started to head out. When he reached the door, he looked back at Barton and raised his eyebrows – as if to ask one more time whether Barton wanted to get something off his chest, maybe confess and bare his soul right then and there.

When the door was about to close behind Bennett, Barton blurted out, "Wait!"

Bennett stopped in his tracks, pushed open the door, and doubled back into the room. He thought Barton might have had a change of heart, maybe he just wanted to explain his actions to his fellow government agent.

"Yes?"

"I just wanted to say a few things," Barton said. He sounded sincere, like it felt good to talk to someone after what happened yesterday. "Off the record."

"Sure, go right ahead."

Barton could not contain his smug grin. "I want you and your buddies to kiss my ass."

Bennett frowned. He didn't like to be jerked around. He wasn't really surprised though. "Anything else?"

Barton lost the grin. He was smart enough to know what he needed to do next.

"Yeah. I want my lawyer."

World War II Normandy American Cemetery and Memorial –
Colleville-sur-Mer, France

President Schumacher and the First Lady were the first of the heads of state and dignitaries to arrive at the Normandy American Cemetery. The sun was out and the sky was clear. A slight breeze rolled in off the English Channel, causing the First Lady's blonde hair to blow gently off the shoulders of her red dress. The President wore a dark blue suit and a red tie over his white dress shirt – red, white, and blue being the colors of the day. The President asked to arrive early so that they might walk amongst the field of white crosses and Stars of David and plant American flags on the graves of the men who gave their last breath for freedom. There are over 9,300 graves at the cemetery, and the markers, each in their perfectly straight rows, seemed to go on forever above the lush carpet of green grass. It was the first time the President had been to Normandy, and the gravity of what happened there hit every patriotic American in the gut. And even more so the current Commander-in-Chief of the United States military.

After the national anthems were played and speeches made, the President took his turn at the podium. He thanked the French President and the other world leaders who sought to honor the men who stormed the beaches of Normandy on that fateful June day.

"We stand here today in the midst of world turmoil – fueled by the angst of an agitated generation. A generation that demands more from their fellow countrymen and women to satisfy the wants and desires of their self-centered lives. Currently, there are protests in Washington, Paris, London, Rome, Munich, where the young of our world demand that their countries provide them with sustenance, education, health care, employment, and retirement. They are the demands of the entitlement generation who believe in a cradle-to-grave mentality of wealth redistribution and government handouts with little or no sacrifice required on their part. Let me read you some quotes taken from those who are currently protesting:

'What we ask for is what we deserve.'

'I have bills, and it is time for the government to pay them.'

'We are the future of this world.'"

The disdain the President felt for the malcontents of society was evident to all who were listening. Some of the liberal TV commentators whispered to themselves that such a partisan political speech was inappropriate for a D-Day memorial service. Their Twitter feeds derided the President and his "boorish" and "obnoxious" behavior. Some called on his speechwriter to be fired. Others called on Cogdon to be fired – but that was just because they didn't like him. Still more apologized to their foreign colleagues and the rest of the world for their President's immature behavior.

But President Schumacher was about to switch gears.

"Contrast a segment of our current generation with the generation who stormed these beaches and scaled the cliffs on the sixth of June 1944. Men who gave their last breath in the air above, on this land below, and in that channel afar. Brave men who did not leave the comforts of their homeland to demand what they felt they were entitled from their government, but to protect what they believed were blessings given to them from their God above. They left the farms, the factories, the printing presses, the doctor's offices to join together in the fight for freedom. Their brothers and sisters across the Atlantic were in desperate need of help against the tyranny of the Axis Powers, and they charged headstrong into the face of evil, knowing the winds of liberty would propel them forward – always forward – with the hand of the Almighty guiding them to victory. The courage and bravery displayed by the thousands of men who landed here can best be described by a citation presented in the name of Jimmie W. Monteith, Jr., a 26-year-old first lieutenant of the United States Army, who landed a short distance away on that unforgettable June day in 1944. Let me read it to you:

'1st Lt. Monteith landed with the initial assault waves on the coast of France under heavy enemy fire. Without regard to his own personal safety he continually moved up and down the beach reorganizing men for further assault. He then led the assault over a narrow protective ledge and across the flat, exposed terrain to

the comparative safety of a cliff. Retracing his steps across the field to the beach, he moved over to where 2 tanks were buttoned up and blind under violent enemy artillery and machine gun fire. Completely exposed to the intense fire, 1st Lt. Monteith led the tanks on foot through a minefield and into firing positions. Under his direction several enemy positions were destroyed. He then rejoined his company and under his leadership his men captured an advantageous position on the hill. Supervising the defense of his newly won position against repeated vicious counterattacks, he continued to ignore his own personal safety, repeatedly crossing the 200 or 300 yards of open terrain under heavy fire to strengthen links in his defensive chain. When the enemy succeeded in completely surrounding 1st Lt. Monteith and his unit and while leading the fight out of the situation, 1st Lt. Monteith was killed by enemy fire. The courage, gallantry, and intrepid leadership displayed by 1st Lt. Monteith is worthy of emulation.'

"First Lieutenant Monteith's actions, 'for conspicuous gallantry and intrepidity above and beyond the call of duty,' resulted in him being posthumously awarded the Congressional Medal of Honor. Along with so many of our heroes, First Lieutenant Monteith is buried here, just a short walk down the way. Although his life ended on D-Day, his courage and bravery continue to inspire us even to this day. Just like him, thousands of brave men put aside their desires for self and marched forward, side by side, upon hearing the desperate cries of the oppressed in this world. The so-called "Greatest Generation" did not turn a deaf ear to that call for help. Their own self-interests were cast aside, and they mobilized to save a country, a continent, and mankind itself.

"Where would we be?" the President said softly into the microphone, looking out over the gathered crowd.

"Where would we be if those men who charged across the ocean to liberate those oppressed under fascist regimes did not come? They came from the Allied nations of Greece, Norway, Poland, Czechoslovakia, Belgium, the Netherlands, France, Australia, Canada, Great Britain, and the United States of America. Where would we be if those brave men had asked, 'What's in it for me?'

"Today we are once again confronted with hostile regimes who seek to impose their violent ideologies on the rest of the world. Those regimes seek to dominate or to destroy anyone who does not follow their belief system. Women are denied the right to vote, teenage girls are sold into slavery or forced to marry against their will, men are beheaded . . . simply for believing in God. There is evil in this world and it must be confronted everywhere just as those who took part in the D-Day invasion confronted evil here on the northern coast of France. I call on this generation to redouble our efforts to support the cause of freedom and liberty throughout the world. Just as we should emulate the courage and leadership shown by First Lieutenant Monteith, we owe it to the Greatest Generation to continue the fight for freedom here and abroad. And we also owe it to the generations who will come after us to preserve for them a life as a free people.

"To the men who lie here in eternal rest, to those who are with us today, and to those around the world, on behalf of the United States of America and the Allied Powers, may I humbly leave you with a heartfelt *efharisto*, *takk*, *dziekuje*, *dekuji*, *dank u*, *merci*, and thank you."

Following the ceremony, the American contingent made its way out of the cemetery and onto the beaches – first Omaha and then Utah – where they looked at the cliffs and the churning waters of the English Channel. As the gusty winds blew ashore, the President knelt down and ran his hand through the sand, trying to imagine what it must have been like to hear the crack of seemingly endless rifle fire, bullets whistling past your ear, the land exploding beneath your feet, and to feel the fear and anxiety that every step forward must have caused as your comrades in arms fell on each side.

Once the President finished his visit to the monument to U.S. Rangers at Pointe du Hoc, he shook the hand of every veteran and current military man and woman he could find. The pictures and autographs took a good forty-five minutes. As he headed for the limousine, Director Stubblefield caught up to him.

"That was some ceremony today," Stubblefield said.

"Yes, it was."

"Mr. President, I just got a call from Special Agent Bennett in Washington. He said Barton lawyered up."

"Probably not much of a surprise."

"No, not at all."

"Well, I guess we'll have to wait and see what comes out. Maybe I should have a chat with the Russian President when I get to London."

CHAPTER 12

Office of the Civil Liberties Alliance – Washington, D.C.

Art Brennan was hunched over his morning newspaper, a cup of coffee to his left, and a cigar burning in the ashtray to his right. A trail of smoke snaked its way to the ceiling. Brennan's office was a cluttered mess – stacks of legal files piled on side tables, in the chairs, on the floor. There were no family pictures anywhere to be found. He had no wife or children, no dogs or cats either. The open spaces on the walls contained framed copies of the front pages of big-city newspapers with Brennan, mouth wide open spewing forth some fiery rant and index finger poking the air for emphasis, as he took his liberal crusade to the people.

Brennan was transfixed with the news from Italy, where rioters were making a mess of the place and political leaders were succumbing to the people's demands. Brennan's rent-a-mob was still on the job on the National Mall. They were a hearty bunch, enjoying the June sunshine without a care in the world. Whether they would stay through the tourist season and the high humidity rolling down the Potomac remained to be seen. He hoped they could hold out at least until the Fourth of July so he could get some good press. Maybe create some fireworks of his own.

The ringing phone disrupted Brennan's train of thought.

"What?" he grunted. He didn't like to be disrupted during his morning coffee and smoke. Any interruptions made him more irritable than usual, and those not wanting a tongue-lashing did their best not to disturb him.

Brennan's secretary, who was used to his abrasive style, did not apologize. "Mr. Brennan, there's a call for you from a Mr. Roland Barton."

Brennan had his eyes on a picture of the Italian rioters and their bandana-covered faces. "I've never heard of him. Take a message."

The secretary thought for a second. She was readily aware that Brennan wasn't very good on the computer. Probably hadn't even turned it on yet. He obviously had not seen the Internet headlines and the announcement that the FBI had arrested a CIA mole in a dramatic chase through the streets of downtown Baltimore. The morning's *Post* was lacking in details, and the name of the spy had not even been mentioned.

"Mr. Brennan, the FBI arrested a CIA agent who was spying for the Russians."

"Yeah. So?" He threw the cigar in his mouth and gave a good satisfying puff.

The secretary couldn't believe she was having to spell it out for her boss. "His name is Roland Barton."

Brennan almost lost his cigar in his lap. He sat up straight and shook the cobwebs from his head. He wasn't sure if he heard correctly.

"Mr. Brennan, Roland Barton is on line one."

Brennan leaned forward and dropped his cigar in the ashtray. He was slightly disoriented at the news. He took a sip of coffee to wet his lips and cleared the smoky phlegm from his throat. "I'll take the call, Mary."

He could not believe it. His first spy. A man after his own heart – the destruction of the American way of government. And from the inside no less. He tried to control his breathing. He didn't want to sound too interested lest it throw Barton off. Deep breath, he told himself.

"This is Art Brennan," he said calmly.

There was a silence on the other end. Barton had been hanging on for three minutes and he was wondering if he had been cut off. He figured it was just the Feds trying to listen in on his conversation.

"Hello?" Brennan asked, fearing his dream client had hung up on him. The red light on the phone indicated someone was still on the line. "Hello?"

"Hello, Mr. Brennan, this is Roland Barton."

Yes! Brennan thought to himself. He still had him. "Roland, please, call me Art," he said. No need for formality, he thought. They were comrades, buddies, soldiers in the same cause. Maybe even twin brothers separated at birth. "It is good to hear from you. How are you doing?"

"Well, I've been better. I take it you have read the news and know who I am?"

Brennan spun around in his chair and furiously tried to find the button to turn on his computer. He needed to get his Internet up and running. He thought about yelling to his secretary for help.

"Yes, I've read what happened yesterday."

"Mr. Brennan, I am in need of legal counsel."

Brennan smiled from ear to ear. He hadn't heard such good news since one of the 9/11 conspirators signed on with the CLA's team of lawyers. Muqtada Abdulla was his most high-profile client, and his mug shot could still be seen in some of the papers hanging on Brennan's ego wall. Of course, Abdulla was eventually on the receiving end of a lethal injection, but Brennan had done the best he could with a guilty terrorist. The case had brought him much acclaim from thugs across the world.

"I can imagine."

"Those bastards in the Justice Department are going to try and railroad me and then send me to prison for life."

Brennan could not agree more. He liked the sound of Barton's anger. "Sons a bitches," he grumbled in full support of the man on the other end of the line.

"Can I count on your help?"

"Absolutely!" Brennan gushed. He was already starting to plot strategy, his legal mind preparing to maneuver through his client's minefield. "Let's not say any more over the phone. You never know who might be listening."

"I hear you." Barton should, of course. He being a former member of the clandestine services at the Central Intelligence Agency.

"I have an initial appearance at the federal courthouse in one hour."

Brennan jumped out of his seat. He needed to get moving – he needed his best suit and he wanted to start scheduling his TV appearances that would surely follow the hearing. "I will be there and then we'll talk some more afterwards."

"Thank you, Art. I just have one more thing."

"Go ahead," Brennan said eagerly. Anything you want was his tone.

"I don't have any money. The Government has frozen all of my accounts. I've got nothing to pay for an attorney."

Brennan thought nothing of it. "Don't worry about that, Roland," he said. "I'm on your side, and the CLA will gladly represent you free of charge."

"Thank you, Art. I look forward to seeing you."

The Embassy of the Russian Federation – London, England

To the west of Kensington Gardens in central London, the Harrington House, constructed in 1852 and located at No. 13 Kensington Palace Gardens, is home to the ambassador of the Russian Federation in the United Kingdom. The Soviet Union and Great Britain first established diplomatic relations in 1924, which were suspended by the Brits in '27, and then reestablished in '29. In 1999, the Russians and the United Kingdom entered into an agreement extending the Russian lease for another 99 years. The annual price – one pound sterling.

The Embassy up the street was relatively quiet in the early afternoon – there being no parade of foreign nationals traipsing to the Embassy in search of a visa to start a better life in the former Soviet Union. Of course, the Embassy staff handling visa application forms was well-known for being rude and abrasive at those looking to peacefully invade Mother Russia.

The black Mercedes with tinted windows and diplomatic plates barely drew a second glance as it made its way through the gates and stopped at the rear entrance to the residence. Cars just like it were seen on a regular basis throughout London and that section of Kensington Gardens was home to multiple foreign embassies. The plates were registered to the High Commission for Pakistan in the United Kingdom. Located just to the southwest of Kensington Gardens, the quick jaunt to the Russian Embassy was one that was made on a regular basis.

Aleksei Dubrovsky met the man at the foot of the grand staircase.

"Mr. Khan, it is nice to make your acquaintance," Dubrovsky said. He was the Ambassador Extraordinary and Plenipotentiary of the Russian Federation to the Court of St. James and, unlike his staff, he was always welcoming and played the gracious host. He had been on the job for two years now and he was well received in the diplomatic community.

But his own people kept him in the dark.

"I was told you were coming." He didn't know why. "And I wanted to personally welcome you to our embassy." He was hoping someone would fill him in.

"Thank you," Khan said, shaking Dubrovsky's hand as he surveyed the surroundings.

Pervez Khan was a naturally suspicious man. He didn't get to be Pakistan's intelligence chief by trusting people. Other than his father, who was Pakistan's Interior Minister, Khan trusted no one. He kept his friends close and his enemies closer.

"I will take you upstairs to our conference room," Dubrovsky said, showing the way to the elevator. He had no clue as to whether other guests would be arriving for the meeting.

On the second floor and seated at the conference table was Vladimir

Patrenko. He had a glass of Stolichnaya vodka in one hand and a Cohiba Lancero cigar in the other. The vodka was Russian, which reminded him of home. The cigar was Cuban, which reminded him of how a country should be run. He admired the Castros, and he longed for the hard-line days when a Russian like Khrushchev would threaten to bury the United States and impose his will in every corner of the globe. As the smoke rose to the ceiling and the vodka made its way into his bloodstream, Patrenko sat back and waited. He was feeling lucky today.

The Impaler had fled the United States soon after Barton showed up unannounced in the Alexandria library. Once a mole starts breaking the rules of the game, Vlad knew it was time to move on lest he be caught in the middle of the mole's eventual slip-up. His flight proved right, given that it wasn't long after they had met that U.S. law-enforcement agents obviously became suspicious of Barton. Patrenko knew he would get nothing more out of the man, and now it was time to utilize the goods Barton had delivered prior to his arrest.

The door to the conference room opened, but Patrenko did not stand to welcome his guest of honor.

"Vladimir, this is Pervez Khan," Dubrovsky said as introduction, waving his guest over to the table. Dubrovsky then excused himself.

Patrenko nodded and motioned for Khan to take a seat. Patrenko knew full well who the man was. He was just the man he wanted to see. Khan, however, decided to stand for the time being. Perhaps this would be a short meeting, he thought. Nothing was said for ten seconds. The men just eyed each other.

"Would you like a drink?" Patrenko asked, breaking the ice and pouring himself another glass. The vodka was 80 proof, but Patrenko gulped it down like it was tap water.

Khan shook his head in the negative. He looked Patrenko over, wondering if he was the Russian President's bodyguard. The use of alcohol by Russian security men while on the job was not out of the question. Some in Moscow thought the men were more alert when slightly lubricated.

"I thought I was going to meet with President Yaroslavsky," Khan said. He thought he deserved an audience with the top leaders of the Russian Federation. He had never even heard of Patrenko, didn't even recognize his face as being one of Russia's higher-ups in government.

"He will not be arriving in London until tomorrow morning," Patrenko said. He then motioned Khan to the chair closest to him. "Please sit down."

A reluctant Khan took a seat, his body language indicating he wasn't comfortable.

"How are things in Pakistan?"

Khan still did not know who the man was, and he was prepared to walk if the mystery lasted much longer. "I didn't know my country was a concern to you, Mr. . . . ?"

"Vladimir."

Khan nodded. Now they were getting somewhere. "Vladimir . . .?"

Vladimir leaned forward and smiled. "I like to go by Vladimir, Mr. Khan. I can tell that you want to know more, but let's just say that we work in the same line of business."

Khan's back stiffened slightly, and he squinted his eyes. He was not very fond of Russian intelligence agents, and he distrusted the SVR more than any other spy agency in the world. Those in the SVR would stab a friend in the back without a second thought.

"Same line of business. Is that so?"

Patrenko nodded and again reached for his glass. He took another sip and closed his eyes in ecstasy as the vodka slid down his throat. "I have some very important information that my superiors want the good people of Pakistan to know about."

Khan's mind was spinning wildly, trying to remember any Pakistani operatives who might have been snooping around Russian interests. If Patrenko confronted him with information on any Pakistani spies, he would deny the allegation and leave.

"And what would that information be, Vladimir?" Khan asked, not showing an ounce of concern.

Patrenko pushed his empty glass away. He cleared his throat and looked straight into Khan's eyes. "We know where your brother is."

Although Khan said nothing, his wide eyes gave away what he was thinking. He had not heard from his brother in over a week and, while that was not unusual, Khan always had ways to contact him in case of emergency. Whether it be a cell phone, the Internet, or courier, Pervez Khan could reach his brother Assad if necessary.

Two days ago, the United States launched a drone attack in northwestern Pakistan at a camp used by a group of resurgent Taliban fighters. Needless to say, those in the upper echelon of the Pakistani

Government were none too happy with the American military and the Schumacher Administration.

And they were determined to put a stop to America's aerial invasion on their homeland.

Pervez was now in need of his brother because the Pakistani military was planning an assault with Taliban fighters on a U.S. base across the border in Afghanistan. Assad Khan would be the one to coordinate the attack.

"Where is he?" Khan asked, trying to hide his concern. "It is important that I talk to him."

"I know it is," Patrenko said. He didn't try to hide the fact that the Russians knew full well what was going on inside Pakistan. The Russians had eyes and ears all around the world.

"Well?"

Patrenko relished the mayhem he was going to cause by divulging the secret information. He leaned in closer and whispered. "The Americans have him."

It took a few seconds for it to sink in, but once it did the fury inside Khan shot out.

"Damn them!" he yelled as he pounded his fist on the table. With nostrils flaring and fire in his eyes, there was no holding back his anger any longer. "I knew something had happened to Assad. He would have contacted me by now, especially after that U.S. drone strike. Those fuckin' Americans are going to pay!"

Patrenko sat back to watch the tirade. He was very pleased with the response. It was even better than he imagined. This might be easier than he thought.

"How do you know the Americans have him?"

"One of our operatives passed along the information to us."

"Where did they get him?"

"Milan."

Khan slammed the table again. Milan. Of all places, he thought. A part of him was mad at his brother for screwing around in Italy, risking his life and the secrets of Pakistani leaders to satisfy his horny urges. Assad had promised this would be his last trip to Milan, but now he was at the mercy of the CIA.

"Where is he now?"

"His last known location was at a CIA black site in the Seychelles."

Khan mouthed the word "Seychelles" to himself but said nothing. He pushed his chair away from the table and stomped around the room. For a fleeting moment, he actually considered a rescue attempt – a glorious victory against those infidel Americans. But the chances of the Pakistani military invading an island in the middle of the Indian Ocean and grabbing Assad Khan from the hands of the CIA were zero. With the rescue plan now jettisoned, he only had one thought on his mind.

Revenge.

"When is President Schumacher coming to London?"

Patrenko could see the wheels turning in Khan's mind. He was starting to like the man. "Tomorrow. Around noon," he said, like he knew the American President's complete itinerary.

Khan continued pacing, slamming his right fist into his left palm. "I'm going to kill that son of a bitch myself," he fumed under his breath.

Patrenko said nothing. He just emptied the last drops of vodka into his glass.

Khan stopped in his tracks, trying to put what he learned into some prospective. He wondered if he was missing something. "Why are you telling me this, Vladimir?" he asked, suddenly curious why the Russians would divulge such explosive information without even a hint of money being involved.

"The information about your brother just came to our attention within the past several days," he said, licking his lips after emptying the glass. "We thought you would want to know. The Russian Federation values its friendship with Pakistan."

"Thank you," Khan said. Maybe the real reason would come out someday, but Khan had things to take care of, plans to make. "I hope I can repay the gesture sometime in the near future," he said, holding out his hand.

Patrenko rose from his seat and gave a firm shake. After Khan excused himself, Patrenko could not help but smile as he looked out toward the Gardens. Without any advice, without any prompting, he set the wheels in motion for the demise of the United States. Soon the Russian bear would be drowning in oil profits once again.

And Russia would regain its rightful spot as the world's lone superpower.

CHAPTER 13

Albert V. Bryan United States Courthouse – Alexandria, Virginia

The TV satellite trucks had staked out their positions the night before as the United States Government prepared to initiate proceedings against the CIA spy. Cameras panned up and down the sidewalk showing security agents patrolling the grounds. Well-manicured cable news reporters lined the grassy area and told their viewers about the double life led by Roland Barton.

The CIA had its fair share of moles and turncoats throughout its history – Barnett, Nicholson, Ames. All of them spied for the Soviets and Russians.

And none of them did it for free.

Aldrich Ames, a CIA counterintelligence officer and analyst, outed American double agents in the late '80s and early '90s in exchange for large sums of money. He pleaded guilty for spying against the United States in 1994 and will remain a permanent resident in a federal penitentiary for the rest of his life. Harold Nicholson sold intelligence secrets for $300,000. Upon conviction, he was sentenced to 20-plus years in the federal pen.

With the promise of riches tempting those with knowledge of information somebody is willing to pay for, the CIA is and always will be at risk from within. And the Russians, with plenty of cash and an unquenchable thirst for American secrets, were always lurking to entice their next sell-out.

"All rise," the court marshal cried. "The Honorable James Madison IV presiding."

Those who were strangers to the courtroom – out-of-towners, rookie reporters covering their first trial in the Eastern District of Virginia – always had a look of wonderment when Judge Madison strode to the bench. The regulars could see it in their wide eyes. Did they hear correctly? Could it really be? Was this man before them a relative of the great man himself?

No, they were later told much to their disappointment. The men were not related, not even distant cousins.

Virginia's own James Madison Jr., standing all of five-four and weighing a hundred pounds, was known as the "Father of the Constitution," authored the *Federalist* with Hamilton and Jay, became the fourth President of the United States, and once lived in Montpelier with a wife named Dolley.

James Jr., however, had no offspring.

James the Fourth, six-six and two hundred, was known as the father of two boys, coauthored a law journal article on the suspension of *habeas corpus* in the Civil War, became the thirty-sixth president of the local bar association, and lived in Manassas with a wife named Molly.

A Republican appointee, Judge Madison had worked in the United States Attorney's office in the District of Columbia for ten years before taking a position in a reputable D.C. firm focusing on corporate litigation. At fifty-six years of age, he was known to have a sharp mind, a good sense of humor, and a future destined for a seat on the U.S. Court of Appeals for the Fourth Circuit in Richmond. As a federal judge for seven years, he had gained a reputation for being tough on crime. Although, he was often quoted as saying he was a firm defender of "his Uncle James'" Bill of Rights.

"Thank you. You may be seated."

Every seat in the courtroom was taken. Reporters from every newspaper, TV and radio network, and Internet news outlet sat poised with pen and paper for the proceedings to begin. A sketch artist sat on the left side of the room ready to provide a rendering in the land of no cameras.

Judge Madison situated himself in his high-back leather chair. His dark hair was combed over to the left, and an observer could see the top of his white dress shirt and red tie underneath his black robe. He handed a piece of paper over to the court clerk and received one in return. After making a notation, he looked out at the lawyers' tables in front of the bench.

"We will begin today with the case of the United States of America v. Roland Barton," Judge Madison announced. "The record will show the appearance of Mr. Waters for the United States and Mr. Brennan on behalf of Mr. Barton."

At that moment, the side door to the courtroom opened and in stepped two U.S. Marshals followed by Barton and two other Marshals. Those in the gallery leaned forward to take their first look at the Russians' spy inside the CIA. Barton wore a jailhouse-issued orange jumpsuit. The handcuffs around his wrists were attached to a chain around his waist. The only sound in the courtroom was Barton's leg irons clanging against the floor as he shuffled his way in front of the bench. The black and yellow bruise above his left eye was very noticeable. The sketch artist went to work and got every detail right, even the butterfly bandage over Barton's left eyebrow.

"Gentlemen, are we ready to proceed?"

Two tables full of lawyers stood and stated they were ready to begin battle. At the point for the United States of America was H. Daniel Waters, a University of Virginia law grad who was the first U.S. Attorney nominated by President Schumacher. His first two months on the job had been uneventful, but his former career in the Department of Justice prepared him well for the war that Brennan and the Civil Liberties Alliance would soon unleash on him. To his left were two assistant U.S. attorneys looking to add to their list of convictions. All three men wore dark suits, conservative ties, and American flags on their lapels.

At the table to Judge Madison's left stood the stocky pit bull Art Brennan for the defense. He wore dark slacks and a gray jacket over a like colored shirt. Dark tie. No flag. Two other CLA lawyers sat behind him but otherwise kept out of the way – Brennan wanting the courtroom optics to show it was one man defending his client from the evil and all-powerful United States of America.

Brennan made his way next to Barton and both exhibited a smug defiance that could be felt by everyone in the room.

"Are you Roland Barton?" Judge Madison asked, looking down from the bench.

"I am."

"Mr. Barton, you, as a United States citizen, have been charged with nine counts of transmitting national defense information under the Espionage Act, 18 United States Code, section 794(a), and conspiracy to commit espionage under section 794(c)."

Judge Madison read through the specific allegations in the charges laid out in the FBI's affidavit in support of the criminal complaint – the signal sites, the dead drops in the library, the cash payments, the sensitive nature of the information handed over to the Russians, the compromised operatives. Reporters tried to keep up, some already on the third page of their note pads. The details would be repeated on every major network that evening.

"Mr. Barton, do you understand the nature of the charges?"

Barton stood tall, his head held high. "Yes, sir," he said in a strong voice.

"Pursuant to the Espionage Act, if found guilty, you could be required to forfeit any proceeds from such a violation. You could also be sentenced to prison, including life without the possibility of parole. Or," Judge Madison said, the short pause that followed indicating something important was about to be spoken. "You could be sentenced to death."

The word "death" reverberated throughout the courtroom. Even though no one but the judge was talking, the breaths being held in seemed to suck the oxygen out of the room given the severity of the admonition.

"Do you understand the nature of the penalties you are facing, Mr. Barton?"

Barton nodded his head up and down.

"Is that a 'yes'?"

"Yes."

"You are entitled to an attorney, Mr. Barton, and I see you have Mr. Brennan here to represent you today."

"Yes."

Apparently thinking he hadn't spoken enough for his liking, Brennan puffed up his chest and made himself heard loud and clear. "Your Honor, I am proud to be here today in the Eastern District of Virginia to represent my client, Roland Barton." The volume began to increase. "On his behalf and with the full support of the Civil Liberties Alliance, I want to enter a plea of one-hundred percent not guilty and demand a trial by a jury of Mr. Barton's peers pursuant to the Sixth Amendment to the United States Constitution!"

Judge Madison reached for his gavel but restrained himself from bringing down the thunder of the court. He wasn't going to let his courtroom be turned into a circus sideshow with Brennan acting as the ringleader.

"Mr. Brennan!" he bellowed, each syllable rising over the last. "I'm familiar with the constitutional rights afforded to your client and he will receive all that he is due." After a short pause and seeing that he had sufficiently stopped Brennan's diatribe, Judge Madison calmly rattled off his necessary findings. "Let the record show the defendant is present in custody and represented by counsel. He pleads not guilty and requests trial by jury. Mr. Waters, I take it discovery will be forthcoming?"

"Yes, your Honor."

"Okay, we will proceed accordingly." Paperwork was then exchanged and calendars were checked and documented for the next hearing.

Brennan inched forward, obviously with something to say. "Your Honor, if I may. I would like a chance to consult with my client after the hearing."

"Very well. You can do so in the attorneys' room."

The hearing ended without any further theatrics. Brennan was content to save it for the cameras and reporters later.

After Barton shuffled out of the courtroom under heavy guard, he sat down at the table in the attorneys' room and waited for his lawyer. The walls of the room were painted white, the table was government issue, and the chairs were Carter Administration plastic. It smelled like sweat, less so than his cell but still noticeable, like those who frequent the place only get to shower once or twice a week.

Barton started to wonder just how long this process would take. He was fifty-six years old, and if Brennan didn't save his ass, he would be shuffling in and out of these smelly holes in the wall for years to come. He had no family who would claim him. It would be him and his attorneys. For now, he would just have to sit and wait. With patience not being one of his strong suits, his right foot started furiously tapping the carpeted floor. Going on little sleep, he didn't even try to stifle his yawn. With a deep breath preparing for the long journey ahead, he brought both of his cuffed hands up to scratch his nose.

When the door to the room opened, Brennan entered with a file folder and his yellow legal pad. He took one look at Barton, stopped in his tracks, and turned back to the door.

"Guard!" he yelled. He didn't care to wait for a response. "Guard!"

One of the jail guards returned in a huff, thinking his prisoner had escaped or passed out on the floor. He looked in the window of the door and turned the door handle.

"What is it?"

"Take those damn handcuffs off!" the snarling Brennan barked. "My client is innocent until proven guilty and I will not have him treated like some sort of mangy animal!"

The jailer restrained himself from rolling his eyes. He would be happy to take off Barton's cuffs, and if Barton happened to strangle Brennan during their meeting, well, that would just be too bad.

"Now get out," Brennan snapped, a thank you not being in his vocabulary.

Barton stood and shook hands again with his attorney. It felt good to have someone on his side. Someone who would fight for him. He massaged his wrists and sat back down.

Brennan finally got a good look at the man who would be one of his most high-profile clients. He could barely believe it. His first spy. The man sitting across the table tried to sell out the United States of America. Brennan could not wait to hear his story.

"Did those scumbags do that to you?" Brennan asked, pointing to his own eye. He had pen in hand to take down names and dates so he could file motions to suppress any confession the Government obviously beat out of his client or a civil suit for police brutality and violating Barton's civil rights.

"No," Barton said, his left hand gently touching the bruise.

"I am going to give you this file folder so you can keep track of all the motions that I will be filing."

"Thank you."

"And there will be a lot of them. How have they been treating you so far?"

It hadn't even been two days yet since his arrest. "Fine for now," Barton said. How he would hold up over time couldn't be answered yet. He had spent most of the time lying on his bed and staring at the ceiling. He was ready to get the process rolling.

"Getting enough to eat?"

"Yes."

Brennan went over some preliminary matters – the mountains of discovery that they would receive from the Government, the motions to suppress that Brennan would inevitably file, and the path toward trial, if it even got that far given Brennan's assurance that Barton would be a free man in the near future.

"I'm sure they'll have surveillance videos. So we'll watch those together while we work on the defense."

"Good."

"Once we get the names of the CIA agents who worked on your case, we'll dig into their backgrounds, check their performance files. Maybe some of them don't like you, maybe they tried to frame you to get you out of there."

Barton nodded. This was good, he thought.

"We'll make it so difficult on the CIA that they'll be begging you to take a plea to a lesser charge to save their own asses."

"I'll start thinking of the guys who might have held a grudge against me," Barton said. Brennan's strategy had already taken hold of him. He would love nothing more than to take down some of his former colleagues.

"I imagine they are probably going to keep you in solitary confinement."

Barton nodded. A part of him probably preferred it. He didn't want to spend his time talking to some idiot. It was bad enough that he had to put up with them at the CIA, he thought to himself.

"But if they put you in a cell with someone, do not under any circumstances talk about this case," Brennan said, his stubby index finger stabbing the table for emphasis. "Not one word. The only reason they would give you a cell mate would be to tape record your conversations and hope to use the snitch at trial. And even if you are in solitary, don't talk out loud to yourself. I know of a case where the Government bugged a guy's cell, literally caught the man confessing to himself, and used the statement against him at trial."

"I understand."

After an hour of questions and answers about the legal proceedings, the meeting was beginning to wind down. But Brennan was dying to delve deep into the mind of the American traitor sitting across the table from him.

"Why did you do it?" Brennan asked. Did Barton hate the United States? Was it America's slave past? Was it for dropping the bomb on Japan? Was it the wars for oil? Was it for corporate America polluting Mother Earth? Was it for the same reasons that Brennan so despised the U.S.?

Barton thought for a second. He didn't know whether Brennan wanted a long and involved answer but the reason was pretty simple for him.

"Money."

Brennan sat there with his mouth open. Money? That was it? Greed. Simple greed.

"Plus, I couldn't stand some of those idiots I worked for. I could have run that place a whole lot better than them."

Brennan nodded his head. He was disappointed his spy didn't hate America like he did. It didn't matter, he told himself. He would represent him like they had the same interests at heart.

After the two men shook hands, Brennan told Barton he would be in touch every day. He promised to make sure the case was resolved quickly and in his favor. Once they parted ways, Brennan prepared for his shining moment, the moment when TV cameras and microphones would, once again, make him a household name around the world.

When he stepped out the front door and made his way down the steps, he noticed the swarm of media coming at him. TV cameramen and photogs jockeyed for position on the sidewalk. Newsmen and women hurled their questions at Brennan, who could feel the blood coursing through his veins. This was why he did what he did.

"Mr. Brennan, can you tell us about Mr. Barton!?" one reporter yelled before Brennan had even reached the microphone set up at the bottom of the stairs.

Brennan looked around at the gathered throng. He was happy with its size. He noticed some pedestrians walking by, and he graciously gave them time to walk over and gawk at the show he was about to put on.

"I met with Mr. Barton for the first time this morning," he said. "As the head of the Civil Liberties Alliance, I am proud to call Mr. Barton a client."

"Is he guilty of spying against the United States!?" another reporter asked. It was a question with an obvious answer. Barton had not even been tried yet. But that wasn't the point of the question. The reporter simply wanted to light a fire under Brennan and get the ball rolling on some good copy.

"My client is absolutely, one-hundred percent not guilty!" Brennan thundered. "This is nothing more than a crackpot theory by this Administration to take people's minds off all of the crap that is going on in this country!"

"Was Mr. Barton caught with money hidden in his pants!?"

Brennan's face reddened. He was ready to fight. "Mr. Barton is one-hundred percent not guilty of these charges! There is not one shred of evidence to convict. And I look forward to seeing the Government's case go down in flames in the near future. My client will be completely vindicated!"

With that, Brennan stomped away from the microphone. Reporters trailed behind, thrusting a microphone in his face, practically goading him to say something of shock value – something for tomorrow's headlines.

"This is nothing but a fucking conspiracy to frame my client!" Brennan bellowed as he took a seat in the CLA's limousine. "And I intend to show the President, the FBI Director, and the CIA are attempting to frame my client to cover their own sorry asses!"

Brennan's bleeped-out comments would make the rounds of every network news program later on that evening. With a final snort of rage, the red-faced Brennan slammed the door shut and sped off.

CHAPTER 14

Palazzo Chigi – Rome, Italy

Prime Minister Scarponi's secretary found him at his desk, his aching head in his hands. He had not answered her on the intercom. He had not slept in two days, and the bloodshot eyes and sagging face indicated the political turmoil was taking its toll on him. Calls for his resignation seemed to come from every corner of Italy, protesters burned him in effigy, and friends distanced themselves from him.

"I have brought you some aspirin for your head," the secretary said, placing the medicine and a bottle of water on his desk. "Can I get you anything else?"

On any other day, Scarponi would have made some crack comment about how beautiful his thirty-something secretary looked, maybe fondle her buttocks right there at the desk. Neither one was married, and they had fooled around on the job and after-hours on a number of occasions. But no one was in the mood for hanky-panky today.

"No, thank you," he said weakly. He plopped two pills into his mouth and swallowed. The coolness of the water made him feel slightly better, like he simply needed a little refresher to recharge his batteries.

It would be another long day for the Prime Minister.

The Prime Minister's chief of staff, Luciano Rossi, knocked softly on the door as the secretary left. It was Rossi's job to gather all the information he could and tell the Prime Minister how bad it was. And it was bad.

Rossi took the seat next to Scarponi's desk. He looked over at his boss, who had his head tilted back and his eyes closed. Rossi placed a folder on the desk, making just enough noise to let Scarponi know that they had better get started.

Scarponi let his head fall forward and blinked the weariness from his eyes. "How bad is it?"

Rossi did his best to give it to him straight. "It is very bad," he said as he opened up the folder. "Another woman has come forward. She says you raped her in a Milan hotel room a year ago."

Scarponi slowly shook his head like he couldn't believe it. He tried to remember a woman in Milan. There had been so many of them across Italy that he lost track. But he was sure it was not rape. He had never raped any woman. At least not in his mind. With his money and power, he had women of all types throwing themselves at him. And if they became pouty, disgruntled, or pregnant, the money would flow for fancy clothes, ritzy apartments, and complete silence. The money made it consensual.

When the money dried up, however, the scorned women brought out the long knives. Within the last ten months, four women claimed to have given birth to a Scarponi love child. Italian tabloids plastered the women's faces on the front page and printed the salacious details of the Prime Minister's bed hopping up and down the Italian peninsula.

"I don't remember a woman in Milan," he said.

Rossi wasn't surprised. "She just turned eighteen," he whispered. "A prostitute."

Scarponi let out a deep breath. The public had always laughed off his late-night trysts, but underage sex crossed the line.

"I don't remember her," Scarponi said. Had he, he might have repented to Rossi, although it was doubtful he would do the same to his countrymen. But he had played the game long enough to know that politics is a dirty business. The blood started flowing again. The fight in him was coming back. "The opposition is just making it up. Someone is paying her to make up these allegations. They do it all the time." He then sat up in his chair. "But they sometimes forget that we have money too."

Rossi nodded and made a note on his pad. Next order of business.

"The economy," he said, moving on. "Your supporters are upset over your austerity measures, your opponents are upset over the growing debt crisis. That doesn't leave a whole lot of people in your corner. The confidence vote in Parliament is scheduled for two o'clock this afternoon."

Scarponi nodded. He had been on the phone throughout the night – begging, pleading, bribing his supporters to stick by him this one last time. They owed it to him, he lectured repeatedly. He wasn't afraid to remind some of them that they took part in some of his insider deals and would be implicated if he was ousted. The veiled threats had already turned five votes back to his favor.

The Italian Parliament is a bicameral legislature, split up into the lower house, the Chamber of Deputies, and the upper house, the Senate of the Republic. In the 630-seat Chamber of Deputies, the opposition party called for a confidence vote in hopes of ousting Scarponi once and for all. He had survived numerous confidence votes over the last five years but his margin of victory kept shrinking with each one.

"What are the numbers?" Scarponi asked. As with most politicians around the world, it all came down to the numbers.

Rossi pulled a list out of his shirt pocket. "We have 304 votes in your favor," he said before adding. "But that was thirty minutes ago."

Scarponi grabbed the remote on his desk and clicked on the TV. It was wall-to-wall news coverage of the Scarponi mess – sex scandals, corruption, parliamentary votes. Split screens showed a parade of the Prime Minister's beauties over the years – some luxuriously on his arm, others disheveled with a hand in front of their faces to hide their identities. The other side of the screen went back and forth between the riots in the streets and the fisticuffs in the Chamber of Deputies. Two members of Parliament had already come to blows that morning after one accused the other of being in bed with "that snake Scarponi." There were even some risque gestures thrown in for the benefit of the hearing impaired.

"We need twelve more to change their votes."

Scarponi winced at the number. One or two would be easy, a piece of cake, but twelve would take some doing. Rossi handed over the names of those whose arms could be twisted if just the right type of pressure was applied. Scarponi used his pen to check off the names and, before he knew it, he had fifteen prime candidates. Six members could be bribed relatively easily, six could be imprisoned for complicity in the Prime Minister's shady dealings, and three would cave once Scarponi's Mafia connections paid a surprise visit to their families.

Scarponi smiled. He could almost taste the victory. It's what he loved about politics – the wheeling and dealing, the arm-twisting, the threats, some veiled, others blatant. He believed he would once again survive the slings and arrows of his enemies. And he vowed to crush them when his loyal supporters defeated them in Parliament.

"I can get these fifteen easily," Scarponi boasted. He was fully refreshed, the tired eyes gone. "Start lining them up on the phone."

"Yes, sir," Rossi said, grabbing his folder and his list as he made his way to the door.

Scarponi grabbed the phone and placed his first call to his longtime friend, Luigi Pizzano, from Naples. A member of Parliament for six years now, Pizzano had risen to power on the generous donations of his friend the Prime Minister. But recently, Naples had been hit the worst by the bad economy – fires burned as firefighters walked off the job after budget cuts, the streets began to stink after garbage collectors called in sick for three weeks straight. Naples hadn't seen this much turmoil since the bombings of the Second World War. Government was to blame, the Neapolitans cried. And first and foremost to blame were Scarponi and his good buddy Pizzano.

Hoping to save his political hide, Pizzano had taken to distancing himself from the Prime Minister and debunk the popular myth that he was just another one of Scarponi's puppets in Parliament. It seemed to be working, and Pizzano had promised to seriously consider a vote of no-confidence against his friend.

"Luigi!" Scarponi bellowed into the phone. The old-school charmer was in fine form as he leaned back in his chair. "My friend, how are you?" They had not spoken in weeks. Scarponi swiveled his chair around and threw his fine Italian shoes onto his desk. He never saw the door open behind him.

"Sir! You can't go in there! The Prime Minister is on the phone!" The secretary, as attractive as she was, proved no match to the man entering the office. "Sir, please!"

Viktor Zhukov, Russia's head of the Ministry of Gas Industry, barreled forward with a good head of steam. Scarponi lost in his own political world never heard a sound.

Zhukov came up behind and swung Scarponi's chair around, the Prime Minister's feet kicking the phone, a bottle of water, and a tower of paper onto the floor in a great calamitous crash onto the floor.

"What the . . !?" Scarponi yelled out, now face to face with the Russian.

"Morning," Zhukov said without a hint of sincerity.

Scarponi stood and shoved his uninvited guest away from him. "Get the fuck away from me!"

Scarponi straightened his suit and then picked up the cradle of the phone off the floor. "Luigi," he said, wondering if he was still there. "I'm going to have to call you back. Something urgent has come up."

Scarponi hung up the phone. He then went on the warpath. "I don't know who the fuck you think you are, Mr. Zhukov, but I am the Prime

Minister of Italy! If you cannot show some manners when you come in here, I will have you arrested!" The outburst felt good.

Zhukov smiled as he looked over the irate Scarponi. "It's nice to see you again too, Mr. Prime Minister."

"Mr. Zhukov, I'm kind of busy today. What the hell do you want?"

Zhukov turned to look out the window, as if he felt the need to take in the view. "I understand you are facing yet another confidence vote later on today." He didn't wait for any kind of answer. "We don't have much of a need for confidence votes in Russia," he said smugly. "When the Russian people speak, that is the end of the matter."

"More like when the Russian people are told who to vote for, then that is the end of the matter," Scarponi responded. He was in no mood to discuss the differences in electoral processes. "I asked you once. What the hell do you want?"

Zhukov turned and took a step closer, the round ball of a man looking like he was going to pounce on his prey. The bug eyes bulged from behind his thick glasses. "The Russian Federation took a vote last night and we have no confidence in you," he said, pointing an accusatory finger at the Prime Minister. "We have no confidence that you are going to repay the billions of dollars you stole from us. And I have come to give you a chance to change our minds."

This was not what Scarponi needed today. He was facing political ruin, and the only thing the Russians could think about was their money.

"I did not steal your money, Mr. Zhukov," Scarponi said. He was even less convincing now then in their first meeting on the matter.

Zhukov took another step closer. He was willing to go as far as it took to get Russia's point across. "Let's not go down that road again, Mr. Prime Minister. Where's our money?"

"I don't owe you any money, and you can't prove I do."

One step closer. Zhukov was now within five feet. He could see the Prime Minister swallow hard and crouch slightly as if preparing to defend himself. Zhukov reached into his jacket and pulled out his iPhone.

"Mr. Prime Minister, I told you the last time that we can prove you have stolen ten-point-three billion dollars from Russia. Now, we are willing to let you repay the money without mentioning it to the press. I'm sure news of the theft would not play well in your upcoming confidence vote in the Parliament."

Scarponi did not have the time to fight this battle right now. He had to save his political ass. Then he could worry about the Russians.

"I will get you the money," Scarponi promised, hoping Zhukov would believe him and leave.

"This is your last chance, Mr. Prime Minister."

"You'll get the money," Scarponi promised like any good politician. It didn't matter if you could keep the promise or not, just make it and figure out how to wiggle out of it later.

Zhukov wasn't ready to take Scarponi's word at face value. He thought a little extra incentive would help. He held up his iPhone so Scarponi could see it. When the video started, Scarponi knew this couldn't be good.

There on the screen were the Scarponi brothers at the Italian villa that they had purchased from their illegal kickbacks. They were laughing, almost counting the money that they had stolen from the Russians. Not a particularly good move on their part. They insulted Russian President Vitaly Yaroslavsky and Prime Minister Nikolai Grigoryev while they were at it. They discussed bank accounts in Switzerland and the Bahamas. All the details were there.

"How did you get in there?" Scarponi asked, finally snapping out of his shock at seeing the video.

"That should not be a concern of yours. Just let it be known that the leadership in Moscow is not happy with your actions. They thought you were an ally, a partner in the global community."

"I am," Scarponi protested. He did not sound convincing. "I will be a strong partner with Russia."

"I'm not sure I believe you."

Scarponi knew he had to come up with a plan, but first things first. "I will get you the money," he told Zhukov. "But it will take me a little more time. I have to survive the no-confidence vote first. Then I will get you the money." He sounded sincere in his promise to get the Russians their $10-billion refund.

Zhukov was willing to give Scarponi some leeway, but he would keep a tight hold on the leash. "Mr. Prime Minister, you have three days to return the money." He held up three fingers to make sure Scarponi heard him correctly. "If we do not get the money, your little video might find its way into the public domain."

Scarponi had enough. He regretted ever getting into bed with the Russians. "Get out," he snapped. "I've got work to do."

CHAPTER 15

Office of the Civil Liberties Alliance – Washington, D.C.

With sleeves rolled up and an unlit cigar in his mouth, Art Brennan was in the middle of a meeting with the CLA's top lawyers. They were itching to get to work on Barton's espionage case. Attorneys for other spies were contacted and questioned on legal tactics. A legal defense fund was created, and foreign sympathizers had already donated large sums of cash to fill the CLA's coffers. Investigators were hired and told to gear up for war. Brennan and the CLA were going to free Barton and take down the FBI, the CIA, and the President of the United States while they were at it.

"I want the Government's discovery," Brennan barked. The five lawyers around the table looked on with great anticipation, like nervous ballplayers before the big game. Brennan, the coach, was firing on all cylinders, exhorting his team to fight like hell and leave nothing on the field of battle. He stood up and pounded his desk. "Those assholes at the Justice Department probably think they're going to bury us with affidavits, witness statements, surveillance videos, and crap like that! But they don't know yet what's in store for them! We are going to kick their asses! Now, let's get to work!"

The team members stopped short of jumping up and down but the adrenaline was definitely pumping. Each lawyer, now sufficiently energized, grabbed his materials and headed to separate offices to execute the battle plan. The red-faced Brennan continued to stomp around his office – he couldn't wait to fight.

"Mr. Brennan?" his secretary asked over the speakerphone.

"What!?" Brennan yelled from across the room toward the phone. The secretary could hear him through the walls.

"There's a Max Warner here to see you."

With the espionage trial, Brennan had forgotten all about his meeting with the billionaire Warner. Most of the protesters on the National Mall had returned to their parents' basement or their college campuses. But

Brennan had not given up on his plan for more civil unrest. He had contacted some of his friends in Europe, and the anarchists and socialists were out in full force in London. They had even shut down the tube from Heathrow to downtown. It was a fine mess the Brits had on their hands. Brennan hoped his cause would gain momentum overseas and follow President Schumacher back to the United States.

"Send him in, Mary," Brennan said, once he got back to his phone.

The dapper Warner walked in the office. The frown on his face indicated he was not happy.

"Max, how are you?" What with the espionage case on his mental docket, Brennan was in good spirits.

"I'm a little lighter in the wallet," Warner said, obviously in a bad mood. "First, the President's energy plan screws me out of a couple hundred million dollars and now your rent-a-mob has disbanded and gone home. I guess they think global warming is over now?"

Brennan tried to soothe Warner's feelings – in part because he wanted to take care of his customer. With the money Warner had in his portfolio, it was important to keep him happy. "Can I get you a drink?"

"No." Warner wasn't thirsty. He wanted to know what he got for his investment because he couldn't see it at the moment.

Both took a seat on the couch. The well-dressed Warner, with his perfectly creased slacks, draped his left leg over the right. The rumpled Brennan, with his shirttail coming untucked, rested his foot on the coffee table.

"Max, we're in a bit of a lull right now," he said, gesturing out toward the National Mall. "It will pick up."

Warner started shaking his head. "I was promised chaos, maybe something just short of revolution."

"You'll get it," Brennan promised. "We're not done yet."

"I think you've moved on to the Barton trial and put me on the back burner."

"Nonsense," Brennan huffed. Remember the money, he told himself. "I can juggle more than one ball at a time, Max."

"I'm not sure that you can."

"Listen, Max. There is upheaval all over Europe. Maybe not so much in England, but Italy is a powder keg. It could explode at any time, and the President is heading right for the heart of it the day after next. I've got my people working on it."

Warner was not impressed with Brennan's noisy parades and sit-ins. He wanted results. He wanted his bank account to look like it did before President Schumacher came to office. That meant more drastic measures needed to be taken. And he had his own ideas.

Warner looked at the coffee table. "Is that today's *Post*?" he asked.

Brennan lifted his scuffed shoe off the paper. "Yep," he said, handing it over.

Warner flipped through the first section, bypassing the news on the spy trial and the President's European trip. He then found what he was looking for.

"Here," he said, pointing at the headline. "Marundi takes the stand at International Criminal Court."

Brennan nodded his head and then glanced at the story. He wasn't sure what he was supposed to get out of it. "Yeah. So another African warlord is on trial for genocide. What about it?"

Headquartered in The Hague, Netherlands, the International Criminal Court is the tribunal used in the prosecution of state leaders, warlords, and other worldly thugs for crimes against humanity, genocide, war crimes, and crimes of aggression. In the mid '90s, prior to the establishment of the ICC, tribunals were established by the United Nations to prosecute war criminals in the former Yugoslavia like Slobodan Milosevic, Radovan Karadzic, and Ratko Mladic.

Seeking a permanent tribunal, the International Criminal Court was established in July 2002 by the passage of the Rome Statute, of which 115 countries are parties, including Germany, Italy, Spain, Mexico and the United Kingdom. Russia has not ratified the Statute, and the United States decided to unsign it during the Bush Administration. In 2006, Congolese warlord Thomas Lubanga Dyilo had the dubious honor of being the ICC's first suspect based on his recruitment of children to be used as soldiers in the Congo's bloody civil war. Current cases before the Court also involve African murderers and despots in countries like Sudan and the Central African Republic.

Warner jabbed his finger on the article. "This is the war you should be fighting."

Brennan was slightly confused. He had a Harvard law degree, but he rarely dealt with the law of foreign courts. He was failing to see the connection.

"This is how we get the President." Warner was done with the rookie-league strategies. He wanted to go big. It was the only way to get the President out of the picture.

Brennan, however, was searching his mind for the holes he just knew had to be in the plan. "The President is not going to submit to the court's jurisdiction," Brennan scoffed. Anyone with half a brain could see that. Plus, he added. "The United States is not a party to the treaty establishing the ICC."

The ICC has jurisdiction over an accused who is a citizen of a signatory of the Rome Statute or if the alleged crime took place in the territory of a signatory nation. The Office of the Prosecutor conducts the investigations and initiates the prosecution of the alleged criminal. Three judicial divisions adjudicate the case from the pretrial stages to any appellate proceedings.

But Warner had done his homework. He had contacted his friends overseas, and they all told him that he was on to something. "The U.S. might not be a party, but that doesn't mean the President won't show up in a nation that is."

Brennan was still dubious. "So . . . , we have Germany or Italy arrest him when he steps off Air Force One? Come on."

Warner looked again at the article. He then pointed to a name. "See this. Judge Romancini. He is one of the biggest left-wing radicals Italy has ever produced. He was huge in my global-warming campaigns. When a spot opened up on the court, I was in full support of his candidacy. He owes me."

"One judge? That's all you got?"

Warner had more. "I also have Raul Gonzalez on my side."

"And he is?"

"He's the new prosecutor, just elected to a nine-year term last May," Warner said before pausing for his next dramatic statement. "He's also from Venezuela. And those communists down there hate the President and America more than you do. Gonzalez conducts the investigations and decides whether to bring charges. He will be inundated with calls to prosecute the President if the situation calls for it. His countrymen would love nothing more than to strike back at the United States. Chavez's henchmen will threaten to kill his family if he doesn't. And think of the Venezuelan oil profits when the price of a barrel goes through the roof."

"That's all well and good but it still doesn't show how you're going to get the President before the ICC."

Warner flipped over the paper again. "That's where you come in. The CLA has friends in Europe right?"

Brennan nodded.

"You need to start spreading the word. Quickly. Mention the President in the same sentence with 'war crimes' and 'crimes of aggression.' We get him on his prosecution of the war on terror. Have people start snooping around. Maybe they uncover something. The leftists will run with it."

"Then what?"

"Then we get one of these signatory countries undergoing civil unrest to arrest the President. The liberals, the anarchists, the anti-capitalists throughout the land would rejoice."

"What about our foreign allies? Even the Russians and the Chinese would balk at arresting the President of the United States. It would be chaos."

Warner smiled. "That's right. It would create chaos the world over."

"And you would laugh all the way to the bank."

Warner did not disagree. He had already thought of what he would buy and what he would sell when the market inevitably crashed to the bottom.

Brennan's head started to hurt. He was still trying to get his mind wrapped around the plan. "What evidence do we have that could be used against the President?"

"We'll just make it up if we have to," Warner said, his hands now folded between his knees as he leaned in closer to Brennan. "Don't you have somebody who can give us some dirt on him? For goodness sakes, you've represented terrorists who want to destroy America and President Schumacher. You had to have learned something."

Brennan's mind stopped spinning. His thoughts immediately turned to Barton sitting in the jail cell on charges of espionage. The Russians, he thought.

"I know just who to ask."

CHAPTER 16

Thames House – London, England

Tyrone Stubblefield had been busy since he awoke at 5 a.m. While he accompanied the President on the trip, Stubblefield had no desire to listen to foreign leaders at the G-8 Summit or even take in the local tourist attractions – Big Ben and the London Eye could wait for another day. His trip was centered solely on security – at home and abroad. Earlier in the morning, he met with the City of London police and then it was over to Scotland Yard. Notes were compared, strategies were discussed, new gadgets put to the test. They were good meetings, and Director Stubblefield solidified working relationships with his British counterparts.

With the President in town, Stubblefield always had him in the back of his mind. The President's itinerary was on a list in the pocket of the Director's jacket. He had pulled it out several times during the course of the day as he traveled from meeting to meeting. With his confidence growing as to his counterparts' war on terrorism, Stubblefield felt reassured that London was as safe as Washington, D.C.

For the time being at least.

At 6:30 in the evening, Stubblefield and his FBI entourage met with the Director General of Britain's Security Service, otherwise known as MI-5, the U.K.'s counter-intelligence and security agency, at its headquarters at Thames House on Millbank overlooking the Thames. The head of the agency was Barney Walsh, a former member of the Royal Air Force. He grew up just outside of London and spent his youth worrying about whether the IRA would bring its bombs to his neighborhood. With relative peace and quiet coming from Belfast, he and the 3,000-plus employees working at MI-5 now focused their attention on the worldwide threat coming from al-Qaeda.

Standing six-three, the Director General could almost see eye to eye with Stubblefield. He wore a black jacket and tie over a white dress shirt. He looked uncomfortable wearing a suit, and it wasn't long before the jacket came off and the sleeves were rolled up. Both Walsh and

Stubblefield took their jobs like the life of their country depended on it. The safety and security of their homelands were the first thought on their minds in the morning and the last thing they thought about before going to sleep at night. Joining Walsh was Paul Hill, himself a security-minded chap, and the head of MI-5's Joint Terrorism Analysis Center.

The working dinner meeting started off with a talk about families, all the kids were grown, and then sports. Although the English love their soccer, Walsh and Hill were impressed that the man sitting across from them used to play the American brand of football for the Oakland Raiders. The small talk, however, didn't last long. With the G-8 Summit in town, leaders from around the globe had to be shuttled to meetings, out to dinners or parties, and then back to their temporary residence. Then, of course, were the anarchists who followed the G-8 leaders around like rock-star groupies. Every summit had them, and each host country dealt with the protesters in different ways. The local Londoners usually decided it was the best time for holiday. The Brit security services decided loading up on the water cannons and tear gas was the way to go – just in case the riotous yobs and hooligans needed a gentle reminder to follow the law. In anticipation of the G-8 summit, Walsh had raised the U.K. threat level up from "substantial" to "severe" – warning Brits that a terrorist attack was highly likely. Walsh and Hill, already running on fumes, thought they would be lucky to get an hour of rest during the next twenty-four. Although they only had to get through tonight and the departure ceremony tomorrow, they couldn't wait for the G-8 to go away.

The meal was light – fish, chips, and Cokes, which gave them plenty of time to discuss security without a four-course dinner weighing down the conversation. The TV monitors on the wall gave impressive views of greater London – underground, at street level, and a bird's-eye view. Closed-captioned broadcasts from CNN and the BBC ran off to the side.

"I understand your FBI has captured a spy inside the Central Intelligence Agency," Walsh said. Both of the men kept close watch on what was going on across the pond.

"Yes," Stubblefield said. "A career analyst in the CIA. He was selling secrets to the Russians."

"I'm sure President Schumacher was not happy," Walsh said. Like many Brits, he pronounced Schumacher as "Shoe-macker," the latter half like "packer."

"He was not," Stubblefield said, stating the obvious.

"What type of information was compromised?"

"We're still trying to figure out the extent of the information as well as the damage. We believe at least three U.S. operatives were killed based on the divulged intelligence. The CIA Director is supposed to call me once they determine the full extent of the breach. It seems to expand every day."

"What have our friends the Russians had to say?"

Stubblefield grinned slightly, like the answer to follow would not be a surprise.

"Nothing," he said. "We don't have a name of who Barton was selling the intelligence to, but we believe the man is Russian. We are still investigating the matter, poring over surveillance tapes and phone taps. Needless to say, the Russian Federation has not offered to help us in our investigation."

"What a shock," Walsh said. The Russians were never very forthcoming with him either, only when it was in their best interests.

The buzzing on Stubblefield's hip broke up the meeting. He grabbed his phone and looked at the screen. "Excuse me, I need to take this," he said, pushing back his chair.

Walsh and Hill stood, kindly English gents that they were.

Stubblefield exited the room and stopped in the hall. "Director Parker, this is Ty. Whattya got?"

Across the ocean and six hours behind, Director Parker was standing at his desk at CIA Headquarters, a folder with fresh information on the Barton investigation in his hands. "Ty, I wanted to let you know what we have uncovered since we last talked. The intelligence Barton downloaded spans a period of about three months. Obviously, he had access to the material for a lot longer time, but the last three months is all he downloaded on his own flash drives. In the last two weeks, intelligence was downloaded regarding the capture of Assad Khan and his interrogation by the CIA in the Seychelles."

Assad Khan. Pakistan. Terrorism. More bad news Stubblefield thought. He started pacing the hallway. "All right, good work, Bill. You want to go ahead and call the President to fill him in. I'm sure he'd like to know just in case something comes up tonight." He pulled out the President's itinerary – it noted the President and the First Lady were to have afternoon tea with the Queen at Buckingham Palace. The First Couple had a great relationship with the royal family, and the British people marveled at the First Lady – the most beautiful blonde they had seen since Lady Di.

"He's probably preparing to leave the Palace for the G-8 dinner."

"I will put a call in to him right now and see if I can get him."

After ending the call, Director Stubblefield stopped in the hallway and stared the wall. He wasn't the only one in the U.S. that distrusted Pakistan, and the information from the CIA didn't allay his concerns. He reentered the room with the MI-5 brass, apologized for the interruption, and sat back down.

"That was Director Parker from the CIA," Stubblefield said. "He called to inform me that intelligence regarding Pakistan may have been compromised. I know you guys will keep this confidential, but the CIA recently captured Assad Khan in Milan, Italy. He was taken to a CIA black site in the Seychelles for interrogation. We have received a vast amount of intelligence from him, including the names of operatives and the locations of secret hideouts in Afghanistan used by the Taliban. But on an even more disturbing level, we have also learned that the Pakistan Government was involved in the attack on U.S. and coalition troops recently. I know there were some British special forces who were also killed."

The men across the table nodded and gritted their teeth. Pakistan claimed to be a friend of the United Kingdom, but the Brits had also doubted the sincerity of the friendship.

"We also believe the Pakistanis have been in on other plots involving U.S. troops, tipping off terrorists to our plans or setting us out on wild goose chases. We don't know whether this intelligence was sought after by the Russians or whether it was just part of the intelligence sold to them. It's possible Barton downloaded it and did nothing with it. But we do know it was downloaded by him. I'm not exactly sure what the Russians would do with the information anyway."

Director Walsh turned his head toward Hill, their eyes meeting and showing grave concern. MI-5 was tasked with protecting the homeland from terrorists, saboteurs, and mischievous agents of foreign governments. And recent events had raised some red flags.

"Director," Walsh said, turning back to Stubblefield. "I don't know whether there is any significance, but we have observed members of the Pakistan Embassy visiting their counterparts at the Russian Embassy on a number of occasions over the last couple of days. It might be nothing."

Stubblefield pushed away his plate and leaned his massive forearms on the table. He was trying to put the pieces together to see if they fit. Maybe it was just the Pakistanis paying a diplomatic call on the Russians, maybe an import/export deal was being discussed. He tried not to think the worst. There was probably an innocent explanation for the meetings, just a coincidence.

"Do you know who from the Pakistani side was meeting with the Russians?"

Walsh thought for a moment. His desk had been so full of other matters that a meeting between Pakistan and Russia did not reach his radar screen. He was more worried about the terrorists trying to blow up the Tube or take down Big Ben just up the street. He grabbed the phone on the table and issued his orders. "This is Walsh. Can you pull up the surveillance video of the vehicle from the Pakistani Embassy going to the Russian Embassy?" He stopped for a second. "Yes, within the last five days."

Stubblefield started tapping his foot underneath the table. He was starting to get that bad feeling again.

The TV screen with the test pattern on the far right of the room flickered to life.

"This is a video from a couple of days ago," Walsh said as they all looked at the screen. "Again," he said, pronouncing it "a-gain," like "a-plane." "It could be nothing."

London has more closed-circuit surveillance cameras per square mile than anywhere in the world. London police, Scotland Yard, MI-5, MI-6 – all of them kept a watchful eye on every public act that every Londoner takes. The all-seeing eyes could record faces and license plates and cross-check them with a computer database of every criminal in the U.K. and across the world. Some of the citizenry resented Big Brother watching their every move, while big cities around the world wanted to know more about London's vast system of cameras and how they could implement it in their own countries.

One of Walsh's technicians entered the room and manned the computer controlling every live-feed surveillance camera and the massive storage that kept track of every video MI-5 had logged.

"Tighten up on that Mercedes there," Walsh said, pointing at the main screen in front of him.

The technician went to work, zeroing in on the Mercedes and its occupants. "It's going to be difficult with the tinted windows," the young man said. Despite the technological wizardry the Brits had in their employ, the cameras could not peer through the darkened windows. When nothing of substance revealed itself, the tech went to the next camera and caught the Mercedes sitting at a stoplight.

"Let's see if we have anything here," the man said.

"The back seat," Walsh directed. "Take a closer look if you can."

Assistant Director Hill was already on his own laptop, bringing up every person who walked into and out of the Pakistani Embassy. Some of the people had been identified, others were still a mystery.

The technician slowed the video, looking frame by frame. It wasn't long before a smile appeared on his face. Luck was on their side. A long-legged brunette had just sashayed her way down the sidewalk and past the stopped Mercedes. She was beautiful in every way – coming and going. Khan, apparently hoping to get a better look, had rolled down his window and ogled the woman. He stopped short of asking her if she needed a ride but he did admire her backside for a good long time. All the while, a nice full-on head shot appeared on the screen.

Assistant Director Hill didn't even need to look at his list of Pakistani Embassy officials. He already knew the man. "That's Pervez Khan," he said. "He's the son of Pakistan's Interior Minister."

A cold chill went up Stubblefield's back. The news just kept getting worse. "He's also Assad Khan's brother," he said, the dread in his voice clear.

The computer geek let the video play out, and the Mercedes made its way to the Russian Embassy. With no cameras at the back door, no one saw Khan walk in. An hour later, another video showed the Mercedes leave and return to the Pakistani Embassy. Khan, or whoever occupied the back seat, kept the windows rolled up on the return trip.

"Coincidence, Director?" Walsh asked of Stubblefield.

"No." No one believed it was a coincidence that the Pakistani brother of a man secretly captured by the U.S. and surreptitiously learned by the Russians just happened to get together for a chat with those Russians on a normal London day. "Son of a . . .," he muttered to himself.

Walsh then stated the obvious for everyone to kick around. "I think it's safe to say the Russians and Pakistanis know you are holding Assad Khan. What they plan on doing with that information I don't know."

Stubblefield pulled out the President's itinerary from his jacket pocket. He traced his finger down the page until he stopped at 8 p.m. It listed "G-8 dinner/G-20 announcement."

"The President's schedule tonight indicates he is going to have dinner with the G-8 leaders and then they are going to make an announcement regarding the G-20. Any idea what that is about?"

The G-8 Summit consists of leaders from eight of the most powerful countries on earth – France, Germany, Italy, Japan, Canada, Russia, the United Kingdom, and the United States. The group started out with six members in the mid '70s and grew to seven with Canada and then eight with Russia. The G-8 countries meet on an annual basis, the location rotating every year, to discuss economic issues, foreign trade, and international terrorism.

Not wanting other countries to feel left out, the G-8 countries are also part of the G-20. This group of twenty countries sends its foreign ministers to summits around the world to discuss financial matters. China, Australia, South Africa, South Korea, and Brazil are all members, just to name a few.

Walsh was unsure of what was on the agenda. Like Stubblefield, his mind worked solely on security. Politics did not interest him. Assistant Director Hill reached for a copy of the *U.K. Telegraph* behind him. He quickly turned the pages, looking for "G-20" in a headline.

"Here it is," he said. "Following the G-8 dinner tonight, a special presentation will be made to welcome Pakistan into the G-20 and making it the G-21."

"Pakistan!?" Stubblefield blurted out.

Pakistan had lobbied hard to get into and have a seat at the G-20 table. Saudi Arabia, Turkey, and Indonesia were already on the membership list, and Pakistan pointed out it had a fast-growing economy and wanted to be a partner in the global marketplace. Oh, and by the way, Pakistani leaders mentioned it would someday soon become the largest Muslim country in the world. As a majority of other countries did not want to be seen as politically incorrect, they welcomed Pakistan into their midst with open arms.

"Who's going to be there?" Stubblefield asked.

Neither Walsh nor Hill knew of the guest list. They weren't the Prime Minister's security guards. "Maybe your Secret Service would know," Walsh said.

Stubblefield pushed his massive body away from the table and grabbed his phone. "I have to find out where the President is," he said in a rush.

Walsh did not hesitate. He already knew. "Ty, your President is leaving for the Russian Embassy," he said, pointing to the CNN broadcast. The screen showed the President and the First Lady in an explosion of camera flashes as they said goodbye to Her Royal Highness and the Duke of Edinburgh and then headed for the limousine. "He's heading that way right now."

"Shit! Put your police on alert!" Stubblefield hurried to the corner of the room and started punching in numbers. "Schiffer," he whispered into his phone without any identification. "Get the Phantom team ready."

The door to the room never closed as Walsh's underlings filed in – some on their phones, others manning the computers. No one knew what they were looking for, just anything suspicious. They knew, however, it was not a drill. The command center across the hall was a flurry of activity – eyes looking at a massive wall of TV screens showing video feeds of nearly every square inch of London, urgent phone calls and alerts being issued.

Director Stubblefield had a fleeting thought to call the President and explain the situation but instead he dialed the number of the head of the President's Secret Service detail, Michael Craig, who was currently in the front passenger seat of the President's limousine as the motorcade made its way to the Russian Embassy.

"Yeah, what is it?" Agent Craig said abruptly. Now was not the time to disturb him. Transporting the President anywhere was an activity filled with great tension. He, along with the thirty other Secret Service agents surrounding the President in a cocoon of heavily armored vehicles, was on high alert. Craig had an earpiece listening in on the Secret Service command channel as "The Beast" rumbled away from Buckingham Palace with its collection of bulletproof black Suburbans and decoy limos in tow. While he would not normally take a call while on the motorcade route, only two people had the number to the cell phone now next to his left ear – Director Stubblefield and the Secretary of Defense.

"Mike, it's Ty Stubblefield."

"Go ahead," Craig said, scanning the area ahead of him. Notwithstanding the rain in London that evening, there was a good crowd waiting at the gate to wave at the American President and his lovely wife.

"I've just concluded a meeting with MI-5 Director Walsh and have learned the Pakistanis have met with the Russians in the last couple of days. I think the cat is out of the bag."

Craig knew what he meant. "And?"

"I have a bad feeling about the President going to the Russian Embassy tonight."

Craig needed to make a decision quick before they got to the Embassy. If the President got to the front door and then left, a diplomatic uproar would ensue. It was only a five-minute drive, three-and-a-half if the driver picked up the pace. The President's limousine had just left the protective gates of Buckingham Palace, and the sirens were being turned on. The motorcade had planned to drive up Constitution Hill and take South Carriage Drive until they got to Kensington Gardens.

Craig made the announcement on the command channel. "All units, we're taking the alternate route. Repeat, alternate route to the Russian Embassy."

A Suburban and a limo in front of The Beast made a quick right and led the way down The Mall – away from Buckingham Palace and in the opposite direction of the Russian Embassy. Instead of going west on the southern edge of the near rectangle that was Kensington Gardens and then north along the western edge, the route would head north on the eastern edge and then west. It was a controlled change of plans – the route was clear, and with the added length, it gave Craig time to think things through.

Agent Craig turned around in his seat and made eye contact with President Schumacher. "Ty, I'm going to give the phone to the President."

Craig lowered the window separating him and the driver with the President and the First Lady in the back seat. "Sir, it's Ty," Craig said, handing him the phone.

The President reached for the phone and put it to his ear. "Ty, what's up?"

Director Stubblefield gave his recitation of the events with MI-5 and the video of the Pakistanis at the Russian Embassy. At a leisurely pace for Secret Service standards, the motorcade made its way down to the end of The Mall, turned left at Trafalgar Square, and then made a right turn on Regent Street.

Across town, a small scramble was underway. The Secret Service had kept two routes open for the President's motorcade to approach the Russian Embassy. With the call for the alternate route, a group of ten agents shifted their positions and headed to the entrance on the north side to prepare for the President's arrival. They informed the head of the

Russian security team and waited.

One member of the Russian security team, however, did not wait with them.

The man radioed to his command post regarding the change in the Americans' plans. This led to a call to the Pakistan Embassy. Change of plans, they were told. The motorcade supposedly carrying the Prime Minister of Pakistan was supposed to trace the same path as President Schumacher's initial route. The plan called for the ten-car Pakistani caravan to cause a traffic jam at the front door of the Russian Embassy. This would cause the Secret Service to stop on the roadway and wait for the line to move on. A second wave of Pakistani officials would come up from behind on Kensington Road. With their own flashing lights, diplomatic plates, and other security paraphernalia to indicate that some VIP was on board, they would barely be given a second look as they roared up in the President's rear-view mirror. Two vans would speed toward the President's motorcade, screech to a halt on both sides of the limousine, and detonate enough explosives that even The Beast could not withstand.

But now the southern entrance was being blocked off. A traffic jam wouldn't do any good now.

Pervez Khan was in the lead car of the second wave, the two security vans full of explosives right behind him. This was his plan. None of the higher-ups in Pakistan's Government knew of it. The Russians didn't even know what was going on. A few thought Khan wanted to make a show when President Schumacher exited the limo, maybe get in his face or poke him in the chest. If the President was embarrassed at the Russian Embassy, oh well, such is life.

But Khan was out for revenge. He had a death wish, and it would be spectacular. If he was killed in the explosion, he would be a martyr to his people, a man who sought retribution for the kidnapping of his brother. He would bring down the leader of the free world to honor his family.

"Go to the north entrance!" Khan yelled into his phone. "We have to get to the north entrance before the President gets there!"

The driver of Khan's black Mercedes floored it and the caravan flew down Kensington Road. The vans packed with explosives were right on the tail of the Mercedes. Sirens from all of the vehicles echoed throughout the grounds of Kensington Gardens. It looked and sounded like a typical diplomatic motorcade.

"You're going to have to take Kensington Church Street," Khan told the driver. Khan had one hand clutching his phone and the other holding onto the door handle. "Then a right at Notting Hill Gate onto Bayswater Road! We'll get them head on! Faster! Faster!"

President Schumacher's motorcade made it to Oxford Circus and then a left on Oxford, which becomes Bayswater Road. The President was still on the line with Director Stubblefield.

"Sir, if the Russians obtained the information on Assad Khan from Barton and told it to the Pakistanis, there could be problems tonight," Stubblefield said, almost out of breath.

The President didn't want to believe the leaders of Pakistan and Russia would be in on anything to throw mud on the President and the United States. Maybe the meeting was simply to talk about the party tonight, maybe go over the menu one last time. But with Pervez Khan being the one who showed up, the meeting probably wasn't about food.

"Ty, are you on the treadmill or something? You sound like you're running?"

Stubblefield had been running down the stairs. The Phantom team was outside in a waiting van ready to offer one extra layer of protection to the President. Stubblefield was hurrying to get suited up just in case there was trouble.

"Sir," he huffed, "I'm going to meet you at the Embassy."

When the side door to the building opened, the Phantom team van was pulling up. In the front passenger seat was Special Agent Duke Schiffer in full battle dress uniform, an MP-7 slung around his neck. He stepped out, handed a bulletproof vest to the Director, and slammed the sliding door shut after Stubblefield hopped in. The four bodyguards that followed the Director wherever he went hustled to their parked car.

"We need to get to the Russian Embassy," Stubblefield directed. "And fast!"

MI-5 Headquarters on the Thames River is southeast of Buckingham Palace. Both Khan and his suicide caravan and the President's motorcade were traveling away from the Phantom team's current position.

"We need to pick up the pace," Stubblefield said. With traffic light because of all the road closures, the van and follow-up car reached the west side of Buckingham Palace and then headed west on Kensington Road. "Come on, come on, come on." Stubblefield reached for his phone and dialed the President again.

"Mr. President, where are you?"

The President looked out the window and into the gloomy darkness. "I think we're nearing the Embassy."

Across town, Khan's Mercedes and two vans reached speeds of sixty miles per hour. In a quarter of a mile, they would reach the final turn and be ready to charge head on into the President's motorcade.

"Faster!" Khan yelled at the driver. "We're almost there!"

The driver of the Mercedes had sweat pouring down his face, the tension of the moment getting to him. He had not practiced any high-speed driving before, and definitely not any with two vans loaded with explosives following closely behind. To top it all off, the rain was coming down in sheets. The windshield wipers made a valiant attempt to wash the deluge away. The driver weaved in and out of traffic, crossing the centerline in his mad dash. They were almost there.

The approaching sign read Notting Hill Gate. The driver didn't see it, but Khan did.

"Stop! Turn here! Turn here, you idiot!"

The driver slammed on the brakes, but the tires failed to grip the wet pavement. The driver tried to make the turn but the Mercedes slid sideways right through the intersection. When the Mercedes came to a screeching halt, both the driver and the Khan looked back from they just came.

And all they saw were the two vans skidding right for them.

"Ty, I think we're about to make the . . ." the President said before the phone line cut out.

From their position on Kensington Road, the Phantom team members could feel the jolt from the explosion, the ground shaking underneath them, a massive fireball shooting into the night sky.

"Mr. President, can you hear me?" Stubblefield asked. "Mr. President?"

Before the Phantom team even made it within a quarter mile of the blast scene, the streets were becoming clogged with emergency vehicles – police, fire, ambulance.

"Shit! I've lost him!" Stubblefield said, looking east at the fire that was spreading to a nearby bookstore.

CHAPTER 17

London, England

The Sky News team had been on the scene all night long – nonstop through the early hours while a horde of firefighters doused the flames of the burning wreckage and the destroyed bookstore and now as the sun peeked through the clouds over London and investigators went to work. The late night rain had helped keep the fire from spreading through the entire block of businesses. The acrid smell of smoke filtered through the air along with the distinctive odor of burnt chicken – the charred shell of the KFC indicated it wouldn't be serving any finger-licking goodness anytime soon. The only thing left of the retro clothing store was the display racks – the merchandise having been incinerated.

Yellow police tape surrounded the scene. The usually bustling Notting Hill Gate area was vacant. The ubiquitous double decker busses and taxi cabs detoured around the area. The cameras looking down the street recorded tourists and locals gawking at the horrific scene behind police barricades.

"Let's begin the top of the hour with a live report from the scene. Rachel, what can you tell us?"

Rachel, the Sky News reporter, had on a blue raincoat, but with the rain now stopped, she took down the hood to show off her wavy red hair. With microphone in hand, she turned sideways and pointed to the rubble.

"Phillip, I can tell you that some people have described it as a war zone," she said dramatically, as the camera zoomed in down the street at the carnage. "At approximately 7:30 p.m. last evening, a Mercedes carrying Pervez Khan, the son of Pakistan's Interior Minister, failed to navigate the slippery wet streets and crashed into a light pole. It then jumped the median and came to rest on the sidewalk. Two vehicles, both registered to the Pakistani Embassy, also failed to make the corner at Notting Hill Gate and plowed into the Mercedes. It is believed all three vehicles were traveling at a high rate of speed. The crash apparently ruptured the fuel cells in each of the three vehicles, causing a massive fireball that one witness said sounded like a bomb going off.

"Mr. Khan, as well as five other Pakistani officials, was killed in the accident. I can tell you Mr. Khan was on his way to the Russian Embassy where he and other Pakistani leaders were set to celebrate Pakistan's membership in the G-20."

The camera zoomed out and focused again on the red-haired reporter.

"As you can also see, several businesses have been destroyed in the fire. Brigades from as far away as Lambeth joined in the effort to put out the blaze. The investigation into the crash continues, and the area of Notting Hill Gate surrounding the scene has been cordoned off and is not expected to open until later on this evening. Phillip, back to you."

Two miles from the scene of the crash, Peter Daniels, the White House correspondent for Fox News, was beginning his live report back to the still sleeping United States. The "Breaking News Alert" had interrupted what was an otherwise normal late night of programming. At Grosvenor Square just outside the fortified gates of the American Embassy, the mood was quiet. A line of visa seekers chatted about the explosion from the night before.

"Guys, I can tell you that President Schumacher was on his way to a social gathering at the Russian Embassy last evening at approximately 7:30 p.m. His motorcade had just left Buckingham Palace when a torrential downpour deluged the London metro area. Out of an abundance of caution, the Secret Service decided to wait out the storm on the secure grounds of the American Embassy behind me. During that time, the President received word of the accident involving the Pakistani delegation. Because of the loss of life, it was decided that the party at the Russian Embassy to welcome Pakistan to the G-20 would be postponed. I can tell you the President stayed here at the Embassy last night and greeted staff members this morning before heading to the airport and Air Force One. He is expected to begin the last leg of his foreign trip in Rome later on this afternoon. Back to you."

Air Force One

President Schumacher and the First Lady had said their goodbyes to Prime Minister Philip Martin and other British officials at the departure ceremony. The President thanked the Prime Minister for the visit to 10 Downing Street and invited him to Camp David next July. After the Fourth, of course. Now on board and in the air, William Cogdon, Director

Stubblefield, and Agent Craig met with the President in his office. CIA Director Parker, the Secretary of State, and the Secretary of Defense were also on board via video conference.

"Mr. President," Secretary of State Mike Arnold said. "All the TV reports are saying it was an accident."

The President leaned forward and spoke into the receiver so everyone back in the States could hear. "We've seen the pictures and the reports."

"And this was no accident," Stubblefield growled. "That blast was too big for a three vehicle collision. They weren't driving Pintos."

"I agree with Director Stubblefield, Mr. President," Defense Secretary Javits said, seated with his hands folded at a desk in the Pentagon. "A fuel cell explosion wouldn't cause that crater in the street. And it wouldn't have demolished that building – maybe blow out the windows but not bring the facade down." He then pointed his finger at the camera. "Those were two truck bombs. I guarantee you that."

The President sat back in his leather chair and rubbed the back of his neck. He closed his eyes and listened to the hum of Air Force One's four massive General Electric engines purring in the air at 35,000 feet.

"So another terrorist attack?" President Schumacher asked, although he already knew the answer.

"That's what it looks like to me, Mr. President," Secretary Javits said.

"I agree, Mr. President," Director Parker said from CIA Headquarters.

Stubblefield had already made his thoughts known to the President but shared them for those who weren't privy to prior conversations. "I also believe it was a terrorist attack. My contacts at Scotland Yard and MI-5 are looking at the surveillance video right now. They are going to try and determine where the attack originated and see if other vehicles might have been involved."

"And we are sure I was the target?"

Director Parker decided to speak up first. "Mr. President, that's what it looks like. Obviously, we can't be one-hundred percent sure until we get all the facts. But if the Pakistanis knew about our capture of Assad Khan, which we do believe they knew about given the information passed on by the CIA mole, then it would give them a motive to retaliate against you."

Everyone else nodded in agreement with the assessment.

"So today is probably not the right time to say we are going to move Assad Khan to Guantanamo Bay and try him before a military tribunal for committing terrorists acts against the United States?"

Everyone also agreed it was not the right time – except for Wiley Cogdon, who thought they should make the announcement and promise they'd continue the fight against terrorism everywhere in the world.

"Secretary Arnold, this is probably not going to help our relations with Pakistan any," the President noted.

The Secretary of State tried to sound optimistic. "Sir, I'll work on that here at the State Department. Once all the facts come out on Assad and Pervez Khan, the Pakistanis will be hard pressed to claim victim-status. The world community will be behind us, I assure you."

"Okay, thank you everybody," the President said, closing up the meeting. "We can mend these cracked or broken fences. Let's hope this little incident won't bubble up into something worse."

Russian Embassy – London, England

"Fuckin' amateurs," Vlad Patrenko grumbled under his breath. He was standing in front of the TV looking at the destruction just down the street. The glass of vodka in his right hand was nearly empty.

President Yaroslavsky and Prime Minister Grigoryev had just delivered messages of condolence on the front steps of the Russian Embassy, aired live with translation on Sky News. Both remarked at how they had hoped to celebrate with the Pakistani delegation last evening but were shocked and saddened to hear about the tragic events that took the life of the Interior Minister's son and others. They looked forward to meeting with Pakistan officials in the near future, once the grieving process played out.

"Do you think they know?" The man at the other end of the room looking out the window at the smoldering smoke still wafting into the air was Viktor Zhukov, the head of Russia's Ministry of Gas Industry.

Patrenko didn't respond and took a breath. Today was supposed to be one of celebration. He walked over to the credenza, fully stocked with bottles and bottles of Stolichnaya, and refilled his glass. He took a good sip and let it slide down his throat.

"Do they know what?"

Zhukov looked over at his comrade. Even though they were in Russia's very own Embassy, he wasn't about to take chances. Somebody might be listening on the inside or the outside. Having a deeply suspicious nature was a requirement when working in today's Russian Government. He walked over to the credenza, filled himself a glass, and walked over to

Patrenko who was back looking at the TV news.

The Russians knew full well that the blast down the street wasn't just the product of a couple of fuel tanks rupturing in an unfortunate vehicle collision. It was two carefully crafted car bombs that went off prematurely.

"Do you think the Americans know about the Pakistani plot?" he whispered.

Patrenko put his glass on the table. "I think they can put two and two together. They captured Pervez's brother and whisked him off to somewhere so they can torture him or whatever they do to those terrorists. And then Pervez and two car bombs show up last night just as the President of the United States was supposed to show up. I think they know what the Pakistanis were up to."

Zhukov raised his glass to his mouth. "But what about us?" he whispered.

Patrenko took a step closer, and put his hand in front of his mouth. Not even the best hidden camera could read his lips now. He leaned in and spoke with the confidence that came with years of experience growing up behind the Iron Curtain. "With the arrest of Barton, we can assume the Americans know we have the information about Khan. Now, whether they think that we would give the information to the Pakistanis, I don't know."

"But it's possible."

"Yes, it's possible."

"What if the Brits show Khan arriving at our Embassy?"

Patrenko thought for a moment, then paced back and forth across the carpet. With the surveillance cameras on every street corner, that was a possibility. He came up with an answer. "We have the Embassy pass it off as trade deal negotiations. The Pakistanis will go along with anything we say. They aren't going to let the cat out of the bag. Plus, President Yaroslavsky and Prime Minister Grigoryev have no knowledge of anything that has really gone on."

"So you think we're in the clear?"

Patrenko nodded. "But we still haven't solved our problem."

"The American problem?"

Patrenko nodded again. "Oil prices are continuing to fall, and we must do something soon if Russia is going to restore itself as the world's sole superpower."

Zhukov had been taking the angry calls and rants from all his Gas Industry deputies and suppliers. And the Russian oil tycoons were the worst – calling him two or three times a day to curse and swear that something needed to be done because they were losing money at an alarming rate. They of course didn't care what happened – blow up an oil rig, or a pipeline, or a refinery. Anything to raise the price of oil and make them some money.

"I'll make some calls."

"You need to think of something, because if the President makes it back to America that's it for me," Patrenko said. "I can't go back there."

Zhukov nodded. "I will come up with something. Just stay close. We might need to leave quickly."

Patrenko grabbed his glass and downed the rest of his vodka. He went back to staring at the TV with its pictures of the burned wreckage. He couldn't stop shaking his head in disgust.

"Fuckin' amateurs."

CHAPTER 18

Albert V. Bryan United States Courthouse – Alexandria, Virginia

With the sun rising over the nation's capital, Art Brennan exited the back seat of the CLA's limousine outside the courthouse in Alexandria. His briefcase was packed with legal papers, file folders, and two Butterfinger bars. The latter was a request from his number one client – Roland Barton. Once everything was carefully X-rayed and checked, all under Brennan's watchful eye to make sure the Feds didn't rifle through his work product, Brennan marched his way to his meeting with Barton.

"Roland, how are you?" he asked, entering the attorneys' room.

Barton had been fidgeting in his seat for the last five minutes. He needed a cigarette, but there was a no-smoking policy in the courthouse and the resultant nicotine withdrawal was causing quite a shock to his system. He stood up from his seat and extended a hand. He looked tired, like he hadn't slept well. The orange jumpsuit he wore hung loosely on his shoulders. It was too big for him, and it still reeked of days-old perspiration.

"I'm as good as can be expected, Art."

"You look like you have lost weight. Have you been eating enough?"

"I'm sure you can imagine that the food sucks here. Bologna on stale bread. Toast that is rock hard. Even the coffee tastes like crap."

Brennan nodded. He made a mental note to raise some hell at the next court hearing, maybe claim the food constitutes cruel and unusual punishment. He would demand a better menu for his client. He then remembered his goodie bag.

"I brought you some Butterfingers," he said, reaching into his briefcase. "You mentioned the other day that you liked them."

Barton's eyes lit up when the candy bars made their appearance. He handled them like they were bars of gold. But that didn't last long. He ripped open one of the yellow wrappers and chomped down on the bar. He took a seat and smiled.

"Thank you," he said with half a mouthful. Oh, it tasted good. He took another bite, chewing slowly, desperately trying to savor the crunchy goodness. He would keep the other one for later.

"I thought we would go over some of the surveillance videos. See if we can find anything helpful to our defense."

"Sure, sounds good," Barton responded. It's not like he had anything better to do.

Brennan turned on the TV in the room and inserted into the DVD player the first of many disks that the Government had provided as part of the discovery process. Brennan's team of lawyers was hard at work back at the office, but he liked to watch surveillance videos with clients to immerse himself in the case and ask questions as they went along. They would have to watch every hour of every one to see what the Government already knew about the secret life of Roland Barton.

"First one here is the surveillance video on the morning of your arrest."

Brennan pushed the play button and waited. With a couple of court-authorized wiretaps, the FBI had entered Barton's residence to bug his phone and insert a hidden camera in the TV of his living room. The phone recordings revealed nothing. Barton was smart enough not to contact his Russian handlers with his home phone.

Although Barton always checked for hidden cameras, he never took apart his TV set. The gadget gurus at the National Security Agency kept making the surveillance cameras smaller and smaller, and detection was almost nonexistent. The one in the TV sat behind the "On" light inside the TV. It was actually a camera disguised as the "On" light. The NSA had different colors depending on the color of the light that came with the TV. Barton's Sanyo had a blue light. Motion activated, it would record everything in the room in black and white when anyone walked in. When someone turned on the TV, the only difference was the video picture would turn to blue and white. Agents tapped the cable line and recorded everything the camera captured.

Brennan fiddled with the remote. Like any tech device, he had trouble working those too. He hit "Play" again and waited some more. The screen was nothing but black for thirty seconds, just long enough for Brennan to wonder if the Feds had erased some exculpatory evidence from the tape. He jotted "*Brady* violation" down on his legal pad just in case. A press of the fast-forward button finally revealed a blue screen with the title "United States v. Roland Barton" in big white letters as the opening credits.

Brennan put the remote on the table beside him, leaned back with his feet up on his briefcase, and settled in his seat with a legal pad in his lap. "I guess I should have brought some popcorn for us," he said, smiling to Barton and trying to lighten the mood.

The blue screen faded away and the first pictures just missed Barton as he turned the corner and walked into the kitchen. Given the pictures of the living area, it was obvious Barton did not do well in the divorce. The bachelor pad looked like a rat trap – dilapidated furnishings, faux wood paneling from the '70s that did not age well. Fast-food bags littered the floor, a pile of dirty laundry stacked in the corner. No way Barton was getting his security deposit back.

When Barton reappeared from the kitchen, the video showed him in black and white and definitely *au naturel*.

Brennan's eyes suddenly got very wide.

Barton wore nothing as he walked around his dump of an apartment. Unfortunately, nature had not taken kindly to him – a nice spare tire rolled around his gut, his old-man breasts drooped toward his toes. Back into the kitchen he went and then back again to the living area. He scratched himself and posed a bit too long in front of a full-length mirror at the opposite end of the TV. The viewer could almost read his mind, almost hear what he was telling himself – once he skips the country he was going to start working out in the warm Brazilian sun, maybe lift some weights and run along the sandy beaches every day. Before he knew it, his buffed and bronzed self would have hot strippers on each arm for the rest of his life.

Brennan started to wonder what in the hell his eyes were seeing. Something had to be wrong. He grabbed the DVD sleeve and looked at the date written on it.

"I thought this was from the morning of your arrest?" He wondered why a mole would be prancing around naked in his living room on the day he planned to skip town for good. Shouldn't he be preparing for his cloak and dagger getaway, maybe hide the guns and cash or promise the beautiful girl he'd return for her once things quieted down.

"I don't wear any clothes around the apartment, Art," Barton said dryly.

Brennan let that unknown fact rattle around in his brain. "Oh," he said, finally nodding in acknowledgment. "Okay."

"I find it liberating."

"I see."

Yes he did. Unfortunately so. Apparently, Barton was not only Brennan's first spy but also his first nudist.

The video showed Barton taking a seat on the couch and then lighting a cigarette. He grabbed his remote from the end table and pointed it at the TV. The picture on the video turned a light blue but Barton was still clearly in the buff. He scratched and puffed some more as he flipped through the channels – *Headline News*, *SportsCenter*, *The View*.

As the right hand tapped the edge of the ashtray on the end table, Brennan saw Barton's head tilt back as his left hand headed south. It didn't take long before the ladies on *The View* had Barton at full attention.

"Aw, jeez," Brennan bellowed, almost falling out of his chair as he feverishly tried to find the remote on the desk. "Aw, jeez." He grabbed the remote, pointed it at the TV, and repeatedly jabbed the fast-forward button. Unfortunately for him, the batteries must have been low on juice. "Come on, come on," he begged, pressing down as hard as he could. Please, make it stop.

Finally, the connection was made and the video hurried forward. After Brennan pushed "Play," the video showed Barton finishing his cigarette with one last long drag.

A red-faced Brennan sat back in his seat. He didn't know what to say. He wiped the sweat forming on his forehead and tried to make a joke of the matter. "I guess we'll have to keep that part from the jury."

Barton was not amused.

The two men returned their focus to the video. The naked Barton stood up from the couch and left the room, kicking a McDonald's bag out of the way as he went. He returned with his attire for the day and draped the clothes over a chair. On went the underwear, much to the red-faced Brennan's relief. Then came the socks. Barton then walked over to his briefcase, opened it, and pulled out an envelope that he had stuffed with lots of cold hard cash. He fingered through it just to make sure it was all still there.

"Shit," Barton whispered as he watched. The hidden camera caught the whole thing. Right there in blue and white for all to see was Barton sealing the envelope before he strapped it to his ankle. At trial, the Feds would have a nice picture of what remained after Barton took a dip in the harbor later on that day.

Barton put his slacks on next and checked the look in the mirror. He raised his leg to see if the envelope stood out. It didn't, he thought. He then gave his leg a good shake to see if anything fell out. Everything seemed secure. The shirt went on next, then the watch. He put the ticket to the Orioles game in his back pocket, and when he faced the mirror again to check his look the camera even caught the section and seat number on the ticket.

"Shit," he whispered again. This time, the weight of the evidence was starting to stack up. And he hadn't even made it out of the apartment yet. There would be a mountain of evidence before the Government was done with him. He stewed in his seat. The video ended with a fully clothed Barton leaving his apartment for the final time.

"Can you get that thrown out?" Barton asked, hoping against hope that the jury wouldn't have to see him in his birthday suit and his related activities.

"I'll try," Brennan said. "I'll file a motion arguing the FBI didn't have probable cause to get a warrant, or the warrant was defective, or an agent lied to the magistrate who signed off on it. I'll argue something."

"What are the chances of success?"

Although Brennan never lacked for confidence, he hadn't seen any problems yet in the materials the Government had handed over to him. "Slim to none."

With all the legal issues having been discussed, Barton did have some questions. "Art, they won't give me a newspaper and my cell doesn't have a TV so I haven't been able to learn the latest news. Have people been talking about me?"

Brennan repositioned his chair so he could look his client in the eye. "Absolutely. You have been all over the networks, the cable news shows, the Internet, newspapers." Brennan stopped short of mentioning that he had been all over the news too. "You're getting a whole lot of press. So much so, I might file a motion to transfer venue and claim the jury pool around the Beltway area is too tainted to give you a fair trial. Maybe we could move the trial to Richmond or Charleston."

Barton seemed to be happy with the coverage of his crimes. "What else is going on? I worked as an analyst for thirty years and I hate not getting the daily news."

"Next time I'm here I'll make sure to bring some newspapers. And some more Butterfingers."

Barton had already finished both bars.

"Let's see," Brennan said, looking at the ceiling. "You probably didn't hear that an official in the Pakistani Government was killed in an explosive car crash in London last night on his way to the Russian Embassy. Huge fireball. He was killed along with five other Pakistanis. President Schumacher was supposed to attend but cancelled at the last moment."

Barton didn't respond right off. He was definitely curious. He and Brennan had not yet discussed the classified information that he had passed on to the Russians.

"What was the name of the Pakistani official who was killed?"

Brennan had to search his mind for that one. He had only glanced at the story that morning, and the guy was not a well-known figure. "I think his last name was Khan."

Barton nodded his head. "Pervez Khan," he said, like he had intimate knowledge of the man.

"Yeah, that's the guy. You know of him?"

Barton tapped his fingers on the table. "Art, I guess it can't hurt to say anything now. Some of the information I passed on to the Russians involved classified intelligence indicating CIA agents had captured Assad Khan, Pervez's brother, and took him to a black site to interrogate him. The President signed off on it. The father of the Khan brothers is the Interior Minister of Pakistan."

Brennan started jotting down notes on his pad.

"If the Russians told the Pakistanis that the U.S. was holding Khan, someone in Pakistan might have decided to take matters into their own hands."

Brennan's eyes widened again. He was starting to put together the pieces of Barton's puzzle. "So you don't think it was an accident what happened last night in London?"

Barton shrugged slightly, but he thought he had a pretty good handle on things. "I don't know the specifics, Art. I'm just telling you what I know and what some people might do if they had that information."

Brennan slowly began to realize the truly sensitive nature of Barton's security breach, along with the unsavory individuals on the other side who would be willing to use that information. Those people most likely followed no higher authority, did what they wanted to do without fear of world consequences. He then remembered his conversation with Max Warner and the grand plan they had hoped to hatch. Brennan was getting nowhere, but Barton had given him an idea. The President was on his last stop before returning to the United States. Something had to be done.

Quickly.

Brennan put down his pen, leaned forward, and lowered his voice. "Roland, I have a friend who, let's just say, would like to make President Schumacher's life very difficult. My friend is not doing well financially under the Schumacher Administration and was hoping regime change might turn things around."

Barton nodded like he understood. "Go on."

"Do you know of anybody that might be able to help him out, somebody overseas he could contact for assistance?"

Barton looked to his left, his mind running through the names of his Russian handlers here in the United States and abroad. He was beginning to think he might be able to wreak some havoc even while behind bars – maybe stick it to the government that screwed him over. The power trip pumped up his ego.

"You should try to find a guy named Patrenko."

Brennan flipped through his legal pad and found a clean page. He clicked his pen and wrote "Patrenko" on the top line. He then underlined it twice.

"Vladimir Patrenko," Barton said.

Brennan added the first name to the page and then asked the next obvious question. "Any idea where I can find him or get in touch with him?"

Barton thought for a minute. He hadn't seen Vlad since that final time in the library. He had no idea where he was.

"Did the FBI arrest anybody else in my case?"

"No."

"Mention any Russian suspects?"

"No names come to mind."

"Kick any Russian Embassy officials out of the country?"

"Not that I am aware of."

Barton nodded. Patrenko must have gotten away. Maybe he had been spooked and decided not to go to the game in Baltimore.

"Well, Patrenko probably left the country. He could be anywhere right now."

"Any ideas?"

"You or your friend could call the Russian Embassy," Barton said before he started shaking his head back and forth like it was a bad idea. "But the FBI and CIA keep their eyes and ears on the Embassies in Washington and Moscow. Chances are they would be on to you pretty quickly. If I were you or your friend, I would drop a dime to the Russian Embassy in London. They might know how to get in contact with Vlad."

Brennan wrote "London" on his legal pad and tapped his pen on the paper. He couldn't think of any other questions. "This is going to very helpful, Roland," Brennan whispered as he jotted down a couple more notes. He started collecting his materials.

"If I can think of anyone else, I'll let you know."

With a final click of the pen, Brennan stood and started packing his briefcase. "I need to get in touch with some people ASAP." The wheels in his mind were spinning fast. He needed to get back to the office. The clasps to the briefcase were snapped shut. "I will be back the day after tomorrow and we'll discuss where we are."

Brennan stuck out his hand and grasped Barton's. "Thanks for the insider information."

"My pleasure," Barton responded, a sly smile forming at his lips. "And don't forget to bring some papers next time."

"Will do," Brennan said. Anything his spy wanted, he told himself.

"And some more Butterfingers too."

CHAPTER 19

The Vatican – Vatican City

The presidential motorcade rumbled down the Via della Conciliazione in as silent a procession as one could imagine from the fifteen-vehicle armored fleet. The sirens were off and the red and blue flashing lights were dark – a sign of respect as President Schumacher and his entourage entered St. Peter's Square. Tourists intent on viewing the sites of the Holy See got a bonus as the President of the United States made his first visit to the Vatican.

The motorcade made it around the Largo del Colonnato and pulled to a stop.

"All units, Craig. Stand by." Agent Craig turned in the front seat of the presidential limousine and scanned the landscape. The tourists were kept back at an acceptable distance, and all of them had gone through metal detectors by the Vatican's Gendarmerie to get to their current position. Advance agents had been on the ground for a week checking with Interpol and Italian authorities on the local crazies. A guy who had threatened the Pope was under constant surveillance just in case the voices in his head told him to go after a new target.

Two Secret Service Suburbans now shielded both ends of the Beast for added protection. Agent Craig was as satisfied as he could be considering his protectee was on foreign soil. Although he was slightly worried that the men on the roofs of the Largo del Colonnato were not Secret Service snipers. The Vatican didn't like armed foreigners, but Craig was at least allowed to have his men on the ground armed to the teeth under their suit coats. He exited the limo and stood by the rear door.

"All units, Craig. Shadow and Sunshine are coming out."

Once the back door opened, President Schumacher stood and acknowledged the cheers to his left and to his right. A flurry of tiny American, Italian, and yellow and white Vatican flags waved back at him. Once the First Lady joined him, they took a minute to look at the Square, the 56-foot columns, all 284 of them, framing each side, and the 2,000-

year-old Egyptian obelisk in the center pointing toward the heavens. They then marched toward St. Peter's Basilica, the giant saintly statutes on the roof looking down upon them from on high.

The First Couple walked inside where His Holiness was waiting to meet them. Dressed in his white robe, he needed help to rise from his seated position. The Pontiff was eighty-three years old and time had taken its toll on his body. He stooped slightly, and shuffled slowly as he moved forward. Two aides were never more than three feet away lest he trip and fall. When he wasn't carrying the Crucifix down the aisle of St. Peter's, he relied on a hand-carved wooden cane that he also liked to use to point out the many architectural wonders of the Vatican.

"Your Holiness, thank you for inviting us to the Vatican," President Schumacher said in a strong voice. He had been told the Pontiff had trouble hearing. The President reached out with both hands and gave a firm handshake, which the Pontiff received with equal firmness.

Although almost six-feet tall, the Pontiff's stoop caused him to look slightly upward to make eye contact with the President. He was fluent in eleven different languages, and his best was his native German, followed by Italian and English. He reached out his left hand and brought the President in closer.

"As the Bishop of Rome, and the head of billions of Catholics around the world, I welcome you to the Vatican," he said. He was at times hard to hear, his voice weakened by the strains of being the head of state as well as his advancing years. But in the quiet stillness of St. Peter's, devoid of any tourists, the President and First Lady heard every word clearly.

The Pontiff then turned to his left, and with a twinkle in his eye, he welcomed Danielle Schumacher with a kiss on her hand. "Welcome. It is a pleasure to meet you."

The President and First Lady presented the Pontiff with a wooden cross – hand carved by an American artisan who just happened to be their neighbor back home in Indiana. The Pope handled it with great care, inspecting it from every angle. He thanked them and said he would hang it in his personal office.

Following the exchange of pleasantries, the Pontiff's aides helped him into a wheelchair, his preferred mode of transportation since his hip surgery just three months ago. The wheelchair would be discarded whenever the cameras were on however, the Pontiff always seeming to gather the strength and determination to walk down the aisle for Christmas

Mass or on the balcony of St. Peter's to give his Easter address.

The tour of the massive St. Peter's Basilica would be one to remember even if not led by the Pope. There was Michelangelo's *Pieta* behind bulletproof glass. And the altar under which are said to be buried the remains of Saint Peter himself.

The group moved on to the Sistine Chapel, where the Pontiff, as tour guide, pointed out the famous works like a seasoned docent – the *Last Supper* by Rosselli, the *Temptation of Christ* by Botticelli. He pointed his cane here and there, a maestro with artwork as his symphony – Michelangelo and *The Creation of Adam* with the hand of God reaching across the ceiling and *The Last Judgment* towering behind the altar.

After the tour, the Pontiff and the President sat together in a gilded meeting room where they sat and shook hands for the lone cameraman allowed into the meeting. There were warm smiles in the two men. The schedule then called for a thirty-minute meeting; afterwards the Pontiff would need to rest. The only ones allowed in the room were the Pope's aides and Agent Craig. All three of them stood near the door and out of hearing range.

As they sat side by side, President Schumacher leaned over closer to hear the soft-spoken Pope. "I have read about your trials and tribulations in the United States, Mr. President," he said quietly. "You seem to be a marked man."

The President nodded in acknowledgment. "Unfortunately, yes. But I am hoping the worst is behind us. I'm sure you can understand the position carries with it great responsibilities and not everyone is supportive of my policies. They feel violence is the answer."

The Pontiff nodded. He heard every word. "Violence is never the answer," he said, hoping for peace throughout the world. But he understood fully. As head of the Catholic Church, he too was a marked man. As was every other Pope. That is why he requires 24-hour security and the armored Popemobile for travel.

He picked up his cane with his right hand, raised it, and pointed it at the President's chest. He had other matters to discuss. With a stern look in his eyes, he growled. "I hear you are affiliated with the Lutheran Church."

President Schumacher's eyes widened and he bit his tongue. He wondered if his regular attendance at St. John's Lutheran Church in Silver Creek, Indiana, would come up. The Pontiff looked serious, and the cane seemed poised to be thrust into the President's ribs if he answered incorrectly. The President's mind suddenly had a vision of Luther pounding in his *Ninety-Five Theses* into the door of the Catholic Church in Wittenburg and his subsequent ex-communication and life as an outlaw. For goodness sakes, the indulgences Luther so complained about just happened to finance the rebuilding of St. Peter's Basilica where they had just walked. The President decided he should tread lightly.

"Your Holiness, I just came from England where my American forefathers had a bit of a spat with Great Britain some time ago. We have made great peace together since the days of the Revolution. I hope, and pray, that you and I can continue the relations our forefathers have had in the centuries since the Reformation."

The Pope lowered his cane and tapped the President on the knee. A wicked smiled crossed his lips. "We welcome all believers here." He winked.

"Thank you," the President said, feigning great relief at the Pope's decision. "Thank you very much."

"Even the Lutherans."

The Pope wanted to know more. Although his aides had prepared a lengthy biography of the President for the Pope to study, he wanted to hear it from the man himself. A bit of a papal test.

"What is your favorite hymn?"

The President gulped and shifted in his seat. Was it getting hot in there? It had been awhile since he had been under this type of interrogation. He didn't dare lie to the Pope though.

"*A Mighty Fortress is our God,*" he said.

The Pope's eyes widened and he tapped his cane against the President's knee with a little more force than the last time.

"*Ein fest Burg ist unser Gott!*" he exclaimed in a loud German accent. He instantly recognized the hymn and made it seem the President had some nerve to mention it inside the Vatican. "Written by Luther himself!" Another strong tap to the knee with the papal cane.

"Based on Psalm 46, I believe," the President responded, hoping to save himself from the Pope's wrath.

The Pope nodded, his body settling back down in his chair after the faux outburst. The smile indicated he would forgive his guest.

"A fine hymn it is." He lowered his cane and grew serious. He motioned with his finger for the President to move closer. "I have been impressed with your focus on the sanctity of life," he said.

"Yes, we are trying to restore a culture of life to our country. The First Lady is also heading a campaign for adoption. It is very important to us."

The Pope nodded. "That is good. We must all be champions of life, and be a voice for those who cannot speak for themselves."

They talked for five minutes on the pro-life movement, and the hope that abortions throughout the world would someday be a rare occurrence. The conversation then went on to terrorism, third-world development, and the need to free Christians who have been persecuted for their beliefs in countries like China and Iraq. The President agreed to talk to his allies on the world stage to bring the issues to their attention.

"Your Holiness, I would like to invite you to the United States. You have not visited since you became Pope. The American people would like to welcome you to Washington and the White House."

The Pope smiled. "I would like that," he said.

"Maybe we could take in an American baseball game."

The Pope laughed with great energy. Even though the thirty minutes were almost up, he did not appear to be losing strength. He grabbed his cane again and tapped the President on the shin. He then pointed the cane at him. "Cardinals," he said. It had been part of the biography.

"Yes," the President said, laughing. "I'm a big fan of the St. Louis Cardinals."

The Pope thought for a second, searching his mind for the right word.

"Musial," he said quietly. The Pope's father was German, but his mother was Polish. And every Pole worth his or her salt was well aware of Stanislaus Franciszek Musial.

"Yes, Stan Musial," the President responded in recognition of the famed St. Louis slugger. "The greatest Cardinal of them all."

The Pope then grasped his cane with both hands and swung it like a baseball bat in front of him – a decent impression of "The Man" himself.

The President gave a strong clap of his hands as he roared with laughter. He was wonderfully impressed with the man sitting next to him. And anyone, especially a foreigner, who knew of and could imitate the swing of "baseball's perfect knight" was a man of worldly talent and intellect.

With yet another wink in his eye, he pointed his cane toward the door. "I have my own team of cardinals right here."

The President and the Pope had a splendid chat. The Pope, he of partial German descent, even asked President Schumacher if he was related to the German racing Schumachers.

"Michael and Ralf?" the President said. Michael being the seven-time Formula 1 world champion and Ralf his younger brother. The President smiled and shook his head like he might be fibbing to the Pope. But he went ahead with it anyway. "I think we might be cousins," he said with a wink. "At least that's what I like to tell people."

Those in the presidential entourage were waiting patiently for the meeting to end. Except for Cogdon, who was pacing the floors hoping that the President didn't mention that he was Lutheran causing the Pope to chase him and the rest of the heathens out of the Vatican. He kept checking his watch. The President was supposed to meet with Prime Minister Scarponi and then have dinner with him. Cogdon worried that the President might be taking too long. He was always worrying.

Across the way, Director Stubblefield was getting the tour of the Vatican from Monsignor Silvio Regazzoni. Standing at a diminutive five-five, the seventy-five-year-old Regazzoni was dwarfed by the massive Stubblefield. With a head of wispy white hair and horn-rimmed glasses, Monsignor Regazzoni spoke perfect English with a strong Italian accent. He walked quickly, hurrying here and there, pointing to this and talking about that. He was high strung and tightly wound, and his nervous energy must have burned thousands of calories off his thin frame. He looked frail in his black cassock, and the clerical collar looked too big for his skinny neck. He seemed a bit intimidated by the barrel-chested Stubblefield as they fast-walked through the Vatican, but he made every effort to please his guest.

Regazzoni was a legend in the Vatican and the Catholic Church throughout the world. Second only to the Pope in popularity, Regazzoni wowed crowds with his knowledge of papal history and church architecture. Utilizing his God-given selective retentive, easy-access memory, he could remember names, dates, and bits of trivia that rivaled most historians and, some would say, even the best computers. Pointing to a picture and asking, "Who's that?" would lead to a half-hour discussion on the person and his importance in the Church. The listener would be so enthralled with Regazzoni's brilliant recall that he would mention it to others rather than the saint or martyr he had just heard about. They came away amazed that so much material could come from a man of such small stature.

Regazzoni and Stubblefield had visited the Pope's motor pool so the Director could take a look at the modified Mercedes-Benz M class SUV and kick the Popemobile's tires. They then met with several members of the Pontifical Swiss Guard of Vatican City – the Swiss military guards in their traditional red, orange, and yellow Renaissance uniforms.

Monsignor Regazzoni stopped and knocked on the door of Alberto DePaolo, the Commandant of the Swiss Guards.

"*Mi scusi, Signore DePaolo*, Director Stubblefield is here," Regazzoni said.

DePaolo stood up and walked around from behind his desk. "Director Stubblefield, it is a great pleasure to meet with the head of America's famed FBI."

"It is a pleasure to meet you, sir."

"I trust that Monsignor Regazzoni has been a good tour guide." The Monsignor's reviews were always stellar.

"Oh, absolutely. He's been wonderful," Stubblefield said. Regazzoni nodded in humble embarrassment at the praise. "I have learned a great deal."

"No one knows the Vatican, not to mention all of Italy, like Monsignor Regazzoni."

"I am coming to find that out."

"He is one of the Vatican's most prized assets."

A blushing Monsignor Regazzoni excused himself but told Stubblefield that he would be right outside if he needed anything. He reminded him that he and several officials from the Swiss Guards would be having an early dinner. But, no need to worry, Regazzoni promised that he would remind him and keep the Director on schedule.

"*Grazie*," Stubblefield said in thanks.

Regazzoni nodded and shut the door behind him. He worked off some more calories as he paced outside DePaolo's office.

Stubblefield and DePaolo sat down for their conversation on security. Stubblefield was interested in all forms of law enforcement and security organizations. He was always trying to learn how to make his FBI better.

The Swiss Guards has over 130 members and acts as the security force in protecting the Pope as well as the Apostolic Palace. The halberdiers, or privates, are Swiss nationals of the Catholic faith, and new recruits must be within the age range of 19 to 30. They must all be no shorter than five-eight-and-a-half.

"Director, usually it is with your country's Secret Service that I have the pleasure of meeting to talk about security."

Stubblefield sat back in his chair. "I am always on the lookout for new ways of doing things. You and I might have different job parameters, but I am just as interested in security as our Secret Service is."

"I can imagine," DePaolo said.

"Plus, since it is a federal crime in the United States to harm our President, I feel it is my duty to help in any way I can to protect him."

"You and your President have both had close calls."

Stubblefield nodded. "Too close. And too often."

DePaolo went over the history of the Swiss Guards, their uniforms, their various forms of ceremonial weaponry – the long sword, the halberd.

"And any firearms?" Stubblefield asked. He hoped his tone wasn't one that said he hoped they had something other than swords and long-handled hatchets to respond to an emergency.

"We do have an assortment of small arms," DePaolo said. "But as you can imagine, we hope to never use them here at the Vatican."

"I can understand that."

"We do our best to safeguard the Pope and the Apostolic Palace by making sure no weapons of any type come in from the outside world."

"Sure. I would like to see your surveillance rooms. Maybe I can get some tips on how to protect some of our historical buildings and architecture in America."

"I would be happy to show you our control room. But first, I must introduce you to my staff. And then we shall eat."

CHAPTER 20

Palazzo Chigi – Rome, Italy

Prime Minister Scarponi's headache had returned. He thought he had brought his country back from the brink of economic collapse but now he was not so sure. The European Union was all over his ass, demanding concessions for the bailout that he had begged for, the one that he had promised the Italian Parliament and the Italian people. He had survived the no-confidence vote, but the riots in the streets of Rome seemed to be growing by the day. The citizens were not happy, and the protests were picking up. He blamed most of it on President Schumacher's arrival – lamenting that the camera hungry anarchists and socialists that followed the American leader around had set Rome aflame. He was at his wits' end on how to calm the crisis. He had purchased the Prime Minister's position with his billions, but he could not seem to buy the answers to put out the fires.

"Mr. Prime Minister," his secretary said over the intercom. "The Russian Ambassador is here to see you."

Scarponi was pacing back and forth across his office. He had thrown out his chief of staff after a heated argument. Then he started drinking – first with the whiskey and then with the vodka. He had not slept in two days.

Now the Russians were calling again. Could his day get any worse?

The door to the office opened and Ambassador Aleksandr Tkachenko walked in. Followed closely behind were the bombastic Russian duo of Vladimir Patrenko and Viktor Zhukov.

Scarponi's shoulders slumped. "Aw hell," he muttered to himself, along with a choice assortment of Italian profanities.

Yes, it could get worse.

"Good afternoon to you, Mr. Prime Minister," Ambassador Tkachenko said. He had a dignified air about him, like every foreign diplomat thought he or she should have. But he was on no diplomatic mission today. He was simply there to make sure Messrs. Patrenko and Zhukov got in the door to bust the Prime Minister's balls.

"Hello," Scarponi said. It was not a welcoming greeting. He wished the Russians would get lost. "What do you three want?"

Ambassador Tkachenko stepped forward. "Mr. Prime Minister, on behalf of President Yaroslavsky and Prime Minister Grigoryev, I ask that you please grant Mr. Patrenko and Mr. Zhukov an audience."

Scarponi knew he couldn't say no. Patrenko and Zhukov weren't going anywhere. Still, he didn't feel the need to make it easy on them. "I don't remember those two being on my schedule for today."

Ambassador Tkachenko understood his duties. "Sir, if you would permit them to speak, I'm sure those in Moscow would be most appreciative."

Scarponi huffed in disgust. "Whatever," he said before turning his eyes on Patrenko and Zhukov. "What do you want?"

Ambassador Tkachenko stepped to the side of the two men and thanked the Prime Minister for his time. To Scarponi's surprise, he then left the office.

"Aw hell," Scarponi muttered under his breath. Let the ball busting begin.

The bug-eyed Viktor Zhukov, the head of Russia's Ministry of Gas Industry, took the lead. He wore all black with a silver tie. He unbuttoned his suit coat. "Shall we sit down?" He motioned the Prime Minister over to the couch.

The Prime Minister took a seat on the end and Zhukov sat facing him on the other end. The round mound of Vlad the Impaler stood next to Zhukov, as if readying himself to pounce on Scarponi if the spirit moved him to do so.

Scarponi thought he would do his best to get yet another surprise meeting with the Russians off to a good start by letting them know what he had been up to. "I have been working hard to return your money." The fake sincerity didn't fool anyone.

Vlad Patrenko shook his head slowly. He felt the need to crack his knuckles like he was going to use them in the near future. "We still don't have the money. You obviously have not been trying hard enough."

"I told you once before that I would get it!" Scarponi snapped, the alcohol giving him a bit of a boost. "I am the Prime Minister of Italy!"

Yes, Patrenko and Zhukov were well aware of that. And they had heard that line too many times before to have it mean anything to them now. Neither believed Scarponi's claim that he would get the money. That's why they were there.

The Russian Embassy in London had received an interesting call from Art Brennan, head of the Civil Liberties Alliance. He had mentioned that he was friends with Max Warner and they had discussions that the Russians might like to be a part of. After a few phone conversations, Patrenko and Zhukov were on a plane to Rome.

And their mission was to make a deal with Scarponi that he could not refuse.

Zhukov brushed some minuscule piece of dust off the knee of his black slacks. Threats came easy to him. It was a part of doing business with foreign leaders. He took his time because he knew he had the upper hand.

"The Russian Government would very much like for you to make good on your promise to reimburse $10.7 billion that you stole."

"$10.7 billion!?" Scarponi exclaimed in some matter of shock. "You told me last time it was $10.3 billion!" He made it sound like the Russians were attempting to screw him, which, of course, they were, and he would have none of that!

"It was $10.3 billion last time we met," Zhukov said matter-of-factly. "But with interest and late charges, your bill keeps going up and up."

Patrenko found the Prime Minister's mini-bar and helped himself to some vodka. He poured a second glass for Scarponi. He was going to need it.

"We want our money, Mr. Prime Minister," Zhukov said again. "And we want it right now."

Scarponi slumped farther down in the couch. He felt like he had gone ten rounds, and the pummeling he had taken was wearing him down. He wondered if the pressure would ever end. When Patrenko walked over and handed him a glass of Stolichnaya, he accepted with a nod of acceptance.

The Russian tag team knew he was beaten. And now they were ready to pounce.

"Mr. Prime Minister," Zhukov said. "We would like to propose a deal that would enable you to pay off your debts to the Russian people."

A deal? The silence that followed indicated Scarponi was interested.

"What kind of deal?" His voice was growing hoarse, his throat hurting every time he spoke.

Zhukov looked Scarponi straight in the eye. "We are willing to wipe out the $10.7 billion debt you owe us," he said.

Scarponi's eyes widened, probably too much so. "All of it?"

Zhukov nodded. The Russians could tell he was eager to please in exchange for cancellation of his debts. "Every cent," Zhukov said.

Scarponi was almost afraid to ask. "What is it you want from me?"

Zhukov leaned forward in his seat. He then moved to the center of the couch. Just two feet separated him from the Prime Minister. Scarponi gulped, which aggravated his throat. He took a sip of vodka.

Zhukov adjusted his thick glasses. "We want you to give us the President of the United States."

Silence.

Scarponi blinked his eyes and shook his head to clear the cobwebs. He wondered if he was drunk and heard incorrectly. He thought Zhukov mentioned the President of the United States. But how did he fit into all of this? The U.S. had nothing to do with Scarponi's mess with the Russians.

"What?"

Zhukov leaned forward and laid out the plan. "We want you to deliver the President of the United States to the International Criminal Court at The Hague."

Silence. Then another shake of the head.

"What?"

"The International Criminal Court. The President is to be tried for crimes against humanity."

"Are you two out of your freaking minds!?"

Zhukov leaned over and poked his stubby index finger in Scarponi's chest, hard enough for the Prime Minister to flinch.

"No, sir," Zhukov grunted. "We are very much serious about this matter."

"He hasn't done anything to warrant a trial. The United States is not even a party to the ICC. He can't even be tried."

"He cannot be tried unless he is arrested in a country that has signed on to the Rome Statute. Italy has done so."

"But what crimes has he committed?"

"Crimes against humanity," Zhukov said, ticking off the allegations like they had already been proven. "Bombing innocent civilians in Iraq, Afghanistan, Pakistan."

"They are at war," Scarponi protested.

"He has even authorized the kidnapping of foreign government leaders on Italian soil."

"What?" He was not expecting to hear that.

"That's right," Zhukov said, reeling Scarponi in. "Didn't know about that did you? He authorized the arrest of Pakistan's Assad Khan off your very own streets of Milan. Right under your nose."

"I never heard about that."

"Just like that cleric from Egypt," Zhukov reported.

"Omar," Patrenko said.

"That's right. Abu Omar was picked up off the streets of Milan by U.S. CIA agents and then tortured in Egypt. Italian courts convicted the CIA agents *in absentia*. Meaningless, of course. Now the U.S. is right back at it, abducting people right off your own streets. That is a crime against your country!" Zhukov exclaimed in grand legal fashion.

"I don't think that is enough to . . . ," Scarponi said before Zhukov lunged at him.

"I don't care what you think, Mr. Prime Minister," Zhukov growled. His meaty left forearm was draped across Scarponi's chest, his left knee poised perilously close to Scarponi's crotch. "If you want us to forget about your little debt with us, then you will do what we say."

"The ICC wouldn't do anything anyway," Scarponi said. He was desperately trying to wiggle out of Zhukov's body block.

"The Office of the Prosecutor is controlled by Raul Gonzalez, a citizen of Venezuela and a prominent socialist. One of the judges is your countrymen – an anti-capitalist if there ever was one. The President has violated the sovereignty of your country. They will act accordingly."

Zhukov knew they would. Because the Russians had bought them off years ago.

Scarponi would have none of it. He would rather pay back every last dime to the Russians. He had the money. Even if they played the tape of his kickback deals, he could resign in disgrace and still retire in luxury. Some might even consider him a hero for screwing the Russians and stealing their money.

"No," he said defiantly. He was a man of honor, he told himself. "I won't do it."

"They will hang you in the street like they did Mussolini," Zhukov said.

"No. I cannot do it."

This time it was Vlad the Impaler's turn. With Zhukov holding the Prime Minister against the couch, Patrenko leaned in and wrapped his right hand around the front of Scarponi's throat.

"I warned you not to fuck with us," Patrenko growled. With just enough of a squeeze to let Scarponi worry about what was going to happen, he released the pressure and stepped back. He reached for his iPhone and searched for the video.

"I've already seen your damn video," Scarponi hissed. "I told you I'll pay back the money."

Patrenko leaned in again and held the iPhone about a foot from Scarponi's face. "You have not seen this video before."

The quality of the picture was decent, good enough to let the viewer know it was taken by a hidden camera in a hotel room. If Scarponi had trouble seeing himself, the voice on the video was clearly his and he was clearly drunk. He was with a young woman, and after the door to the room closed, the clothes came off with remarkable speed. Then the bed shook and rattled for a good couple of minutes. But when the naked woman began to protest, Scarponi turned a deaf ear and continued on. When she started to push him off, he became violent – first with his fists to her head and then his sex organ to her privates. The sound of open palms to bare skin seemed to get louder with every whack. The screams would not play well in an Italian court, and definitely not in the court of public opinion. A video of the girl crying her heart out would be the end of his political career. When the screams grew louder, the inebriated Scarponi wrapped his hands around her neck to quiet her. The grip grew tighter until the screams went silent. If a jury saw Scarponi squeeze the last breath out of her, he knew that would be the end of his life.

Scarponi was starting to remember now. He had been in the mood for a prostitute that evening and he told his people he didn't care what she looked like or where she was from. He couldn't remember her name but he thought she had a Russian accent.

"You should have stuck to screwing Italian women, Mr. Prime Minister," Patrenko growled. The Impaler was ready to gut the Prime Minister right then and there.

The video continued on. First with the Prime Minister panicking when he realized he had killed the woman – suffocated her right in the bed. Then the frantic phone calls where he mumbled incoherently for help to save himself. Finally, the video showed the Prime Minister's henchmen, wrapping the prostitute in the bed sheets and hauling her out to the Dumpster – to be thrown out like yesterday's garbage.

Scarponi had to exert great control from relieving his bladder. He was no longer thinking about losing his position as Prime Minister. He had thought he could always retire with his billions and move to Monte Carlo or Switzerland or one of his many villas around the world. Now his thoughts were focused on spending his golden years in an Italian prison.

Zhukov could tell Scarponi was seeing only one way out.

"All you have to do is get the President in here and don't let him leave. You order your police to cordon off the area. You tell the President he is being detained for trial at The Hague. We'll take it from there. We have everything and everyone we need to pull it off."

Scarponi could not restrain the tears running down his cheeks. He was shocked at the level of planning made by the Russians. And with no sleep, the pressures of the office, and now their ultimatum, Scarponi wanted to end it all now. His shaking hand brought the glass of vodka to his quivering lips.

"You will be a hero to your countrymen," Zhukov said, trying to sweeten the deal. "Our friends will also take care of your protesters. They'll call them off and you will once again have peace in the streets."

"What about peace in the world?" Scarponi croaked.

Patrenko looked like he wanted to replay the video again. Zhukov backed off from the Prime Minister. He stood up from the couch and straightened his jacket. "You have two choices, Mr. Prime Minister. Either you face life in prison for your crimes or you give us the President of the United States so he can stand trial for his."

Vlad Patrenko took a step closer. He opened his jacket revealing the knife on his left hip and a gun on his right. "Today's the day, Mr. Prime Minister," he said, ominously. "It's D-day for you and President Schumacher. What's it going to be?"

Scarponi licked his dry lips and closed his eyes. It didn't take long for him to make up his mind. He nodded slowly.

"I will do it," he whispered. "I will give you the President of the United States."

The Vatican – Vatican City

After Cogdon had looked at his watch for the umpteenth time, the doors to the meeting between the Pope and President Schumacher finally opened. The Pope's aides entered, as did Cogdon. The President was saying goodbye to the Pontiff and again offering to host him in Washington, D.C. The Pope indicated he hoped to travel to the United States in the very near future. After a final round of handshakes, the President started to back away when the Pontiff, now seated in his wheelchair, raised his hand and motioned that he had one more thing to say. President Schumacher bent down slightly, but the Pope motioned him down further, come closer, he seemed to say. When the President took a knee next to him, Wiley Cogdon almost had a panic attack. Luckily, he held his tongue long enough to realize there were no cameras in the room.

The President leaned in his with his left ear. The Pope moved forward in his seat. He put his right hand around the President's neck. "Mr. President," he said softly. "You be careful out there."

The President felt a strange power flow through him at the Pope's words. He looked in the Pontiff's eyes – the seriousness of the look could not be questioned. The Pope leaned in closer and said it again. "You be careful." The Pope then placed his left hand on the President's head and made the sign of the cross with his right. He mumbled a prayer heard by no one but God.

The President stood, reached out with both hands, and grasped the Pontiff's hands for the final time. "Thank you," he whispered.

The Pope's aides slowly wheeled him away to his apartment. The President and Cogdon stood but said nothing.

"All units, Craig," Agent Craig said into his microphone as the entourage made its way to the elevator. "Prepare for departure."

The Beast rumbled to life out in St. Peter's Square. A second limousine arrived to take the First Lady to visit the American Embassy and, if her security team deemed it safe, a tour of the Colosseum. The First Couple then planned on meeting at the airport for the ride back to the U.S. later on that evening. They hoped to be back in their own bed in the White House at a decent hour.

"All units, Shadow and Sunshine are coming out."

The President and First Lady walked out into St. Peter's Square and took in the warmth of the late afternoon sunshine. After they waved to the crowds, the President gave her a kiss on the cheek and told her he would see her later.

Agent Craig scanned the crowds and waited for the President to get into the back seat of the limousine. When the door closed, he looked over his troops. One last trip, he said to himself. Get through this and it's off to the airport and the safety of Air Force One. He took a seat in the front of the Beast and shut the door. He shook off the feeling that they were about to enter the lion's den.

"All units, Craig," he said into his microphone. "To the Palazzo Chigi."

CHAPTER 21

Palazzo Chigi – Rome, Italy

Once the presidential motorcade left Vatican City, the Secret Service lit the lights and sounded the sirens. It made its way east across the Tiber River and traveled along the Lungotevere until it reached the Via del Orso. It wound its way through the narrow streets until it reached the northern side of the Italian Parliament where it turned south on the Via del Corso. From there, it was only a few blocks south to the front door of the Palazzo Chigi.

"Stagecoach, this is Andrews," the Secret Service agent outside the Palazzo Chigi said. "Recommend a quick entrance. We have protesters to the west. Do you copy?"

"Roger that," Agent Craig said. He was worried about that. The protesters had caused enough trouble throughout Rome that it raised concerns for the Secret Service, which persuaded the President to cancel a planned overnight stay in the capital city. Craig turned around in his seat. "Mr. President, if you could proceed directly into the Palace we would appreciate it."

"No problem."

The motorcade came to a stop under the Column of Marcus Aurelius and a team of security agents fanned out across the Piazza Colonna. Agent Craig then made the call. "All units, Shadow is coming out. Straight inside."

President Schumacher exited the back seat and looked to the west. The protesters were in full song, chanting something he couldn't hear. Maybe they were yelling profanities at him in Italian. He gave them a quick wave and started walking toward the front door of the Palace. The tense swarm of security moved quickly, almost prodding the President to move faster. The agents wanted him out of the danger zone. It was then that something to the right caught the President's attention. It was a red hat, sticking out like a sore thumb in a sea of color. A small crowd had been handpicked by the Prime Minister's public-relations people to welcome the President to the Palace. All had been plucked off the nearby streets – some were locals, others simply tourists at the right place at the right time. They were a peaceful bunch, none of them with any violent agendas. And all had been fully frisked. They had waited for hours to catch a glimpse of the President of the United States and give him a warm welcome.

The President zeroed in on the red hat – he had seen the make and model a million times. He even had the same one back home. The white STL on the front indicated the man had impeccable taste in sports teams. Not wanting to disappoint those hearty souls who had patiently staked out their positions and wanting to compliment the man on his hat, the President darted to his right, nearly startling Agent Craig and the rest of the President's detail in the process.

It's called a "breakaway" in personal security parlance – the protectee going off script to press the flesh or say hello to a donor or a constituent. The agents on the protective detail hated the "breakaway," figuring little good could come of it from a security standpoint because it brought way too many variables into the equation. The agents practically begged their protectee not to do it. President Schumacher usually complied with their requests.

But not today.

"Shadow is going to work the line," Craig said through gritted teeth into his radio. Ever the professional, he restrained himself from letting his true feelings known. He wanted the President inside pronto. The security detail made a hard right toward the barrier. A wall of suits then separated the President from the protesters to the west.

The President made a beeline straight for the Cardinals fan and extended his hand. "Nice hat," he said.

The man in the hat had a name tag that read "Bill" along with the name of an Italian tour outfit. "Hello, Mr. President." The accent was definitely American. Most likely the Midwest.

"Oh, Americans?" the President asked, happy to hear English in a foreign land.

"Not only are we Americans, we're from Silver Creek, Indiana," Bill said.

The woman next to him, Bill's wife, "Sharon," according to the name tag, stuck out her hand next. "We live next door to Floyd Revson."

The President could barely believe it. Hometown folks in the middle of Rome, Italy. And neighbors to the President's friend and former boss to boot.

With laser-like focus, Agent Craig's eyes zeroed in on the two Hoosiers. The name Floyd Revson got his attention real quick. Craig had heard of Revson, even met him a couple of times. His security-minded brain ran through the possibilities. Could it be a diversion? An attempt to distract the President while he worked the rope line? No. Craig's eyes scanned the couple, determined them to be harmless, and moved on to the next person in the sea of hands and cell-phone cameras.

"Well, tell ol' Floyd that I said hello. I haven't seen him in awhile," the President said before moving to his right.

As the security scrum moved along with the President, Agent Craig could feel the pressure building behind him across the Piazza. The angry hooligans were banging on the gates holding them back, looking like they were ready to charge. One of them set off a smoke bomb, and Secret Service agents put a finger to their ear trying to hear any commands over the growing clamor. In all the noise and commotion of the moment, Agent Craig leaned into the President's ear and forcefully whispered, "We need to get inside, sir."

No one else but the President heard it. Agent Craig didn't need to say it twice. The President nodded and backed away. He had deviated from the plan and needed to get going. "Thank you all," he told the crowd with one last wave.

For a split second, Agent Craig thought about escorting the President straight to the limo and getting him out of there. His instincts told him something didn't feel right. He didn't like the protesters being so close. As he reached out to get the President's attention, the President took a quick right and headed up the steps of the Palazzo Chigi and in the front door.

Agent Craig followed right behind him. He was still on edge but at least he had the President inside now. The secure walls of the Palace gave his anxiety some relief. The Prime Minister and several leaders from Parliament approached to greet President Schumacher.

"Mr. President, welcome to the Palazzo Chigi," Scarponi said, extending a hand. He spoke decent English, but his words seemed slower than usual.

The President thought he smelled alcohol. It was getting close to dinnertime, he thought. Maybe Scarponi had started early.

"Mr. Prime Minister, thank you for welcoming me to your residence. It is a pleasure to be in your beautiful country of Italy."

"Will the First Lady be joining us?"

"No, she sends her regrets. She has a speaking engagement at the Embassy this early evening. And she really wanted to see some of the sites before we return to the United States later on tonight."

The Prime Minister could only manage a weak nod. The President sensed his disappointment. Perhaps the ladies' man in him really wanted to see the First Lady in person, maybe ask her to dance.

The two leaders posed for the photographers before their handlers ushered them into the Hall of Globes, so named for the two globes that date back to the 1600s. There, ensconced in large chairs, the two discussed trade deals, terrorism, and the world economy. It was short on specifics given that Scarponi's mind seemed to be elsewhere. He kept nodding in agreement at everything the President said. He also kept glancing toward the door. Although it was a quick meeting, the parties would call the get-together productive – one where both sides promised to work with each other and forge a new friendship between the countries. It would be a mutually beneficial partnership.

Once the meeting was over, the Prime Minister motioned for President Schumacher to meet him in the corner of the room for a private word.

"Mr. President, I was hoping to have a more private chat with you in my office upstairs," Scarponi whispered into his ear. "Maybe have a quick drink prior to our dinner."

"Sure," the President said. He didn't see the need to be so secretive about it.

The President, Cogdon, the Secret Service, the Prime Minister, and his bodyguards all walked up the stairs. They stopped at the Hall of Gold on the second floor. Scarponi pointed out some the 17th century artwork in the Palace and gave a short history. The fourth floor included a tour of the Chigi library. When they reached the door to his fifth-floor office, he turned and looked at the assembled group. It was clear he thought they should stay out in the hall.

"Mr. President, I was hoping we could have a moment in private. One on one."

The President said that was not a problem. "Give us a few minutes guys," he said, motioning to Cogdon and the Secret Service.

Agent Craig stepped forward. With security being his sworn duty, he had no qualms about disagreeing with the President or offending some foreign leader so he spoke up. "Mr. Prime Minister, if I could just have a quick look in your office."

The Prime Minister was indeed offended and looked as if the President should call off his security man. The President, however, trusted Agent Craig with his life, and he did his best to accommodate the Secret Service whenever possible. And remembering his "breakaway" earlier, he thought he would make up for it with a request of his host.

"Just a quick look, Giovanni?"

Scarponi, obviously flushed, opened the door and waved Agent Craig inside. Craig made a quick scan of the room. He walked to the south side of the building and looked out over the Piazza. He checked the windows and they all seemed secure. The only two people in the room were a short stocky bald man and what looked like his slightly taller brother with thick glasses. Their black attire was covered by a white butler's jacket. Each carried a tray with glasses and alcohol. Both stood ready to serve their master.

Craig looked at the two men and then at Scarponi. "Staff!" the Prime Minister barked. He stopped short of asking Agent Craig if he wanted to frisk the help.

"Thank you, Mr. Prime Minister."

Scarponi waved the man away, cursing in Italian, insulted at the intrusion.

As the President walked in, he gave a friendly tap on Agent Craig's shoulder. "Thanks, Mike," he whispered. "No worries."

Agent Craig shut the door behind him and took up his position. A nervous Cogdon took to pacing the floors, his head down, mumbling to himself. He walked in and out of open rooms hoping the President would get by without his political guru by his side to prevent any unwanted gaffes.

President Schumacher and Prime Minister Scarponi entered the latter's office, the sunlight from the western sky filtering in through the southern windows.

"Giovanni, you didn't say much downstairs," the President said.

Scarponi could feel his throat tightening, his tongue heavy. His churning stomach made him want to double over, but he fought through the urge. "Mr. President, can I get you a drink?"

"It's Anthony, Giovanni, you know that. I'll take a Diet Coke if you have one."

Vlad the Impaler walked to the mini-bar and poured a can of Diet

Coke into a glass full of ice. He and Scarponi didn't make eye contact. The Prime Minister grabbed the President's glass and poured himself a half a glass of vodka. He brought the Diet Coke over to the President. He had to grip the glass hard to keep it from shaking.

"*Grazie*," the President said. He took a swig and the cool soft drink felt good. The caffeine brought a bit of energy to him. "Giovanni, you have a beautiful country. I hope my wife and I can come back some day on a more leisurely trip and take it all in."

The Prime Minister nodded and raised his glass. There was no smile, just heavy burdened eyes.

"You said you wanted to talk in private. What's on your mind?"

Scarponi looked out the window, his head almost in a fog. He took a drink, which didn't help. "There is a lot of unrest out in the world, isn't there, Mr. President?"

The President walked over and stood by the Prime Minister. "Yes, I guess there is. You have problems here. I have problems back home. I guess it goes with the territory. We are given great authority and with that comes great responsibility."

"Yes it does."

As the two men faced out the window, Patrenko slowly walked to the other end of the room and pretended to straighten up. He worked his way along the wall before stopping at the door. He reached for the knob and gingerly turned the lock. He turned his back toward the door and waited. That was the signal for the Prime Minister to go about holding up his end of the bargain.

Scarponi cleared his throat. "Mr. President, I have been advised that you are wanted at the International Criminal Court."

That was what this secret meeting was about – the International Criminal Court. "They want me to speak at the ICC?" Really? the President wondered. "The United States is not even a member. And given my political background, I doubt they would want to hear from me."

Scarponi shook his head. "No, Mr. President. You are wanted as a defendant."

"A defendant?"

"Yes, a defendant. To stand trial for crimes against humanity."

The President was not following. He hadn't heard anything about it, although there was always some leftist around the world calling for the U.S. President to stand trial for something. "What are you talking about,

Giovanni?"

Scarponi took a step closer. His eyes narrowed and his voice quivered slightly. "You're under arrest, Mr. President."

The President started laughing. "Giovanni, are you drunk?"

The unmistakable sound of gunfire erupted inside the Palace. From the kitchen, fifteen Russian mercenaries dressed as butlers made their way upstairs or out of locked rooms. The lids of the dinner trays were lifted and Russian Uzis were fired in all directions – down the halls, up the stairs, over the balconies.

The President spun around toward the door. He could hear yelling out in the hall. He reached into his right pants pocket for his panic button and pressed it. Agent Craig was attempting to kick down the door, the pounding growing louder as another agent joined in.

The President took a step toward the door to see what was going on. The gunfire was getting closer. Scarponi put out a hand. "Hold it right there, Mr. President."

"Get out of my way, Giovanni."

The President pushed past him and headed for the door. Vlad Patrenko then opened his butler's jacket, pulled out a gun, and pointed it at the President.

"You're not going anywhere, Mr. President," he said in his distinctly Russian tone.

From the other side of the room, Viktor Zhukov brought out his Uzi from underneath the mini-bar.

"Mike!" the President yelled toward the door. "Mike!"

Patrenko moved in, the gun pointed at the President's head. "Not one more word."

Had it just been Patrenko, the President might have thought of going after him, maybe resort back to his FBI days and disarm the man with the gun pointed at him. But Zhukov was moving in. And the chaos out in the hall meant there were others just like the two Russians surrounding him. Then the President heard the click behind him. It was Scarponi cocking the hammer of the snub-nosed revolver that he had kept in his desk. Now the President had three barrels pointed at him.

Out in the hall, Agent Craig and the President's inner security circle were taking fire.

"Shots fired! Shots fired!"

Wave upon wave of Russians appeared from every corner. They had taken over every floor of the Palace. "We want the President! We want the President!"

Agent Craig took down two from his spot behind a pillar, but when a bullet tore through his shoulder, his SIG-Sauer P229 pistol flew out of his hands. He staggered to his knees.

"Shadow is . . .," Agent Craig said, weakly into his microphone.

The Secret Service command post, codenamed Horsepower, was set up at the American Embassy in Rome. It coordinated all of the President's movements from the arrival at the airport until the departure. It was connected to Secret Service Headquarters in Washington, D.C. And those manning the radio transmissions did not understand the last call.

"Uh, Craig, Horsepower. Your last transmission was garbled. Say again."

Craig could only whisper now. He had taken another bullet in the chest. "AOP in progress." The microphone remained on but nothing was heard but a man gasping for breath. "Agents . . . down."

"Craig, Horsepower. Say again." No response. A call that there was an attack on a protectee and agents down was as serious as they come. "Agent Craig, do you copy?"

There was no response, just more gunfire.

"Agent Mullins, Horsepower."

Mullins was standing guard outside the President's limo in the Piazza. The radio transmission had already caused a flurry of activity outside as the agents manning the motorcade prepared for action. "Horsepower, Mullins. Go ahead."

"Are you in contact with Agent Craig?"

"Negative. He is inside. There has been radio traffic of 'shots fired.'" Mullins then looked left before reaching for his weapon. "Horsepower, I have Italian police vehicles approaching."

The intensity at the command post just went up a notch. They hadn't been notified of any police movements.

"Mullins, Horsepower. Are they dealing with the protesters?"

"Negative. The protesters have left."

"Say again."

"The protesters have left their positions!" Mullins then watched as the armored personnel carriers started to ring the grounds of the Palace. "Horsepower, we might have a serious problem here. Recommend immediate evacuation."

"How many are there?"

Mullins was never able to respond. A Russian had stepped out front and fired his Uzi into the sky. Another joined him and put a gun to Mullins' head. His weapon and radio were taken away. He and six other Secret Service agents were marched inside the Palace, where they were cuffed, hooded, and watched over by three Russian thugs.

"Agent Mullins?" No response. "Mullins, Horsepower." Nobody was responding. "Craig, Horsepower."

The phone connecting the command post to the Joint Operations Center at Secret Service Headquarters in D.C. started ringing. "Horsepower?" the agent manning the phone said.

"Yes, Director Defoe is requesting a situation report?" The bells and alarms had been going off in D.C., where everyone was watching and wondering what was going on.

"Sir, we have lost contact with Agent Craig and Agent Mullins. It appears the Palace is being surrounded."

When Director Defoe came on the line, everyone knew this was no run-of-the-mill problem. "We have a possible AOP in progress. Coordinate all commands with Horsepower. Where is Sunshine?"

An unknown agent broke the silence. "Sunshine is on the tarmac at Da Vinci preparing to board Air Force One."

"Roger that," Director Defoe said. "Keep the airport locked down and get her on board." He hung up the phone and then picked it up again. "Get me the Vice President and the Secretary of Defense! And hurry!"

CHAPTER 22

The Vatican – Vatican City

Director Stubblefield was enjoying a meal of veal parmigiana and toasted ravioli along with a dessert of chocolate mousse. The conversation with Commandant DePaolo and several of his Swiss Guards staff was lively and, while law-enforcement matters were discussed, many of the questions from Stubblefield's foreign counterparts again were focused on his former, albeit short, career with the Oakland Raiders of the National Football League. Given their proximity to Rome and the rest of Italy, soccer was often on the minds of the Swiss Guards. They were big fans. But they were intrigued by the American brand of football. They asked if he had ever played in the Super Bowl and whether he knew Tom Brady. No and Yes, he responded.

When Monsignor Regazzoni hurried in, everyone took notice – the trembling hands, the pale white skin in his face. He looked like he might drop dead at any moment.

"Monsignor, what is it?" DePaolo asked with great concern in his voice.

"*Mi scusi,*' Regazzoni said weakly. He approached the table and turned to Director Stubblefield. His trembling increased, his lower lip quivered in fright. "Dir. . . Dir. . . Director Stubblefield," he stammered. Tears were beginning to well up in the old man's eyes. "*Signore,* there has been a problem with your President."

"What!?" Stubblefield barked, the force of the exclamatory blast almost blowing the Monsignor off his feet.

Regazzoni staggered a bit before grabbing hold of the back of a chair. "Your President is in trouble."

The massive Stubblefield pushed back his chair and towered over Regazzoni. He reached out his hand to support the Monsignor, who looked like he was going to faint. "Tell me what happened," Stubblefield ordered.

"Your President arrived at the Palazzo Chigi to meet with Prime

Minister Scarponi," Monsignor Regazzoni said, whimpering as he went. "There was gunfire. And your Secret Service has been hit."

"What about the President?"

"I do not know. I am sorry."

Stubblefield ripped open his jacket and reached for his phone. The flummoxed Regazzoni was helped to a seat. He looked like he might need a doctor. DePaolo also reached for his phone and started throwing out orders. Swiss Guards of every rank hurried into the room and then back out again. The Vatican was going under lockdown.

"Schiffer!" Stubblefield blurted into his phone over in the corner of the room. "Get the Phantom team ready. Now! Meet me at the Vatican garage!"

DePaolo held his hand over his phone. "Director, whatever you need. I have been given full authority from His Holiness himself to offer any assistance to help your President."

"Good, thank you." Stubblefield said. He put the phone back in his pocket and looked at his watch. "I need to get down to the motor pool." He stopped briefly, his mind already thinking of a plan. He had one request of Commandant DePaolo. "And I need Monsignor Regazzoni to come with me."

"Me!?" a frightened Regazzoni shot back. A part of him worried that Director Stubblefield was going to shoot him for being the bearer of such bad news.

"Yes, I hear you know Rome better than anyone. We might need your expertise, Monsignor." Regazzoni, however, was vigorously shaking his head back and forth. Stubblefield looked at DePaolo for an answer.

"Take him," DePaolo shot out with a wave of his right hand, much to Regazzoni's horror.

"Thank you," Stubblefield said, grabbing the Monsignor out of the seat by the arm. "Let's go."

With their shoes echoing off the marble floors, Stubblefield and Regazzoni hurried down to the papal garage where Schiffer and the Phantom team were roaring to a stop in a Fiat Ducato van. The van was painted Vatican white with no other markings. It had no windows on the passenger sides or the rear, just solid white panels. Dressed in black attire with a white clerical collar, Schiffer exited the front passenger seat and met them twenty yards from the van.

"Do you know what's going on?" Stubblefield asked before they got there.

Schiffer gave the scant details that he knew. "Italian police moved in on the Palace. The Secret Service lost contact with its agents on the ground."

"Is it a coup or what?" Stubblefield asked.

"I don't know. The Secret Service has had no contact with the President."

"Son of a . . ."

The driver and three other members of the Phantom team stood next to the van waiting for their orders. They were all dressed like priests – large priests, but, nonetheless, they would blend in nicely when in Rome. They had been out scouting the area when the call came in. Now, the intensity in their eyes indicated they were ready to go.

"Gentlemen," Stubblefield announced. "This is Monsignor Regazzoni." He said it in such a calm fashion that it appeared the Monsignor was just another piece of the Phantom team puzzle. "He will be joining us and offering any assistance that he can give us. We are going to the Palazzo Chigi. Or somewhere nearby so we can survey the scene. Let's saddle up."

Director Stubblefield took the front passenger seat and three members squeezed into the rear seat. Monsignor Regazzoni stuck his head inside the van and it was clear that he was thinking twice about getting in. His mind wondered how he had gotten involved in this mess. He raised his right leg then lowered it. Then he did it again. He might have needed a step stool to get in.

No need.

"Here, let me help you there, Padre," Agent Schiffer said, hoisting Regazzoni up off the ground by his belt and armpit and placing him into the van and the seat behind the driver. Schiffer took the seat behind Director Stubblefield and slammed the door shut.

"Do you need anything from us?" DePaolo asked Stubblefield through the open window.

"We just need you to keep it quiet," Stubblefield said, pointing back to his men.

"You got it."

"Let's go," Stubblefield ordered.

The Phantom team van went west out of the Vatican garage. Stubblefield pulled the maps out from the glove compartment as they proceeded on the northern edge of Vatican City on the Viale Vaticano. Schiffer opened up the weapons bag next to his seat and Monsignor Regazzoni let out a yelp that startled the whole van.

"*Signore!*" he exclaimed, his voice shaking. He looked like he had seen a ghost. The excitable Regazzoni probably hadn't seen a gun since his days as a kid watching Clint Eastwood shoot 'em up in his old-time spaghetti westerns. And about all he remembered about the plots was that the guns were the law of the land.

"*Signore*, we do not allow foreigners to have weapons in the Vatican." Even in distress, the Monsignor was a stickler for Vatican protocol. "*Per favore*, sir."

Stubblefield turned his head and looked at the frightened yet dignified Regazzoni. He then turned to Schiffer and nodded his head, as if to say let's give the guy a break for the time being. Schiffer looked at Regazzoni, then zipped up the bag.

"Monsignor, what's the best way to get across the river?" Stubblefield asked.

"The Ponte Umberto Bridge will give you the best route to the Palazzo Chigi and other side streets if you want."

Stubblefield looked over his maps and started surveying the layout of the Palace grounds. Little was said as they prepared for whatever they were about to encounter.

When the van hit the outskirts of Vatican City on the Via Crescenzio, Agent Schiffer leaned over and with a polite smile on his face lightly tapped Regazzoni on the knee. "Excuse me, Monsignor. What does that sign say?" he asked, pointing at the green sign.

Apparently because of the tour guide or historian in him, Monsignor Regazzoni was beginning to feel useful and gladly translated for the man seated next to him. With great flourish, he said, "It says that we are leaving the Vatican and entering the city of Rome."

Schiffer smiled in appreciation. "Good. That's what I thought it said."

With one long swipe, Schiffer reached down and unzipped the bag. He reached in and pulled out a Glock 17 9mm pistol. The 17-round magazine met his approval and he jammed it into place. He then yanked back the slide and slammed it shut with such flare that Monsignor Regazzoni's eyes nearly bulged out of his head. He jammed the gun into the holster on his thigh.

"Oh my!" Regazzoni exclaimed, startled yet again.

Next in Schiffer's bag of goodies was an MP-7 submachine gun with its 30-round magazine. He pulled it out, slid back the slide, checked it over, and then slammed it shut. He turned on the laser sight and the red dot just happened to dance up and down the right side of the Monsignor's cassock.

"Oh, *Dios mio*," he cried softly.

Schiffer slung the MP-7 around his head and under an arm. From under the seat, he then pulled out his baby – a Remington .308 sniper rifle. He opened the telescopic sight and checked the view of the van's wall next to Regazzoni.

The Monsignor could be heard mumbling to himself. Schiffer looked like Santa Claus on Christmas morning – passing out firearms and spare magazines to his compatriots. Various forms of weaponry were being checked and passed around the van. Stubblefield thought he might have heard Regazzoni reciting the *Our Father* or maybe it was a *Hail Mary*.

Taking his eyes off the map, Stubblefield turned his head and saw the Monsignor shaking in his seat, almost afraid to even look at Agent Schiffer, who just seemed to keep piling on the weapons. The Director took notice and smiled.

"Don't worry, Monsignor. He won't shoot you unless you piss him off."

Schiffer then handed the Director his own Glock 17. He slid back the slide, slammed it shut, and jammed it in the empty holster inside his suit coat. After all the weapons were handed out, the radios went on.

"Check, check, sound check," Schiffer said in his microphone.

"Copy that," Stubblefield said.

The van crossed the Tiber River and turned left heading east on the Via Orso before the driver, Special Agent Zach Olivera, slowed to a halt. "We've got a roadblock ahead."

"Turn right here and try the next street down," Stubblefield ordered, pointing over to his right. He laid the map on his lap and circled the Palazzo Chigi with a red marker.

They went down to the next street and again saw the road blocked. The next street showed another barricade of police vehicles.

"Pull over," Stubblefield said, pointing to the side of the road. It was hard to get any bearings in this area of Rome. The roads were narrow and the closely packed buildings averaged five stories high. Stubblefield rolled down the window and stuck his head out. The streets were eerily quiet.

The protesters had scattered in fear, not knowing what the Italian Government was doing. If they had killed or captured the President of the United States, they would kill the citizenry without a second thought.

"Shit!" Stubblefield said, slamming his fist against the door. He needed to think of something. Storming the Palace through the front door was probably not an option. They had no air support. They were unsure of whether the President's Secret Service agents were incapacitated. If that was the case, the Phantom team might be the President's only hope. The Director forced himself to take a breath before turning around in his seat.

"Monsignor," he said calmly. "The President of the United States is in trouble. We need to get into the Palace to see if we can help him. How do we do it?"

Regazzoni looked at Stubblefield and thought for a second. He then folded his hands in his lap. He glanced over slightly in Schiffer's direction, making sure he did not have a gun pointed at him. Schiffer didn't, but the glare in his eyes indicated he hoped the Monsignor had an answer.

Regazzoni took a deep breath. There were a thousand churches in Italy, and Regazzoni could tell you something about every one of them. He was an expert in church architecture – from their construction to preservation. He even wrote a coffee table book showing some of Italy's most famous places of worship. He knew it all, every nook, every cranny.

"We should go to the Church of Saint Ignatius of Loyola. It's a couple of blocks east of the Pantheon. It was built between 1626 and 1650 . . . ," he said. He went on and on, his reflexive memory not knowing when to stop.

"Hey, Padre," Schiffer interrupted, tapping Regazzoni on the knee. "Why do we need to go there?"

"Oh," he said, snapping back to reality. "There is an underground tunnel from the Church to the Palace. You can enter there."

"An underground tunnel?"

"Yes."

Stubblefield picked up the map. "Show me where the church is located."

Regazzoni reached forward and pointed to the map. "Here is the church. Here is the Palazzo Chigi." He then moved his finger down the map. "We are right here."

"Outside of the perimeter," Schiffer said.

"Only by one street, though," Stubblefield said, looking out the front window. "If we can get close enough to exit the vehicle, we might be able to fight our way into the church."

"That could get noisy," Schiffer warned.

"You're sure there's tunnel access from the church, Monsignor?" Stubblefield asked.

"Yes."

Stubblefield looked out the front window again. He had to make the call. "Well, that's our best chance right now. We're going to have to fight our way in."

A worried Regazzoni let out a deep breath and closed his eyes. He didn't want any gunplay and especially in and around a church. He mouthed a few words to himself, perhaps asking for guidance in silent prayer. The whole Phantom team had their focus on him. When his eyes opened, he took another deep breath and looked at the Director.

"*Signore* Stubblefield, I think I can get you into the church."

Stubblefield shifted his body in his seat. "Let's hear it."

"We need to approach the police men at the roadblock," Regazzoni said, pointing out the window in front of him. "I believe I can get us through."

"How do you plan on doing that?" Schiffer asked.

"I know it will work," he said. "I think it would be best if I drive."

Stubblefield's eyes suddenly grew large. "Excuse me?" he asked in disbelief. "You want to drive the van?" Was the Monsignor nuts? Stubblefield looked around at the rest of the team. Their eyes indicated they thought it was a bad idea, like Regazzoni might prove to be more dangerous than the men holding the President. "Have you ever driven before, Monsignor?"

"It has been awhile but I can do it," he said, unbuckling his seatbelt. He was a man on a mission. "We must get going."

Stubblefield was just about to throw up his hands, but he had no other ideas. He hoped he didn't end up regretting his next decision. "Let's give it a shot. Get him out."

Schiffer opened the sliding door and held a hand out for the diminutive Regazzoni. They walked him around the van and gave him a boost into the front seat.

"Here, let me move the seat up for you, Padre," Schiffer said, reaching for the lever underneath the seat.

Monsignor Regazzoni sat on the very edge of the seat and gripped the steering wheel. He hadn't driven a vehicle in thirty years, and that was his brother's battered Fiat Uno, not an eight-passenger van filled with six FBI agents. He felt good in the driver's seat though. Perhaps he was feeling better just because he was out of the back seat with the fully armed Schiffer.

He looked over the gauges and then down at the pedals. He was ready to go. "Here, Director, hold this for me," he said to Stubblefield, passing over the rosary that had received quite a workout in just the last ten minutes.

"You remember how to do this, Monsignor?" Stubblefield asked. The Monsignor's co-pilot seemed worried.

"Yes, I think so." He then turned slightly toward the rear of the van. "If you could lower your weapons, it would help greatly."

Stubblefield snapped his fingers and the weapons, helmets, and vests disappeared as fast as they came out.

"*Signore,*" Regazzoni said to Agent Schiffer. "If you could have that empty duffel bag ready, please."

"You got it."

"Okay, now put your foot on the brake and put it into drive," Stubblefield said, motioning over to the steering column.

Regazzoni cranked the shifter to drive and hit the gas. The van lurched forward before he slammed on the brakes throwing everyone in the van forward in their seats. He pressed the gas pedal, then slammed on the brakes, then the gas, then brakes. The men inside felt like the inside of a pinball machine.

"Monsignor! Stop! Stop!" Stubblefield yelled, bracing himself against the dash. "Just take it easy there, Mario."

Regazzoni still had a death grip on the wheel. With his love of Italian history, he couldn't help but smile at Stubblefield referring to him as the legendary Andretti himself. He so badly wanted to gun it.

"Don't worry about the gas, Monsignor. We'll just idle up to them slowly and you can depress the brake pedal to stop it. Nice and easy. Okay?"

"Yes," he said. He made the sign of the cross. "I think I've got it now." Once more, he wrapped his bony fingers around the leather wrapped wheel and onward they went.

With the checkpoint nearing, Stubblefield counted six men – all with automatic weapons and determined looks on their faces. The FIAT 6614 armored personnel carrier blocking the road had a .50-caliber machine gun ready to fire. One man, dressed in his Carabinieri dark blue, had a Beretta 92 on his hip and an M12 submachine gun slung over his shoulder. He took one last drag off his cigarette and threw it to the ground in disgust, like he was ticked off at the intrusion. The scowling man now had his hand out ordering the approaching driver to stop. The others raised their weapons. Everyone inside the van knew this could turn ugly at any minute.

"All right," a tense Stubblefield said under his breath to those in the van. He buttoned his gray jacket and tried to make the bulge in the holster less noticeable. "Let's everybody be cool now."

Schiffer had his left hand behind his back ready to whip his Glock out of his belt. His right hand slowly pulled up his pant leg revealing an ankle holster and a five-shot .38 Smith & Wesson J-Frame revolver. Schiffer was not a man to go down without a fight.

Regazzoni guided the van to a stop like a pro and rolled down his window. When the Italian guard came up to the driver's side, he could barely believe what he saw. The scowl vanished from his face. He raised his M12 over his head but stopped short of firing it into the air.

"Monsignor Regazzoni!" the man bellowed, his face lighting up. He then heaped a great Italian welcome on one of the most famous Vatican officials in all the land. "*Buon giorno! Buon giorno!*" The guard then turned to his fellow soldiers, his arms raised in celebration. "It is Monsignor Regazzoni! Monsignor Regazzoni!"

The Phantom team looked on in surprise, wondering what in the world was happening. Agent Schiffer took his hand off his Glock.

"*Buon giorno*," the smiling Regazzoni said, waving to them all like a seasoned politician at a Labor Day parade. Hello, my people, he seemed to say. "*Buon giorno.*"

"What are you doing here, Monsignor?" the guard asked, the smile indicating he was so happy to see him. He acted like he knew Regazzoni. Of course, every Italian Catholic thought they knew the man. But his mood quickly turned somber. "The streets are very dangerous this evening," he warned.

"What is going on down at the Palazzo, my son?"

The two conversed in Italian for close to half a minute, some of it was in whispers but all of it was very serious. At one point, Regazzoni slapped his hand against his pale white forehead like he couldn't believe the news he was hearing. Stubblefield and his men only got bits and pieces of what was discussed.

"The Prime Minister called for the Carabinieri," the guard said. He was vague on the details, like he wasn't at all clear about what was going on. "Something about the Americans becoming hostile. Apparently, the President of the United States has done very bad things. We are to keep the streets clear and let no one in until the Army gets here. That's all I know."

"I see," Monsignor Regazzoni said calmly, taking it all in. He then went to work. "My son, His Holiness wants to make sure the relics at the Church of Saint Ignatius are protected and secured. That is why he has sent me."

The guard's eyes narrowed, his mind trying to understand what was just said. His Catholic history was a little fuzzy on what priceless artifact was housed at St. Ignatius.

"The relics?" he wondered out loud. Really? The Pope sent Monsignor Regazzoni himself to Rome to secure some relics?

"Yes, the relics in the church. We are to secure the relics. They are very important to the Holy Father." He was very convincing. He gestured with his right thumb to Stubblefield and his men. "I have brought some muscle," he said. He then flexed his bony arms. "I cannot do it myself."

The guard looked over at Stubblefield, who was handling the rosary beads like a lifelong Catholic. The guard then looked in the back at Schiffer and the rest of the Phantom team. They were not small men, but with their black attire and clerical collars, they outwardly appeared to be in the same profession as the Monsignor. It was clear the guard was debating whether he should let the van pass. Why did they need six men to secure some old bones?

"They are from the Vatican?" he asked, nodding at the others in the van.

"Yes, the best Swiss Guards we have," Regazzoni said in praise of the men.

The guard nodded, knowing full well the Monsignor would never lie to him. But he still had concerns. "I don't know, Monsignor." Orders were orders, the guard thought to himself.

"We have a bag to secure the relics just in case."

From his seat in the middle of the van, Schiffer held up the empty duffel bag. It was like they had practiced the plan a hundred times.

"Monsignor, I'm not supposed to let *anyone* inside the perimeter."

Regazzoni nodded like he understood. "My son, I will only drive to the side of the church over there," he said, pointing across the way. "You will see the van at all times."

The guard looked around. A Carabinieri office sat just across the piazza from the church, and he wondered if his superiors were watching. Yes, he was under strict orders, but it was Monsignor Regazzoni. The guy was an absolute legend in Italy. It was like having Elvis drive up and ask a favor. No Italian in his right mind would turn down the Monsignor. And certainly no one of the Catholic faith. A part of him thought he might get in trouble if he turned down Regazzoni's request – maybe get himself a nice long letter of reprimand in his personnel file. After a couple of seconds of thought, he made up his mind.

"Go ahead, Monsignor," he whispered. "But be quick so nobody sees you. Or I will get in trouble with my superiors."

Regazzoni thanked him. He then placed his left hand on the guard's head and blessed him. "I will tell the Holy Father of your good works."

The guard shouted at his fellow officers and waved the van through. He then pointed toward the archway down the street. "Be safe, Monsignor Regazzoni."

"Just let off the brake," Stubblefield whispered out of the corner of his mouth. As the van slowly rolled forward, he added. "That's it. That's it."

The Phantom team let out a collective sigh of relief. Regazzoni waved to the men as he passed by them. He had parted the Carabinieri like Moses and the Red Sea. Why the guard decided to let the van through was beyond anyone's comprehension. Maybe it was divine intervention. Whatever it was, Regazzoni had come through without a shot being fired.

"Nice work, Padre," Schiffer said, tapping the Monsignor on the shoulder.

"Just turn here," Stubblefield said, using his left hand to help steer the wheel. "Get close to the door under the archway. That's it. Now hit the brakes." When the van lurched to a stop, Stubblefield reached over and slammed the shifter into park. He then turned around in his seat and gave the order to his men. "Get everything you need."

Monsignor Regazzoni sat in the driver's seat, unsure of what he had just done. A part of him could almost hear the bells in Maranello pealing throughout the city in recognition of his driving exploits. He prayed his little white lie would do no harm.

"Come on, Monsignor," Stubblefield said, opening his door. "We're gonna need you."

CHAPTER 23

The White House – Washington, D.C.

"What the hell is going on!?" Secretary of State Mike Arnold yelled, barging into the White House Situation Room. His face was red, and it was clear from his mismatched clothes that he had dressed in a hurry. Arnold was a deliberate man – the perfect guy for the State Department because he handled diplomatic crises with calm back-and-forth negotiations at fancy venues across the world. On those occasions, the outcome was usually a foregone conclusion and all that needed to be done was for the diplomats to sign on the dotted line and then smile and shake hands for the cameras.

Today was not one of those times.

Defense Secretary Russell Javits was huddled around the end of the table with CIA Director Parker and Joint Chiefs Chairman Hugh Cummins. No one answered Secretary Arnold. They had all rushed to the White House – Javits and Cummins from the Pentagon and Parker from Langley. The TVs on the wall were tuned to CNN and Fox News. Neither of those networks knew what was going on or where the President was. The only pictures from Rome showed a roadblock down the street from the Palazzo Chigi.

"Does anyone know what the hell is going on?" Arnold asked again, tucking in his shirt while he was at it.

General Cummins unfurled his massive frame from his seat. He wanted to calm the situation down. He didn't particularly like a lot of yelling at national security meetings. It didn't help any, and it usually led to hasty decisions being made that ended up doing more harm than good. "Sir, we don't know what's going on. We are having trouble contacting the Secret Service agents on the ground."

"Do we even know what happened?"

This time it was Secretary Javits who rose from his seat. His suit coat was off, and his tie was loose. He kept rubbing the back of his neck. "Mike, somehow, someone got to the President."

"We think someone got to the President," Cummins said, still unsure and wanting to deal with what they did know.

"Has he been shot?"

"We don't know," Javits said, obviously worried – a thousand thoughts were racing through his mind.

"Where's the Vice President?" Arnold asked.

"She's on her way back from Hawaii," Javits said.

"Damn!" Arnold exclaimed. "It's going to take her forever to get here. It's gotta be a ten-hour flight."

"We can reach her on Air Force Two," General Cummins said.

Arnold started looking around. Now he was starting to get worried. "Who's in charge here?"

Javits and Cummins looked at each other. Neither of them wanted to have their own Al Haig moment. According to the Presidential Succession Act of 1947, the Secretary of State stood behind the President *pro tempore* of the Senate in the line of succession. Then came the Secretaries of the Treasury and Defense followed by the rest of the cabinet members in order of the creation of their departments. So, as it stood in the White House, Secretary of State Arnold was the highest-ranking member in the presidential line of succession.

But he had no idea what he should do.

Sensing Arnold's unwillingness to act, General Cummins took the lead. "As Defense Secretary, Russ should take the lead here at the White House and coordinate with the Vice President." He looked around to see if there was any objection. Secretary Arnold was nodding his head up and down like it was a great idea. Seeing and hearing no objection, Cummins added, "At least until we hear from the President."

Now relieved of any leadership duties, Secretary Arnold turned his focus to Director Parker. "Did your boys have any idea that there might be a problem?" His tone was much too accusatory.

"What are you saying, Mike?" Parker shot back. "You think I knew about this?"

"Well," Arnold said, throwing his palms up into the air. "Your agency hasn't had the greatest track record with this President."

Cummins looked at Javits. The General didn't want to lower himself to the level of dressing down Secretary Arnold. But he was clearly over the line.

Javits, however, had no problem lowering the boom. "Mike, that's enough," he snapped. "We have to figure out what we're doing here."

Javits took out a pen and flipped open a legal pad. He had a whole list of questions that needed to be asked and even more orders that needed to be made. "Do we know who might be involved other than the Italians?"

"No."

"Where's the First Lady?"

"She's at Da Vinci airport on Air Force One."

"Tell the Secret Service and the Air Force to get her in the air. I don't want Air Force One sitting as a stationary target on the runway."

"Yes, sir," General Cummins said, scribbling down notes.

"Have the pilot circle over the Tyrrenhian Sea close enough that he can land if and when the President is en route. And get an in-flight refueler in the air just in case."

"Yes, sir."

Javits made a note and stopped writing. Running through his mental checklist, he moved on to the next order of business. "General, have you heard from Major Swanson with the nuclear football?"

"No."

Javits nodded and made another note. The situation kept getting more dire by the minute. "General, let's put the state of military readiness at DEFCON 2."

"Yes, sir."

General Cummins put down his pen and reached for a secure phone to give the order. Within ninety seconds, bells would ring and alarms would blare across the world – on land, in the air, and under the sea. Before another ninety seconds could pass, LGM-30 Minuteman missile silos in Montana and North Dakota would be readied for launch, B-2 Stealth bombers would roar off the runway in Missouri and take to the skies over the heartland of America, and Ohio-class Trident submarines in every corner of the globe would prepare for nuclear war.

"Let's put up combat air patrols over the capital and New York City just in case."

"You got it," General Cummins said, relaying another order to the person on the other end of the line.

"Alert the Speaker of the House and the Senate Majority Leader," Javits said to no one in particular. "And the rest of the Cabinet."

"What else?" General Cummins asked, his hand over the receiver.

"What type of resources do we have in the region right now?" Javits asked.

Cummins hung up the phone and searched his mind. "We have the *USS Mount Whitney* on its way back from Greece and a carrier group of the Sixth Fleet going through the Suez Canal right now."

"Once the carrier gets through, tell 'em to hightail it up the Mediterranean. What about in Italy?"

"We have two fighter squadrons at Aviano Air Base in northeastern Italy. The 510th and the 555th – F-16s, A-10 Thunderbolts."

"Get 'em in the air and down to Rome," Javits ordered. "And start thinking of a rescue operation."

"Yes, sir."

"We need to alert the nearest SEAL team."

"I'll do it," Cummins said.

"Mike," Javits said to Secretary Arnold. "I think it might help if you get on the horn to Prime Minister Martin and President Chiron to see if they know anything."

After taking a bit of a breather, the Secretary of State agreed and headed for the phones.

"And find out where the Italian President is. He's in charge of their military," Javits said before adding, "Although he's been known to be a bit of a lightweight and a tool of Prime Minister Scarponi."

National Security Adviser Carl Harnacke hurried into the room with a cell phone to both ears. He ended the calls and asked if there was any news. Javits said no and closed his legal pad.

"Have you been in contact with the Vice President?" Javits asked of Harnacke.

"Yes, she's over the Pacific. We can try to get a secure conference call to Air Force Two."

Javits nodded and leaned his elbows on the back of the leather chair he was standing behind. Sweat was beginning to form on his forehead. He pulled out a handkerchief, wiped his brow, and forced his mind to continue. He looked around the room, taking note of those present. He suddenly realized somebody other than the President was missing.

"Where's Director Stubblefield?" he asked to anyone who was listening. Javits definitely wanted him there.

Director Parker spoke up first. "He's on the ground in Rome."

"What?" Javits asked, obviously surprised. "He's with the President?"

"He was with the President on his foreign trip," Parker said. "I don't know if they were together when this all went down."

Javits gave out another order. "Why don't you find out. Call the FBI and see who we might be able to contact in Rome."

"I'm on it," Parker said.

A knock on the door to the Situation Room grabbed the attention of everyone inside. A military aide opened the door and in walked Kimberly Carmi, the President's spokeswoman. A trusted member of the White House inner circle, she had known the President for over ten years and first worked for him during his days in Congress. She was the calm and cool voice of the Schumacher Administration and well respected by members of the media.

"What are you doing here?" Javits asked of her. Shouldn't Carmi be with the President on his foreign trip?

The attractive Carmi placed her suit coat over her dark blue blouse and set her long brown hair over the collar. She was getting ready just like the rest of them. "I stayed stateside to celebrate my parent's fiftieth wedding anniversary. Once I saw the news, I came right in. Are we going to make a statement?"

The men in the room looked at each other. They had been so busy seeking information and handing out orders that no one had thought of telling the American people what was going on. Carmi, however, knew the public needed to know.

"Guys, we have to say something," she said. "There are stories floating around on the Internet claiming the President has been assassinated."

"Oh my God," Arnold said, his hand slapping his forehead.

"Shouldn't we wait for the Vice President?" Harnacke asked. He was still trying to contact her 35,000 feet over the Pacific Ocean.

"I don't think we can wait that long," Carmi said. She had dual degrees in political science and journalism and was well aware of the optics of the current situation. And right now, the United States Government was adrift on stormy seas without a captain. Something needed to be said to calm the waters.

"Who should speak?" Arnold asked, becoming more flustered by the minute. "What would we say?" He was full of questions but no answers.

Javits looked at the ceiling trying to think. After sufficient contemplation, he gave his thoughts. "I think Kimberly should give a statement," he said. "We don't want to look like we're panicking. She can tell the nation that we are in contact with the Vice President and everything is under control here at the White House. Maybe mention we have been on the phones with our allies in Europe. She can also reassure the world that the United States is determined to get to the bottom of this matter."

"The First Lady is safe?" Carmi asked, scribbling down her notes.

"Yes. She's at the airport on Air Force One."

"Excuse me, Director Javits," Parker interrupted, a phone to his ear. "I have made contact with Director Stubblefield."

"Thank goodness," Javits said.

Everyone around the table breathed a sigh of relief. They all felt Stubblefield would give them what they needed most – information.

"Put him on speaker," Javits ordered. Once Parker gave him the thumbs-up, Javits leaned closer to the table and everyone listened in. "Director Stubblefield, this is Russ Javits. Can you hear me?"

Through the speaker on the phone came the deep voice of the FBI Director. "I can hear you, Russ."

Javits then asked the question everyone hoped Stubblefield would have the answer to. "Ty, what the hell is going on?"

From inside the back door of St. Ignatius, Stubblefield told them what he knew. He had no contact with the President. It was reported that Secret Service agents were down but he could not confirm that.

"Right now we are planning an insertion into the Palace," he told them.

Javits looked at General Cummins, who obviously didn't have any idea what Stubblefield was talking about. "Insertion? Who is planning an insertion?"

"I am," Stubblefield barked, the voice booming throughout the Situation Room. He was ready to get moving.

"You and who else?" Javits asked. He really wanted to ask "You and whose army?"

"I have the Phantom team ready to go."

More confused looks. Glances were exchanged across the table. General Cummins shrugged his shoulders at Javits. No one knew what Stubblefield was talking about.

"Phantom team?" Javits asked.

The impatient Stubblefield was ready to end the call. "I've got five FBI agents with me ready to lead an assault on the Palazzo Chigi and rescue the President."

"Ty, you don't even know what you're up against," Secretary Arnold said in disbelief. "You're going to get the President killed."

Although nobody outwardly agreed with Secretary Arnold, the same thoughts were on their minds.

"Listen, Mike," Stubblefield said, obviously irritated. "I don't have time to argue with you. I'm on the ground and I am going to get the President back."

Javits thought he had better put an end to any rogue FBI squads. It was too risky. "Ty, we're attempting to coordinate a military response from Aviano as we speak. Let's let the professionals handle it."

"We don't have time to wait for Aviano!" Stubblefield yelled into the phone. Then the line went dead.

"Ty, are you there?" Javits asked into the speaker. "Ty?"

"Oh, man," Secretary Arnold muttered, his right hand rubbing his throbbing forehead as he anxiously paced the floor. He started mumbling to himself. "This is not good. This is not good."

CHAPTER 24

Palazzo Chigi – Rome, Italy

"Hand it over, Mr. President," Vlad Patrenko growled. He was four feet away but still with a gun pointed at the leader of the free world. The rabid look in his eyes indicated he desperately wanted to use it.

Zhukov was off in the corner keeping a watchful eye on Patrenko and the President. He was yelling into his phone – a combination of Russian curses and demands. When he saw Patrenko moving in closer to the President, he gave one last order and hung up the phone. A part of him feared Patrenko would kill their prized catch.

"I said hand it over!"

The President wasn't sure what he was talking about, and he sure wasn't going to help his captor out. The President knew he was in trouble. The cavalry hadn't showed up. Obviously, a very well-planned attack had taken place if the best security detail in the world had been disarmed or disabled. The President needed to start thinking of his own way out of this mess. And the sooner the better.

Patrenko took a step forward and stabbed the air with the gun. "I said hand it over right now!"

Zhukov walked over, the Uzi now slung over his shoulder. He tried to sound reasonable. "Your locator device, Mr. President. We know you have one."

The President locked eyes with Zhukov. The intense glares from both Russians indicated they weren't in the mood to negotiate. But being unarmed, the President was at a distinct disadvantage. He reached into his right pants pocket and pulled out the oversized Lincoln penny. The panic button also gave the Secret Service a constant indicator of the President's location. He tossed it over to Zhukov. The penny would be sent down to street level and given to a motorcycle courier, who would be told to take it as far as the tank of gas would allow. Those looking for the President would be sent on a wild-goose chase through eastern Italy.

"And the card for the nuclear football."

The President had not even thought about the nuclear football. The Air Force major who followed the President around wherever he went lugging the black briefcase containing the nuclear launch codes was most likely incapacitated out in the hall. The President, however, had few qualms about handing the card over. He knew the codes would have been changed by now given the circumstances. Under the National Command Authority, the Secretary of Defense would be calling the shots if nuclear weapons were needed. The President reached into his right pocket of his suit coat and pulled out the plastic card. He tossed it over to Zhukov.

"And your cell phone."

This time it was the left pocket inside his suit coat. The iPhone with the presidential seal emblazoned on the back was turned off. The President handed it over.

"Make him take his jacket off too," Patrenko said, apparently believing Zhukov was in charge. "He might have a hidden locator device sewn inside."

Zhukov agreed. "The jacket, Mr. President."

The President took off his suit coat and tossed it over to the couch. Patrenko started rifling through it – inside and out. He found a couple of pens and some scraps of paper with notes on them.

"I guess it's a good thing I didn't bring my wallet today," the President said dryly.

"Shut up," Patrenko shot back. "Sit down."

The President took a seat on the couch and made eye contact with Prime Minister Scarponi. The man's eyes seemed to be growing redder by the minute. He still had the gun in his hand. Of all the armed men in the room, the President most worried about Scarponi. The man was obviously unstable, and the President thought he was the most likely of the three to start shooting.

The President leaned on the right armrest. Out of the corner of his eye, he kept watch on the door, wondering when the Secret Service would break it down and start firing. With the passage of time, however, he knew a rescue wouldn't be forthcoming any time soon. The slight twitch in his nose told him tear gas had been used, and whoever unleashed it would now be in control of the Palace. The President thought he might be able to talk his way out of this mess. Or at least find out what was going on. He figured he might as well get comfortable.

"Giovanni, how about another Diet Coke?" the President asked. "Or, as you folks call it over here, a Coke Light."

A soda? That was the first thing out of the President's mouth? He just wanted another Diet Coke? After thinking over the rather benign request, Scarponi slowly walked out from behind his desk. His eyes never left the President's – as if he was in fear that the President might spring from his seat across the room, tackle the Prime Minister, and disarm him. The President had thought about it, but given the looks of Scarponi's revolver, there was a good chance it wouldn't fire. And then he'd be no match for the Russians' Uzis. Scarponi grabbed a can from the mini-bar and walked over to the President – stopping well short and out of arm's reach. He tossed the can over and then backed away.

The President opened the can and took a drink. Ahhhh. "Thank you," he said. "I needed that." He then settled in for the long haul. "So what's the plan, gentlemen?"

Scarponi looked over at Zhukov. The Prime Minister had no idea what the plan was. His only job of getting the President into the room was complete.

"We are waiting to transport you to The Hague," Zhukov said.

The President nodded. "The Hague. I've never been there," he said, almost like he was looking forward to seeing a new place. He didn't fully believe the statement, the thought of a trial before the International Criminal Court a bit of a stretch. Charges might be brought, but a trial? Sure there were leaders around the world who would like nothing more than to have the American President marched before the court for whatever crime they thought he or his country might have committed. The President decided not to respond to Zhukov's travel plans. "Giovanni, you realize a trial is never going to happen."

"Don't be so sure, Mr. President," Scarponi said, shaking the gun at him like a wagging finger. "You have committed crimes against my country. Crimes that you must answer to in a court of law."

The President took a good long gulp of his Diet Coke. In quick fashion, it was almost empty. "What crimes are you talking about?"

"You authorized the capture of Assad Khan right off the streets of Milan. The streets of my country!"

The President shrugged his shoulders like it was something that had to happen. "Giovanni, Assad Khan is a terrorist financier. We have hard evidence to show he was involved in planning the ambush of ten American soldiers. We also believe he beheaded an American defense contractor. You should be thankful we took him off your streets."

"The people of the world are tired of the United States violating the boundaries of their sovereign countries in your endless wars, Mr. President. In Iraq, Pakistan, Afghanistan. Now in my own country of Italy!"

The President sighed. "I guess we'll just have to disagree, Giovanni." The President thought about mentioning his country's need to go after terrorists in every corner of the world to prevent another 9/11 attack. Or that Islamic terrorists had exported their violent acts to countries like Spain, France, Britain, and even to Italy, killing innocent civilians along the way. But the lecture would probably fall on deaf ears anyway. The armed men in the room had no desire to listen to a presidential speech. He shook his empty can of Diet Coke, the back and forth with Scarponi making him thirsty. "Could I get another one please?"

The gun-toting Patrenko smiled. If only the American people could see their pathetic President now – obviously frightened, shaking in his boots and unable to handle the crisis. He laughed at the weak-kneed American leader. He resisted the urge to taunt the man.

Zhukov grabbed a can and tossed it over.

The President opened the can and wet his lips once again. "So what's your story?" he asked of the Russians.

Zhukov smirked. "We have no story, Mr. President."

"You sound Russian. Do I know you?" The President had welcomed a Russian delegation to the White House following his inauguration and wondered if he and Zhukov had met before.

"No, you don't know me," Zhukov said gruffly. He didn't like the questions. And he wasn't going to give any unnecessary information.

The President finished off his second can in a matter of minutes. "Giovanni, what have you done to get into bed with these two?"

"Screw you, Mr. President." The agitation in the Prime Minister was growing. He didn't like it that they were just sitting around waiting. He wanted the President out of there. "Screw you."

"Giovanni, for goodness sakes, put the gun down."

"No!" Scarponi yelled, stepping forward, the gun pointed at the man on the couch. "You don't get to call the shots any longer. You have caused all of this."

The President rolled his eyes. "Giovanni, how much are the Russians paying you to do this?"

"Shut up!"

The President relented. He wasn't going to get anywhere with Scarponi. And he didn't appear to be getting anywhere with the Russians. Without knowing what was going to happen next, the President decided he needed to insert himself into the equation. Maybe shake things up a bit. But first, the Diet Cokes he had downed necessitated a pit stop. He started squirming in his seat, at one point almost crossing his right leg over his left.

"Man, I gotta go to the bathroom."

Patrenko let out a loud Russian belly laugh. He could hold his taunts no longer. The President is such a weak man, he thought. The Russian Prime Minister, Nikolai Grigoryev, was a black belt in jujitsu, wrestled alligators, and hunted big game – machismo being the greatest asset of the Russian leader. And here is the so-called leader of the free world about to piss himself.

"Oh, the President of the United States has to go pee," Patrenko mocked. "Poor little baby."

Zhukov got a good laugh out of it.

"Maybe we should get you a diaper so you don't pee your pants," Patrenko said, piling the insults on thick. "We'll even put the presidential seal on the back side for you."

The President exaggerated his movements some more. "Come on, guys."

"Let him go," Zhukov said with a wave of the hand. "We don't want Amnesty International or the Red Cross telling us we are mistreating our prisoners like the Americans do."

The three captors laughed at the President's expense. Zhukov told his cohort to escort the President to the bathroom. The sneering Patrenko held out his hand and pointed the way. Oh how he wanted to take a few swipes at the President for all of Mother Russia. The two men walked into the Prime Minister's private washroom. The President gave it a quick look but noticed there were no windows. There was just one air vent, but with the circumference of a telephone pole, no human was going to be crawling in or out. There would be no rescue attempt via this route. The President fronted the toilet and unzipped. He could feel Patrenko eyeing him from behind.

"Do you mind?" the President said before conducting his business. He made sure it sounded a bit snippy. "A little privacy please."

Patrenko scanned the room again.

"I'm not going anywhere," the President said, his hand pointing to the walls and the ceiling.

Patrenko gave in. He would resume his mocking once the President was done. He backed away and stood at the door.

"Hurry up!" Patrenko ordered.

CHAPTER 25

Church of St. Ignatius of Loyola – Rome, Italy

The Phantom team members took up their positions in Lancelotti Chapel in the right transept of the Church. Therein lie the remains of Saint Aloysius Gonzaga. While Stubblefield and his men assembled their gear, Monsignor Regazzoni went to check on the relics – just like he told the guard. That way he could feel better about his little fib. Nearby he found the remains of Cardinal Robert Bellarmine, who died in 1621. In the left transept, Regazzoni found the grave of Saint John Berchmans – the patron saint of altar servers. Everything seemed secure, the Monsignor thought.

"Everything all right, Monsignor?" Stubblefield asked as Regazzoni rejoined the group.

"Yes, I believe so."

Stubblefield checked the magazine of his MP-7 before jamming it into place. He then screwed in the suppressor. The Director took notice of Regazzoni, who was staring wide-eyed at the men in his midst. "Gonzaga," Stubblefield said, pointing over to the urn and trying to engage the Monsignor to help him feel a little more comfortable considering the circumstances. "Is that the Gonzaga of Gonzaga University?"

"Yes," Regazzoni said. His encyclopedic mind then went to work. "Aloysius Gonzaga was an Italian Jesuit who lived from 1568 to 1591. He was beatified by Pope Paul V in 1605 and then canonized in 1726 by Pope Benedict XIII. He is the patron saint of young students and plague victims." Regazzoni then looked at the date on his cheap digital watch. "And his feast day is right around the corner on June 21st. Saint Aloysius was a student of Cardinal Bellarmine, who also has a university named after him in your country."

The Phantom team listened but had other things on their mind.

"Are we all ready to go?" Stubblefield asked when the Monsignor finished.

"I think so," Agent Schiffer announced. The clerical collars were all gone, replaced with Kevlar and helmets. Schiffer then looked over at the diminutive Regazzoni, still in his black cassock and obviously unarmed. Schiffer took off his bulletproof vest and handed the body armor over to the Monsignor. "Put this on, Padre."

Regazzoni stood wide-eyed looking at the vest. He didn't like the thought of why he needed it. After he tried it on, he looked again at Agent Schiffer. "*Grazie*, my son."

"Just in case." Schiffer said, helping Regazzoni strap the Velcro together. The vest was so big it protected the Monsignor down to mid-thigh. Schiffer then looked at the Director. "We're ready."

Stubblefield nodded. "Okay. Jenkins and Alvarez, you two are in the lead. Schiffer and I will follow with Monsignor Regazzoni. Olivera and Guerrero will cover the rear. Monsignor, where do we go?"

Regazzoni pointed the way toward a door on the side of the altar. The men, fully armed except for one, marched through the silent church, their eyes taking in the grand structure. The frescoes by Andrea Pozzo seemed almost lifelike. The cupola on the ceiling seemed almost real. It wasn't, however. Just a painting on a flat ceiling.

Behind the altar, the men walked down two flights of stairs, the decrease in temperature indicating they had gone subterranean. Regazzoni kept pointing the way – first to his left and down a corridor and then to his right. At the end of a dark hall, the men came to a door. Regazzoni motioned for someone to open it. Agent Jenkins grabbed the handle and gave it a tug. Nothing budged. The door probably hadn't been opened since the Second World War. He grabbed the handle with both hands and pulled back with a grunt. The layers of dried paint broke free and a rush of cool stagnant air filled everyone's nostrils.

Stubblefield moved to the head of the line and looked in. His flashlight failed to show where the darkness ended. He didn't particularly like what he saw. "Great," he said with a heavy sigh. "More tunnels. Just what I need." Nothing he could do about it now. "Lights on and let's go."

The men lit the flashlights attached to the barrels of their weapons and headed in one by one.

"Pull that door closed, Olivera," Stubblefield whispered. "That way we'll hear if someone is coming up behind us."

Underneath the streets in and around Rome lie a labyrinth of catacombs that are famous the world over. Some of the tunnels date back to the first century, and Jews and Christians were known to use them to bury their dead. But the Phantom team need not worry about running into any skeletal remains in this tunnel. It was lined with cement blocks, and the dust covering the poured floor indicated it hadn't seen much use since the war. The Italians built the passageway in case the Allied Powers decided to more aggressively bomb Rome and target the Italian Parliament and the Palazzo Chigi. The Italians figured a bombing campaign would not include the Colosseum or the Pantheon and definitely not some church. They thought the Church of St. Ignatius would be the perfect getaway.

After what felt like two city blocks of brisk walking, Director Stubblefield ordered a halt when they came to a door on the side of the tunnel. He pulled out his map and looked at the streets of Rome between the church and the Palace. "Monsignor, give us an idea of where we are."

Regazzoni traced his finger from the church to the north. "Right here," he said, pointing. "We're probably about to go underneath the Piazza Colonna to the south of the Palazzo Chigi. It is where the column of Marcus Aurelius stands."

"What is this area here south of the Piazza?" Stubblefield asked, his finger pointing to the ceiling above him.

Regazzoni thought for a moment. "It is full of shops."

"Shops? What kinds of shops?"

"Clothing," Regazzoni said, his mind trying to remember the collection of storefronts that he never frequented. "And Rolex." He then put his right hand, with pinkie and thumb pointed out, to his ear.

"Cell phone dealer?"

"Yes."

"Is there anything above the shops?"

Regazzoni thought some more. "Yes, apartments."

"How many floors total?"

"Five or six."

Stubblefield decided this was the best place to recon the area, get a view of the Palace, and come up with a strategy before they made their final move to rescue the President.

"Olivera," the Director said. "Get the bolt cutters and open this door."

The padlock on the door looked like it might have been put there by Mussolini himself. Olivera wiggled out of his massive backpack. As the tool man of the group, he had an impressive array of knives, wrenches, hammers, screwdrivers, drills, and hand axes. He also had one very large pair of bolt cutters. With one snap from his beefy arms, the padlock proved no match and hit the floor in a clank.

Agent Olivera opened the door a crack and saw a ray of light coming down the staircase above him. Seeing and hearing no one, he opened the door wider and let the Director take a look inside the stairwell.

"All right, let's make it quick," Stubblefield said. "And be alert."

The six FBI agents with weapons drawn plus Monsignor Regazzoni hustled up two flights and hit the ground floor. The empty hallway showed several doors with the names of a different business on each one. This was the back entrance to the businesses. Probably never used except when the trash needed to be taken out. Agent Jenkins turned the handle on the door on the opposite side and found another staircase. The men snaked their way single file, not making a sound, guns at the ready. Once they reached the fifth floor, they could go no higher. The door to the stairwell opened and the hallway revealed a collection of apartments – just like the Monsignor said.

Even with their earpieces, the agents could hear the silence of the place. Stubblefield figured the building must have been evacuated by the Italian police. Having nobody around was a good thing. The only sound was the wood floorboards creaking with every light step the men took.

"Compass?" he asked to no in particular.

Agent Alvarez stepped forward and brought out the directional compass. He pointed to the wall in front of him. "North," he said.

"Olivera, get this door open."

With his MP-7 slung over his shoulder, Olivera stepped forward and took a quick look at the lock. On the flight from London and upon arriving in Rome, the master locksmith had been briefed by the CIA on every known lock used in Italy. He was a master at shimming, bypassing, raking, picking, and destroying anything that was meant to secure a door from those on the outside. He could jimmy a lock in total darkness just by feel. In a former life, he could have been Houdini's apprentice. If the situation called for stealth, he could enter as quiet as a mouse. If speed was needed, the battering ram would make quick work of almost any lock. Just in case the apartment was still occupied, Olivera went with the ram and busted in.

The men hustled into the apartment, guns drawn, looking for anyone who might be hiding inside. The men proceeded cautiously, making their movements quick, and keeping their bodies out of the middle of the windows. No one was home. The apartment overlooked the Piazza

Colonna and had a head-on view of the Palazzo Chigi. The drapes were pulled back and the shutters opened. Time for reconnaissance.

"Five floors," Schiffer whispered, now surveying the scene across the way. "Bars on the lower level windows. There's a security camera at the southeast corner of the roof."

"The President's limo is still in the Piazza along with two Suburbans," Stubblefield said. Through his small binoculars, he could look north down the street and see the Italian Carabinieri still at their checkpoint. The Piazza showed no signs of life below. It looked like a ghost town, like all of the occupants vanished into thin air without a trace.

"Now what?" Schiffer asked.

Stubblefield looked at the roofs of the buildings across the way. He saw no movement, no snipers. He wished he could get an idea of how many people were currently in the Palace and where they were located. He trained his binoculars on every window of the Palace, looking for signs of life.

Now what? he thought to himself.

With his mind preoccupied, Stubblefield barely noticed the beeps coming from Guerrero's cell phone. Guerrero pulled the phone off his hip. He wasn't expecting a call. It wasn't his personal cell phone. It was just a single line phone, and there was only one person who had the number.

"Director!" Guerrero whispered as loud as he could across the room. When he made eye contact, he held up the phone and did his best not to shout. "It's the President!"

Director Stubblefield didn't understand what he meant. He thought Guerrero said something about the President. "What?"

As he hurried in a crouch across the room, Guerrero held up the phone. "It's the President! The President's ChapStick device has been activated!"

Stubblefield looked at Guerrero's phone in disbelief.

"Son of a bitch," he whispered to himself.

The Director had forgotten all about it. He didn't know for sure whether the President was alive or injured, and now it was possible that he was trying to contact them. Stubblefield could barely remember what he was supposed to do. He took the earphone jack out of his portable radio and inserted it into the phone. Then he scrolled down, entered the last number, and took a breath. It was the most nervous he had been all day.

"Let's hope this works." With his hand over the microphone, he whispered as quietly as possible. "Mr. President, can you hear me?"

Although the wait was only five seconds, it felt like a lifetime before the President responded with one click yes.

Stubblefield's broad smile lit up the room. He gave the thumbs-up to his men. He then reminded himself to follow the plan. It was possible someone had taken the ChapStick from the President and each click might lead them down a path of no return. He had told the President that there would be some preliminary questions to confirm identity.

"Mr. President, is my son's name Michael?"

Two clicks no. Michael was the name of the President's son, David that of Director Stubblefield's male offspring.

"Is my wife's name Tisha?"

Two clicks no.

"How about Tina?"

One click yes.

"Okay, I read you, Mr. President," he whispered with great relief. The President of the United States was still alive. "Good to have you with us. Sir, are you injured?"

Two clicks no.

"Copy that. Stand by, Mr. President. We are in the area." Stubblefield then turned to his men. "Schiffer, get your rifle ready just in case. If we go in, I want you here giving us a bird's-eye view."

Stubblefield then took another look out the window and across the Piazza. He still saw no movement in the windows of the Palazzo Chigi. He put his hand back over the microphone. "Mr. President," he whispered again. "Are you alone?"

Two clicks no.

"Are there more than five with you?"

Two clicks no.

Stubblefield took a stab in the dark. "Three?"

One click yes.

"Are they friendly?"

Two clicks no.

"Do you know where your detail is?"

Two clicks no.

"Are you on the fifth floor?"

One click yes.

"Okay, guys," he reported to his crew. "We have the President on the fifth floor, three men with him, no security." Agent Jenkins was writing it all down just in case.

"Mr. President, is the Italian Prime Minister one of the men with you?"

One click yes.

"Is he involved?"

One click yes.

"Copy that." Stubblefield wanted to get working on the rescue, but he did want to give the President some good news. "Mr. President, the First Lady is safe on Air Force One. Okay?"

Although it took a few seconds longer that the other responses, the President clicked off a thankful yes.

"We're devising a plan. Do you copy that?"

One click yes.

CHAPTER 26

The White House – Washington, D.C.

The tension in the White House Situation Room had gotten worse. Secretary Arnold's frantic pacing back and forth brought the temperature up a couple of degrees. He was growing increasingly grim, and his pessimism did not help the situation. He wanted to take things slow – as most diplomats would.

But the men around him appeared to be hell-bent on bringing the full force of the United States military down on Italy. In one outburst, Arnold had referred to Javits as "Mars," the Roman god of war, for the way he took over and went about throwing around U.S. military might. For his part, Javits had already yelled at Secretary Arnold twice to keep quiet unless he had something positive to add. Arnold, now pissed off and with nothing productive to add at that time, stewed in his seat at the head of the table.

Paper maps of Italy and Rome covered the conference table, and satellite views from above filled the TV screens. A tray of deli sandwiches sat untouched in the corner. The only thing going down was strong black coffee – and lots of it.

Kimberly Carmi was sitting in a chair in the corner of the room, jotting down notes as information came in. When there was a lull in the action, she spoke up.

"Guys, I still think we need to get out there," she said, her voice sounding more urgent. "Let the people know everything is under control." She stopped for a second before adding, "At least we make it seem like everything is under control."

"I agree," Javits said. One by one, the rest of those in the Situation Room agreed.

"Kim," Arnold said. "Should we all stand behind you?" That was something productive he could do, he thought. Plus, it would put him on TV and let the world know that he was helping guide the ship in the storm.

"I think off to the side would be better. That way I can point to you if necessary. The press will highlight your appearance. If we have too much of a crowd it might be hard for us all to control our emotions. We just want one voice from the White House."

She pulled the buzzing iPhone off her hip. Reporters were bombarding her nonstop with questions. One asked who was running the country. Another asked if martial law would be declared. The questions were over the top and it would only get worse if the Administration did nothing.

"The stock market is down 200 points!" Secretary Arnold spouted out, reading the ticker across the bottom of the TV screen. His eyes kept getting bigger. "And oil is up to $150 a barrel!" The sky is falling! The sky is falling! would most likely be the next words out of his mouth.

"We need to get up to the briefing room," Carmi said.

"You two get up there," Javits said. "General Cummins and I will monitor the situation from down here. Make sure you let America know that."

"I will," Carmi said.

Carmi led the way out the door followed by Secretary Arnold, NSA Harnacke, and Director Parker. They solemnly marched up the stairs, through the subdued first floor of the West Wing, and past the empty Oval Office. All four stopped outside the press briefing room and took a breath. Carmi could feel her heart pounding. Billions of people around the world would be watching her every facial movement, listening to every syllable she uttered, analyzing the rise and fall of her chest as she spoke.

The briefing room was stuffed with a hungry pack of reporters – ready to shoot questions and demand answers. Carmi looked the men in the eye and received the green light. She walked in and those in charge took a spot against the wall.

Carmi cleared her throat. Her solitary diamond necklace rested against her blue blouse. Like most in the Schumacher Administration, an American flag pin decorated her left lapel. She arranged her scant notes and looked at the sea of faces and then into the cameras.

"Good afternoon," she said with a strong voice.

Back downstairs in the Situation Room, Javits was glad to have some breathing room. They turned their attention away from the TV showing Carmi beginning her statement and looked over the maps again. A Black Hawk helicopter full of Navy SEALs was in the air and two hours away from Rome.

"Sir," a military aide announced to Secretary Javits. "It's Director

Stubblefield on the line."

"Put it on speaker," Javits said. Finally, they reestablished contact, he thought. "Ty, what is going on?"

"Russ, we have made contact with the President."

Javits and Cummins looked at each other. What a relief. "Is he okay?"

"He is not injured."

"What did he say?"

"Russ, I have not spoken with the President. I can talk to him but he cannot talk to me. He just responds with clicking yes or no."

"What have you been able to get out of him?"

"He is away from his security detail. It is not clear if his agents are down or restrained in some way. There are three men with him at the present time on the fifth floor of the Palazzo Chigi."

Both Cummins and Javits looked at the screen. The military aide maneuvered the mouse and zeroed in on the Palace. Cummins pointed to the screen after Stubblefield noted his present location.

"We're formulating a plan right now," Stubblefield said.

Javits still was not convinced a rescue attempt was prudent at this juncture. "Ty, I don't think that's a good idea."

Stubblefield wasn't going to be convinced otherwise. "Russ, the President has given the go ahead. And we're going ahead."

Javits knew when to end a fight, especially when Director Stubblefield was involved. "Ty, we have satellite images ready to go. Give us a call if you need anything. We have a SEAL team two hours out."

"Thank you, Russ," Stubblefield said before adding, "I need you to send me whatever the Defense Department has on the Palazzo Chigi. If you or the CIA has the interior plans of the Palace, e-mail them to me."

"Director Parker and I will get right on it. We'll send you whatever we have."

"Thanks. One more thing, Russ. The Italian Prime Minister is involved."

Javits shook his head, like things just kept getting worse. "Understood. We're still trying to contact the Italian President. He's on a cruise somewhere off the coast of Alaska. Until we can get a hold of him, you might be wary of Italian police and military."

"Will do," Stubblefield said before hanging up.

Upstairs and behind the podium in the White House pressroom, Carmi continued with her statement.

"At approximately 11:30 a.m. Eastern time, President Schumacher was meeting with Italian Prime Minister Giovanni Scarponi at the Prime Minister's residence in Rome, Italy. Shortly thereafter, Italian police moved in on the Palace and has cordoned off the area. We have had no contact with the President at this time."

Reporters were scribbling as fast as they could, others furiously tapping on their smartphones and laptops. They could barely believe what they were hearing.

"Here at the White House, Defense Secretary Javits, Secretary of State Arnold, Joint Chiefs Chairman Cummins, National Security Adviser Harnacke, and CIA Director Parker are monitoring the situation with Vice President Jackson, who is on her way back from Hawaii. Security precautions have been taken here in the United States and at embassies and military installations around the world."

The door to the briefing room opened and a flushed Secretary Javits entered. He did his best not to look winded, but the blood running up to his face indicated he had been huffing and puffing up the steps. He swallowed hard. He could tell Carmi was nearing the end of her statement – she had no other facts to report. Javits walked up and placed the note on the podium. Carmi looked at it and then at Javits. He nodded, as if to say go ahead. She took a breath and then looked directly into the living rooms of millions of Americans watching on TV. Without a quiver in her voice, she showed no fear – even though she was about to make the most stunning announcement in American history.

"Ladies and Gentlemen," she started somberly. "The President of the United States is currently being held against his will by a foreign government."

CHAPTER 27

Palazzo Chigi – Rome, Italy

While he was in the washroom relieving himself of the Diet Coke, the President had reached into his left pants pocket and retrieved the tube of ChapStick. With uncanny deftness, he popped off the white cap and then the balm cup. With a steady stream of urine still filling the bowl as well as the ears of Vlad the Impaler guarding the door, the President placed the tiny earpiece in his right ear and then closed up the container. He hoped and prayed that he would hear the voice of Director Stubblefield.

The voice came when the President had returned to the Prime Minister's office where Scarponi and Patrenko were both busy wondering when their ride was going to show up. The President kept the ChapStick hidden in his closed left hand, and he would place his hand in his pocket every so often. He had to restrain himself from smiling when he first heard from his old friend. He just looked out the window and gave a quick click with his index finger and thumb. It was good to have a friend in his ear.

"Mr. President," Stubblefield whispered. "Can you hear me?"

The President shifted on the couch. One click yes.

"We're still working on a plan."

The President was looking at the two Russians. Zhukov had his back to him and was saying something to Patrenko, who was keeping an eye and a gun on the President. He overheard them talking about a helicopter, and Zhukov twice pointed to the roof. Both glanced at their watches. It was obvious they were not on schedule.

The Phantom team had set up shop in the empty fifth-floor apartment of what appeared to be a twenty-something college coed. Hanging on the wall were pictures of young Italian lovebirds in the arms of each other at various Rome landmarks – the Colosseum, Trevi Fountain, the Arch of Constantine. It was definitely a female's place – the scented candles, the moisturizing lotions, the pink towels in the bathroom.

Stubblefield really needed to come up with a plan. "Monsignor? Do you know Prime Minister Scarponi?" he asked.

"I have met him many times."

"Do you two get along?"

Regazzoni held out his hand and shook each side up and down. The response was very telling coming from such a polite man. But those in the Vatican frowned upon Scarponi's rampant womanizing.

Stubblefield, however, was hoping to put Regazzoni to good use. Having such a well-recognized man of the cloth on his side was a good thing. "Have you ever been involved in a hostage negotiation?"

"No."

Stubblefield figured he wouldn't worry the Monsignor but he was thinking today might be the day. The Director then looked out the window and put the microphone back up to his mouth.

"Mr. President, can you get to the window on the southeast side of the building?" Stubblefield asked.

Agent Schiffer had commandeered the dining-room table and was presently lying on top of it – black cheesecloth covering his body and his legs overhanging the table but propped up by a small armoire pulled away from the wall. He had his Remington .308 sniper rifle fixed on the fifth floor of the Palazzo Chigi. The apartment window was open and the cheese cloth concealed him in the relative darkness of the room. Through his Leupold MK4 20x scope, he moved the crosshairs from window to window trying to pick up movement from inside the Palace.

The south wall of the Prime Minister's office had an impressive collection of old books – many of them rare. Works on Italian history and tomes on Roman mythology were some of the more prevalent topics. The President, still seated on the couch on the opposite side, focused his eyes on a row of Bibles. With the Russians still talking on the southern end and the armed Scarponi sitting at his desk on the north side, the President got up and walked slowly across the room. The three captors watched him, eyeing him all the way and wondering what he was doing. They didn't seem to care much – it wasn't like he was going to jump out of the windows. They didn't open anyway.

The President selected a Bible off the shelf – it was well worn with a green cover and binding. He couldn't make out the version but it was in English. The date indicated it was printed in 1896, and it might not have been opened since that time considering the President had to practically pry the pages apart. He began flipping through the Bible with care – not wanting to tear or rip any of the pages. He happened upon Psalm 56, verses 3 and 4:

When I am afraid, I will trust in you. In God, whose word I praise, in God I trust; I will not be afraid. What can mortal man do to me?

With his head down and eyes studying the verses, obviously in deep contemplation, his mind was taken back to his conversation with Wiley Cogdon just a couple of weeks ago. The inquisitive Wiley had asked about the motto "In God We Trust." A hollow feeling struck the President in his gut. He realized he hadn't heard from his chief of staff, had no idea where he was. He feared Wiley might be dead or dying out in the hall. With the Bible still in hand, the President looked at the door to the hall. Then, remembering Stubblefield's request, he slowly walked toward the southeastern corner. He stopped in front of the last window, the light from the early evening sun still strong enough to brighten the President's face.

"I got him," Schiffer announced, the President now in the center of the crosshairs. "Southeast window."

Standing at the end of the dining-room table behind Agent Schiffer, Director Stubblefield grabbed his binoculars and saw the same. "All right, Mr. President, we have you in sight. Good to see you, sir. South side across the Piazza, fifth-floor apartment."

The President glanced up from his biblical study and looked across the Piazza. He squinted his eyes and counted up five floors. He saw nothing except the darkened windows of the apartments on the top floor.

"Can you see us?"

With the open Bible in his right hand, the President slowly reached into his left pocket and gave two clicks.

"Good," Stubblefield whispered into his microphone. Now to the next order of business. "Mr. President, is that glass bulletproof? If so, close that book you're reading."

The President stepped closer to the window. It was obviously not a single pane, definitely thick enough to stop a bullet. The Prime Minister's security would have called for ballistic glass years ago. The President closed the Bible and backed away.

"Roger that," Stubblefield said.

Schiffer saw movement through his scope and focused his attention on two men behind the President. "I have two men in sight, Director."

Stubblefield adjusted his binoculars. From that distance and with the shadows, it was difficult to get a good read on the men.

"Mr. President, are the two men behind you Middle Eastern?"

Stubblefield was beginning to wonder if this was some sort of Islamic terrorist plot.

Two clicks no.

"Are they Italian?"

Two clicks no.

So they weren't homegrown Italian terrorists or Middle Eastern Muslim extremists.

Schiffer adjusted his scope once more. "Sir, I've got a better look at them now. Two white males," he said before adding, "very white."

Two "very white" males, Stubblefield said to himself. He was starting to put it together. With the Barton mess in the United States and the attempted attack at the Russian Embassy, Stubblefield figured out why the men were "very white." They were "Siberian white" – the cold climate of much of Russia not being the best place to tan one's skin.

"Mr. President, are the two men Russian?"

The President put the Bible down on a credenza and reached into his pocket. He pulled out his ChapStick and hid it in the middle of his fist. He gave it one click.

"So it is Scarponi and two Russians?"

One click yes, the President signaled, still looking out the window.

"Jenkins," Stubblefield whispered. "Send a text to Secretary Javits that two Russian males are holding the President along with Prime Minister Scarponi."

Agent Jenkins pecked away at his encrypted cell phone providing a direct line to the Secretary of Defense at the White House.

"Anybody else with you?"

Two clicks no.

With the sunlight still illuminating the President's face, Vlad the Impaler noticed the President's left hand and a white object he was holding.

"Hey! He's got something in his hand! He's got something in his hand!"

Oh shit, the President thought. With his mind worrying about the whereabouts of Wiley and his ear now filled with Stubblefield's questions, the President had taken the ChapStick out of his pocket without even thinking about it.

Patrenko rushed over and threw the President up against the window. With his beefy hands grabbing the President's white shirt, the Russian's eyes bulged out of his head like he was going to tear the President apart. The President could smell the vodka on Patrenko's breath. He turned his head to the right, just in case Patrenko got close enough to look into his right ear and discover the hearing device.

"Oh shit," Stubblefield said.

Across the way, Agent Schiffer slammed the bolt handle down on his Remington, closed his right eye, and readied himself to pull the trigger to take out the white Russian – bulletproof glass or not.

Watching through his binoculars, Director Stubblefield wrapped his right hand around the microphone. "Easy, Duke," he whispered calmly. "Easy now."

Patrenko took some joy in roughing up the President of the United States. "I saw something in his hand!" he told Zhukov and Scarponi, both of whom were now walking over to see what the President was hiding.

"Just ChapStick," the President said, feigning a bit of fright and holding up the container. "It's just ChapStick. I always have some with me."

The President hurriedly took off the cap and showed it to his captors. He then applied the balm to his lips. He made sure his hand was shaking enough for everyone to see.

"Hand it over," Zhukov ordered, holding out his right hand.

The demand turned the President's stomach. At that time, his super-secret ChapStick was his only lifeline to the outside world. Going against Director Stubblefield's orders never to give it up, the President put the cap back on and handed it over. He had no other choice.

Zhukov looked at the container and turned the dial a couple of times. Across the way, Stubblefield heard the two clicks in his earpiece. Zhukov brought the container to his nose and gave it a smell. It was classic ChapStick. The cold-weather Russians were big users of lip balm – chapped lips not making a man more macho.

"It's just ChapStick," Zhukov said. "I saw the President show it to everyone in a debate last year." It was nothing for the Russians to concern themselves with. "It's not like he's going to use it against us." The two Russians shared a laugh.

Zhukov tossed it back to the President, whose heart rate and those across the Piazza slowed at the sight. The President put it back into his left pocket.

"Come on," Zhukov said to Patrenko and Scarponi. "It's about time to go."

CHAPTER 28

Rome, Italy

From the side of the room, Director Stubblefield slowly made his way to the window of the apartment and looked down at the Piazza below. There was still no movement, the Italian Carabinieri continuing their blockade and preventing any vehicles from entering the area. Two Russians and the Italian Prime Minister were holding the President on the top floor of the Palazzo Chigi. He still did not know how many others might be involved – possibly more Russians or some group of Italians sympathetic to the Prime Minister. But he couldn't wait much longer to find out.

"Guys, we're going to make our way over to the Palace," Stubblefield said. "Let's get our gear. Agent Schiffer will stay here and cover the exterior."

Agents Jenkins, Alvarez, Guerrero, and Olivera headed for the door. Stubblefield kept Monsignor Regazzoni in front of him. They went down the still silent hallway and then the staircase to the ground floor. Before heading down to the tunnel, Stubblefield decided to take a look outside.

"Jenkins," he whispered. "Check this room."

Agent Jenkins pulled out a micro-camera with a fiber-optic cable and snaked it under the door. The clothes on the racks indicated it was women's fashion – fairly high-end merchandise given the location. Jenkins maneuvered the snake to the left and right – the black and white screen of his handheld TV showing no one inside.

"It's clear."

"Olivera," Stubblefield said. "Open this door." He then thought it over a second longer. "Quietly."

Although Olivera had several state-of-the-art tools at his disposal, a quick glance indicated this would be an easy job. The lock was pre-war, and an experienced cat burglar would be inside in short order. Olivera reached into the pocket of his bulletproof vest and pulled out his Phantom-issue American Express card. He never left home without it. The name of the cardholder was Donald Trump. With one swipe, the lock clicked and the door opened.

Stubblefield looked in. "Guerrero, you're coming with me," he said. "You three stay here and watch over the Monsignor."

Stubblefield and Guerrero crawled in on their hands and knees – not wanting to show themselves to anyone who might be watching from the outside. They maneuvered around clothing racks and ladies' mannequins. Stubblefield stopped when he could see outside the window. He grabbed his binoculars and looked across the Piazza – the Secret Service's Beast and the Suburbans still there. When he saw movement on the front steps of the Palazzo Chigi, he zeroed in on the three men standing outside the door. White males, probably more Russians. They were all armed but none were wearing military uniforms. A few more could have been the Prime Minister's bodyguards.

"I have two males at the far southeast window on the first floor," Guerrero reported. "Two more at the second window."

"You copy that, Duke?" Stubblefield asked into his microphone.

"Copy," Schiffer responded from upstairs.

Neither Stubblefield nor Guerrero saw any movement on any of the other floors of the Palace.

"All right," Stubblefield whispered to Guerrero. "Let's get out of here."

Back out in the hall, Stubblefield informed his men that there were at least seven men inside the Palace. They left the door of the fashion boutique unlocked just in case. They then headed down the stairwell and found the tunnel as cold and quiet as before. They marched on, the flashlights on the barrels of their assault rifles leading the way.

When the tunnel came to a T, Stubblefield figured they had reached the outer edge of the Palazzo Chigi. Now he had to figure out which way to go.

"Monsignor," Stubblefield said. "Have you ever been down in these tunnels?"

"Not in the tunnel on the Palace side," Regazzoni said, shaking his head.

Stubblefield grabbed his iPhone and opened the e-mail message from Secretary Javits. Javits and Director Parker had found the interior layout of the Palazzo Chigi in the vast archives of the Defense Department and Central Intelligence Agency. Collected from years of cameras secretly hidden on U.S. diplomats as they mingled during the multitude of holiday receptions held at the Palace, the intelligence community had gathered reams of data on floor plans, entrances and exits, and hidden passageways in the home of the Italian Prime Minister. Now it was time to put the information to good use. Stubblefield flipped through each page – showing his men the interior and the route upstairs to the Prime Minister's fifth-floor office.

"Have you ever been in the basement, Monsignor?"

"I have been in the Palace's wine cellar. Over three thousand bottles. One of the best in all of Italy."

Stubblefield didn't need to stop Regazzoni from rambling on because the shaking ground quieted the Monsignor.

"What the hell is that?" Stubblefield wondered aloud, the rumbling from above growing louder.

"It's not a tank, is it?" Olivera asked.

The Phantom team members were all looking toward the dark ceiling of the tunnel, their ears straining to recognize the thump-thump-thump that they were hearing. Then the call came from above.

"Director!" Schiffer whispered loudly into his microphone. "Incoming chopper!"

Stubblefield looked at his watch. Javits said the SEAL team was two hours out. And that was about thirty minutes ago.

"Shit!"

"Director, it's coming for the President!" Schiffer said louder than before. "It's hovering over the Palace!"

Stubblefield punched in the number. "Mr. President, are you on the move?"

One click yes.

"Shit!"

Stubblefield didn't know which way to go. He didn't know what lay ahead inside the Palace. All he did know was that he could not let the President get on that helicopter. If he did, Stubblefield and the Phantom team would have no chance at a rescue. He decided to go back.

"Back to the apartment!" he told his men as they took off back down the tunnel. "Schiffer! Schiffer!" he yelled into his microphone and now in full sprint. "Do not let the President get on that chopper!"

Schiffer had thrown himself off the dining-room table, his prone position not giving him a clear shot at the helicopter above the Palace. He crouched in front of the window but still nothing. He took off running back into the hall, trying door after door to find the entrance to a stairwell that would lead him to the roof. He found one door at the end of the hall on the far south side. There was no number on it, no indication that it led to someone's fifth-floor residence. He tried the knob but found it locked. He didn't have any of Olivera's tools.

"Schiffer! Get to the roof! Get to the roof!"

Schiffer pounded on the door with his boot. "I'm on my way," he huffed. Another boot to the door. Then another. Then the shoulder. "Come on!" he yelled to himself. He was one shoulder thrust away from shooting his way in. He hurled himself into the door and barreled through, crashing into the steps. He raced up the stairs and unlatched the lock to the door to the roof.

With a gun in the President's back, Patrenko forced him up the stairs to the roof – Zhukov and Prime Minister Scarponi following behind. Vlad the Impaler had cuffed the President's hands to his side at his belt – that way he could not use them as weapons. The President still had his ChapStick in his left hand.

"Hurry up!" Patrenko ordered.

Stubblefield and his men were back on the ground floor and hugging the wall of the fashion boutique looking at the sky above them. To the north, they could see the whirling blades above the roof.

"Schiffer!?"

Agent Schiffer had to sprint toward the north side of the building, scrambling up the face of a five-foot wall with his Remington slung over his shoulder. He could see the chopper a hundred yards in front of him. He fell to the roof underneath a small covered archway and behind a row of planters.

"Schiffer!?"

Patrenko held the President by the collar and pushed him forward, yelling over the roar of the chopper's rotors to move it. There was no helipad on the Palazzo Chigi's roof, which was littered with heating and cooling units and satellite dishes. The outer edges of the roof slanted toward the street. The only way for anyone to board the eight-person chopper would be for the pilot to hover near the edge of the open-air courtyard in the center of the Palace and make the passengers step on board via a skid. One wrong step could lead to a five-story free fall.

Patrenko waved his right arm at the chopper pilot, motioning for him to turn his tail rotor to the north so they could get on board from the left side.

"Move!" he yelled at the President over the roar of the rotor wash. Dust and dirt were being thrown into the air and into the faces of those on the roof.

Through his squinted eyelids, the President looked to his south, wondering where Stubblefield and his team were. He knew full well he could not get on the chopper. He turned to the side and acted like he would go no further.

"I said move!" Patrenko yelled again. "Move or you're a dead man! I'll throw you off this roof if I have to!"

Seeing the President's refusal to move, Zhukov stepped forward and pushed both Patrenko and the President forward. "Get on board, Mr. President!" he yelled into his ear. Now just forty feet from the chopper's skid, Zhukov grabbed the President's collar and pushed him forward. The President did his best to push back.

"Schiffer! Do not let him get on board!" Stubblefield yelled, a feeling of helplessness falling over him.

Agent Schiffer's heart was pounding at 110 beats per minute. Breaking down the door and sprinting across the roof of the apartment left him nearly out of breath. Now surveying the scene, his options were fraught with risk. If the President got on board the helicopter, it was game over for the Phantom team. If Schiffer shot the pilot, the rotors of the helicopter spinning at 500 rpms could kill everyone unfortunate enough to be in their path. He had to do something.

"Director, tell the President to get down!"

From inside the apartment building, Stubblefield yelled with all his might. "Mr. President, get down! Get down!"

Barely able to hear over the rotors, the President intentionally tripped over his own feet and fell like a dead weight next to an air-conditioning unit, which provided him some semblance of cover. This gave Schiffer just the opening he needed. With his Remington steadied on a ledge, his right hand jammed the bolt handle down. He exhaled what air was left from his lungs and closed his right eye. The crosshairs found their mark on the chest of the pilot, who was having difficulty keeping the chopper steady. The chopper was all over the place – the main rotor downwash hitting the roof on the left but nothing but the empty chasm of the courtyard on the right. With the vortex ring out of kilter, the pilot was constantly maneuvering the controls to keep the bird level.

"Schiffer!?"

Bam!

The shot whistled through the Rome sky and caught the pilot in the left shoulder. The skid of the chopper hit the inside of the Palace, and the two Russians and Scarponi dove for cover. While trying to maintain control, the pilot took his right hand off the stick to see if his left shoulder was still there. It was, but not much of it. The pilot, now in paralyzing pain, his mouth open screaming in agony, inadvertently pushed down on the right foot pedal, causing the rear of the chopper to veer to the left where the spinning tail rotor clipped a satellite dish and sent shrapnel flying all over the roof. Without the tail rotor stabilizing the chopper, around and around in circles it went. Schiffer would see the pilot trying to regain control with his one good arm before the tail would swing around again. Schiffer closed his right eye and waited for the out-of-control chopper to spin around once more. He needed to end it right here.

Bam!

Schiffer timed it perfectly and sent another shot into the pilot's skull. The left skid slammed into the roof and when the chopper edged forward with its nose down the main rotors crashed into the southern roof of the Palace, gouging a hole in the southern roof and sheering off the blades. The now powerless chopper nosedived into the courtyard below and erupted into a ball of flames. The explosion that followed rocked the whole area.

"Get up, you son of a bitch!" Patrenko yelled to the President. "I said get up!" He grabbed him by the collar and yanked him up from behind the AC unit, putting the President in between him and whoever was shooting from across the Piazza. "I ought to shoot you right now, you bastard!"

"Get him inside!" Zhukov yelled, hiding behind a planter on the roof. "Get him back inside!"

"Schiffer, if you get a shot!" Stubblefield yelled into his microphone. "Take it!"

Schiffer had cycled the bolt on his Remington and had the crosshairs on Patrenko, who kept darting his head in every direction behind the President's as they tried to make their way back off the roof of the Palace.

Schiffer exhaled the air out of his lungs. "Director, tell the President to move his head to his left," he said with hardly an ounce of emotion.

Stubblefield hesitated ever so slightly until he remembered it was

Schiffer on the other end – the best sharpshooter in the arsenal of U.S. law enforcement. "Mr. President, move your head to your left!"

Schiffer had his right eye closed and the index finger on his left hand on the trigger. The President ducked to his left and exposed Patrenko for a split second, but no shot came. Patrenko grabbed the President by the neck and fired his Uzi across the Piazza. He then jammed the barrel of the gun against the President's head and pulled him inside.

"The President is back inside, Director," Schiffer reported. If he had a shot, he would have taken it. Now fully drenched in sweat, he topped off his magazine just in case he got a second chance.

"Copy that," Stubblefield said. "Good work, Duke." He then turned to his men. "We gotta get over there. Let's move!"

The White House – Washington, D.C.

Following the press conference, Secretary Arnold, NSA Harnacke, and Director Parker returned to the Situation Room where Secretary Javits and Joint Chiefs Chairman Cummins were holding court. Javits told them two F-16s would be over Rome in less than thirty minutes, the SEAL team in less than an hour.

When Secretary Javits felt a buzzing on his hip, he reached for his cell phone and looked at the text message.

"All right," he said. "Everybody listen up."

When the players around the table quit talking, Javits made the announcement.

"I just received a text from Director Stubblefield. He says that two Russian males are involved along with Prime Minister Scarponi."

NSA Harnacke started shaking his head. The worry on his face was evident. "This changes everything."

The President's security and defense brain trust figured this was another terrorist operation. Maybe the Italian Prime Minister was involved, but they all thought it had to be an extremist plot to capture or kill the American President.

"Probably has something to do with that traitor Barton," Harnacke said, thinking out loud in frustration.

"Mike," Javits said to Secretary Arnold, "get on the horn to your Russian counterparts and find out what the hell is going on. And don't pussyfoot around either."

Secretary Arnold walked over to the wall and picked up the direct line to Moscow. He didn't even have to dial a number – just pick up the phone and a friendly Russian operator would direct the White House caller to anyone in the Kremlin.

"This is Secretary of State Mike Arnold. I want to speak with Foreign Minister Chernakov." He waited two seconds before stating, "Right now!"

When Minister Chernakov came on the line, he stated his concern for the American President and hoped the ordeal would come to a peaceful conclusion for him and the American people. He stated the Russian Government would help in any way possible, but he did have cause for concern.

"You have cause for concern!?" The nerve of the man!

"Yes, we have reason to believe that your armed forces have been acting aggressively in the last few hours," Chernakov said, sounding very worried and even more offended that the Americans would do such a thing. The Russians, of course, were well aware of the increased readiness of U.S. forces. Russian satellites had picked up U.S. long-range bombers in the air along with a flurry of activity at U.S. missile silos. What was more worrisome to the Russians, however, U.S. nuclear submarines had seemingly vanished into the depths of the Pacific. And that could mean only one thing.

"American belligerence will not be taken lightly by the world community, Mr. Secretary," Minister Chernakov lectured. "And it will not be tolerated."

"Cut the crap, Leonid!" Arnold shot back. No more diplomatic niceties. "We have solid intelligence that two Russians are involved in the abduction of the President of the United States!"

The line suddenly went silent. The charge was as extreme as ever could be made. "Mr. Secretary," Chernakov said calmly but seriously. "I can assure you that no one in my government is involved in this matter. Further, I can assure you that no one has presented me with any information that something like this might take place."

Secretary Arnold only half believed him. It was the old "Trust, but verify" way of doing business with the Russians. "Let me tell you something, Leo. There are going to be eyebrows raised around the world if what you are telling me is not true. I've already been on the phone with several EU leaders who have promised the most draconian sanctions imaginable if we find out Russia is officially involved. I suggest you get on the phone to Prime Minister Grigoryev and President Yaroslavsky and figure out what is going on."

Chernakov agreed. He was not about to spout off some old Soviet-style bluster Arnold's way. He did not know what was going on. And a large part of him worried some of his countrymen might have set back U.S./Russian relations to the Cold War days. "I will call them, Mike. We will get to the bottom of this. But, like I said, I can assure you that my government has had no involvement in this matter."

When Arnold hung up the phone, his face was as red as a tomato. He could be a charming diplomat when he wanted to be, but he kind of liked being a prick and a hardass in dealing with the Russians. He thought he might do it more often.

"Well?" Javits asked.

"I seriously don't think he knows what's going on, to be honest with you," Arnold reported. "I just didn't get that feeling they're trying to hide something or cover up a plot to capture the President. Or, at least, I don't get that feeling from him."

"Maybe I should call their defense minister," Javits said.

"Russ, look," General Cummins said, hitting Javits on the arm with the back of his hand and interrupting his conversation with Secretary Arnold. He pointed to the wall. "Look on the TV."

The screen showed a billowing black cloud rising over Rome. The Sky Italia news chopper in the air was ordered to keep its distance by the Italian military, but the news crew still had a decent view.

"Turn up the volume," Javits said to his military aide.

The news reporter was speaking in Italian, but an American translator provided a recap of what the man was saying.

"At approximately 6:30 p.m. this evening, a helicopter crashed into the courtyard of the Palazzo Chigi, the residence of Prime Minister Scarponi. It is unclear why the helicopter was in the air. It has been reported that the President of the United States is being held inside the Palace but that cannot be confirmed. The Carabinieri has blocked off the streets around the Palace and no one is allowed inside the perimeter."

As the chopper moved in as close as it could, the cameraman zoomed in. The pictures showed the smoke growing thicker. With the sun having set, the early evening darkness helped to highlight the orange flames licking the south wall of the Palace's courtyard.

The voice of the Italian newsman could be heard in the background growing more excitable by the minute. But the American translator continued on with little emotion – just the facts. He ended with a description of what everyone watching on TV could plainly see.

"The Palazzo Chigi is on fire."

CHAPTER 29

Palazzo Chigi – Rome, Italy

"It's all your fault, you son of a bitch!"

Vladimir Patrenko was seething with rage. The Russians' planned escape had crashed down into a ball of flames. And he was placing blame for their current predicament squarely on Prime Minister Scarponi.

"You told us your police would keep everyone out!"

Scarponi was seated on the couch with a gun in his face. "I don't know what happened," he responded weakly. He was a tired, beaten man. He had never envisioned the violence that had happened and would most assuredly happen in the near future.

Patrenko and Zhukov had forced President Schumacher down off the roof of the Palace and were now holed up in the Prime Minister's office trying to figure out what to do. The President was at the other end of the couch, his hands still shackled to his side. He watched as Patrenko angrily paced back and forth between him and the Prime Minister – cursing and threatening both of them.

Vlad the Impaler was getting desperate. A part of him wanted to shoot the President and get it all over with. The fury in his eyes indicated he might just do it.

"We only have one choice left," Zhukov said to Patrenko. Zhukov had been hiding behind the curtains as he peeked out the windows. He wondered where the shots had come from and where they would come from next. In contrast to the combustible Patrenko, Zhukov knew they needed to come up with a backup plan. There was still time, he told himself. Still time to finish off the President and slip back under the radar to their home country and keep Russia from taking the brunt of the blame.

Zhukov walked over to the other side of the Prime Minister's office. The black smoke in the courtyard was billowing past the windows, flames starting to lick the walls two stories below. It wouldn't be long before the whole side of the Palace would be engulfed in flames. Zhukov dialed a number into his cell phone and made the call. He didn't tell the person on the other end who he was. He didn't need to. It was his own private backup plan.

"Minister Khan, if you want him," Zhukov said, cryptically. "Come and get him." There was only one question put to Zhukov. "Yes, at the Palace. Come in from the northeast corner. That's where the fire trucks will be." He then stopped before giving one last message. "He's all yours."

Zhukov thought the Pakistanis were Russia's way out of the mess. Zhukov had the goods on Scarponi and the Pakistanis wouldn't rat out the Russians. It was the perfect plan. Scarponi would say nothing. And the Pakistanis would pump up their chests and claim they were the brains and brawn behind the whole operation.

When the President heard the name Khan, he knew things were about to get a lot worse. He looked over at Scarponi, who looked like he knew this was the end.

Zhukov ended the call, walked over to the couch, and pointed his own gun at Prime Minister Scarponi. "It's time for you to make a call," he growled at the defeated man beneath him.

Scarponi could barely raise his bloodshot eyes to look at Zhukov. He was visibly shaking. He was the Prime Minister of Italy, he thought to himself. It wasn't supposed to be this way. Zhukov held out the phone to him.

"Giovanni, if you make that call, we're all dead," the President said.

"Shut up!" Patrenko shouted. He then planted his steel-toed boot in the President's kneecap to show he meant it.

The President lurched forward as the pain shot through his body. He wasn't sure where Scarponi's call was going, but he had a pretty good idea it wouldn't help his cause. "Giovanni, don't do it."

"I said shut up!" Patrenko shouted, louder this time. He then pistol-whipped the President across the forehead.

Zhukov waved the phone in front of the Prime Minister's face. "If you don't, we'll release the video," Zhukov said. "And we'll let everyone know of your involvement in taking the President hostage."

"No," Scarponi croaked. The hostility for the Russians was evident even in his shaking voice. "I did not sign on to this."

Zhukov lunged in and wrapped his meaty left hand around the Prime Minister's throat. He then cocked his pistol, the click of the firing pin echoing in Scarponi's ear. "Do it or you're dead."

Zhukov jammed the barrel farther into the Prime Minister's ear. It would create a fine mess when he pulled the trigger. With tears beginning to fall down his cheeks, Scarponi nodded. He had decided to save himself.

Zhukov released his grip. He then punched in the numbers and handed Scarponi the phone. "Tell your police to stand down and let the firefighters in. They are also to allow in two diplomatic vehicles from the Embassy of Pakistan."

Scarponi grabbed the phone and looked over at the President, who said nothing, a stream of blood running down the side of his face. When a Carabinieri commander came on the line, Scarponi gave the orders – send in the firefighters and two vehicles from the Pakistani Embassy. Without ending the call, he dropped the phone onto the floor.

"Good," Zhukov told him. He then turned to Patrenko. "Let's get ready to go."

Seven stories below, the Phantom team was huddled in amongst the dusty bottles of Italian wine in the Palazzo Chigi's darkened cellar. It was there that they discovered the remains of the Russians' staging area. Zhukov and Patrenko's operatives had hid in the locked cellar, completely invisible to any Secret Service security sweeps, and waited for the signal. Now the empty Uzi cases and extra tear gas canisters put the Phantom team on notice as to what they would find upstairs.

"Schiffer, do you copy?" Stubblefield asked into his mike.

"Go ahead."

"Do you have a visual on the President?"

Schiffer, who was still on the roof of the apartment building across the Piazza from the Palace, scanned the fifth floor for any signs of movement. "Negative," he said. "Be advised, Director. The inner courtyard appears to be on fire. I hear sirens en route."

"Copy that," Stubblefield said. "Mr. President, can you hear me?"

One click yes.

"Are you still on the fifth floor?"

One click yes.

Stubblefield gave a thumbs-up to his men. "Stand by, Mr. President, we're coming to get you."

The Phantom team assembled on the steps leading to the basement of the Palace. At the back of the line stood Monsignor Regazzoni. He had followed them this far and wasn't sure what to do now. Stubblefield took notice. He grabbed the Monsignor by the elbow and led him to the darkest corner of the wine cellar. He unholstered a flashlight from his vest and handed it over.

"Monsignor, I want you to stay right here. If we're not back in twenty minutes, you get back in that tunnel and head to the church. You got that?"

"Yes."

Stubblefield reached out his massive hand just in case. "*Millie grazie, my friend.*"

"Be safe," Regazzoni whispered back. He took his spot in the dark and started to pray.

Stubblefield rejoined his men. "All right, guys. I want the President back safe and secure," he said, stating the obvious. "I want Prime Minister Scarponi alive too. But if he has a gun pointed at you, I want you to take him out. You understand?"

With their flashlights illuminating their faces, the team nodded in unison.

"We have to expect ten to twenty armed men. Most likely on the first two floors and then maybe more on the fifth outside the Prime Minister's office. Let's be quick."

With the flashlight attached to his MP-7, the Director shined it on his tool man. "Olivera, I want you to cut the power to the place. Night vision everyone."

Agent Olivera crept silently into the basement above the cellar and found the electrical closet, the janitorial staff having abandoned it hours ago. Olivera didn't need to cut anything. He just prepared to pull down the red handle.

"Stand by for power loss," he said into his mike.

"Copy that," Stubblefield said. "Pull the fire alarm while you're at it. Schiffer, you are clear to engage any and all targets."

"Roger that," Schiffer said.

"Do you have the bag of flash-bangs with you?"

"Affirmative."

"On 'Go' I want you to throw the multi-bangs down to the street on the east side of your position."

"Roger that," Schiffer said as the Palazzo Chigi suddenly went dark.

"Go!"

Agents Jenkins, Guerrero, Alvarez, and Olivera, followed by Director Stubblefield, snaked up the stairs and hit the first floor. They heard the muffled explosions from Schiffer's flash-bang grenades outside the Palace and echoing through the empty streets. The multiple blasts made it sound like the U.S. Army was rolling into position. With the Russians distracted by the darkness, the fire alarm blaring in their ears, and the blasts out front, it was total sensory overload.

The Phantom team silently raced through the west hall, like the angel of death riding in on a cold winter wind through an open door.

But the Russians saw no one.

It was as if ghosts with automatic weapons had descended upon them in the darkness. The Phantom team struck with equal part stealth and force. Their steps were quiet, their bodies fluid, their guns silent but deadly. Those inside the Palace started dropping one by one. The low-level whistle would be followed by a thud to the skull, the distinctive sound like someone thumping a melon. When one Russian would fall to the floor in a heap, his comrade standing next to him would turn around to see nothing but an MP-7 round between his eyes.

When seven Russians rushed back into the Palace through the front door, the silenced MP-7s took them down one by one. From his rooftop perch, Schiffer could see the bright flashes illuminating the first-floor windows and then the second. An endless stream of Russian gunfire echoed off the marble walls. They were firing at shadows. The Phantom team quickly made their way up the stairs, shell casings clanking off the floor, enemies falling at their feet.

"Floor three," Stubblefield announced, barely out of breath.

The acrid smell of smoke from the courtyard fire filtered into the Palace. Six Russians held their positions behind marble pillars until Alvarez rolled a grenade in their direction. The blast ripped a hole in an interior Palace wall – plaster and stucco shrapnel flying through the air.

Schiffer saw the flashes on the fourth floor before his attention was drawn to the street below. The fire department was showing up followed by two vehicles that didn't look like they came from the stable of the Italian military.

"Floor five."

Through the AN/PVS Universal Night Sight attached to his Remington, Agent Schiffer could see the outline of Zhukov in the darkness through the fifth-floor window. The Mad Russian was yelling into his phone, demanding to know what was going on and why his men had shut off the power. When he didn't receive a response, he realized the line to those downstairs was dead. His comrades were also dead. He ran to the window and looked to see what was going on. Just then, Schiffer squeezed the trigger on his Remington and sent a round through the Italian sky. Zhukov flinched as the outer glass of the bulletproof window cracked like an eggshell. He took a step closer, curiosity getting the better of him. With the streetlights below aiding his view, Zhukov's eyes zeroed in on the head-high object stuck inside the window, a hole definitely forming behind it. He then realized it was a rifle round. Agent Schiffer was coming after him. With another hard smack, a second bullet hit the first, the cracked glass now looking like a spider web. Finally, coming to his senses, Zhukov realized the next round would be heading straight for his brain.

"Look out!" Zhukov yelled to the others while diving for cover. Schiffer's third shot broke through the glass, the bullet lodging in the Prime Minister's desk. Zhukov pushed himself off the floor and grabbed Scarponi off the couch by his collar. "They're coming for the President! Let's get out of here!"

Patrenko grabbed the President off the couch and tried dragging the recalcitrant Schumacher to the back exit. Their faces were lit by the orange and red flames lapping the north side of the Palazzo Chigi. The President, his wrists still shackled at his waist, could do little more than pull his body away.

"Move or I'll kill you right now!" Patrenko yelled as the gun went up.

"Mr. President, we're right outside the office!" Stubblefield yelled over the radio.

Upon hearing the Director in his ear, the President leaned into Patrenko and head-butted him. With a little more distance between them, his right shoe then planted the presidential seal on Patrenko's testicles. The big Russian bear staggered backwards, growling in pain, his nuts now throbbing.

"Mr. President, hit the deck!" Stubblefield ordered.

The President kicked the gun out of Patrenko's left hand and then fell to the floor. The snarling Impaler reached for his knife and prepared to drive that stake into the President's heart.

Boom!

The main door to the office blew open on the strength of Olivera's battering ram. Alvarez stepped in, found the bald Patrenko with his knife in the air, and fired one round into his chest followed by two more to the head. The Russian fell backwards against a bookcase. His lifeless body then crumpled to his knees and fell forward onto the President.

Jenkins took the armed Zhukov down with a shot to the chest and two more through the left lens of his thick glasses.

"Don't move, Scarponi!" Guerrero yelled. The Prime Minister better not because he was in Guerrero's sights.

Director Stubblefield entered the room and found the President underneath Patrenko. Through his night-vision goggles, Stubblefield could see the dark blood on the President's shirt and forehead.

"Mr. President, are you okay?"

"I'm okay," he said, rolling Patrenko off of him.

"You're bleeding!"

"No, I'm okay. It's just my head."

"Let's get you up, Mr. President."

"Get on your knees!" Guerrero yelled to the Prime Minister across the office. Scarponi did not fight back. He had no fight left in him. Guerrero zipped the flex-cuffs onto his wrists and then gagged his mouth.

"Schiffer, Stubblefield," the Director said into his microphone. "We got him."

From the roof across the way, Schiffer didn't like what he was seeing. Out of two vans came a horde of men in olive-colored garb. Even in the darkness, Schiffer could tell they were not Italian Carabinieri or military. The Kalashnikov rifles at their sides indicated they were not Italian, but they were definitely looking for a firefight. In the middle of the scrum was Minister Khan himself, looking to exact revenge on those who captured one son and "caused" the death of another. Khan told the men he wanted the President dead. With the order given, eight armed men hurried inside. "Director, we have non-firefighters coming through the front door. Eight of them armed with Kalashnikovs."

"Roger that," Stubblefield said. "We're on our way down." With the President standing next to him, he looked him over. "Olivera. Snap off these restraints."

Olivera pulled out his bolt cutters and gave the President freedom to move his arms. Stubblefield took off his bulletproof vest and put it over the President. Alvarez and Guerrero covered the main entrance to the office. Agent Jenkins went through the pockets of Patrenko and Zhukov and collected a cell phone from each of them.

"We gotta move, guys," Stubblefield announced. "Move! Move!"

As they hustled down the back stairs, the Director instinctively counted his men – Olivera, Alvarez, Jenkins, Guerrero. Only Schiffer was missing. They made it down to the basement then the sub-basement and finally the wine cellar. The relative silence that followed the shootout was broken by the sounds of shouts coming from above.

Somebody was looking for them.

Halfway down the tunnel under the Piazza, Stubblefield radioed to Agent Schiffer. "We're heading back to the church. Meet us in the tunnel."

"I'm on my way."

Stubblefield guided the President by the elbow as they broke into a run – the Director's mind running just as fast. Olivera, Alvarez, Jenkins, Guerrero. Schiffer was on his way. The Phantom team had five members – six if the Director included himself. The team was all here, save for Schiffer who was on his way down. They had their catch – the President. Their surplus – the Prime Minister – threw Stubblefield off on his numbers. As the thumps of their boots echoed off the tunnel walls, Stubblefield went through it again – Olivera, Alvarez, Jenkins, Guerrero, Schiffer. It was then that he stopped in his tracks.

"Shit!" Stubblefield said.

"What's wrong?" the President asked, out of breath. Then the rest of the team stopped and wondered the same thing.

"I forgot Monsignor Regazzoni."

"Who?" the President asked.

Going against his instincts to get the President out of harm's way as fast as possible, he knew what he had to do. He couldn't leave a team member behind.

"I got to go back and get somebody," he said, looking back north down the tunnel. "Olivera, Alvarez. Cover the President and get back to the church. Jenkins and Guerrero – lead the way. Schiffer and I will meet you guys there."

Director Stubblefield took off back down the tunnel. He had taken off his night-vision goggles in preparation for entering the church so the flashlight on the barrel of his MP-7 led the way. He made it back to the T and followed it around to the wine cellar. Then he forgot where he put him.

"Monsignor?" he called out in a whisper. "Monsignor Regazzoni?"

He went down row after row of racks – bottles and bottles of Brunello di Montalcino, Barolo, and Chianti. The rows were so numerous

Stubblefield wondered if he would be able to find his way back out if he ever did find Regazzoni.

"Monsignor?"

The voices above were getting louder, and the shouts were definitely angry. Somebody was asking where the President was. And the tone indicated they were going to find out.

"Monsignor?"

Stubblefield wondered if Regazzoni had high-tailed it back to the church. If that was the case, Stubblefield needed to get moving. He turned down the last row when he heard a click behind him, causing him to freeze in his tracks. He spun around, raised his weapon, and prepared to fire.

"It's me, *Signore!*" Regazzoni said, shaking in his cassock, the flashlight now under his chin. "It's me!"

Stubblefield lowered his weapon. He hurried over, picked up Regazzoni, and tucked him under his arm. He then made like a running back and sprinted down the tunnel. When they reached the door that led to the apartment, Stubblefield could see Schiffer's light as he made his way to the church.

"Schiffer!" Stubblefield yelled out, just loud enough for only Schiffer to hear. "Schiffer! Stubblefield coming up behind you!"

It was a wise and intelligent man who didn't sneak up on Agent Schiffer.

"Where's the President?" Schiffer asked, as he waited for the Director to catch up with him.

"I sent them on to the church," Stubblefield said, releasing Monsignor Regazzoni from his grasp. He then pointed over to the man of the cloth. "I had to go pick up somebody."

The Phantom team, along with the President, the Prime Minister, and Monsignor Regazzoni, reassembled in the Church of St. Ignatius – the place they had started their rescue operation, which felt like days ago. The Church was silent, the only light from a table full of candles flickering in the rear.

"Let's get out of here," Stubblefield said as they made their way to the rear entrance from where they came.

"Where are we going?" Olivera asked, he being the driver.

Stubblefield didn't have an answer. He had to stop to think. He hadn't thought it this far through.

"The Embassy?" the President offered. "Or the airport?"

The FBI had an attache office at the American Embassy, which was less than two miles away. It would have a handful of agents as well as Marines on duty for security. But Stubblefield knew the streets of Italy might not be the best place for them at the present time. And the airport was a good forty-minute drive west of Rome. Although they had Prime Minister Scarponi if they needed a bargaining chip, it was risky to trust anyone in the Italian police or military right now. The Director looked at Monsignor Regazzoni, who was starting to shake in the chill and excitement of the evening. Stubblefield made his decision.

"We need to get back to the Vatican," he said. "It's the safest place for all of us until we can get reinforcements here to get the President to Air Force One."

"Back to the Vatican," Olivera responded, firmly confident that he knew the route.

As they approached the back door, Stubblefield rattled off his instructions. "Tie up the Prime Minister and put him on the floor in the back. Alvarez and Guerrero – take the rear seat. Schiffer and I will cover the President and the Monsignor in the middle. Then it's Olivera and Jenkins up front."

With guns drawn, Alvarez and Guerrero cautiously opened the side door to the church and the others followed out behind them. They all stopped in the empty archway.

Director Stubblefield couldn't believe what his eyes were seeing. Or what they weren't seeing.

"Where the hell is the van?"

CHAPTER 30

Church of St. Ignatius of Loyola – Rome, Italy

The Phantom team hustled back inside the church. Stubblefield tried to think of where the van went. They were in the right place. He remembered Monsignor Regazzoni was the last one to drive the van. Maybe they forgot to take the keys out of the ignition. Maybe some local kid stole it during the lockdown.

"I have the key to the van right here, Director," Olivera said, holding up the key. He had read Stubblefield's mind. Each team member instinctively reached up to his breast pocket – they each had a spare key just in case and all were accounted for.

The screeching tires the team heard on all sides of the church told them the perpetrators hadn't taken the van out for a joy ride. Whoever it was who took the van was now back in search of the occupants.

"Everybody back in the tunnel," Stubblefield ordered. "Move! Move!"

The Phantom team, along with the President, the Prime Minister, and Monsignor Regazzoni hurried to reach the tunnel. Once inside, they waited.

"Olivera," Stubblefield said. "Secure that door."

Olivera pushed the door shut with his shoulder. If those on the other side knew about the secret tunnel, it would only be a matter of minutes before they came looking.

"What's the plan, Ty?" the President asked.

Stubblefield didn't like feeling boxed in. If the Italians were coming from the church and the Pakistanis were coming from the Palace, it could leave those in the middle in a heap of trouble. They had no way out. Stubblefield pulled back his watch – the SEAL team was still ten minutes out. But Stubblefield didn't have ten minutes.

"We need a vehicle," Stubblefield said.

"I can hot-wire anything," Agent Jenkins offered.

Stubblefield nodded. It was a possibility. Any other ideas?

"What about the Beast?" the President asked.

The presidential limousine, Stubblefield thought. It was still in the Piazza Colonna with the two Secret Service Suburbans. At least they were still there the last time he looked. If they were left idling, they still might have enough fuel to get back to Vatican City. If the keys to the Beast were gone, Stubblefield could at least get the President inside and hope the bulletproof windows and blast resistant doors held during any type of an onslaught.

"I think that's our best bet right now," Stubblefield said.

He ordered Jenkins to text the plan to the Secretary of Defense so he could inform the SEAL team. He then ordered a check of weapons. The ammunition was growing thin.

"Let's get back to the apartment building."

Agent Guerrero led the way back down the tunnel. The Phantom team was beginning to know every square inch of the place. When they reached the door that would lead to the apartment building above, they stopped to listen. When they heard voices from the Palace end, they hurried upstairs.

The team took up position in the back of the clothing store.

"It's still there," Stubblefield whispered to the rest of them. "The Beast and the two Suburbans."

The Piazza Colonna was buzzing with activity – three fire trucks were on the scene and firefighters were dragging hoses into the Palazzo Chigi. Stubblefield could see a handful of men just off the main entrance – and they weren't discussing how best to put out the blaze. He grabbed his binoculars and zoomed in. The men were definitely Pakistani – the diplomatic plates noting their presence. One other man appeared to be Italian, and they argued back and forth. When the Italian motioned his hand underneath the Piazza, the eight Pakistanis who had already searched the Palace took off inside in a rush, hungry to find their hidden prey. They weren't interested in transporting the President to the ICC. They wanted him dead, and they were hell-bent on making it happen. Five more men stood outside by the cars, their weapons ready should the President show himself.

It was only a matter of time now.

"Okay, we gotta go," Stubblefield said, huddling up in the back. "Schiffer, give the President your side arm."

Without a second thought, Agent Schiffer ripped the Velcro straps off his thigh holster and handed his Glock pistol over to the President, who promptly strapped it on like he had done it a thousand times before.

"Duke, I need you on that roof to provide some cover."

"Roger that," Schiffer said to him, taking off for the stairs with his Remington.

"Guerrero, I need you to secure the door to the tunnel," Stubblefield ordered as Guerrero grabbed his bag. "And hurry!"

Agent Guerrero ran back down the stairs. He was an expert in underwater demolition. And he was just as lethal on dry ground. He quickly rigged up a grenade to the door – whoever was unfortunate enough to open it from the other side would wish he hadn't done so. He hustled back upstairs to rejoin the team.

"Schiffer, do you copy?" Stubblefield asked over his radio.

"I copy," Schiffer said. "I am in position to cover the Piazza."

"What do the roads look like?"

"On the east side of the Palace heading north is your best bet. They're clearing a path for the emergency vehicles."

"Copy that," Stubblefield said. Now it was time for the ex-football star to draw up a play. They moved to the front window. "Olivera, I need you to get to the limo. You're driving." The driver's side was facing them so it would give Olivera and the team a protective approach. "Jenkins, you take Monsignor Regazzoni. I'll cover the President."

"Why don't I cover the Monsignor?" the President asked, the ex-FBI agent offering his own thoughts on the game plan. The rest of the team was somewhat taken aback by the thought. "Ty, you need your hands free. We'll follow you."

Stubblefield looked at Regazzoni. "You got your running shoes on, Monsignor?"

"Yes," he said, looking down on his fine Italian footwear. Good enough for a mad dash, he thought.

"Monsignor, I want you to stay right behind the President. He'll follow right behind me and we'll get to the limo. Okay?"

"Yes, I can do that."

"Okay, now Olivera gets to the driver's seat. I'll get to the rear door and get the President and Monsignor Regazzoni inside. Alvarez, Jenkins, and Guerrero – I want you to head for the closest Suburban. It will give you some cover. Alvarez, you drive."

The Phantom team members nodded.

"If the vehicles are operational, we're turning around and heading north on the Via del Corso. Then west across the river and to the Vatican."

Out of the corner of his eye, Director Stubblefield saw the President removing his bulletproof vest. "Mr. President, what are you doing?"

The President handed the vest over. "If you're going in front of me, you need this more than I do."

"Mr. President, I can't let you do that."

"Ty, if you get hit, it's not going to help any of us. I doubt that the Monsignor and I can drag you very far."

"Sir . . ."

The President would have none of it. "No. You put it on, and that's an order!"

Stubblefield relented.

"Now what about him?" the President asked, pointing over to the corner with his now unholstered pistol.

The team looked over at Prime Minister Scarponi – bound, gagged, and most likely a dead weight in their plan to get the hell out of Rome.

"I'll leave it up to you, Mr. President," Stubblefield said. "We could use him as a bargaining chip but . . ."

The explosion rocked the floor beneath them – bits of plaster from the ceiling above falling to the carpet.

"We gotta go!" Stubblefield yelled.

The group of eight Pakistanis searching for the President found the door to the apartment in the tunnel below. When they had opened the door, the Phantom team's explosive device killed two of the men; the six others were blown back but not deterred. Once the smoke cleared, Agent Guerrero dropped his last grenade down the stairwell. The blast one floor down caused the Pakistanis to unload with their automatic weapons – the bullets blasting off the store's back door.

"We gotta go! Grab the PM! Schiffer! We're coming out!"

The two blasts in the apartment building grabbed the attention of the five Pakistanis across the Piazza. They were now heading toward the shops.

"Schiffer!"

From his vantage point, Stubblefield watched three armed Pakistani terrorists fall to the ground one right after another. Schiffer cycled the bolt – the pungent aroma of gunpowder filling his nostrils and intoxicating his sniper's brain. In a span of five seconds, Schiffer had cleared the field below him

At least for now.

"Go!"

Olivera burst out of the front door of the store – his MP-7 raised and ready. Stubblefield was next in line to the left, followed by the President and Monsignor Regazzoni, then Alvarez to the right, and Jenkins and Guerrero pulling up the rear.

"Go! Go! Go!" Stubblefield yelled.

Three more Pakistanis came running out the front door of the Palace – their guns ablaze and firing across the Piazza. Their comrades had made it up the stairwell from the tunnel and were now heading out the front door of the store.

Schiffer took out one more across the way before something caught his eye below. "You got some coming behind you! And a chopper en route!"

Stubblefield's MP-7 lit up the night sky. The President had both hands on the Glock firing across the way. Monsignor Regazzoni crouched as close as he could behind him, his hands covered his ears, his teeth were clenched tight, and he flinched with every shot. Agents Jenkins and Guerrero fired off multiple rounds into the clothing shop, the glass windows shattering to the ground.

Olivera reached the limo first, and he discovered the keys were still in the ignition. Stubblefield's MP-7 went silent just before he reached the back door of the limo. He had no more ammunition. He opened the back door. The President stopped, grabbed Monsignor Regazzoni, and threw him in. He then landed on top of him. And then Stubblefield landed on top of both of them.

Alvarez made it to the first Suburban, but Jenkins and Guerrero were bogged down by the Pakistanis from the rear. Schiffer scattered the men below long enough for Jenkins and Guerrero, who had thrown Prime Minister Scarponi over his shoulder and hauled him through the gunfire, to get inside.

"All in!" Alvarez radioed. "It's running!"

"Go, Olivera!" Stubblefield ordered. He scrambled from the back to the front passenger seat. "Go!"

Olivera jammed the Beast into drive and slammed on the accelerator. Bullets ricocheted off the limo, its tires squealing. The Suburban turned left and followed behind.

"North!"

Stubblefield looked behind him – the President and the Monsignor were okay and the Suburban was right on their tail.

"Left up ahead!"

Olivera made the hard left on the Via Fontanella Borghese and gunned it. He didn't like what he saw ahead of him in the darkness. "Roadblock!"

Stubblefield surveyed the scene ahead of him – an armored personnel carrier blocking the road and a handful of men preparing for battle. The men manning the checkpoint were not dressed in Carabinieri blue but the civilian clothes of Russian operatives. In case their chopper didn't show, Zhukov and Patrenko had planned an escape route, one that would be free of Italian interference and give them a clear shot out of Rome. Now their comrades were looking to settle the score. Stubblefield saw the only room was on the sidewalks and it wasn't wide enough for them. He had to make a call. "Alvarez, get up here and clear us a path on the north side! Don't stop!"

Agent Alvarez slammed on the gas pedal and overtook the limo. His last look at the speedometer showed 45 mph. "Hold on!"

"Don't stop!"

The Suburban barreled into the end of the personnel carrier – the crashing steel mangling both vehicles. The Suburban wedged itself between the carrier and the building to the north, and the revving engine indicated it wasn't budging.

Olivera only had one choice. "Brace yourselves!" He mashed the gas and rammed the Beast into the back of the Suburban, edging it forward slightly but not enough. Now they were both wedged in.

The Russians responded with gunfire on the two vehicles – those in the Beast able to do nothing but watch the bullets bounce off the bulletproof glass. The Suburban, which was only partly armored and with its windows down, meant Alvarez and the agents inside had to return fire. But pretty soon they would be out of ammunition. And, even worse, they weren't moving anywhere.

The President leaned forward from the back seat. "Ty!" he yelled, pointing to the dash. "The red switch on the right! The red switch!"

Stubblefield flipped the switch and the Beast's tear gas cannons shot out a massive cloud, enveloping the whole area around the wreckage. " Alvarez, roll up your windows!"

In the suffocating smoke, the Russians' guns stopped firing – their eyes burning in agony, their lungs feeling like they might explode.

"Alvarez, floor it!"

When Alvarez slammed on the Suburban's accelerator, the tires spun in place, the burning rubber and smoke further clouding the whole area. The Suburban was still wedged in between the building and the armored personnel carrier.

"We're stuck!" Alvarez yelled.

"Back up!" Stubblefield yelled to Olivera. "Back up!"

Olivera jammed the Beast into reverse and squealed the tires back thirty feet. Then, he hit the gas and used the eight-ton limo as a battering ram into the rear of the Suburban, breaking it free from its sandwich.

"Go! Go! Go!"

The Suburban and the Beast hauled ass to the Ponte Vittorio. It was there that Director Stubblefield looked out the window and the chopper closing in from the passenger side. The spotlight shining on him blinding his eyes. "Hurry up!" he yelled to Olivera.

They crossed the Tiber River, turned left, and had a straight shot down the Via Della Conciliazione into St. Peter's Square. But the chopper overtook them and then spun around to meet them head on.

"Keep going!"

Stubblefield grabbed the shotgun stashed in the side of the Beast's door. He'd use it on the chopper if he had to.

As they neared the bright lights of the Vatican, it was then that Stubblefield saw out the front windshield that the chopper had an American flag painted on its fuselage. That, along with the chopper's M240H machine gun and its GAU-19 Gatling gun, finally let Stubblefield breathe easier. Olivera steered the Beast around St. Peter's Square and screeched to a halt, the battered Suburban pulled to a stop on the driver's side. The UH-60 Black Hawk full of SEALs landed to the south. No one else would be getting in tonight.

"Let's get the President inside," Stubblefield said into his radio. He then turned around in his seat. "Wait here, Mr. President."

Stubblefield exited the limo and checked on his agents in the Suburban. They came through unscathed, as did the still-bound Scarponi in the back seat. The same could not be said of the vehicles. Both were a mess. The Suburban's engine was smoking, bullets holes riddled the left side but none penetrated the interior. The Beast had a long gash down the side – the presidential seal on the side barely identifiable.

After surveying the wreckage, Stubblefield walked toward the Black Hawk, its rotor still spinning at a good clip. He met the man coming at him.

"Mr. Director, I'm Commander Alexander at the President's service," he yelled into Stubblefield's ear. "Is the President safe?"

"Yes, thanks for coming. I need some of your men to escort the President inside the Vatican."

"No problem. Whatever you want."

Stubblefield looked back across St. Peter's Square at the crumpled mess of vehicles parked at the front steps of the Vatican. Out of habit, the names started running through his head again. The President, Monsignor Regazzoni, Prime Minister Scarponi, Olivera, Alvarez, Jenkins, Guerrero. He then looked at Commander Alexander and the Black Hawk.

"Commander, I need five of your men and your chopper," Stubblefield said, pointing at the helicopter.

The Commander was six-four, so he could look the Director directly in the eyes. But the Commander looked confused."What?" Alexander asked, the chopper's 1,800 horsepower turboshaft engine still thumping around in his eardrums. He thought Stubblefield was asking to borrow his $20-million, tricked-out, top-secret helicopter.

And that's exactly what he was asking for. Stubblefield leaned into the Commander's ear. "I have a team member left behind! I gotta go get him!"

Commander Alexander motioned his team leader over and gave the order. Stubblefield ran back to the limo and told the President that the SEALs would get him and Monsignor Regazzoni inside. He then started walking toward the chopper.

"Where are you going?" the President asked.

"I gotta get Schiffer!" Stubblefield yelled back.

"Wait!" the President shouted. He hurried over to the Director and ripped off the pistol and holster strapped to his right thigh. "Here," he said, handing it over to him. "Just in case you need it. Tell Agent Schiffer I owe him a few rounds."

Stubblefield grabbed it, thanked him, and hurried to the chopper. Once inside, he saluted the President and gave him a thumbs-up. The Black Hawk lifted off from St. Peter's Square and thundered back into the smoke-filled Roman night.

CHAPTER 31

Leonardo da Vinci Airport – Fiumcino, Italy

President Schumacher and the First Lady reunited on Air Force One, the long hugs a welcome feeling for both of them. The President had spent a few minutes with the Pope, thanking him for his prayers, and safely returning Monsignor Regazzoni to the Vatican. After Director Stubblefield and the SEAL team plucked Agent Schiffer off the roof of the apartment building south of the Palazzo Chigi, they returned to St. Peter's. The Italian President, still on his Alaskan cruise, restored order with a couple of phone calls and had the military and police secure the streets of Rome. Once the area was deemed safe by the Secret Service and the U.S. military in, around, and above Italy, the President boarded Marine One and headed for the airport in the early morning hours.

"Mr. President, we're ready when you are," Colonel Marty Washington, the President's pilot on Air Force One, announced.

In the President's cabin on Air Force One were the First Lady, Wiley Cogdon, and Director Stubblefield. There was someone missing and they all knew it, felt it in their hearts.

"Marty, we're not leaving until I can bring my guys home."

"Yes, sir."

When the three military transport vehicles hit the runway, the President walked down the steps from Air Force One. The six caskets draped in American flags were offloaded, and under the watchful eye of the President, they were placed onto Air Force One.

Six agents from the United States Secret Service had been killed in the attack on the President, including the head of the detail, Michael Craig. More would have been killed had they not been rounded up and barricaded in the Palazzo Chigi by Prime Minister Scarponi's security team. Six agents were on their way to Ramstein Air Force base in Germany for treatment but were expected to fully recover.

Once the caskets were secure, the President returned to the aircraft. Air Force One then roared off the runway, banked east, and settled in the blue sky over the Atlantic for the final trip home.

The only picture would show the President of the United States, alone with the flag-draped coffins, his hands folded in prayer.

EPILOGUE

The White House – Washington, D.C.

"It is always an honor to be here on a day like this," the President said behind the podium in the East Room of the White House. The entire room was packed with individuals from all three branches of the U.S. Government – Cabinet members, a delegation of Representatives and Senators, and several Justices of the Supreme Court. "We have come here today to recognize the contributions of seven of our greatest Americans."

The ceremony was to posthumously award the Presidential Medal of Freedom to Agent Craig and the five Secret Service agents who lost their lives in the defense and protection of the United States. It was the highest civilian honor the President could bestow on an American citizen. The President took his time, highlighting the heroic lives of the slain agents. He welcomed their families, thanked them for their sacrifice, and closed with a reading from the thirteenth verse of John chapter fifteen. The tears and smiles helped in the recovery process.

Along with the members of the Secret Service, the President had one other American he wanted to honor with the medal – FBI Director Tyrone Stubblefield.

"I have known Director Stubblefield for over thirty years now. We first met at the FBI Academy when I was just out of law school and he was just off the football field. Since that time, there have been few men in this country who have served with as much dignity and determination as Director Stubblefield. He has worked to uphold the rights of American citizens here and abroad and risked his own life on numerous occasions to preserve, protect, and defend the American people, and the Constitution of the United States. This country owes Director Stubblefield a debt of gratitude that cannot be repaid with mere words. But, today, I hope he will accept this award on behalf of the American people for his dedicated service to this great country."

Given his height, Director Stubblefield had to remain seated as the President placed the medal around his neck. Once the medal was secured,

Stubblefield rose and turned to his old friend – the President of the United States. They shook hands and then hugged. The standing ovation lasted for three minutes.

Stubblefield had asked that he not be awarded the medal, humbly believing the honor should be solely focused on the members of the Secret Service. But the President thought the honor was appropriate. Stubblefield had already been recognized with the Congressional Gold Medal, numerous other law-enforcement awards, and another spot on the cover of *Time* magazine – with the headline reading "The Future President?"

The Phantom team members were not at the East Room ceremony – they wanting to remain anonymous. They did, however, privately receive the Public Safety Officer Medal of Valor from the President for their "extraordinary valor above and beyond the call of duty."

Agent D.A. "Duke" Schiffer was on the White House grounds during the Medal of Freedom festivities – on the roof of the mansion with his Remington, always on duty, just in case. He and the rest of the Phantom team would remain in the shadows but fully operational in the defense and protection of President Schumacher and the United States of America.

After reading the salacious details of the plot between the Russians and Italian Prime Minister Scarponi in the newspapers, Roland Barton decided to save himself and plead guilty to espionage – quickly. He would spend the rest of his days as a guest of the federal government.

Prime Minister Scarponi had been taken into custody by the Phantom team and then handed over to U.S. authorities. He was brought to the United States and tried for the deaths of the six Secret Service agents and the attack on President Schumacher. Seven members of his inner security circle were also in custody. The Russian phones taken by the Phantom team provided the most damning evidence against Scarponi. The jury found him guilty, and the federal judge sentenced him to death for his crimes. An uproar followed from Italian authorities, who wanted to put Scarponi on trial for his crimes in Italy. Moreover, Italy cried foul over the sentence, given that it did away with capital punishment years ago. People on both sides of the political spectrum weighed in – some wanting Scarponi to rot in jail for the rest of his life and others wanting him to hang in the streets like Mussolini. In the end, President Schumacher decided to commute Scarponi's death sentence to one of life in prison. The evidence indicated Scarponi had demanded that the Russians keep the killing to a minimum, which saved the lives of twenty Secret Service agents who were held hostage on the first floor of the Palazzo Chigi. The deciding factor for the President, however, was a personal note from the Vatican asking for mercy for the Prime Minister.

It was signed by honorary Phantom team member Monsignor Silvio Regazzoni.

Silver Creek, Indiana

Once the summer tourist season was in full force, the President and First Lady loaded up Air Force One for a nice long vacation back home again in Indiana. There, they doted over their grandchildren and otherwise took in the lazy summer days along the Wabash River.

Wiley Cogdon was pacing back and forth in the front yard – plotting strategy for the mid-term elections that he said were "just around the corner." He was lucky to be alive. He was recovering nicely from a broken nose and two black eyes. When the attack in the Palazzo Chigi started, he took the butt end of an AK-47 to the face. He remembered nothing after that. He was out cold when the paramedics arrived on the scene. If the Coyote was a cat, he had about three lives left.

While President Schumacher needed the rest, things were looking up. The economy was booming and gas prices continued to drop.

The Russian Government, of course, denied any involvement in the attack on the President, as those in Moscow were want to do when the evidence proved otherwise. The world would watch as the macho men in the Kremlin steadily lost their dictatorial hold on power.

The Pakistanis would claim rogue elements of their government were behind the assault on the President – a personal vendetta by the late Minister Khan to engage in his own brand of violent diplomacy. The Pakistanis promised to improve relations with the United States. The U.S. Government would proceed cautiously.

President Schumacher, however, had everything he needed. He had the world community behind him, his lovely wife by his side, and a fresh container of FBI-approved ChapStick in his left pocket.

THE END

Acknowledgments

A special thanks to Mom and Dad for offering their editorial assistance and the opportunity to visit many of the places that found their way into this book. Also, a big thank you to Special Agent Dave for his law-enforcement insight and willingness to answer all of my questions.

Rob Shumaker is an attorney living in Illinois. *D-Day in the Capital* is his fourth novel.

To read more about the
Capital Series novels, go to

www.USAnovels.com

••• •••• ••‾